IN PURSUIT OF FREEDOM

The Price of Apartheid

CHRISTOS MELIDONIS

iUniverse, Inc.
Bloomington

In Pursuit of Freedom
The Price of Apartheid

iUniverse books may be ordered through booksellers or by contacting:

iUniverse
1663 Liberty Drive
Bloomington, IN 47403
www.iuniverse.com
1-800-Authors (1-800-288-4677)

ISBN: 978-1-4502-8485-1 (sc)
ISBN: 978-1-4502-8486-8 (ebook)

Printed in the United States of America

iUniverse rev. date: 5/3/2011

Dedication

This novel is dedicated with hope, respect and admiration
To those who resist oppression in pursuit of freedom.

And to

My beloved wife Greer Melidonis, a faithful friend who stood by me at all times.

And to

My sons Georgios and Arion Melidonis,
and daughter-in-law Yvonne
Companions in the growth of compassion and understanding.

Thanks and acknowledgements

To Philip Grundy who did the initial translation from Greek to English.
To Greer, for many hours, translating and revising the manuscript.
To George, Yvonne and Arion for editing the manuscript
To all those who read the drafts and made suggestions

Table of Contents

Foreword

It is always a struggle to live in freedom and equality with others so that love, peace and justice flourish on earth as the various gods of mankind have willed.

Chains give a stifled groan
Cold iron bites fiercely into flesh
Wrists are inflamed
Blood drips red.
The captive cries out in lamentation
Condemned to fear and pain
Who is he? You ask
No, not Prometheus
Just another sufferer
In pursuit of freedom

Christos Melidonis

CHAPTER 1 Face of Apartheid

It was just at the beginning of September. Summer had arrived early that year, very hot, with a clear light blue sky. The sun was a flaming disc that burned the coastline where two great oceans meet; the Cape of Good Hope. A flock of seagulls dived noisily in spectacular show into frothy waters teeming with sardines. People swam and others, scantily clad sunbathed under large colorful umbrellas. A large square sign declared with huge letters, WHITES ONLY.

A lonely walker strode slowly along the limitless sandy beach. He longed to swim in the crystal fresh waters but the last time he had tried; armed policemen had violently dragged him out and imprisoned him because his skin was darker than theirs. He turned away from the beach and climbed up a high sand dune, his face gaunt and harsh under the bright sun. He held a flat parcel wrapped in brown paper under his armpit. At the summit of the dune, he looked across to Table Top Mountain which dominated the terrain amid a vast backdrop of ocean. He gazed out proudly. This was his land, his country and he loved it. He sat on the warm sand withdrawing into his thoughts. He stayed like that for over an hour. The brown packet now drenched with his sweat. He turned to it, and carefully unwrapped the package. He examined it thoughtfully, as if for the first time. It was a German sheaf knife, wide and almost ten inches long, ending in a thin pointed sharp edge. As he tensed his grip on the wooden handle, the blade seemed to fill him with strength and power. He raised it slowly and menacingly to the sky. The steel blade flashed in the sun's rays.

The South African parliament was in session. The beloved and popular Prime Minister, Dr. Hendrick Verwoerd, sat on the front bench of the House of Assembly preparing his speech for the assembled ministers. He planned to discuss his improved economic development program, as well as his separate development policy of apartheid, involving the continued resettlement of the Bantu homelands. A man in a parliamentary messenger uniform, walked across the lobby toward where the Prime Minister was seated. He carried a stained brown paper package under one arm. His eyes reflected the cool peacefulness of one who has embraced fate. He stopped purposefully behind the Prime Minister. He felt surprisingly relaxed, even though his senses had never felt more acute. With calculated speed he reached out and yanked back on the Prime Minister's hair. The brown, crumpled, paper sheath began its gliding descent towards the floor. The knife itself glinted visibly for the lesser part of a second, before it was thrust vertically into the left side of the Prime Minister's throat.

"My name is Dimitris Tsafendas," the armed man shouted exultantly, before he plunged the knife three more times in quick succession.

A quickly subdued cry of pain and surprise escaped the lips of Dr. Verwoerd. The Prime Minister's pale face had transformed into the quintessential mask of agony. He tried in vain to turn his eyes toward his assassin, but Verwoerd's vision quickly lost its focus as his blood splashed out, spraying nearby people and furniture. It was the sixth of September 1966.

The Nationalist Party immediately announced that John Vorster, a hard-core right-wing Nationalist, would take leadership as the new Prime Minister. John Vorster declared that he would intensify the hard line taken by Verwoerd on apartheid and separate development. Total power must remain in the hands of the Boers. The Republic of South Africa wrapped itself in a cloak of mourning as special editions of the newspapers announced the tragic assassination of the Prime Minister. Later editions revealed that the assassin was Greek. His motivation was totally unclear to the flourishing Greek community who could not believe or accept the shocking news.

"Who is he? Why? Where does he come from?" they asked, while they rushed to close their businesses for fear of retaliation. The first repercussive attacks from incensed white Afrikaners had already begun. The next day, police headquarters announced that the assassin was a colored man. His father was Greek and his mother, a black woman from Mozambique. Newspapers then asked how it was possible for a colored man to work as a messenger in parliament.

Andreas Magdalos came down the stairs to join his mother for breakfast. She was reading her newspaper with more intensity than usual. She wore a disturbed expression on her face.

"What's the matter Mom?" Andreas enquired.

"They should have sent him to the gallows, not to a psychiatric hospital," she felt bolstered by her anger.

"Who mother?" Andreas asked.

"That horrible monster, Tsafendas! He murdered the best Prime Minister we ever had. Poor Dr. Verwoerd! He was a visionary, the architect of apartheid. He liberated this country from the goddamn British. It was he who helped realize the dreams of the Voortrekkers, who had fought so hard against the English and Zulus. You must understand Andreas! It was he who brought recognition to our Afrikaner ancestors. Our people who spilt rivers of blood so that we whites could have this land. Our fatherland."

Andreas observed her silently.

"Worms in his stomach indeed!" continued his mother. "That heinous criminal! Out and out madman! And to think that he has the cheek to call himself a Greek. Is it likely that a Greek would marry a black kaffir woman and have a child with her? He has brought so much shame on your Dad and me and the whole Greek community.

"Do you have to use words like that? Selina is black and she's not a kaffir!" Andreas could stand to listen no more.

"Of course she is! You can never trust any of them. Give them a hand and they will take an arm," his mother quickly retorted.

"Oh, but you could trust her with me?" Andreas long knew how to bring his mother's blood to boil.

"You annoy me. Now that you are getting older you need to wake up to the realities of this country."

Andreas swallowed his anger and turned his back on his mother. He knew it was futile to argue with her.

"You're probably right." He said it lethargically.

She tried to dismiss the sarcasm in her son's tone. She needed him to come around. She missed him. Why couldn't he share her anger over this tragedy? Why was he always so abrasive? Why couldn't he see? But, this was no time to be soft. The boy got enough of that from his father. She needed to set a strong example.

"You're bloody right, I'm right!" she stated as she turned and forced Andreas to look her in the eye, "and it's about time you finally grew up!" she added.

Andreas bowed his head and retraced his steps upstairs. His thoughts drifted to an early memory when for the first time that he had realized the 'realities' of his country. Christmas had been approaching. With joy and expectation of a young child, Andreas Magdalos had impatiently looked out of his bedroom window at the heavy iron gates that formed the entrance to his home. His father had promised that they would deliver the tree that morning, but it was already almost eight o'clock and it had not yet arrived.

"Andreas, come and have your breakfast," he heard his mother's voice.

Without much enthusiasm, he removed himself from his window view and made his way to the dining room. He found his mother sitting in her usual seat, her face hidden behind the morning newspaper. Mrs. Lanie Magdalos, a youthful woman in her late thirties, was wearing sweat pants and a stained top. She had just returned from an exercise class at the gym and her blonde hair was still tousled and tied up in a knot.

"Can you believe it?" remarked Andreas. "They have not yet brought the tree!"

His mother put aside her newspaper and rang a little bell on the table imperiously.

"Be patient! Perhaps it will arrive after breakfast?" She gave her words the air of a promise and affectionately ruffled his hair.

Selina and Maria, both dressed in starchy white uniforms, appeared from the kitchen, carrying two silver trays filled with food. They set them down on the table, which they had earlier set for breakfast. The room filled with the pungent smells of bacon, sausages, fried eggs and freshly brewed coffee. His mother threw a quick surveying glance at the table. Satisfied, she gave the servants a tight lipped smile of approval.

"Would you like anything else, Madam?" Selina asked with a tone of practiced servility.

"No, that's all. You can go now. Just listen for the bell. And ah, Maria, before you go, fill my bath, but don't make it scalding like the last time! I have to leave immediately after breakfast."

"Yes Madam. I will be very careful this time." Maria said.

The truck arrived just as they finished breakfast. Old Tom, the gardener, brought in the tree with the aid of the truck driver. Just like every other year, they stood it in the same position in the middle of the living room, between the two marble bowed staircases that led to the upper floor.

"Oh, Tom! You are always so careless and clumsy! You have dirtied my floor again!" Mrs. Magdalos called out with a tone that was somehow both hurt and angry.

"Selina," she continued.

"Yes Madam."

"Send Sylvia to clean the floor. Then I want you to stay with the young master. I have to leave right away."

"The tree is so huge; it must be over seven feet!" Andreas shouted with excitement. "Don't you think so Mom?"

She nodded in reply, "Yes, it's beautiful. Your father chose rather well. But now Andreas, I have to go. I am already late. I have so much to do for the party and I have to get on with my shopping."

"Aren't you going to decorate the tree with us?" Andreas asked with disappointment.

"I'm sorry, Andreas, my boy. I promise you I will try to come back as soon as I can. In the meantime, your Dad will be home soon and you and he can start as soon as he arrives."

She gave him a quick kiss and departed to get ready.

When they were alone, Selina's face relaxed and she gave him a big smile.

"Andreas, what a beautiful fir tree! It smells so fresh and good. I am sure that this year we will have the most magnificent tree in the whole neighborhood."

"Let's go and get the decorations from the store room," Andreas said excitedly.

"Don't worry. I have already told Tom to get them, together with the ladder. We are going to need it!"

"I want to start decorating right away!" he stated impatiently.

"No my boy, this is a job for you and your father. But tell me, what would you like to do until he comes?"

Andreas looked at her with some disappointment. He looked up at the bare tree. He yearned for his father to arrive so that they could begin decorating. He longed for the presents that always appeared in stacks around the base of a heavily festooned tree. He loved the feeling of warmth and excitement that came with the holidays.

"Well, can you tell me a Christmas story?" he asked her without much enthusiasm.

"I don't think I know any Christmas stories. Anyway, I am not very good at telling stories."

"Come on Selina!" Andreas's interest was piqued by Selina's refusal.

"Tell me about a special Christmas that you had?" he persisted.

"Well, I'm not sure if it's a good story but I can tell you about a Christmas that I remember every year?"

The boy's attention was on her now. For a short time he would forget about the tree. Selina began to lose herself in the past as she started her tale.

"You were still very young back then. Your parents decided to spend Christmas in Greece. The big boss gave me leave and my salary for two whole weeks. It was the first time that I was able to spend Christmas with my family. I remember that the train trip to my homeland seemed so long. Those were the most joyful days of my life," she said, now at the mercy of nostalgia.

"I remember that I wanted to do something out of the ordinary, so I bought a pretty little plastic tree with some nice decorations. It was my children's first tree. I also bought them some clothes and toys as presents. My God, as long as I live, I will never forget the joy and excitement I saw on their faces when they saw that tree. The picture is so alive in my mind that it has remained with me all these years and keeps me company especially at this time of the year."

Andreas looked at her in surprise.

"You never told me about that. You have family and children and you never told me about them?" he asked her puzzled.

"Oh yes, Andreas," she replied. "I have a husband and six children. Matthew is the youngest and he is nearly the same age as you."

"But where are they? Where do they live? Why have I never seen them?" he asked.

"My husband works in a gold mine in the Transvaal and he lives in a hostel. We meet every now and then, when he and I can get a day off. My kids live back in the homeland with my old mother. They don't have passbooks, so the law does not allow them to live in the white areas."

Andreas felt a little jealous. He loved Selina and did not want to share her with anybody else. She was his second mother. She had brought him up. He had learned his first words from her, in her dialect. He had played his first games with her. The reality that she had her own family hit him not unlike a thunderbolt. Is it possible that nobody had ever spoken to him about them? It was hard to believe that he knew so little about her life.

"Selina look! Tom is here with the decorations. Let us go and help him." Andreas's mind was quickly brought back to the present.

"Tom, take your shoes off," Selina shouted.

At the very moment, Frixos Magdalos arrived, carrying a bag filled with even more ornaments.

"Daddy, Daddy!" Andreas shouted and ran to embrace his father, with great excitement. "It's a beautiful tree. Let's start decorating. Selina can help us!"

The three of them went to work in a chain of life fashion. Selina opened the decorations and gave them to Andreas who passed them to his father. Andreas excitedly yelled directions as to the placement of the elegant and delicate glass ornaments.

"Dad, when did you have your first Christmas tree?" Andreas asked. He was still thinking about Selina's story.

"Andreas, you are lucky to have all these things. When I was a child in Greece, under Nazi occupation, we did not even have food, never mind a Christmas tree."

"So you never had a tree?" Andreas enquired.

"I was more than twelve years old when my father first took me to buy a tree. We had had to wait for two wars to end; first the war against the Germans, and then the civil war. I remember that it was a cold and windy day. My father and I had huddled together as we walked to the market near the church of St. Nicholas in Kaisiariani, a suburb in Athens where our home was. Unlike here, Greece is cold during the winter. My father bought a branch of a fir tree and we made it into our first Christmas tree. I remember the pride on my father's face, and my excitement as we carried it home to our house. Still, we had no money for Christmas presents in those days."

Within a couple of hours the tree was finished. Andreas felt that it was magnificent, with all its decorations and lights. The tree had succeeded in turning his home into a fairyland.

"We did a great job! Mom will be very proud of us. By the way, Selina, ask Maria to make us some lunch. We deserve it after all this hard work," instructed Mr. Magdalos.

"Dad, you never told me that Selina is married and has children," Andreas asked when she left the room.

"Are you sure? I thought you knew," his father replied. "By the way, she asked my permission to bring her youngest boy to spend Christmas holidays with her. We can't let her go because we have a big party coming up and your mother needs her."

"What did you tell her Dad?"

"To tell you the truth, I had forgotten all about it."

"Are you going to permit it?"

"I will have to ask your mother"

"You should. I would like to meet him. I want to know what he is like."

'I guess he is kind of my half-brother,' Andreas thought to himself, already aware enough to not speak the notion aloud.

"Alright, I will have to ask you mother first, though. I don't need any extra trouble around the holidays."

A few days later, Matthew arrived. He was an attractive child with big black eyes and a timid smile. He had a sturdy, wiry frame, and he carried an irrepressible energy that suited his heightened sense of adventure. Andreas was drawn to him like a magnet. He had mostly played alone or with Selina before his new friend's arrival. The two boys would run about, climb trees and play out all kinds of imaginary adventures together. Andreas would return home exhilarated with glowing eyes and shining cheeks. He had loved being outside and away from the house, and despite all the differences that seemed to separate them, he could not reason as to why Mathew and he could not be friends. During the early days of Matthew's stay, Selina took both boys for the first time, to her church in the township, and to local prayer meetings on the banks of a nearby river. Andreas had been awed by the singing and the lively rhythms of the drums, both of which stood in deep contrast to the solemnity of the Orthodox Church of which his parents were members. For the first time in his life Andreas found that God was not completely alien and boring. Those were exciting days for Andreas and he still recalled how he had felt happy and content.

Around the time of Mathew's arrival, Andreas's mother had been busy with the party preparations and her social calendar. Consequently, she had not noticed how much time Andreas was spending with the servants.

Christmas Eve finally arrived. Andreas's parents took him for a trip to town. They wandered happily through brightly decorated city streets, hand in hand. He was treated to a milkshake and a toasted crab sandwich at John Orr's, a large department store. When they set off home the car was loaded with parcels. Andreas insisted on buying a present for Matthew as well. Later on that afternoon, he had played happily on the living room carpet with his father, all the while eyeing the presents under the tree that he knew could not be opened until the next day. As night had fallen, the honored guests began to arrive for the party. It had been a splendid affair. Large chandeliers blazed proudly, while pool fountains danced rhythmically to the sound of their own music. French champagne bubbled in crystal glasses, and single malt whiskey flowed like water. Exotic and pricey hors d'oeuvres of Russian caviar and pate de faux gras were passed out to guests on elegant silver trays.

Upstairs in his room, Andreas felt lonely and deserted. He needed company, and the noise from the party made it impossible for him to sleep. As he lay awake he pondered his options for a little while, before making up his mind to find something to do. He knew that he could not join the party without angering his mother. He put on his slippers, and silently jumped from the open bedroom window onto the balcony roof. He then climbed down to the garden below. He looked around carefully and when he was sure that no one had seen him, he ran toward the servants' quarters. This part of the grounds was deathly quiet. A single weak lamp threw a feeble glow through the window of his nanny's bedroom. He pushed the door open and entered. Inside, he found Matthew sitting on the concrete floor, playing contentedly with two wheels, the remains of one of Andreas's discarded toys. The young umfaan (boy) was startled to see Andreas and jumped to his feet, dropping the toy on the floor. His face was a picture of bewilderment. It was unusual for Andreas to visit the servants' quarters unaccompanied by Selina and especially at that time of the night.

"What are you doing here? Does Madam know?" he asked uneasily.

"Come and play with me, Matthew!" Andreas urged.

"No Andreas, it's too late. You know my mother said I can't come to the big house. Better leave it. Tomorrow is Sunday. We can play at the river."

"Don't be scared, Matthew. It's all right if you're with me. Besides, don't be frightened of my mother, she's a very nice lady. And Matthew, you've got to see my new toys. They're super. Come on, let's go," insisted Andreas.

The black child still hesitated, but Andreas seized him by the hand and pulled him up. Matthew went along with him, afraid yet excited by the word 'toys' and mostly unable to say no to the young white boy. Like a night-moth, the bright lights of the big house attracted him.

Matthew stood in Andreas's room, his mouth agape. Never in his life had he seen such luxury. Little by little, he gained his confidence and started to slide his bare feet pleasurably over the soft carpet. All the toys dazzled him, and he enjoyed what he uneasily knew, must be the sweet taste of forbidden fruit.

The two boys were immersed in an exciting game of Shaka Zulu with imaginary spears and shields when suddenly the bedroom door flew open and in marched Andreas's mother. Mrs. Magdalos had been very angry when she saw that the light was still on in the room and realized that her son was still not asleep. When she saw Matthew on the bed however, her anger turned to rage.

"Oh, my God!" she screamed.

The piercing yell brought Matthew back to reality, and he jumped down from the bed, his small body trembling. Terrified, he looked at the mistress of the house and cringed like a trapped animal.

"I'm sorry, madam, I'm very sorry," he wailed, and looked around for a way to escape.

"What are you doing in my house, you wretched little kaffir?" Mrs. Magdalos shrieked, raising her hand in a threatening manner. "I will kill you!"

Matthew, confused and frightened, with tears in his eyes, bowed his head, ran to the window and leaped out. Andreas had stood motionless and astounded, unable to believe what was taking place.

"M-M-Mom," he finally managed to stammer, "Why are you shouting at Matthew like that? It is not his fault. He's good. He's my friend. I brought him here."

Mrs. Magdalos could control herself no longer and she turned on him, slapping him twice across the face.

"I've told you over and over again, I forbid you to play with blacks. My God, what a nerve you have! Have you lost your mind? What impudence to bring him into my house. And how he stinks, too! How can you stand the smell of them? Oh really, it makes me feel sick!" she shouted as she pressed a scented handkerchief to her nose and violently opened all the windows.

Andreas looked her in the eyes, unable to hold back his tears. "Mommy, stop it!"

"Hold your tongue," she screamed at him furiously, "What in the hell do you know? Next thing he will be letting in all his friends to rob this house. Turn off the lights and go to bed at once! I'm telling your father. He'll fix you tomorrow!"

Andreas was too confused and upset to go to sleep. He felt so lonely and isolated. He could not understand his mother's violence, and knew that he could talk to nobody about what had just happened.

The next morning, Matthew was returned to his village and an enormous sense of emptiness overtook Andreas. He felt trapped within himself and guilty that he had unwillingly caused so much trouble and unhappiness for Selina. It was at that time, as his isolation grew, that he first decided to express his inner feelings of confusion in the form of a diary. After all, he believed correctly that he had nobody else to turn to. Over the years his diary became his faithful friend and confidant, someone with whom he could share his feelings of guilt and pain; feelings that would persist to haunt him for most of his adult life.

"I can't understand," he wrote in an early entry, "how it is that you can live so close to people, let them bring you up, wash you, cook your food, and yet at the same time you are expected to hate them just because of their skin color?".

Over the years, many more unanswered questions arose constantly and persistently in Andreas's mind.

"Why do blacks not have the right to use their talents and abilities in any way they want? Why do they not have the right to vote, to speak freely, or even to have access to a reasonable education? Why are they forbidden to own property? Why do they have to ride in separate lifts, buses and trains? Why should several hundred thousand blacks have to go to jail every year for offenses that have been created simply and solely for the purposes of apartheid?"

Gradually, Andreas came to realize that he could not understand or accept the racist regime of apartheid in South Africa. On the day of his mother's outburst, new questions arose within him, begging to be answered. How could Tsafendas, who was half-Greek, like him, commit a crime like that? Did Tsafendas also hate racism just like he did? Was he a psychotic criminal, or perhaps, just a man who truly loved his country?

CHAPTER 2 Awakening

Over time, Andreas's views had become more and more pronounced. His parents became increasingly concerned about what they believed to be unhealthy and dangerous attitudes on the part of their son, regarding the plight of the black population. At first, they felt that he would outgrow what they saw as childish and romantic notions. However, as Andreas grew into a man his revolutionary ideas intensified. His parents were particularly disturbed when he began to insist on arguing political points with his family. Their household gradually became engulfed in frequent domestic arguments that often ended with Andreas storming out of the house. One event in particular alarmed his parents so deeply, that they decided in their desperation, to send their son far away from South Africa.

High school graduation was approaching. Andreas felt a sense of joy, euphoria and excitement that he could not explain, perhaps because he was turning eighteen and looking forward to life after school. The world seemed to belong to him; all he had to do was grasp it in his hands, squeeze and drink the juice. He had an excellent academic record and his father had promised him a new sports car, and a trip to Europe as his reward.

Andreas always enjoyed eating breakfast on the verandah overlooking the swimming pool. The garden was in bloom and the grass manicured to perfection. The clean fresh pool water shimmered in the sunlight and the waterfall murmured its usual alluring melodies. He thought that life could be beautiful in the Republic of South Africa, under the right conditions. One needed only to be white and rich. Selina and Maria, the cook, arrived with trays filled with an array of breakfast delicacies. There was enough food to feed four people. He had loved those two women and felt loved by them in return. They had raised him from infancy and had been present at every point of his life. He wished that he could ask them to sit and join him for breakfast, but knew that they would be too frightened. Either way, his mother was sitting in the living room, and Andreas did not feel like arguing today. His country had so many problems that bothered him, but on that day he was preoccupied with his upcoming trip. All he could only think of was London, Paris, Rome and Athens. Andreas ate with the zestful appetite of youth and after a swim and shower, he decided to visit his tailor in order to prepare his wardrobe for the trip. As he was leaving the telephone rang and he ignored it.

"Andreas, Andreas! Pick up the phone. It's Carol," his mother shouted.

Cornered by his mother's insistence, he picked up the phone.

"Hi Carol. What's happening?"

"I don't know why I always have to chase you Andreas?"

"Don't be mean. You know that I am running around to get ready for my trip."

"I would like to see you. I miss you. Would you like to go to the drive-in tonight?"

"How romantic! But still, it's not a bad idea. I will pick you up at eight."

It did not bother him which film they would see. Nobody went to the drive-in for the sake of the film.

Anthony's Tailors was located in the heart of the city, on Bree Street. Anthony was one of the best tailors in South Africa, according to Andreas's father. He was a cultured and well-dressed Indian man who had learned his craft from his father. His trade was a source of great pride, a family affair that went back for generations. He was the Magdalos personal tailor and Andreas had known him ever since he was a young child. He had accompanied his father, many times over the years, when he came in for his fittings. Anthony was known for taking a great deal of interest in his customers and he dressed each of them with taste and elegance. His store boasted a luxurious selection of English cashmere and other fine materials, and was perfectly suited to satisfy even the most demanding of customers. A team of

Indian tailors had worked for Anthony since they were young boys and each had mastered their craft by working constantly on sewing machines under Anthony's direction. Anthony, or rather Mr. Lala as he was known around his boutique, was a slender middle aged gentleman of medium height with an honest open face, and delicate facial features. His skin was almost white and only his slightly darker lips showed his nationality. He had rich bushy white hair and his eyes were shiny and bright under his glasses. Andreas's father had often said that the old tailor must have belonged to a higher caste of Hindus. He looked to the old man's light complexion, obvious education and genteel nature as proof of his Brahman status.

Mr. Lala himself was untiring and would do anything to please. He spoke perfect English with a characteristic Indian accent. He was a spiritual man, although well versed in world affairs. Most importantly, he was a master of his craft. He told Andreas that a good garment has to uplift and enhance your personality rather than the other way around, something that only a good craftsman could achieve. Andreas had long felt warmly towards the old man more especially as Mr. Lala managed to hold on to what seemed to be a constant demeanor of zest and joy.

Strangely however, on that day, Andreas found him walking on the pavement outside of his shop in a disheveled state with his hands behind his back. This was a major departure in behavior for Mr. Lala who usually stood by the entrance of the shop door, chewing chili bites while waiting to welcome his customers. Andreas was shocked by the desperation on the old man's face. His skin seemed dry and his shriveled eyelids were stretched over his red eyes. As Anthony paced, Andreas could feel the depth of the old tailor's confusion, even panic.

"Hello Mr. Lala, what is the matter? What is happening to you?" he asked with trepidation. The old man stopped and looked at Andreas as though he saw him for the first time. He had tears in his eyes.

"I am lost," he whispered, "lost," he repeated to himself. "They sent me a registered letter saying that I have until the end of the month to pack up and go. The building has been sold and it is going for demolition. Can you believe that? After thirty five years of operation they are chasing me away, throwing me in the street like a dog."

Andreas had been caught unprepared. He did not know what to say.

"I understand how upset you are Mr. Lala, but it is not the end of the world. There are plenty of vacant shops in the center of the city. You could easily continue somewhere else. If money is a problem, I am sure my father would help you."

Mr. Lala stopped pacing and looked up at Andreas slowly, puzzled as if the young man was an alien from outer space.

"You are young. You don't know. You can't understand my child. Things are not that easy when you are not a first-class citizen. The law forbids Blacks, Indians and Asians to have their own business in the white areas. They want us all out."

"But then how did they allow you to operate over the past thirty five years?" Andreas asked him in confusion.

"While we were under British occupation, they allowed us, more especially the Indians to do business all over the country. When it became a Republic, the apartheid regime introduced new laws. All those who had business were allowed to continue until our leases expired. After that we lost the right to do business in the so-called white areas. Now, if I want to open a business, I have to move to the township, Lanseria, set aside for Indians only. To do what there? The people are poor, most of them unemployed. Who has the money to buy a suit? I don't know what to do. I feel so disillusioned. What will happen to all my workers without a job? How are they going to support their families? How will I manage to support my three kids, two are studying in England and one in Canada? Do you realize they are not allowed to study here?"

Andreas felt awful, as though he was the creator of the problem. He realized that the guilty feeling was indeed familiar to him. He pushed the thought aside and tried to give Mr. Lala courage.

"You must not despair Mr. Lala. I am sure there must be a way."

"Yes there is, but only if I do business under a white man's name. Where am I going to find him? Who would accept to do such a thing for me?"

Andreas could offer no consolation and he could not stand the pain of the Indian man's desperation. His excitement about the trip and his new wardrobe had disappeared. It had been squashed, defeated and now thoroughly replaced by his anger. He became determined to help the old man.

"I will talk to my father this evening," he promised. "I am sure he will find a way. You are his friend. He will help you."

For a split second, Andreas thought he saw a ray of hope in Mr. Lala's eyes, but it quickly disappeared.

"Nobody is prepared to take them on," Lala said, "everybody is afraid. They are too bloody strong."

Andreas left feeling powerless. He walked purposelessly for a little while, on the busy roads of the city. He stopped in front of a building that advertised L.K. Jacobs: Stores, Offices for Rent. He liked the position and he imagined that Anthony's Tailors would do very well there. A black beggar, paralyzed from the waist down, pulled himself toward Andreas. He avoided the beggar and continued his walk, past shop windows displaying expensive furs and magnificent jewelry, made of fine gold and diamonds. Further down, policemen with automatic guns and sjamboks in their hands had formed a blockade. Indiscriminately they stopped black pedestrians who were passing by, to check their passbooks. All the illegal blacks were packed into a waiting Black Maria, an iron caged truck used to transport black people who had been arrested.

Andreas wondered into the well-tended gardens of Joubert Park. A preacher was standing at the entrance talking about the glory of God and the sins of His people. The flowers were in bloom and the park benches were couched neatly under the shadow of climbing roses. Written plainly on each bench were the typical WHITES ONLY signs. Andreas walked through the park before deciding to escape into the art gallery. He had always been uplifted by the expansive display of paintings including Picassos and El Grecos. Normally, the paintings inspired him, but that day the art of titans hang limp and lifeless on the barren walls. He left the exhibits, his heart frozen under the powerful South African sun.

He returned home with much less enthusiasm than when he had departed like a deflated balloon. His parents were sitting on the verandah, enjoying a sundowner while listening to the Moonlight Sonata on the stereo. He knew that this was not the right moment to talk about Mr. Lala's problems. They asked him to join them for a drink but he excused himself by telling them that he had planned to go out with Carol.

Andreas freshened up and put on an outfit that he knew Carol liked. He drove to pick her up at her house in his neighborhood. She was a tall, beautiful woman and the short mini-dress she was wearing made her appear even more enticing. As she approached the car, her playfully sly smile dropped. She had sensed that Andreas was in a bad mood. She kissed him softly before asking him what was wrong. He wanted to open his heart and tell her the story of Mr. Lala. He kept quiet however, because he knew that she shared the same values as his mother as did nearly every white in his community. Instead, he drove in contemplative silence as Carol played with the radio. The drive-in was nearly full that evening but they finally managed to find a spot on the side. They were unconcerned with their tight angle to the screen. Distorted, projected images flooded the white backdrop with scenes from coming attractions. Neither of the young lovers was interested in the movies. Carol eased herself close to Andreas. She was burning with excitement and knew well that she had the power to make Andreas forget his mysterious troubles. As her tongue lined his lips and entered his mouth, Andreas allowed Mr. Lala to escape from his mind. He needed her. After feeling so powerless and alone throughout the day, he needed to feel pleasure and a sense of connection. He embraced her fully and forcefully pulled her upon him. As she straddled him between the front seats, his hands wantonly explored her long and slender form. He had always found Carol irresistible, and seemed never to get enough of her curvy body. His desire was palpable and Carol moaned as he slid inside her.

The problems of the day seemed to evaporate with the passion of love making. They were done well before the end of the movie. Hungry, they decided to go to the drive-in restaurant across the street to have something to eat. They were just finishing their last bite when a black man passed so close to the car that the tray nearly fell off.

"Look at that kaffir! He must be drunk," Carol said spitefully.

Andreas looked at her in disbelief, disappointed by her obvious prejudice. With one word she reaffirmed the sour taste of the day.

Andreas ignored her and focused on the stumbling man. The face of the middle aged black man glowed with a layer of perspiration under the parking lot lights. He was holding his left side, his hand pressed over his heart. All the while, his left hand was outstretched, desperately gesturing for help. He struggling to reach the back-lit window of the drive-in restaurant then fell limply to the ground before attaining his objective. The young waitress, who just so happened to be passing by, screamed. An older white man appeared from inside the roadhouse door and hurriedly moved her inside. The unknown black man remained flat on his face. No one dared to approach him. Andreas had had enough of sitting idly by. He got out of his car and hurried toward the man.

"Where are you going? What are you doing?" he heard Carol's voice. It was shrill and twisted with her confusion.

As Andreas drew close to the injured man, he saw a stream of bright red blood. He kneeled down and turned the man on his back. He was terrified to see a large deep wound in the man's chest. It looked like he had been stabbed with a butcher's knife. He was bleeding profusely, and losing more blood with every beat of his heart. The black man opened his eyes and looked at him pleadingly.

"I was robbed of all my pay. Please help me Boss," he whispered, nearly out of breath.

He did not smell of alcohol. With this man dying before him, Andreas was horrified to realize that he had little idea of what to do. He took out his handkerchief and pushed it into the wound, pressing it down with force. The bleeding seemed to ease and Andreas saw color retuning to the man's face.

"Help," Andreas shouted loudly. "In the name of God, call an ambulance."

Nobody moved or even gave them the slightest attention. Andreas felt trapped as if in a nightmare. The more he yelled, the more people avoided and ignored him. The handkerchief soon became saturated with blood and began gurgling over. Eventually, Carol came over with a disgusted expression on her face.

Andreas ignored her obvious disapproval.

"Carol, go and ask the shop if they called the ambulance. Get some towels to help stop the bleeding."

Carol returned with a couple of kitchen towels.

"They have called," she said to him. "They said they would send someone. Andreas you can't sit here, it is not safe. Leave him alone! He is just a drunk kaffir who's been in a fight."

"But he is dying," Andreas said.

"I don't give a damn! If you don't leave now, I am calling a taxi and I am going home," she protested, but Andreas did not answer.

"Make sure that you never call me again! I have had enough of you and your craziness. I don't ever want to see you again!"

Andreas let her go. He kept pressing down as he tried to staunch the bleeding for nearly two unendurable hours. Every time he reduced pressure, the wounded man appeared to fade away. Andreas looked up, at the sound of each passing car, hoping to see the glaring lights of an ambulance. However, help never come and eventually, the nameless man died in Andreas's arms. He was forced to abandon the body in the parking lot. Andreas walked away, his suit covered in the dead man's blood. The occupants of the other cars glared at him with contempt, as he had left.

The next morning he went to the office of L.K. Jacobs and signed a ten year lease. He had made a decision that from now onwards he would not subject himself to anything he did not believe in, and that he would make even the smallest effort to do whatever he could to make a difference to this inhuman system. Mr. Lala cried like a small baby when Andreas gave him the contract for his new store.

"I would like this to remain between us," Andreas had told him. "I don't even want my father to know about it."

Mr. Lala took Andreas's hands in his and he tried to kiss them with gratitude.

"Your name from now on will be Motobai, which in our language means big brother. You are my brother and I and my family thank you."

Andreas felt awkward with his new title, but he secretly believed that he deserved it. For a moment, he had even entertained the thought of himself as a religious zealot, assured of his place in heaven. Surprisingly, he was not at all depressed to have lost Carol. Instead, he felt a sense of freedom and purpose. He realized that for the first time, he believed himself to be a worthy human being. It was a high that he planned to ride for the rest of his days.

After a week, Andreas left for his European vacation. He spent some carefree, relaxed and happy months traveling around Europe. Truthfully, he would not have minded to stay there, and he returned home with a heavy heart.

He had not yet recovered from jet lag when he received a strange and macabre call. It was not yet eight o'clock in the morning and yet the telephone rang without stopping, waking him up from a deep sleep.

"Yes," he was able to say, unable to hide the hostility in his voice.

"I want to talk to Mr. Magdalos, Andreas Magdalos," stated an authoritative voice on the other side of the line, with a pronounced Afrikaans accent.

"That's me," Andreas murmured.

"This is Pieter Coetzee, Sergeant Coetzee from the Security Branch of John Vorster Square. I want you in my office no later than ten o'clock tomorrow morning or else I will come and pick you up! Do you understand? My address is tenth floor of John Vorster Square, Office 1024," said the sergeant in a threatening manner as he slammed down the telephone.

Every vestige of sleep had disappeared from Andreas's eyes.

"What the hell is going on?" Andreas said out aloud. "What the hell do I have to do with the Security Police? Most probably it is a stupid friend again trying to play a trick on me."

He made himself a strong cup of coffee, but before he was able to taste it, the phone rang again.

"Surely it has to be that stupid friend ready to laugh at his silly joke," he thought.

"Can I speak to Mr. Andreas," Andreas recognized the characteristic voice of Mr. Lala and butterflies of anxiety fluttered in his mind.

"It is me, Mr. Lala. What is happening?"

"Motobai, we have some problems. If you don't mind, come at once so that we can talk."

"What is going on? Can't you tell me now?" Andreas said anxiously.

"No, it is better you pass from here. You can't discuss these things over the telephone."

Andreas understood with certainty that there was some trouble with the contract that he had signed.

"Alright, Mr. Lala, I will be there right away!"

He found Mr. Lala waiting at the entrance of his business, obviously upset.

"Thank you Motobai for getting here so quickly. You are such a good man. Let's go to my office so we can talk in private."

They went inside and closed the door.

"Motobai," he went straight to the point, "yesterday evening and again this morning someone by the name of Sergeant Coetzee from the Security police came by and he wanted to know to whom this business belongs. Naturally, I told him that you are the boss and that I am just your manager. It did not seem that he was convinced and he asked me for your phone number. He told me that he was going to get in touch with you."

"He has already called me and demanded that I come to his office by tomorrow morning," Andreas said.

Mr. Lala tried to reassure Andreas, who actually looked calmer than the Indian man.

"You must not be anxious at all Motobai. I have already spoken with the leader of our community. He is a lawyer and he assured me that I do not have anything to worry about. They can never prove anything. He wants to meet with you and advise you about what you must say tomorrow. If you don't mind we could go now, he is waiting for us."

Andreas did not know what to do. It had all happened so unexpectedly.

"Is it far?" he asked.

"No, it is by the old Indian market, near the slaughterhouse. I won't take us more than half an hour."

"Then let's go and get it over with."

Andreas, who was born and bred in the city, was surprised that he did not know of the existence of the Indian market. It was a pleasant surprise however. He felt transported from Europe to Asia. Narrow streets were filled with little stands displaying a variety of merchandise. Men were dressed in ethnic costumes and women in silk saris. Aromatic spices such as curry, cumin, all spice, masala and others gave an exotic ambience to the old market. Andreas had noticed that the majority of buyers were whites looking for bargains. They entered a bridal store which did not lack any of the products that could be found in the opulent white areas. Although it had been before noon, Andreas noticed that the store was already filled with mothers and daughters. Mr. Lala took him down the stairs. They entered a huge basement filled with bales of materials and then to the private office of the owner.

Mr. Patel was a bent, middle aged man of medium height. He was bald and wore thin frames with heavy myopic lenses. He was a lawyer who had retired from practice and now attended to the family business. Given his experience in community affairs, he had been informally elected as the community leader. He eyes sparkled with intelligence and his wide forehead showed competence and courage. He was dressed in ethnic costume that reminded Andreas of Gandhi. He welcomed them with a smile and a warm handshake. He then offered them freshly brewed tea from a large porcelain teapot. He had obviously been expecting them.

"Motobai," he said to Andreas, "I have heard so much about you. You are a brave young man with guts and humanity. He added, "you have undertaken this difficult endeavor for no reward or payment. If there were many people like you, the world would definitely be a better place." He then served the tea, filling their cups with aromatic brew.

"Listen Andreas, you have nothing to fear. Tomorrow you will go to John Vorster Square with confidence. As long as you stand by and maintain that the business is yours and that Mr. Lala and the rest of the workers are employees, you have nothing to fear. The lease, as well as the trading license are in your name. According to the law, they will not be able to do anything because they do not have any evidence to the contrary. So hopefully, they will not bother you again. Furthermore, I would like to reassure you that the Indian community is behind you and thanks you for what you are doing.

Whatever happens you must know that we will be behind you and you have our full support."

Andreas felt reassured. He had returned home ready to withstand and oppose the establishment on the following day. He had even considered asking his father's opinion but quickly rejected that idea.

The building at John Vorster Square was a tall and modern structure that covered a whole square block. It appeared peaceful and it was hard to believe that it was one of the most hated buildings in the world. It was a stronghold for the Nationalistic government and a Golgotha for anyone who tried to oppose the racist regime. It also housed the Police Headquarters and the Security police. Andreas had parked his car in the prescribed area for Security Police, as he looked around to get his bearings. He took a deep breath and tried to infuse himself with confidence. With a steady step, he entered the main building. He took one of the numerous lifts and pressed the button for the tenth floor. He looked at his image in the mirror and he adjusted his tie. He liked what he saw. He was very elegant in his new suit. The lift was fast and smooth. A bell rang as he reached his destination. Andreas emerged with composure into a long white passage. It was so clinical, cold and empty that it reminded him of a hospital. A man with a fierce face was sitting behind a small desk in the lobby. He had looked at Andreas with disdain and asked impolitely.

"Can I help you?"

"I am looking for Sergeant Coetzee."

He gave him a long searching look.

"At the end of the passage, Room 1024."

Andreas's steps sounded heavy and hollow as he walked on the linoleum floor. What really struck his interest were the heavy metallic iron bars that were fastened in the windows. An incident came to his mind that had made front page news, a few days previously. The realization made him feel uneasy.

The newspaper had reported that an Indian teacher Achmet Timol had been arrested under the terrorist act and questioned by the Security Police. He was accused of unlawful doings against the State. While in custody, in his effort to escape from a window on the tenth floor, he had supposedly slipped to a tragic death. Andreas looked around to see if anyone was watching and he went over to test the sturdiness of the window bars. He had shocked to realize that it was physically impossible for anybody to get out from there.

"How was that possible?" he thought. "Those bars look like they have been in place for ever. The police must have thrown the man off the roof!" He was terrified by the discovery.

He found the office number 1024 in the middle of the passage. He knocked tentatively on the door.

"Come in," stated a gruff voice.

It was an antechamber, sparsely furnished with a desk and two chairs. Behind the desk on the wall were two portraits; one of Hendrick Verwoerd, the founder of apartheid, and the other was of John Vorster, the present Prime Minister. A man, very similar to the one he had seen before in the lobby, was seated behind the desk.

"Yes," he said.

"I have an appointment with Sergeant Coetzee," he replied.

"Go inside and wait. He will be here soon."

The spacious inner room had a large window overlooking Commissioner Street with the same iron bars as in the corridor. There was nobody inside.

A familiar voice behind him said,

"Good morning. I'm Sergeant Coetzee. Mr. Magdalos, I am sorry that I had to bring you over here. I know that you are a very busy young man but there are some things that you cannot do over the phone," he said politely. "Please sit down."

Sergeant Coetzee was a tall rugged, well-built man, about forty years old. He seemed too well-mannered to be a policeman. He was wearing a dark blue suit with a red tie and he had the longest hands that Andreas had ever seen in his life. Without exaggeration, his arms reached down past his knees and his palms looked like spades.

"Would you like some coffee?" he asked.

"No thank you," Andreas replied, confused by the officer's polite approach, so different from their earlier telephone call.

They looked at each other in silent confrontation. Coetzee glanced at his watch as though he was in a hurry as he sat down in his chair behind the desk.

"Well then we can start. The reason that I called you here is to clarify a few things," he told Andreas in a friendly tone.

"Whatever you would like," Andreas replied with increasing confidence.

"Very well. How old are you Mr. Magdalos?"

"I have just turned eighteen."

"What was your purpose in visiting London, Paris and Rome?" he asked with the hint of a scowl.

"I don't believe that it is any of your business. Don't you have more important things to do than investigate my private life?" Andrew asserted. The words of the Indian community lawyer still echoed in his mind that he had nothing to fear.

"Mr. Magdalos, before we continue, I must say that I have a lot of respect for your family. Your father is a successful businessman and a staunch member of the Nationalist Party. Your mother is an Afrikaner, from a very good family. She is one of us. But believe me, if things were not like that, I would treat you very differently. I have a lot of important things that call for my time," he said in a warning tone.

Sergeant Coetzee stood up from his chair and the room filled with his presence. He looked menacingly at Andreas. He smiled sardonically and sat down on the edge of the desk a step away from the young man. Andreas again began to feel insecure. He remembered the windows in the corridor.

"Meneer Magdalos, you have to understand that in this space, I am the boss. Only I have the right to ask the questions. You have only to reply to what I ask you. Do you understand?" he said coldly bringing his face close to that of Andreas.

Andreas said with deference, "I went away for a vacation. May I ask what your interest is?"

"Everything is important to us here in Security. I want to know what you did and how you passed your time."

"As I told you, I was on vacation and I did what all tourists do."

"Ahh, Meneer Magdalos, by the way, I forgot to tell you something else. I don't like lies. Lies turn me into a wild beast. You know this is a complex shared by all people working here in Security. Our fatherland is very important to us and we try to keep it safe. Did you meet with any other South Africans there?"

"No, only the people that traveled with me in the plane."

"Well, we will see about that. By the way, who is the owner of Anthony's Tailor in Plain Street?" he asked suddenly looking at Andreas straight in the eyes.

"I am," Andreas answered.

"Aren't you very young to have your own business?"

"There is no law to forbid it," Andreas said.

"Very well, can you explain why, that in the past few months that we have been observing the store, you were never seen either opening or closing the shop? Or for that matter, why did you never go to the bank to make deposits, or to get pay for your employees?"

Andreas had never thought about the answers to all of these questions, but he tried to reply, "The nature of this business is such that don't have to be there very often. Nonetheless, Mr. Lala and my bookkeeper take care of all of that."

"Mr. Magdalos, I am a reasonable man. First of all, I do not want to harm you, just to help you. I know for a fact that this business is not yours. I assume that you only did what you did because you are innocent, stupid young man trying to help Lala, with no profit in mind despite the laws of the country. If you tell me the truth, I will help you to get out of the mess that you have created for yourself. So I will ask you for the last time, who is the owner of Anthony's Tailor. To whom does this business belong?"

"To me," Andreas said.

Sergeant Coetzee moved so quickly that Andreas did not have a chance to resist. His left hand grabbed him by his tie and he extended his other arm and slapped Andreas with full force on his right cheek. His hand then turned and he smacked him with the back of his hand on the other side of his face.

"You fucking Greek. I will bring the shit from out of your mouth. I told you, I can't stand lies. I am asking you for the last time."

Strong pain and fear engulfed Andreas. He saw many-colored stars, and warm liquid ran down his nose. His face was burning and he felt his lips swelling from the handprints on his face. For the first time in his life, he felt that his knees were made out of jelly, and his mouth became dry from fear.

"You fucking asshole. You want to play the hero with me? What you have committed is treason. You've betrayed your country! I can stick you in a hole so deep that you never see the sun again. All of your father's money will not be able to help you. As you know, I have the power under the law to keep you here as long as I like, and no fucking lawyers or anybody else for that matter will be able to take you out of my hands. I will repeat my question once more. Who owns the tailor shop?"

"I do," Andreas said but with much less confidence.

"I warned you that I can't take lies." The sergeant struck him again and blood trickled out of Andreas's nose. Sergeant Coetzee took out a box of handkerchiefs and he gave them with contempt to Andreas to wipe his face.

"I wonder why you would want to play this stupid hero's game," he said in a softer and friendlier voice, "when yesterday morning after a few rough questions, Lala tried to bribe me with a handsome amount of money to turn my eyes away from the matter. Lala told me that he is the owner and that you are just the nominee. It is so clear that you don't know the consequences of breaking the law here."

"Lies. Mr. Lala would never have done a thing like that."

"You are so fucking naive. If you don't believe me, I will send for him right away to hear it from his own mouth. What do you say about that?"

"I don't believe it. How could he do that to me?" The thought of such an act made Andreas feel dizzy, but nonetheless, he suddenly knew that the sergeant was speaking the truth. A violent anger engulfed him. He hated his country. He especially hated Lala who had betrayed him and brought him into this tragic situation.

"You don't know these people. If you give them a finger they take your arm. You are very young and stupid. I have contacted your parents and they are furious with you. I told them I don't want to harm you so you had better listen to what I am telling you. I only want Lala out of the city. I will let you go now to L. K. Jacobs. Cancel the lease. I want Lala out by the end of the week; otherwise you are going to be in a lot of trouble."

"You must be joking. I have signed a ten-year lease. They will never release me," Andreas managed to say.

"That is no problem. Take my card and go and tell them what has happened. If they don't release you, tell them to call me. You can go now, but as I told you I want him out by the end of the week, or else!"

Andreas left feeling nauseous and desperate like an abused dog. He could taste the iron flavor of blood in his mouth. He felt sadness and shame. He wanted to cry, hit his head against the wall and scream. He wanted to see Lala and spit in his face for the humiliation of his betrayal. As he had descended in the lift, he looked at himself in the elevator's mirror. Coetzee's handprints were obvious upon his face. His nose and eyes were swollen and turning blue. His anger increased against the system of his county, against the sergeant and every other sergeant who had the power to humiliate those who gave them the power.

He then went straight away to the offices of L. K. Jacobs. There, he was once again surprised; with the same ease that they had signed the contract in the first place, they now tore the document into four pieces. It was obvious that they did not want any problems with the Security Police.

Andreas arrived at Anthony's Tailors out of breath with an ugly expression on his swollen face. When Lala saw him he tried to run away. Andreas grabbed him by the back of his coat. Lala turned and looked at him with tears in his eyes. He feebly put his hands over his face as if he was warding off imaginary blows.

"Don't, please don't," the old man pleaded.

"Why?" Andreas asked him.

"From fear Motobai. I was so afraid, that man is terrible."

Tears filled Andreas's eyes. He had understood what Lala meant, because for the first time, he too had felt what fear is.

"I understand, but you must vacate the store by the end of the week."

Andreas left the store thinking about what was waiting for him in the living room of his house. Andreas's parents were so distressed with the call from Sergeant Coetzee that they decided to resort to desperate measures. They made a decision to separate from their only son and send him to Greece. They hoped that a lengthy stay in a country with no racial problems would help him to see the world more realistically. They wanted him to appreciate, what seemed to them, to be the most significant difficulty in life; the plight of surviving without a great deal of money. They felt that struggle would help subdue his political feelings.

When they told Andreas, they were surprised to find him actually enthusiastic about the idea. It was evident that he felt disillusioned and angry with all that had happened. It would be many years before Andreas would return to his country. When he eventually did come back home, he found Mr. Lala operating in the same location on Plain Street. How and why this had occurred, he did not really want to know. Somehow however, his intuition told him that Sergeant Coetzee was now involved in the fashion business.

CHAPTER 3 Tilting at Windmills

The trip to Greece exceeded Andreas's expectations. He fell in love with the scenery that was so different to the beauty of his homeland. Greece had a wonderful light that he imagined only great painters could truly appreciate. The Mediterranean sky was clear and deep blue. In the mornings, before the wind started to stir, it would reach down and mate with the sea. At those moments it became impossible to tell where one ended and the other began. He found the scent of thyme intoxicating as he walked the mountains and drank deep of the majestic views; great panoramas of sparkling sea and rugged, rocky coastline. Everywhere he traveled he was surrounded by the accomplishments of his ancestors, the ancient marble ruins, the legends and traditions, all so vivid and abundant. He experienced a liveliness that encompassed him. He became a worshipper of life and beauty.

To him, Greece was like an aged countess who had preserved her dignity throughout the long trials of an eventful and turbulent life. The country had endured so much; civilizations, wars, philosophers, and gods of every kind. It was as if all those years of trial and turmoil had contributed to making the land calm and tranquil. He found the people to be peaceful and for the most part content. They were hospitable almost to a fault, always able to spare a kind word for a friend and a plate of food for the hungry. Most importantly though, they knew how to dance! When the first notes of the bouzouki or clarinet sounded, they scorned all material considerations and standing tall and brave they became gods, casting off the burdens of the flesh, becoming pure spirit. They danced with a freedom that went beyond style or step.

Andreas's relatives swamped him with love and affection. He found their homes to be less luxurious than his own, but more hospitable and more sociable. His aunt was not as attractive as his mother, but she had a warm personality and she was a great cook. What's more, she made him feel completely at home. His aunt and uncle were easygoing people and Andreas realized how anxious he had always felt around his own parents. He also thoroughly enjoyed the company of his cousins as they engaged in frequent discussions and lively debates concerning a vast array of topics. He was surprised to find them much more liberated and open-minded than his parents or most of his South African friends. For the first time in his life, Andreas felt a sense of inner peace and contentment. Consequently, his parents had no difficulty in persuading him to stay in Greece. Andreas decided to continue his studies and improve his Greek.

The months sped by and Andreas adapted very well to his new way of life. He became engrossed in the writings of the ancient Greek philosophers, and his ability to speak Greek improved rapidly. His warm-hearted nature and his passion for politics had all found a suitable environment in which to develop and mature. Back in South Africa, political conversations were virtually unknown. People there avoided talking about any topics that were either uncomfortable or socially taboo. They preferred arguments about sports like cricket and rugby, which could go on for days. In contrast, politics was a way of life in Greece. Almost every conversation invariably ended up in lively political arguments in the cafes, schools, homes, or the marketplace. Andreas had many debates with his uncle and cousins. He learned that Greece had been governed by a right-wing regime that had been in power for more than forty years. His uncle told him that thousands of Greeks were exiled on remote islands and that the police, in collaboration with the leaders of the army suppressed anyone who disagreed with the ruling practices. Dissidents were labeled communists and subversives. Andreas was attracted to the leader of the opposition, Georgios Papandreas; an experienced and democratic leader who accused the right of undermining the recent elections. He claimed that the entire electoral process was a farce and blamed the right for rigging the votes, and terrorizing the people with violence. He called for the help of the people in the struggle for democracy and the defense of constitutional liberties. Political instability reigned in Greece. It was time of political ferment. Daily demonstrations took place with people carrying slogans favoring higher standards of personal liberty, democracy, and political independence from the military dominance of the government. Andreas took great zest and even joy while participating in the events with family and friends.

His aunt and uncle had encouraged Andreas to enroll at the university. Soon, as a student of political science and a member of the student union, he was participating at the forefront of the struggle. He helped organize student demonstrations that demanded social change. He tirelessly argued that government should work to give people a better standard of life without racial or class distinctions.

It was during one of these demonstrations that he met Rena. She was a tall slim girl with a shy smile. She had long light-brown hair and velvet Mediterranean skin. Her eyes were a beautiful dark green and were framed by typical Greek almond-shaped lids. Despite her shy smile, she was surprisingly assertive and outspoken, with a lively and independent spirit that Andreas admired. He soon found that his life took on new dimensions. The sun seemed brighter, birds sang in trees and flowers bloomed. All nature seemed to celebrate his awakened senses. The calm seas tenderly embraced the golden beaches and the lapping waves sang mysterious songs to the shores. The whole of creation was sending signals to Aphrodite, the goddess of love. He and Rena had taken a trip to the little island of Poros. They enjoyed life as though it was just beginning, as if they were Adam and Eve. Most of all Andreas found that he appreciated the closing of the days. It was as if each day with Rena, was a great accomplishment. After hot hours of swimming, hiking, eating and love making they would sit quietly together and bid farewell to the sun. Sunset was the most idyllic hour, when the declining rays of the sun turned the western sky to gold. The sea breeze blew gently bringing coolness and relief to the inhabitants of the island, who were worn out by the heat. Crowds of carefree people milled about giving the small towns a carnival like atmosphere. Tables and chairs belonging to cafes and restaurants reached right down to the beach, where multicolored fishing boats rocked gently on the tranquil sea.

On their last evening on Poros, Andreas and Rena had chosen a table near the water. The gentle lapping of the waves seemed to be attempting to cast a spell over them. The waiter brought them the ouzos they had ordered, together with bread, tomatoes, cucumbers, octopus and dried fish. They clinked glasses, wishing each other good health, and they enjoyed the combination of the salty snacks with the aniseed aperitif. They were the only passengers on the ferry, which took them back to their hotel at the other end of the island. Captain Stefan was one of the colorful skippers who constituted the local transport system. He was a sprightly old man with a lean, energetic body, white hair and a face scarred by the salt. He had handed over the tiller to Rena, who played the part of captain with delight as she steered the little vessel to shore. Like happy children, Andreas and Rena ran through the thick sand until they came to an idyllic little harbor known locally as 'The Haven of Love'. They threw off the few clothes they were wearing and hurled their warm bodies into the sea. The full moon hung low on the horizon, pouring out its golden light to create a broad avenue of moonlight on the surface of the sea. The gentle waves played with the sand on the beach and a scented breeze blew over them. As lithe bodies joined together, their hearts filled with loving passion as they pulsated in unison on the warm sand. Andreas had never been happier. Their relationship tightened with time, and their love became more intense, overshadowing any considerations of study, idealism or political struggle. For Andreas however, love could only hide the problems of the world for so long.

He would never forget the day that everything changed. It was at a student rally, where he had made a speech about individual liberty and the rights of the citizen. When he had finished speaking, one of a few black students from Africa now studying in Greece asked him a question.

"Congratulations on a speech that was powerful and well-constructed. What I want to ask you though, is how can you refer to all these grand notions of equality and freedom when your own homeland, South Africa, has abolished them altogether?"

Andreas stood motionless. He felt as though he had been struck an invisible blow. His mouth turned dry and he found himself incapable of speech. He remembered his mother's views, her treatment of her servants and of course, Mr. Lala. Mostly however, he found himself suddenly re-haunted by the face of that nameless black man who had died in his arms. It was a face he had almost forgotten thanks to his happiness with Rena. All of his country's problems poured into his soul now, flooding his mind like frightful nightmares, mocking and cursing him.

"Why don't you answer, comrade?" called the man, irritated by his silence.

What could Andreas say? That he had forgotten where he had come from? That he no longer felt as though he identified with South Africa? That he was too frightened to go back?

"I'm a fool," he thought as he left the hall, hanging his head in shame. "Yes, I'm a Don Quixote killing stone windmills with my lance. If I really acted on what I believe, if I wasn't such a coward, I'd be back there at the core of the problem."

Thoughts of South Africa, rekindled by the man at the rally, continued to plague Andreas for months. He was beset by terrible dreams, in which he found himself bathed in blood, screaming, but unable to be heard. He would wake next to Rena covered in sweat, fully aware that he had been yelling in his sleep. He found himself growing more and more distant from all the things that he felt connected him to Greece. He thought himself a fraud and began to avoid political events. He even withdrew from Rena. Once again he turned to his diary for support as he seriously considered a decision to return to South Africa. Eventually, he tentatively approached his uncle revealing very little of the turmoil in his mind.

"Andreas, are you sure you've thought it through?" his uncle asked in surprise. "I have noticed that you do not seem to be very happy lately. Are you missing your family? But don't you think it's a pity to leave your studies uncompleted?"

"I do have my reasons, Uncle, but I am unable to explain them exactly. I'm not sure that I could help you to understand what's happening to me. In any case, I intend to finish my studies over there."

His uncle looked at him thoughtfully as if in search of an answer he hoped he could give to persuade his nephew to change his mind. Knowing Andreas, he recognized that his efforts were not likely to be successful and he whispered sadly.

"Well, you seem to have made up your mind, Andreas and I won't try to change it. I feel like I am losing my own son. Please don't forget us as your father did when he first went to Africa."

The pain of yet another guilt now stirred in Andreas's brain but all he could say was, "I'll miss you all very much. You see, it's a question of responsibility, I feel that I must go back."

"What about Rena? Have you thought about her? Does she know that you're leaving?" his aunt inquired.

Andreas had told Rena about the incident with the black student. He had shared with her from time to time his growing inner urge to return to South Africa. Rena had remained silent through many of these discussions, as though a great struggle was going on inside her.

Finally she told him, "Andreas, my love, I feel so confused. I care so much about you that I don't want to stop you from doing what you think is right, even if that were possible. My heart says that you have to stay because I love you more than anything. My conscience though contradicts me. It cries that I must not be selfish because we share the same goals and ideals. I too am against oppression, just like you. I also would like to see justice and humanity for all people. But the reality is, that for the last few months, I feel that I have been losing a little of you each day. You draw further and further away and I would rather lose all of you, as you are, instead to watch the man I love dissolve away over time. I am going to miss you so much!"

At the time, Andreas was moved and impressed by her words. Nonetheless, it would take some years for him to realize exactly what he had lost that day. On the day of his departure, Hellenikon airport was crowded with people in the turmoil of constant arrivals and departures. Among them were Andreas's relatives, friends, fellow-students and Rena. Andreas felt overwhelmed by the confusion of warm embraces, choked voices, wet handkerchiefs and farewell kisses. An inner voice had begun to question him.

"Where are you going? Why are you going? What are you looking for?"

As he ascended the gangway to board the plane, he was no longer certain of his decision. He stopped suddenly, turned around and began to go down the steps again, only to encounter the air hostess.

"I'm sorry sir, but we're about to take off. If you don't want to miss the plane, please go back on board."

The voice of fate had sounded. Andreas turned around again, and robot-like, he boarded the plane. Many hours later, the jumbo jet glided into the approach path for landing at Jan Smuts Airport. He passed through customs without trouble and emerged at the arrivals hall. His mother ran to him, crying with joy, and hugged him fiercely.

"Oh, Andreas, how you've grown. You don't know how we've missed you. It's so good to have you back."

Next, his father embraced him, trying in vain to hide his emotion. Andreas looked at them both with deep affection and wondered how he could have lived so far away from them for all those years. A chill gusty highveld wind blew into their faces as they went out to the open car park. They stopped in front of an opulent Rolls Royce and the chauffeur jumped out hastily and opened the doors. The young black man looked at Andreas with a grin as if he had known him for years and said,

"Welcome home Baas Andreas. It's good to see you again."

"Thanks very much," said Andreas, puzzled as to whether he knew the man.

Two porters carefully stowed the baggage in the boot, and Andreas shoved his hand into his pocket to look for a tip.

"Don't worry about that, son," said his father, "Matthew will look after that."

Andreas looked at his father and then at the black chauffeur in bewilderment.

"Matthew?" he murmured, "Matthew Matsimani, Selina's son, the young umfaan?"

"For sure," said his father cheerfully, "except that he's a man now."

After a long drive on recently constructed concrete highways, they arrived at their house. It had not changed very much, apart from some minor renovations. In his bedroom, Andreas felt as though time had stood still. Nothing had been altered and for a moment he was overwhelmed by childhood memories. He was tired after his journey. He had not slept on the plane, but after a few hours nap and a hot bath he felt refreshed. The family gathered feeling happily united in the snug warmth of their home. They talked about Greece and their relatives. Andreas poured drinks for everybody and put needle to record, filling the room with music. He sat on a stool, letting his body sway in time, as he did so his mind filled with nostalgic images of Rena.

He felt his father's hand on his shoulder and turned to look at him.

"I still don't understand why you came home so suddenly, son, but believe me; I've been looking forward to this day so much. Pour me another drink, Andreas. I feel quite dizzy and excited. What a small world it is when you can come home so quickly."

Andreas refilled their glasses and he and his father clinked them together as they drank to each other's health. They were emptied in one draught and then refilled. The living room swelled with the wild, proud beat of the bouzouki. In silence, united by drink and emotion, father and son looked at each other and smiled. They stood together, arms on each other's shoulders and then in unison, their feet and bodies launched into a traditional Greek dance.

"Good for you, my son, dance, dance!" shouted Mr. Magdalos, filled with pride and joy.

Speech was no longer needed; the bouzouki and the santouri said it all for them. Sweat beaded on their faces as the pace accelerated. After a while, they seemed to be to be flying rather than dancing. When the music ended, they collapsed into each other's arms, while Mrs. Magdalos burst into wild applause.

CHAPTER 4 Johannesburg, City of Gold

Several days had passed since his return home and yet Andreas was unable to get used to his return. He held on fiercely to his ties with Greece. His letters to Rena became more passionate with every day that he was parted from her. After the initial period of excitement, during which his family had become reacquainted, the household had again relapsed into its normal routine. Andreas's mother resumed her activities and social life, as well as her involvement in various charitable organizations. His father continued with his numerous business interests, busier than ever, building one the largest textile companies in the country. Gradually, Andreas found that he was more and more alone. He felt as though two entirely different worlds were competing for his attention. On one hand, nostalgic memories of Greece and Rena seemed to summon him back to a land that in his mind, had transformed itself into a carefree world of pleasure. On the other, the same old feelings of guilt and anger haunted him. He still felt that he done nothing to change the oppression that dominated his world. He felt despondent and emotionally isolated. He considered his return to be the greatest mistake of his life. He questioned his ability to affect change in South Africa. What prospect was there to fulfill his grandiose visions? Every day proved to him that the political system of the country was so intransigent that it was impossible to make a dent in it. He felt that even black South Africans had grown accustomed to their lot and had accepted apartheid as a way of life. To him, they seemed to be making not the slightest effort to change anything.

Andreas was bitterly forced to agree with government propaganda that proclaimed South Africa to be one of the most peaceful and stable states in the world. There were no strikes or terrorist organizations to disturb the nation's peace. All the country's problems were well camouflaged. The white minority ruled confidently with an iron fist; the face of a totalitarian system enforced by a well-organized army, equipped with the very latest in weaponry. Furthermore, an omnipotent secret police, with unrestricted power and resources could buy or bully any information they wanted from informers that extended into every social class. Like most of the people in South Africa, Andreas felt an increasing sense of despair that there was absolutely nothing he could do that would have any effect on changing this system!

Feeling so depressed and uneasy during those first days back, Andreas decided to set out to rediscover the city, which he had not seen for so long. Surprisingly, Johannesburg seemed somehow unfamiliar to him, huge and impersonally modern. It was well named the City of Gold with its great palatial houses, magnificent gardens, swimming pools and tennis courts. It flaunted a wealth and status which could not even be aspired to in the nearby black satellite cities and reminded Andreas of a Greek proverb: 'One can neither hide a cough nor money!' As he wandered through the city, he noticed tall skyscrapers, attractive modern buildings, broad roads and highway flyovers serving a multitude of vehicles. The city was wrapped in a mantle of green with well-tended parks, artificial lakes, trees, flowers and gardens.

Of course, Andreas knew that the maintenance of the multitude of parks and gardens depended solely upon the availability of cheap black labor. Likewise, the huge business corporations, food store chains, flourishing banks and insurance companies catered only to whites and discriminated against the black workers who cleaned and delivered in the dark hours of the night. Famous stores, selling Persian rugs and antiques, the fashion shops, nightclubs and luxury restaurants were similarly designated illegal for blacks, even though they relied on them as a workforce. Around the city flat-topped mountains of sandy slag, the petrified residue drilled from the bowels of the earth, rose up as symbols of the country's position as a prime gold-producer. Fabulous jewelry shops boasted windows ablaze with gold, diamonds and precious stones, shimmering white riches earned through the sweat and blood of black hands.

"Colonialism will never end," Andreas reflected. "The world is being stripped and shipped, in order to make a few companies and countries exceedingly rich. What will be left of South Africa when her resources are all exported? Even if apartheid ends, what is the role of a country that does not even own its own water?"

His thoughts were interrupted by a heavily armed policeman escorted by a fiercely trained Alsatian German shepherd. The pair stared suspiciously at each bypassing stranger and paused in front of Andreas. They made him feel uneasy, as if they could tell what he had been thinking, as if they knew that he was not on their team. A van passed by with police sirens blaring and Andreas involuntarily jumped at the loud wailing cry. Startled by his nervousness, the police dog lunged against its leash and barked at him menacingly. The policeman gave Andreas a grimace of disapproval and retracted the leash. It was an everyday encounter but still, Andreas felt shaky following the interaction and stopped at the next busy corner. He watched the faces of the passing crowd. A mass of people hurried by on the run as if they were being chased by the slogan, 'time is money'. Their faces were expressionless masks of indifference. To Andreas they appeared like hungry wolves, ranging the city in the ruthless pursuit of more wealth as quickly as possible.

A well-dressed lady stopped in front of him and held out a metal collection tin. "Whatever you can spare for the SPCA, young man," she pleaded. Andreas put a coin in the tin and the lady smiled as she stuck a label on his lapel showing an ailing kitten. It looked like a medal for his services. The lady moved away with a smile, in search of other animal-lovers. Andreas realized that his mother would be standing on some other city corner with just such a tin. He knew that amid all this philanthropy on the part of the rich, an army of countless black beggars was growing like a field of mushrooms. Blind, disfigured by incurable ailments, paralyzed, old and crippled, they stretched out their hands for money to buy some bread. Just a little mealie-meal (corn flour) could help them survive another day. Officialdom offered them not the slightest help. There was no such thing as a shelter for disabled blacks.

"Man and nature have combined," thought Andreas, "to make life hopeless for a crippled black person in South Africa, while a kitten is sheltered and cared for."

Without realizing time and place, Andreas had wandered as far as the entrance to Witwatersrand University. He walked through the huge gate and was immediately surrounded by large grounds adorned with well-kept gardens, fountains, a huge swimming pool, gymnasium, numerous libraries, contemporary lecture rooms, museums, laboratories and cafeterias. Andreas mingled with the cheerful swarms of students wandering through the expansive grounds. Finally, he asked a student the way to the registrar's office and was directed to a large building flanked by Grecian columns, with a great many steps that led up to its entrance. In the Great Hall by the registry, a horde of lively faced white students was talking animatedly. They watched excitedly as one of their numbers wrote a slogan on the big white board provided for public notices. As Andreas approached, curious to see what was being written, the young man placed his final stroke and stood back to admire his work.

The large brush marks and glossy black paint read;

WHEN THE WHITES ARRIVED, THEY HELD THE BIBLE AND WE HAD THE LAND. NOW WE HOLD THE BIBLE AND THEY HAVE...,

Andreas thought he was seeing things. He read the slogan again and again to make sure he had got it right.

"What a splendid admission," he thought, "the younger generation confessing the guilt of their ancestors. Thank God!" he added feeling suddenly empowered, "I'm not the only one!"

That morning he enrolled at the University of Witwatersrand. Despite a renewed involvement in his studies however, Andreas's state of melancholic loneliness persisted. He was tormented by nostalgic memories of Greece and of Rena. In his mind, he heard insistent voices calling him back to the light, to life and to love. During those first few months, he could think of nothing else, and his studies were a life raft that he held on to desperately, in the vain hope of rescue. He tried to use books, in order to quell his feelings of pain and loss. He buried himself in work, to help in the readjustment to his environment. He told himself that he had had no illusions as to the difficulty of his task. He knew that he had to dissociate himself from the past. More importantly, and he had to fill in the gaps left by his prolonged absence from his native country.

He spent much of his spare time in the university library. There, he was shocked to find books written by black and white authors, even though they were officially banned by the government because of their political content. The personal possession of such a book could lead to as much as six month imprisonment. Andreas was almost ashamed to admit that just holding these books gave him a strange feeling of satisfaction. Views that had always made him feel so alien now made him feel connected to a movement larger than himself. In reading, he found a connection to people and ideas that mirrored his own feelings. Additionally, the books put words to many of his thoughts. He felt that they gave him a new platform from where he could add to the discussion.

He discovered the works of the Nobel Peace Prize winner, Dr. Albert Luthuli. Andreas was impressed with the leader's powerful and humane call to blacks and whites to live together in peace and harmony. He was also in awe of the overwhelming love and compassion that Luthuli expressed toward his country. In his famous book '*Let My People Go*', he was one the first writers with the courage to condemn the racist government for the infamous passbook that every black person had to carry at all times. It was Luthuli who called blacks to passive resistance in order to achieve a peaceful revolution. It was his influence that eventually led to the famous Sharpeville incident, where the people of Soweto started systematically to burn their passbooks, the symbols of shame and oppression. Calamity had followed; the powerful white rulers perpetrated yet another holocaust, which the western world, as in so many cases, ignored. The peaceful non-violent demonstrators were shot dead by police, most in the back, attempting to flee from the massacre.

Andreas was deeply moved by the courage of those who had tried to change the system, and the tragedy that had befallen them. Often, he recalled that his sadness would give in to his anger. It was as if his pain was too great to bear, so it was transformed into rage, under the direction of some kind of emotional safety valve. It was then he would remember Dimitris Tsafendas, and he would wish that he was powerful enough to destroy the whole system and all those who enforced it. At other times, when he allowed his mind to settle and reflect, he endorsed the examples set by Dr. Luthuli and Mahatma Gandhi before him. This conflict of ideologies, his sense of isolation and loneliness, and his feelings of frustration and powerlessness were taking their toll on Andreas and he slipped deeper into his melancholy.

Despite the chill of one winter morning, he put on his board shorts and dived into the clear water of the swimming pool. The cold took his breath away, but he soon recovered as the blood surged through his veins. His father's car stopped beside the pool. The door opened and out stepped Matthew, looking smart in his well-fitting and un-creased uniform. He took his cap off and greeted Andreas with a smile.

"Good morning, Baas."

"Good morning, Matthew," answered Andreas heartily as he climbed out of the water. "This is a nice surprise. I'm sorry I haven't had the time yet to come and see to you."

"Baas Andreas, your father sent me to tell you that madam always plays golf on Saturdays. If you're on your own and haven't anything better to do, he'll wait for you at the factory so that you can have lunch together."

"Thanks, Matthew, you've come at just the right moment. Hang on a moment while I get dressed and I'll be right with you."

Andreas ran to his room, hurriedly pulled his clothes on and went out, taking with him the letters he had written.

"Ready, Matthew. Let's go. And if it's not too much trouble, would you mind stopping at a post office so I can send off these letters?"

"No problem, Baas Andreas," answered Matthew, opening the door for him.

Andreas looked him up and down with curiosity and interest. Matthew was a well-built, solid young man with attractive features, intelligent eyes, full lips and gleaming black skin. Andreas felt an impulse to talk with him, to break down the barrier of reserve between them and exchange ideas.

"Matthew, you can't imagine how pleased I am to see you again. I have many happy memories of you from when we played together as children."

Matthew nodded politely as Andreas went on. "Everything is so much the same really, it is quite surprising."

It was peak-hour traffic on the broad avenue and Matthew was driving slowly. Andreas offered him a cigarette.

"And yet there is much that has changed," he continued. "The country has gone ahead, grown prosperous. As for you, I did not see you for years but you were always on my mind. I would like for things to be different. I'd like for us to be friends."

Matthew looked at him in embarrassment, confused and not knowing how to answer.

Andreas rattled on, "Do you remember when we went to your mother's church together?"

"Baas Andreas," Matthew said. "As you said yourself, a lot has changed. I'm not a young boy, an umfaan anymore. Maybe this place is different from where you have been living. You are back in this country now. You and I cannot be friends. You are at the top of the ladder and I am on the very bottom. You are white and rich and I am black and poor."

"Matthew, believe me, you have all the right to doubt me. I know that living here has taught you to be careful, not to trust a white man. And you're probably absolutely right. If I were in your place, I'd probably be just as suspicious. But you've got to believe me. As far as I'm concerned, black, white or yellow, we're all human beings with the same faults and virtues. We're all alike and all equal."

Matthew did not reply. He found a parking spot near a post office and parked the car. The two of them walked toward the post office in silence.

"Come in with me and keep me company, Matthew," said Andreas, "I won't take long."

Matthew simply leaned his back against the granite wall of the building and pointed to a large notice that read EUROPEANS ONLY. Andreas glanced at it, nodded, and went in alone. When he came out,

Matthew was standing waiting for him in the same place under the notice.

"Thanks, Matthew, that's it. Let's go."

As the two men walked toward the parked car, a black man suddenly leapt out and hurled himself in front of them, running like a maniac to get across the pavement. Matthew reacted automatically pulling up to an abrupt halt but Andreas, caught unaware, slammed into the man, falling over from the force of the impact. The careless man did not even notice and he increased his pace as he continued to run through the traffic to the other side of the road.

Matthew swore in his own language, "baleka totzi! (run thief)."

A woman's voice was heard shrieking hysterically, "Thief, thief! Stop him! My handbag!"

Someone in the crowd chased after the man. Andreas had not yet recovered from the sudden shock and Matthew asked him solicitously,

"Are you all right, Baas? Did you hurt yourself?"

"I'm OK Matthew. I must say I'm amazed at the nerve of that thief, the way he just grabbed that woman's bag and ran, not even worrying about anyone being in the way or the traffic, when he crossed the street."

"Baas Andreas, things like that happen every day, they are just part of daily life here. No one takes any notice. You'll soon see a lot worse and you'll come to know, like everyone in South Africa, that life here is pretty rough and not worth much."

A little further down the street, a crowd had gathered. Andreas was curious, "I wonder what's going on, Matthew?"

As they approached the scene Matthew said, "I'm sure they've caught the thief, Baas."

"Well, that was only to be expected. I've never seen such a desperate act." Andreas stated.

"Baas, if you are poor and hungry, nothing is too desperate."

Andreas replied, "Well I am going to have a look."

"If I was you I would not go," Matthew responded, "what you see you may not like."

Andreas ignored him and walked toward the gathering crowd. He started pushing forward, to try and see exactly what was happening.

He could hear an agonized croaking noise, curses, and angry muttering. The cries of pain got louder, increasing his curiosity. Andreas shoved his way through and Matthew followed. It took a great deal of effort to break a path past the tightly packed crowd, to the front. His stomach unintentionally heaved at the sight that appeared before him. The paving stones were awash with blood. The thief's face was a bloody, disfigured mass. One of his attackers, not content, was twisting, with sadistic pleasure, the misshapen head back and forth as though to wrench it from its shoulders. Nearby, an elderly woman stood helplessly clutching her bag, unable to escape through the crowd. Andreas looked round him at the faces of the people. There were countless spectators, black for the most part. They stood motionless, murmuring angrily, not one of them willing to offer the slightest help. It was at that moment that Andreas became conscious of the deep hatred and conditioned fear of the white boss that blazed in the eyes of the Africans.

Andreas choking with rage, turned toward the two white thugs, fury stamped on his face. The blood raced to his head and his muscles tensed like bowstrings under the pressure of his fury. Matthew guessing his intentions, tried to stop him, but Andreas pushed him roughly aside, without even turning to look at him. His hands, fastened like talons on the wrist of one of the white attackers and he squeezed until the man was forced to let go of the thief's black head. Andreas hit the thug as hard as he could, full in the face. The other attacker, terrified by Andreas's sudden onslaught, took to his heels. Andreas dropped the thug in disgust and, panting from exertion and adrenaline, he knelt to pick up the half-dead thief in his arms. Blood and froth was oozing out of the thief's mouth and nose. Andreas was surprised to find that the purse snatcher was only a young boy.

"Matthew," he yelled "help me get him to the car. We've got to get him to hospital."

Matthew grabbed the young teenager's feet, and they both lifted the body moving in the direction of the car, while the crowd opened a pathway to make way for them.

"The General Hospital is the nearest, I suppose. Drive as fast as you can. This guy looks to be in pretty bad shape, he's not even conscious," urged Andreas, when they were in the car.

"But Baas, they won't admit him there. He's black."

"Nonsense, I can't believe that. The man is in a critical condition. Let's go there."

Within a few minutes they were at the Johannesburg General Hospital, but as soon as the porter saw that the patient was black, he flatly refused to open the door.

"But it's an emergency," yelled Andreas, out of his mind.

"The law's the law," the porter shouted back. "We don't admit kaffirs. You'll have to take him to Baragawanath. Who the hell are you anyway? What are you trying here? Don't you know the law?"

Andreas quickly realized they had no choice, but to give in. Matthew reversed the car and drove off at full speed, sounding the horn continuously. Those forty kilometers to their destination had seemed endless to Andreas. He didn't believe that he could to stand to watch another man die in his arms. Eventually they arrived and two black nurses lifted the injured man out of the car and onto a trolley. Andreas and Matthew sat side by side in the waiting room in silence. Time dragged on monotonously and Andreas's anxiety increased with the passing minutes. At last he heard their names over the public address system, summoning them to the information office. He almost ran there in his relief. A middle-aged, grave looking African doctor greeted them.

"I want some additional details from you people. Are you his relative," he said turning to Matthew.

"No sir," said Matthew in bewilderment, "I don't know anything about the patient. We just brought him in after some people nearly murdered him on the street."

"Well the patient is dead. In that condition, he couldn't make it. He choked in his own blood so to speak. If you are not his relative and you cannot identify him, I guess you can go now," said the doctor.

"But shouldn't we speak to the police? I am sure we will be able to describe his attackers," asked Andreas.

"No point," said the doctor. "Do you know how many thousands are brought in beaten up like that every day? There is a murder every second in this area. The police can't come out for everyone."

Like robots, the two men returned to the car. They did not need to talk, each lost in his own despair about the futility of the man's death.

"Let's go home, Matthew," said Andreas wearily as he flopped into the passenger seat.

The following morning promised a glorious highveld winter day. The sun was high and it cast a mild and pleasant heat over the land. Andreas opened the curtains, and his room was flooded with crisp morning light. He leaned out of the window to gaze at the garden. The quiet, almost rustic view gave an impression of perfect natural peace.

"What a puzzle life is," he wrote in his faithful diary. "Yesterday, a man dies for no reason at all. Yet a fresh day covers the wound, and the world forgets as new and unexpected mysteries unfold. New troubles, tears and joys; over which we have no control. We can't stop or divert them at all."

Andreas had had an exceptionally long sleep, the kind of rest that only manifests with acute emotional distress. His bloodstained clothes draped over the chair reminded him of yesterday's horrible incident, the memory of which terrified him. He rolled his eyes as he heard his mother calling him. Reluctantly, he showered and dressed to go downstairs.

He was surprised to find his mother and a number of other ladies in the drawing room, chatting amiably. Mrs. Magdalos hurried to embrace her son, kiss him and put her arm round him.

"Andreas, dear," she said, "I'm so sorry I left you on your own again yesterday."

"Don't worry about me mother. In any case, I've got things of my own to do," he replied.

"Come along, I want to introduce you to my best friends. They're just dying to meet you."

Mrs. Magdalos made the necessary introductions with so much pleasure and pride that Andreas could not be angry at her vanity in showing him off.

"Maternal pride," he thought loftily, and responded with a warm and spontaneous smile.

Andreas's manly physique and his sharp handsome features visibly impressed the ladies. They invited him to take tea with them. They were a refined and educated group of women, with wide knowledge of current affairs. They talked about Greece, about its artistic treasures, its wonderful beaches and picturesque islands.

Mrs. Magdalos tinkled a little silver bell and in a few moments the maids came in with trays laden with food. They looked quite picturesque in their clean white uniforms and their blue headscarves. 'A postcard of happy servitude,' Andreas sarcastically reflected, but of course, kept his tongue. The air filled with the scent of freshly brewed tea, steaming in a porcelain teapot. The conversation twisted and turned to new topics. Andreas, out of courtesy, felt obliged to some extent to follow the discussion and to take part in it. When they began to talk about fashion however, well-known dressmakers, and charitable organizations, his thoughts started to wander far from the confines of the drawing room.

Two well-fed Siamese cats, both with spotlessly clean grey and white fur, were lying on the rug. The sun shone in through a fold in the curtains and cut a swathe of light through the dancing particles of dust. Andreas felt the same delight he had known as a small boy while watching those beams of light. One of the cats caught sight of something in the sunbeam, stood up on its hind legs and tried to catch it with its forepaws.

Andreas heard his mother's voice, "We've collected thirty-nine thousand Rand for the animal fund."

The cat, frustrated by its attempt to catch the light, mewed in protest then jumped and curled up lazily on Andreas's lap.

"Andreas, you've got to see the puppies I've just bought," said his mother, "they're too cute for words. It took me ages to find them, but it was worth the effort, believe me. They're pure bred, you know. Look, here are their pedigrees." With that, she handed him some parchments.

Andreas, obviously puzzled, reached out for them. One of the parchments fell to the floor and as he bent to pick it up, the cat leaped out of his lap and onto the couch to continue its sleep. With some disgust, Andreas looked at the parchments that referred to the family tree and the titles of nobility belonging to each animal. Again he reflected on the irony that people don't spare as much love and pity for their fellow man as they do for their animals. He swapped the pedigrees with a newspaper from the occasional table. Immediately all the drama of the day before rushed back into his mind. He turned the pages while trying to hide his anxiety, expecting to see the whole incident re-enacted in the newspaper columns. But he found nothing.

Matthew's words came back to him, "That's just one minor event of the sort we see every day. It'll pass completely unnoticed."

Andreas turned his attention back to the paper. He was curious as to which events had made its bulky pages? A rugby match between France and South Africa occupied most of the front page. Flipping through pages filled mostly by advertising, Andreas's eyes fell by chance on a microscopic article, the title of which caught his attention. He started to read it.

WHITES ONLY

A black man was arrested last September at Ellis Park railway station and was found guilty by the Johannesburg court of crossing the line by an overhead bridge reserved for whites only. David Matabele, 30, of Soweto, was sentenced to pay 30 Rand or serve 30 days jail.

He folded the paper in disgust and put it back on the table. At that moment, his father entered the drawing room, bright and cheerful as always. He spent a few moments greeting the ladies and paying them small compliments, and then turned to Andreas.

"I've just heard, son, that you had a nasty experience yesterday. It ruined my day to hear about it. But you must not worry. These things happen all over the world. Crime and terrorism have become a way of life. If you want my advice, never get mixed up in matters that don't concern you. There are dangerous people around here who carry guns and you never know what the consequences might be if you interfere like that again."

"What happened?" asked Mrs. Magdalos uneasily.

When Andreas did not reply, his father gave her a brief account of the episode as he had heard it from Matthew.

"Andreas, dear, things have changed a lot in the last few years," said his mother.

'You have to be very careful or you'll find yourself in trouble with the police. They like to behave like a militia, those fellows."

Mrs. Brown took up the conversation. "The situation has become quite a problem," she said.

"These days you cannot walk the streets with all those robberies and rapes. The blacks have become far too bold. I think we should all carry weapons."

"You're absolutely right, my dear," said Lanie Magdalos. "The police do absolutely nothing to protect us. You've simply no choice but to carry a weapon. Personally, I've just started taking pistol lessons."

"The really infuriating thing is the attitude of some of the papers," intervened Mrs. Anderson.

"I simply can't imagine how they're allowed to behave the way they do toward the government and to go on running down peace-loving white citizens like us who've built this country up from nothing. And then they demand changes and more rights. In my view it's high time the government stopped being so flexible and started taking some firm measures."

"Well, we're to blame too, Pat dear," said Mrs. Brown. "We've become too refined. We treat them leniently and kindly. I remember my father always used to say, give a black an inch and he'll take a yard. But if you look at the Free State where the Boers have stayed Boers, you'll find the blacks have stayed blacks."

Andreas invented a pretext, asked to be excused and went up to his room, knowing full well that he would not be able to stand any more of that sort of conversation without butting in.

"It doesn't take long," he thought bitterly "to relearn all about my country and its people."

CHAPTER 5 A South African Story

On his twenty first birthday, Andreas decided to return to Greece. He longed to see Rena again. He developed a plan to persuade his father to agree with his decision.

"I'll try it at my birthday party," he thought, "I'll ask him for a return ticket as a present."

Once he was resolved, he felt relieved and he cheerfully went back to the business of invitations. The house was in chaos on the day of the party. Andreas's mother was giving the domestic staff orders. She pecked him on the cheek and sent him out to the veranda to find his father.

"Andreas! Grab a couple of glasses and come sit down with me. I want to talk to you."

"Now is the right time," thought Andreas.

His father looked at him proudly and happily.

"Many happy returns, my boy! It's unbelievable how the years go by. It only seems that yesterday we were celebrating your first birthday and here you are a man! I'm glad you came back early, Andreas. You've given me a new lease of life. The world's grown very small and I've got big plans for you, for us, rather. I've decided to make you a partner in the company. I want us to expand; there are no limits to how far we can go. I've made some important political contacts that will help us, and my dream is that one day I'll see you in Parliament as the first Greek South African MP."

The direction that the conversation was taking upset Andreas.

"Dad," he whispered, "Thanks very much. I do understand how

you feel. But you've got to understand me, too. I've made a mistake. I want to go back to Greece."

Mr. Magdalos almost had a fit. "What did you say?"

"Dad, I'm in love. I can't live without her."

Mr. Magdalos's face cleared and began to return to its natural color.

"What is she like? Is she a nice girl?" he asked.

Andreas felt encouraged. "Extremely nice. You can ask Uncle Pericles."

"So, you're in love! But that's very important, why didn't you tell us about it before? Why didn't you bring her here?"

"Bring her here?" muttered Andreas uncertainly.

"Of course! Your mother would be delighted. In any case I've always believed that marriage does a lot for a man. It brings him down to earth and matures him. Of course, I don't mean for you to get married right away but in a couple of years, and if she likes it here, it will do you good. Well, why are you sitting there? Go and ring her! Tell her to come here for a holiday."

Andreas went to the phone, not totally comfortable with the conversation with his father but happy to speak with Rena again. He called once but his longing to hear Rena's voice was substituted for an automatic operator that claimed that the lines were busy. He called again and again. He tried his uncle and some friends but only got the same response. In a moment, he was filled with dread. He wanted to be reunited with Rena, but he intuited that something terrible had happened back in Greece. Andreas turned from the telephone with a worried expression.

"Dad," he said, "something must have happened in Greece. All telephone communication has been cut off!"

"Calm down, Andreas. Let's not get melodramatic. What could have happened in Greece, after all?"

"War with Turkey, perhaps?" Andreas exclaimed feverishly.

"Out of the question," said Mr. Magdalos dogmatically. "If there were a war, the entire world would know about it. There's probably some fault in the overseas cables. It'll all be fixed tomorrow."

Mrs. Magdalos came toward them with an air of excitement. She gave a scarcely perceptible signal to her husband who got up, took his son by the arm, and led him to the garage. Inside was parked a brand new, red Ford Mustang. His mother handed him the keys.

"Happy birthday, darling," she said emotionally.

"It's for me?" stammered Andreas in astonishment.

His hands trembled with delight and excitement as he started the car. The dual exhaust made the air vibrate in shock. Andreas felt ablaze with enthusiasm. He put the car into gear and stepped on the accelerator. With a sudden lurch, the car hurtled forward. Out on the highway, he opened the windows and the cool air rushed in noisily. He welcomed the freshness and drove faster.

"To hell with the world and all its problems," he yelled crazily.

By the time he returned home he felt refreshed, lighthearted and happy. The guests had begun arriving and judging by the number of parked cars, his mother had held no expense. His parents, arm in arm, came out to greet him. Andreas hugged and kissed them, as their friends burst into applause and good wishes. The party soon took off on its own accord. Wine flowed, as the hi-fi shattered the stillness of the air. Dancing bodies moved in rhythm, sensuously and provocatively. Andreas drank and danced continuously, feeling free for the first time since his arrival. As the hour grew late the lights were dimmed and gentle melodies replaced frantic tunes. Andreas had gotten quite drunk and he danced freely, not allowing any thoughts to plague his mind.

When he awoke, Andreas felt the warm flesh of a naked body clinging to him. His head was heavy and painful, his mouth tasted bitter and dry. Worst of all, he had no idea where he was. He tried to get up. The woman next to him woke up and began to caress him with experienced hands. His body shuddered as her lips found his. Andreas tried to stop her, but she was locked on top of him, pressing her body against him. Linda was a classmate from the university. It appeared to Andreas that he must have driven her home, to her apartment, the previous evening. He remembered nothing of the trip and secretly hoped that his new car was still intact. She made him a strong black cup of coffee, but it did little to sober Andreas. She tried to persuade him to stay with her a little longer, but he resisted stubbornly. He promised to ring her soon and staggered out of her apartment. As he got into his poorly parked car, he was enveloped by the pain of dissipation and a feeling of extreme guilt. He drove home slowly, the light tearing in his eyes.

His father, sitting in the drawing room reading the paper, called out frantically as soon as he saw his son.

"You were right yesterday, son. Terrible things have happened in Greece."

Andreas grabbed the staircase banister for support, and stared vacantly at his father. Mr. Magdalos waved the paper he was holding.

"There's been a military coup, Andreas. Athens is full of tanks and armed troops."

His father's statement had sobered him immediately. Andreas snatched the paper from his dad with trembling hands, and started to read the headlines:

The cradle of democracy was yesterday seized
by a military coup.
Violence and fear... Tanks in the streets of Athens...
Widespread arrests of democratic citizens.
Martial law has been imposed to calm the cities
and villages of Greece.

Andreas was wringing wet with sweat and a thousand hammers were beating in his brain.

"Oh, my God," he groaned in agony.

"Dad, I've got to go straight away," he said, his eyes blazing.

"Go where, son? All the airports are closed; they've isolated the country completely."

Andreas looked at his father uncertainly, the light dying in his eyes.

"I suppose so," he said, "I will not be able to get in. Those bastards have done exactly what we feared; they have taken over the country."

"Yes it is terrible, son," said his father, "It is the fate of Greece to always be in trouble. That is one of the reasons that I immigrated here after the civil war. Now, when all's said and done, our country is here in South Africa."

Andreas called Greece daily to try and speak with Rena. Eventually, once the military junta had established order, the airports opened and telephone links were reconnected. Finally Andreas heard the phone ring at Rena's home. Rena's father answered and with a broken tremulous voice. He informed Andreas that Rena, together with most of her friends, had been arrested and exiled to a concentration camp on one of the remote islands of Greece. Andreas felt the phone slip from his hand. Once again he found himself filled with a sense of loss and grief. He had not realized the severity of the political problems in Greece before he had left. Perhaps, if he had stayed he could have saved Rena. His pain turned quickly to anger and he cursed all the world's tyrants. He especially hated weapon companies that worked to allow a few short-sighted individuals to easily crush idealism, destroy democracy and trample human dignity.

The days that followed were a nightmare for Andreas. His mind was in turmoil beset by conflicted feelings, as pangs of conscience and rage seemed to eat away at his very soul. When he was not angry, he felt tormented by fear and concern for the lives and fate of his beloved Rena and her comrades. He thought of their sacrifice with pride and awe. The nameless young men and women who deemed their own lives unimportant, compared to the task of safeguarding the ideals liberty and equality. He mourned all those friends, who he imagined being beaten or killed into submission in a dusty internment camp, because they dreamed of a better world. Making matters worse, he began to hate himself. He saw himself as a coward, who had no direction for the expression of his ideals, too easily swamped by the day-to-day trivialities of an upper class, affluent lifestyle. He told himself that he wanted to return to Greece, to fight the system, but at the same time he felt hopeless about being able to do anything to assist Rena and his friends. He continued with his daily life constantly haunted by thoughts of their situation in Greece. It was at this tumultuous time in his life that one crucial incident finally established his purpose for being in Africa and helped him to focus his mind.

Andreas had first spotted Cornelius as a collapsed heap in the middle of the highway. He was forced to swerve his car in order to avoid Cornelius's body, which was huddled on the black tarmac. It was dusk and a heavy rain was pouring down. Lighting illuminated the sky and was followed by loud thunderclaps. The wind was blowing and a mix of hail and rain was beating down with force. Andreas stopped at the side of the road, and went to the drenched and crumpled body. The stranger did not appear to be alive but Andreas found a weak pulse. After dragging the man to the car, Andreas examined him anxiously. He was an elderly black man with a gaunt, wrinkled face. He was wearing wet, worn-out clothes, full of holes and patches. Andreas opened the glove box, took out a flask of brandy, and poured a few drops on to the old man's lips. The strong liquor seemed to bring him around. His eyes half opened and rolled around in fear and curiosity. He became panic-stricken as his eyes focused on Andreas. He had the air of a trapped and wounded animal, ready to run but unable.

Andreas tried to calm him. "Don't be afraid, Madala (old man). I'm not going to hurt you. I just want to help. You look as though you are at the end of your tether. Take another little drink and you'll feel better."

The old man stared suspiciously and then with a trembling hand picked up the flask and raised it to his lips. He took a swig and grimaced as the strong liquor burned his mouth. Andreas lit two cigarettes and stuck one between the old man's lips. The stranger's face lit up as he sucked the smoke in greedily, as if it were something he had been missing for a long time.

"Thank you Baasie."

"There's no reason to be worried, old man. You're safe here and you can leave any time you want. I don't think you're fit enough yet, though. The sensible thing would be to tell me where you live and then I can take you home."

"Don't worry about me, baas. Something just came over me. I'm right now. I'll be able to get to Alexander."

"Alexander Township? It's a long way from here," Andreas stated, "And the weather's appalling. If I hadn't found you on the road, you'd have died of cold in a few hours. That is if someone hadn't run over you first."

The old man's eyes filled with tears that he hurriedly brushed away with the back of his hand.

"I'm tired, baas, very tired. It would be better if you had just left me to die. But, I do want to see my people again, just for the last time. I have missed them much."

"Well at least tell me what has happened to you. How did you end up like this? I promise you, I would like to try and help you any way I can."

The old man lifted the flask to his mouth and sat silently for a while. Then haltingly, he told Andreas his story in a slow, deep bass, monotonous voice, as though in a trance. Cornelius's homeland was Zululand. Zululand was a vast country with long plains for grazing cattle and green hills that reached up into the Drakensburg Mountains. Andreas had seen photographs of Zululand with its lush tropical plants, many-colored birds, wild animals, and all around, the deep blue and mysterious Indian Ocean.

The old man continued his eyes half closed in nostalgia as he described a place with few trees but instead, flowering bushes and tall grass. He talked about the warriors of his tribe who took part in fierce battles. Andreas knew that Zulus had fought bare-chested with spear and shield, battling against wild beasts and enemy attacks. Since he was a child he had loved stories about the Zulu warriors. Many pages had been written, even in white South African history, telling of the bravery of leaders such as Shaka, Cettowayo and Dingaan.

"I was born there many years ago and I was proud to be a Zulu."

Andreas felt a growing respect for this member of a glorious tribe that had fought so fiercely to keep its freedom. He kept urging the old man to continue with his story so that he could appreciate what it meant to be a Zulu. Cornelius said that from the time that he began to understand the world, he was taught the sacred traditions of his tribe. Whites could think that it was primitive, but to him it was all that he valued. The elders passed on to the young ones the stories of the ancestors. When he was a young warrior, he used to run through the fields and valleys with the other youngsters. They held tightly onto their leather shields and weapons, hunting and playing war games. It was a good, free life and he had loved it. Cornelius was lost in the past now and as the brandy relaxed his tongue, he allowed his mind to travel to a time when he worked in the fields and grazed his father's cattle. He told Andreas how he had once danced with other warriors and how at one of these gatherings, he was captivated by a young woman. Cornelius insisted that she was the most beautiful girl in his village. He used to wait for hours, hidden near the well, just to catch a glimpse of her, even from far away. Life became especially sweet for him after they fell in love.

Andreas listened with close attention, and it seemed to him that through the cigarette smoke he could see the feeble old man growing younger, becoming strong again like the warrior he once was. Cornelius said that his parents did not object to the marriage, but he needed to find money for a dowry. He wanted to get the bride price by himself, as was their custom. His opportunity arrived on four wheels, in the form of a gleaming limousine that had mysteriously stopped at the village square. A white boss emerged and spoke to the village in the Zulu language. He said that he wanted workers for the gold mines. Without asking his father, Cornelius seized the chance and signed a contract for eighteen months.

At first, it was a big adventure traveling across the country by train. The city was so different from the country life he had known. Then, he had to face a terrifying change. There he was, a free man, who loved nature and the open air, trapped in the sunless damp of a mine. Every time the lift dropped him at dizzying speed, thousands of meters down into the bowels of the earth, he felt a cold, skeletal hand clutching at his heart. The working conditions were terrible. The heat was oppressive, and the sweat ran down him in rivers. His body stank, and the foul smell never seemed to leave him.

"Believe me Baas, in that place you burn; you waste away in a vast furnace that grinds down your body and spirit, your ideas, your hopes, your manhood and your courage," the old man told Andreas.

The wage was pitiful for the work, and the conditions were worse than the pay. The days passed slowly and monotonously. Always, they endured the same routine with no joy, not even the pleasure of the company of women. The strong satisfied their urges on the weak. Life dragged on in the hostels with day after day of brutal labor. It wasn't much different from life in a prison. Accidents happened on a daily basis but no one cared. One kaffir less, meant one more ounce of gold for the Republic of South Africa. As for replacements, labor was cheap and plentiful and there were always hands to spare. At the end of every month, after he had been paid, Cornelius would go into a quiet corner, open the little leather bag that he always had hung around his neck and count up what he was worth. He would enjoy the smell of the notes and the beautiful feel of them, and he would count them again and again as if he was waiting for some miracle to double them. Then respectfully, carefully, almost like a sacred ritual, he would put them back in the pouch, tie the leather purse strings, and put it back under his shirt.

"How could you stand it? What gave you courage and patience to go on?" Andreas asked the old man.

"What helped me was that every day I saw in front of me the face of the girl I'd chosen," the old man continued, after a long pause as though to catch his breath, "a face that I'd never kissed, of a girl I'd never held in my arms, but loved all the same. She gave me the power to keep on."

Twenty months went by and Cornelius had little to show for his efforts but exhaustion, loneliness, and the agony of saving less than he had expected. At last his dream became a reality; his contract ended and he was ready to go back home and get married. He felt as though he had won. He had survived the mine and had managed to scrape together the money for the bride price. On the homeward train journey, he realized how much he had changed. This time, he was no longer overawed or even curious as he had been on that first train ride into the white man's world.

"It was a funny thing Baas because I felt uneasy when I should have been happy. I had lost my confidence, something of my faith and my conviction. The feeling robbed me of the satisfaction I should have felt and the joy that I had been expecting as my reward."

When his village finally appeared on the horizon, Cornelius was saddened to find it quaint and uninviting. It seemed so small, dirty and poor with its stone and mud brick huts topped with cardboard or corrugated iron roofs. The sun blazed over everything and the earth was bone dry. He felt very self-conscious in his jacket, white shirt and colored tie. He had bought himself a trilby hat and on the train he had polished his shoes so that they shone almost as much as his reflecting dark sunglasses. A horde of kids rushed toward him to offer their services. Some of the kids recognized him and he felt both proud and embarrassed as he heard them discussing in amazement, the way he was dressed and all the treasure he had brought back with him.

A little boy ran up and started chattering about his return to the village, while Cornelius looked around uneasily trying to catch sight of her. The whole village had abandoned its daily routine so that everyone could come and greet him. They greeted him joyfully but he could see that pain and uneasiness lurked in the eyes of many. His grandfather stood waiting for him, in front of his hut. The old man was close to a hundred years old. There was his mother trembling with emotion, and next to her, huge and solid, his father. They looked at each other silently. His father examined Cornelius from head to foot, and then he smiled. He had forgiven him for leaving without his permission.

Before long the house and the earthen courtyard had filled with a noisy, bustling crowd. The women with their shrill voices vied with each other to relate stories of his life. They told the history of his birth, how he had grown and of when the bad spirit, the tokoloshe, had hit him. They welcomed him back with tales of his childhood, most of which he scarcely remembered himself. An old, blind woman, stooped with age and completely toothless, reached out her withered hands and started to feel his face.

"Would you believe it, it's Cornelius," she had whispered.

"Yes Ugogo, grandmother, it is me," Cornelius said as he opened his suitcase and began handing out the presents he had brought. There was great excitement as he passed out toffees, chocolate, tobacco, cigarettes, matches, scented soap and little mirrors. The children smelled the soap and looked at themselves in the mirrors and were overjoyed. Grandfather gave orders for the biggest ox to be slaughtered and cooked. The women started to prepare the food and tswala, the national beer. The party began at sunset and according to custom lasted for three days and three nights. Nearly all the village was invited and within a few hours the fun was on for young and old. Cornelius approached his father.

"Father," he said, "I've made it. I've scraped together enough money for the lobola!"

His father looked at Cornelius for a moment, then picked up a branch and tossed it into the fire in the middle of the courtyard where it flared, lighting up everything around it. Men and women, dizzy with drink, sweating and excited, were dancing in a way that only the Zulu people could dance. Their bodies shone with sweat and the breasts of the young women, erect and quivering, seemed to be alive, waiting for a young man's caress.

"Father," he said again, "I want to marry the woman I love!"

The old man carefully placed another log on the fire and told Cornelius in a muffled voice, "I am sorry my son but the girl you loved has already married six months ago."

Cornelius felt a chasm opening under his feet. He screamed like a wounded animal. The crowd fell silent. With his guts on fire, he grabbed a mug of tswala and drained it at a gulp. He then threw off his clothes and his shoes and started to dance, yelling at the top of his voice. It was a dance to summon up gods, demons and men and he trampled all of them under with his bare feet. The drums hesitantly began to catch his rhythm and then repeated it, faster and faster. Some of the crowd drew aside and started clapping to the rhythm, perhaps aware of the agony that was eating away at him.

"Baas, I think you have had enough of my story. I feel much better. It is time for me to go."

Andreas started the car. "You're right, we can't stay here. I'll drive you home."

Andreas knew too well that a night out in the rain may have killed Cornelius. He pulled the car onto the highway before the old man could muster a protest.

"So tell me. What happened next? How did you get to be here?" Andreas was fascinated by Cornelius's story and he was still searching for the answer as to how Cornelius came to be on the highway that night. The old man paused for some time, surprised at the white man's continued interest and persistence. Hesitantly he continued.

"After three days, I gave the lobola money to my father and left to go far away, to the great city of Johannesburg."

CHAPTER 6 Reflections of an Old Zulu Warrior

As they drove, Cornelius told Andreas pieces of his story. He explained how on his arrival he had lost himself in the vastness of Johannesburg and how he had labored at any job he could get. His pride forbade him from telling Andreas that in those days he had slept on the streets, mostly in or under old abandoned cars. He did not tell the white boy that as his experience grew he had become increasingly and painfully aware of what a curse, what a terrible sin it was to be born black in his own country. He did not tell how he had been to prison so many times, and been beaten up so often, that he had long ago lost count. The old man felt anger rising within him as he relived experiences brought to life by cold and brandy. He was confused at his a need to tell the young man any of his story. He rationalized that he was close to death, that he no longer needed to be afraid. He believed that there was nothing that any man could do to him anymore.

"I didn't have a passbook and was working without permission in the urban areas." Cornelius continued. He was testing the young man, "that's how I got to hate and fear every policeman and even every white, if it comes to that." The old man looked cautiously at Andreas.

After a while, when Andreas failed to protest his remark, Cornelius went on. "I soon realized how useless I was in this modern world, so I decided to improve myself. I attended the township school with the children. As I learned to read and write in English and Afrikaans, I imagined new roads opening up before me. It was hard but in the end, after many attempts and disappointments, I managed to get a passbook and with it permission to stay and to work. I got a job as a cleaning boy in a factory. I stuck to it patiently and after a few years of hard work, I managed to get promoted to machine operator with a wage I'd never have believed possible before, a whole twenty four Rand a month. My life started to take on a new outlook. I could actually afford a second shirt and a second pair of shoes."

The old man described that as the years passed by, he had created a family. He had married a girl named Constance. She was a Sotho woman who worked in the same shoe factory. Together they were able to rent a small house in Alexander Township. His wife had finally stopped working after their seven children were born. He had been lucky because he was able to keep his same job as a machine operator for nearly twenty years. Apart from the usual troubles that accompany bringing up children in the ghetto, life went well for them. He used to get up to catch the bus into the city at three in the morning and come home after dark. He still had to catch another bus once in the city, out to the factory, but at least he could manage to get to work by seven-thirty, if there were no bus strikes. He was proud to tell Andreas that he had never missed a single day, and his old eyes sparkled as he described how he had arranged to be paid on Mondays instead of Fridays, so that the tsotsis could not rob him of his wages on the buses.

During that time, Cornelius said that Johannesburg had grown enormously. Alongside the white areas, new black townships were also emerging. They had no skyscrapers, schools or hospitals. Instead the townships were basically just ugly mud huts, roofed with tin sheets or cardboard. Dirt, poverty, drugs and violence engulfed the poor communities and became a way of life. Every day, more and more mud huts and shacks were built as people moved in from the rural areas, in search of jobs. The new government under John Vorster took various steps to try to prevent the influx, by passing restrictive new laws and regulations. They passed the decentralization laws, encouraging all the big manufacturing companies to relocate to rural areas. At the same time, the police went on a never-ending hunt for vagrants without passbooks. Their armored vans were filled several times a day with blacks, that were carted away first to jails and then back to the bush. After the decentralization laws were passed, Cornelius was called to the office at his factory. He was sacked and given a month's pay severance. The white boss said that he was sorry to have to let him go. That he had always been a good and conscientious worker. Unfortunately, the government had required them to move the factory.

"So Baas, can you believe it? After so many years, I was back where I'd started; only now I had to support a family. I began roaming the streets from dawn to dusk, going from factory to factory and shop to shop looking for work, but no one needed an old man like me. My wife went back to working as a domestic servant in the white suburbs. Thank God, the kids were older. One terrible day as I was wandering the streets, I squatted down on a footpath to rest. A policeman grabbed me roughly by the shoulder, clapped a pair of handcuffs on me and shoved me into a putrid smelling corner, with many other black people. There, on the side of the street, we waited for a paddy wagon to cart us away like a bunch of mangy dogs.

It was a money-raising trick of the government. Every black had to pay up anything from ten Rand to the whole of his wages, for the offence of having been picked up by the police. It was winter and the wind was bitter and chill, gusting in all directions. Our faces were screwed up against the cold, our hands and noses turned blue and our eyes watered as if we were crying. The hours dragged by and the longer we waited, the more anxious we became. It was twilight before an armored paddy wagon arrived, and my belly rumbled with a volatile mix of fear and hunger. The double doors opened and they started to load us in, five, ten, twenty and more. I lost count. One bloke was drunk. He was shouting and waving his arms around, and then he stumbled and fell. In a flash, one of the cops was on him, kicking him with his heavy boots. I watched them with disgust, but I was too afraid to do anything. Then someone shoved me hard into the truck. I would have landed flat on my face if not for a young lad that grabbed my arm and pulled me into the van, next to him. The doors slammed shut behind us. I remember feeling as if I was choking, packed in that van with all those others. We really were like sardines, without room to breathe. The truck moved off rocking crazily as it tore through the streets, but its lurching and jolting didn't affect us much, packed as we were into a solid human mass."

Cornelius wiped slow tears from his eyes with the back of his deeply wrinkled hand. The drive to Alexander was far, and he went on with his story. He described to Andreas how he had finally arrived, after many hours, at the charge room. It was night when the van doors had opened again. A few lamps threw a dim light into the huge courtyard which was framed by cold iron railings. The captives were put in a line and details were written, including their respective crimes. Their passbooks were then taken away and they were and pushed back outside and into a holding pen, where they waited in the cold once more. Every minute that passed had seemed like an hour. Cornelius had wrapped himself as best he could in his overcoat and had rolled himself into a ball, trying to be as small as possible in the face of the piercing wind. With the formalities of the arrest behind him, Cornelius was finally moved back inside into a large cell, where inmates were piled nearly on top of each other. He was beyond exhaustion and his stomach was complaining of hunger. He felt that he would have frozen to death if he had been left outside any longer. He was so cold that he was actually grateful to have had a stranger jammed against him. Shivering, he had closed his eyes and spent what was left of that night in a restless sleep. He was acutely aware that his wife would have no idea what had happened to him. At six in the morning, the inmates were awakened, put back in trucks and taken to the courthouse. The darkness had started to lift from the sky and the sun made a feeble appearance. Cornelius recalled that its winter rays felt like a blessing on his frozen body.

A court official announced the arrival of the magistrate who seemed arrogant and omnipotent in his black gown. It was just another routine day for the magistrate, who tried each case in the shortest possible time, without acquitting even a single prisoner. Cornelius's heart was pounding when the court orderly at last called his name. He was sure that the magistrate would find him not guilty. After all, he had done nothing wrong. He tried to push his way through to the bench. He was so nervous that he dropped his hat and bent down shakily to pick it up. The prosecutor looked at him with distaste.

"Cornelius Thombone, you are accused of being a vagrant and of staying illegally in the Province of the Transvaal. Guilty or not guilty?" the magistrate asked in a monotonous voice.

"Not guilty, Your Honor," he said firmly.

The magistrate glanced at his papers and said in his monotonous drone, "Cornelius Thombone, this court finds you guilty and sentences you to thirty days imprisonment or a fine of thirty Rand. At the expiry of your sentence you will be deported to your homeland. Next!"

Cornelius stood gaping at the judge in disbelief. At last he managed to pull himself together.

"Have mercy on me, Your Worship. I've been living here for thirty-five years and my children were born in Alexander."

His pleas were ignored by the court, and a black policeman grabbed him and started to pull him away. In desperation, Cornelius went on shouting until the policeman started punching him hard, several times, in his stomach. He came back to consciousness on a cold concrete floor. Crushed and helpless, he stood uncomplaining alongside the other prisoners, as they waited for the next step. A white official came up to them and announced that anyone who had money could go to office number seven, and pay his fine. A few got up and shuffled toward freedom, their troubles over, until the next time. Cornelius knew he had to do something. Suddenly, his anguish and lethargy disappeared. He joined the line of men going to office number seven. Once there, he found a scrap of paper and a pencil and wrote a hasty note to his wife. He went up to a young man who was fortunate enough to be able to pay his fine and begged him to deliver her the note. Cornelius was gratefully surprised when the man took the note and promised to get it to his wife.

"There are some things you have to live through yourself; otherwise you can't describe the feelings or the torment. This is why it is hard to give a faithful picture of what it's like to go to jail, without knowing why," Cornelius said to Andreas. "It is terrible to be dealt with like a criminal when you are not; to have your morale destroyed and your nerve broken. I lost all my strength; all I had left was bitterness. The ancient traditions of my people that had once filled my heart with pride had become distant, hardly recognizable ghosts. My imminent deportation to Zululand remained motionless in my mind, like a snake that paralyzed my thoughts, drop by drop, with its poison."

The prisoners were loaded into vans again, at last headed to their final destination. A squad of armed, black police holding sjamboks, cruel leather whips, herded them between jails. The sun had set, but only a patch of black sky could be made out above the high walls. Prison guards took all the prisoners' personal belongings, sealed them in plastic bags and tossed them into a box. They then ordered the inmates to strip for a shower. Obediently, the prisoners took off their clothes and waited in their vulnerable nudity. Cornelius had been the first to go under the shower. There was plenty of water under high pressure. It was so cold that it took his breath away and made his teeth chatter. He recalled that he must have looked completely ridiculous, because the white prison guard and his black underlings were holding their sides with laughter.

After the shower, they gave him overalls to wear and a blanket so worn, that he could see through it. The guards then took the inmates in groups to a long passage of narrow cells that were all already filled to suffocation. The floor was wet concrete. It had been hosed down in advance, and yet it still stank of mold and filth. Two tins were supplied, one with drinking water and the other for all other needs. Cornelius curled up in the least crowded corner and pulled the blanket over him. It was very dirty, and he caught himself deliberating on what color it had been originally. He felt weak and exhausted. The lights had been switched off and no one could see his tears. A fierce quarrel started up at one end of the cell. The darkness was so intense that someone had missed the tin and urinated on a fellow cellmate, who had been seated beside the rancid waste tin. The fight had eventually died down and was replaced by a deathly silence, broken only by deep, anxious breathing.

The door opened, the lights came on, a whip cracked in the air. Terrified and half asleep, the prisoners stumbled to their feet.

"Outside you lazy bastards," yelled the overseer.

It was four thirty in the morning. Cornelius's mouth felt stale and dry and his breath smelt bad. His eyes were encrusted with the tears he had been too weary to wipe away the night before. They took him to the barber's shop where long-term prisoners, half awake and bad-tempered, shaved his head with rusty clippers. Along with their hair, Cornelius felt that the cut had severed the prisoners' last link to the world outside. And so, stripped of their individuality, they were taken to the chapel for the morning service. At that time, Cornelius had liked the chapel. It was warmer, and had a kind of peacefulness that stood in stark contrast with the rest of the prison. He used to sit, his eyes fixed on a large wooden cross hung behind the altar. There he had prayed to God sincerely, with faith and devotion. He recalled however, that instead of giving him comfort, the cross had gotten bigger and bigger in his mind. It swelled until it became a giant gleaming apparition in the air, dripping with a blood-red mist that threatened to flood the chapel.

"Pray for mercy, you sinners who are condemned by God for your sins."

The voice of the minister had jarred Cornelius from his vision, and the cross had returned once more to its normal size. When the service ended, the prisoners were corralled out.

The night had lost none of its blackness. Silent and gloomy, the inmates trailed after the guards. They were each given a metal plate and a spoon. Cornelius realized that he was to be fed. It was the first food he had seen since before his arrest. He told Andreas how his saliva glands had seemed to be working overtime, and as he waited in line, he feared that he would choke on his own spit. His stomach had grumbled continuously and he felt faint from the blinding ache in his head. He had comforted himself with the belief that in a few steps he would be in front of the steaming boiler. As he turned the corner however, he heard the horrible whistle of a whip. Twice and with terrible force, it wrapped itself around him and bit into his cringing back. He let out a wild, animal shriek as he felt his skin slicing open. He went down on his knees in terrible pain. Only an instinct of self-preservation made him realize that if he didn't get up quickly, they'd hit him again. It gave him the strength to pick up his plate and spoon. The whip whistled again and he held his breath, but this time it was not for him. It was for the man behind him. The whip was there for all who turned the corner.

The cook filled his big ladle with the contents of the boiler, looked around, and then emptied it into Cornelius's deep plate so that it brimmed over with food. It smelt wonderful, steaming hot and savory. He brought the plate up to his face, filled his nostrils with the smell, and warmed his frozen face in the hot steam. He put the plate down carefully on the table so as not to lose a single drop. He filled his spoon and lifted it to his lips. It was so hot that it burned the roof of his mouth, but he didn't notice, in fact, the sensation seemed increased the pleasure. He was chewing quickly, with a will, when his teeth clamped down on something so hard, that he thought they'd been dislodged. Grains of uncooked maize acted like landmines in the food, slowing down its devourers.

What peculiar food he had thought; a sort of porridge mixed up with cereal, sugar, salt and dried maize. The old hands among the prisoners were eating listlessly. They didn't like it at all. Cornelius found that he could not eat it quickly enough before it got cold, without breaking his teeth on the hard grains. He carefully collected them, grain by grain, thinking that he could perhaps chew on them later at his leisure. Next to Cornelius, a heavily built man who had just finished eating produced a little plastic bag with tobacco and a torn piece of newspaper, from his pocket. He shoved his plate aside to make room and leaned his elbows on the table. He dipped into the bag, pulled out a pinch of tobacco, placed it carefully on the square of newspaper and dexterously rolled himself a long cigarette. He lit it and hungrily sucked in the smoke, filling his mouth and lungs, before allowing it slowly to roll out of his wide-open nostrils. The smell of the tobacco surrounded Cornelius and he looked at him enviously. The man took no notice of him. He took a few more deep puffs and then, with a careless shrug, handed Cornelius the cigarette.

The sun had finally begun to show its face in the east. Fierce shouting, the crude abuse of the guards brought the prisoners back to the reality that they had all been trying hard to forget. The guards yelled out names and divided the prisoners into work groups. The groups clambered up on to trucks and set off for the various agricultural properties. Given his age, Cornelius stayed behind with about fifteen others to work on domestic chores. They washed the plates and the boilers, and then they cleaned out the latrines. The stink of the tins being emptied into the latrines had made Cornelius feel dizzy and his stomach heaved. He quietly placed the last water tin in its place and then, ignoring the cold, he washed his hands and face. Cornelius remembered his disgust when he realized that the smell had stuck to him. It had soaked into his nostrils, mouth and worked its way deep into his guts.

"Cornelius Thombone, Cornelius Thombone, report to the guard room immediately."

Cornelius stood there frozen for a moment, transfixed by the booming loudspeaker that seemed to mock him with its huge lifeless mouth. The blood rushed to his face. Shaking with fear he set off, mumbling to himself, "why me, for God's sake?" When he arrived panting at the guardhouse, his lips were cracked and dry from fear. Through the window, he could see the warden standing in front of a heating stove. He was playing with his long whip. Cornelius knocked the door with a trembling hand, and entered. He tried to speak but when he opened his mouth only a muddle of unintelligible noises came out. The warden fixed his cold stare on Cornelius, the sjambok twitching in his hands.

"What the hell do you want, you black bastard? Speak up! And shut the door behind you!"

Cornelius stumbled backwards and groped for the door to shut it.

"B...b...baas," he stammered out, "They've been calling me on the loudspeaker to come here."

"You Cornelius Thombone?" a black policeman asked him from the back of the office. The old man nodded weakly.

"Come here." The guard shoved some papers in front of him and told him to sign. "You're free. Someone in your family has paid your fine."

He pushed the nylon bag toward Cornelius in which he found his possessions; a passbook and a piece of paper that turned out to be a travel warrant.

"Take this warrant to the railway police at the station. You're not allowed to stay in the Transvaal any longer. We're deporting you to your homeland. The train for Natal leaves at seven thirty and heaven help you if you're not on it. Understood?"

"Get out of here you dirty kaffir, you stink!" yelled the warden, with a crack of his whip.

With one eye on the whip, Cornelius had gathered his belongings, and scuttled outside. "I'm free!" he whispered. He couldn't believe his good luck. He changed into his clothes and left the prison as quickly as the guards would allow. A large iron door slammed behind him, and he saw the tiny figure of his wife. She ran to him and they embraced. Then giving him her arm to lean on, she started to lead him away.

"Constance," he said, "you shouldn't have done that. It's a lot of money and thirty days would have gone in no time. Besides, how are you going to pay the rent, how are you going to eat? You're forgetting I'm out of work."

She looked at him affectionately and took his arm again.

"Come on," she said simply. "We're going home. You've got to get ready for the journey. They're deporting you to Natal and there's nothing we can do about it. If they pick you up again you will be put back in prison."

They set off in silence. Cornelius turned back and glanced at the prison. The wall was very high and he could see huge bronze lettering, Boksburg Prison. The sun was fully up and it was warm, but the sight of those words struck a chill in his soul.

The old man paused to wipe his eyes, "Excuse me, Baas. When you get old, you know, you get silly and sentimental. I don't know what came over me. I have told you a lot of rubbish. I'd better stop now. I've talked too much."

"No, Cornelius, go on, please. Don't be afraid! I want to know what happened next and I still don't know how you ended up here," said Andreas.

The old man again took up his tale, "I won't describe the painful scene with my wife and children. I just picked up my suitcase and presented myself to the police at the station. The next few hours were a nightmare of yelling and cursing, whistle blowing and shouting, orders and counter-orders. At one stage, I didn't think I would go anywhere, because one set of authorities had no idea what the others were up to. Everything was a complete muddle. Finally, they gave me another bit of paper and shoved me into a train with a crowd of others."

After a long and tiring journey, Cornelius had arrived in Durban where he was instructed to wait in a police station for the next step. Eventually, they called him into an office.

A sergeant looked at his papers and remarked to his offsider,

"Some mistake here. This kaffir hasn't got a job, certainly not in Natal. He hasn't lived here for nearly forty years. Send him back. We've got enough on our hands here without any more!"

Cornelius thought he must have misheard him. They must be talking about someone else. But when he realized that they were in fact talking about him, he could hardly restrain his tears of joy. It came to him in a flash that he could go home and he imagined how happy his family would be.

"There are some decent whites, after all, there is some justice in the land!" he thought. He was so excited that he wanted to go up to the sergeant, kiss his hands and pour out his gratitude. But the sergeant was such a stern looking man that Cornelius didn't dare. Suddenly his suitcase wasn't heavy anymore and he felt young, strong and hungry. The black policeman was summoned to put him back in the train bound for the Transvaal. Cornelius asked him to stop for a moment so that he could buy something to eat, but he was unyielding and only when he promised to buy him a packet of cigarettes did the policeman give in. Cornelius made a grand gesture; exchanging the five Rand his wife had given him for a packet of fish and chips, and two packets of cigarettes. He felt like a king. He recalled that the trip home was the most marvelous journey of his life. He laughed and told stories to his fellow travelers. His stomach was full, he was happy, and he smoked every cigarette right down to the filter. When they arrived, he wanted to jump out before the train had stopped, but the door was locked and the supervising guard was a formidable character. He waited impatiently for the formalities to come to an end.

"Cornelius Thombone," called a fat policeman with thick glasses.

"Yes, baas," he said, taking his hat off respectfully.

"What the devil are you doing here, you son of a bitch? You're supposed to be in Natal!"

Cornelius told him the whole story of how he had been sent back again."

"I don't know about this load of rubbish you're telling me, kaffir. There's an order here for your deportation."

So they sent him back once again. He was reduced to a little more than a living corpse as he wandered the streets of Durban. He was forced to survive on charity and whatever he could scrounge from garbage bins. When he was tired, he would just throw himself down anywhere. Time and rain and sun had no effect on him, and the days bled together in his depression and desperation. After some time he found his way back to his ancestral village. It was deserted and he did not recognize it at first. He knelt and kissed the ground, his tears falling on the dry earth. He looked around in awe, wondering what his departed relatives would make of him, sunk to such degradation. But everything was deserted and all the houses were now ruins. There was a notice board with big red lettering that read:

SOON TO BE RELEASED. LAND FOR SALE
FOR COMMERCIAL UNITS

"What can I tell you Baas to make you understand what it means to be desperate? In the end, I decided to jump a goods train and to come back here. I have walked and walked and I am so near home, but I did not have the strength to continue until you picked me up Baas. I don't even know why I am telling you all this. I just want to see them one more time."

Cornelius stopped, exhausted. He felt afraid and yet amazed that he had spoken truth without any precautions to a white man. Andreas understood his anxiety and hastened to reassure him.

"You're nearly home, Cornelius, and I promise I'll do everything I can to help you."

The highway soon gave way to a muddy gravel road which led into the township. It was a moonless night and the township was pitch, as it had no electricity. The rain was still pounding abusively and it was impossible for the two men to make out any more than the slanted shapes of the shanty dwellings that manifested around them. No one was out on the streets and Andreas had the impression that he had driven into a ghost town. He urged the old man for directions but even Cornelius had difficulty navigating. It was illegal for Andreas to be in the township and both men felt suddenly vulnerable, the ramifications of their situation apparent to them. Andreas knew that Cornelius could not survive another beating if they were caught. Involuntarily, he remembered the barred windows at security police headquarters, and the brutal sergeant with his great ape like hands.

Undoubtedly, he would not release Andreas so easily, the next time he got those hands on him.

Eventually Cornelius led Andreas down a cramped side street. They parked the car and Andreas carried Cornelius to a corrugated iron sheet that was fashioned as a door. Before entering, they both inspected the area nervously, to make sure that no one had seen them. Andreas was acutely aware that he should probably have stayed in the car and driven home; but he had never been to a township, and he was curious to see Cornelius's house. Inside, the house was nicer than Andreas would have imagined from its façade. It was warm thanks to a small fire and smoky from bad ventilation. Old pots caught the rainwater that had invaded from cracks in the aluminum roof. Cornelius's wife was so happy to see her husband that she made Andreas feel like a savior. He left after a cup of coffee feeling very pleased with his efforts. Fear returned as he started the car and he hoped that there would be no roadblocks on the way out of the township.

CHAPTER 7 Youth Encounters

With the township receding into darkness behind him, Andreas finally began to feel safe. Cornelius never left his mind throughout the drive. He reeled at the obstacles that had nearly defeated the old man. Strangely, he felt a powerful ache to share his evening's experience. He wanted to unburden himself, to be rid of the frustrations that threatened to overwhelm him. He realized painfully that he had no such outlet, at least, not anyone he could trust.

When he returned from Alexander Township, he found his world changed. He looked at his house with a freshly formed contempt. 'Nothing but ostentatious wealth and luxury!' he thought to himself as he reappraised the lifestyle which he had taken for granted for so many years. He felt physically ill with guilt and disgust. He strode purposefully to Matthew's room and knocked. The young chauffeur opened the door and stared at Andreas in amazement.

"Good evening Baas. Does the master want me?"

"No, Matthew, I came on my own to pay you a visit. I want to talk to you if you don't mind. I don't have anybody else."

Matthew seemed slightly annoyed, but told Andreas to come in and offered him his one and only chair.

"You look a bit upset, Baas. What's happened?"

Andreas told him, passionately and melodramatically, the story of Cornelius, but on seeing Matthew's indifferent reaction, he became angry.

"I can see your brother's tragedy hasn't made the slightest impact on you. 'Brother' is what you call each other, isn't it?" said Andreas attempting irony.

"Baas," Matthew replied bluntly, "there's nothing new for me in a story like that. Yes, of course I feel sorry for old Cornelius and for all the other Corneliuses in South Africa. But, ask any one of us and you'll hear an equally sad and equally true story."

"I see," said Andreas goading him on, "so we've got to feel sorry for all the blacks, eh? Well, we do feel sorry for you, because you're a bunch of useless cowards. You build up all that hate against the white bosses, allowing it to grow and fester, and then you waste it in fighting amongst yourselves. I think you slaughter each other because you haven't got the courage to turn on your oppressors and demand some respect! As far as I understand, the only leader that has shown any fighting spirit was Luthuli at Sharpville."

"What do you know about Sharpville?" Matthew asked. "I thought all publications were banned."

"I found some books in the university library," Andreas replied.

Matthew remained totally impassive, indifferent almost. Then after a long silence, he replied with no trace of anger or passion.

"You're a strange man, Baas. I don't really quite understand you. The interest some of you white students try to show in us blacks is very puzzling. You live your rich lives on our backs and then you say it is our fault for the troubles we have."

"Well, Matthew, at least you are finally willing to talk to me like one human to another. This is the first time that you have ever told me even something of what you really think! But one thing you haven't accounted for is that I might actually really care for people. We are all the same in my opinion, racial or class distinctions do not matter to me; there are only people, good ones and bad ones. We live in a huge, rich country that could easily feed double our current population, and yet fear and greed keep us separate and disparate. I detest and condemn the present lawless, racist regime. Its existence is an obscene disgrace and my conscience won't let me take part in it or help it on anymore."

Matthew tried hard to control his reactions. When talking to whites it was always best to be careful. He took a deep breath and said, "Alright baas, so maybe you have some conscience. So what? Why must I believe you? Blacks are not easily persuaded to get sentimental over someone's kindness to us, unless we're sure of his motives. People call us ungrateful, but that's wrong. It's just that there isn't anything to be grateful for. No one has ever done us a favor without wanting something in return. You try to be kind but I don't know what you're aiming at. It can't be a question of profit, since we haven't got anything of equal value to exchange. Don't tell me you're showing interest in someone like Cornelius from pure benevolence! What makes you so different from all the others?"

"I'm different because I truly believe that if things don't change, then this system will lead us all to disaster. I ask you, why should people like Cornelius suffer so? I am certain that the loss of liberty for one will soon mean that there is no justice for any of us. This is my country and I will fight to make sure that it is not only remembered as a symbol of what is wrong and inhuman."

"Those are fine words Andreas. University words for sure. But who are you fighting for? What do you really know about our lives?" asked Matthew. "As a white person, you have everything you need. There's no way you could ever understand how degrading and humiliating life is for blacks in this country. You cannot imagine what it's like to be born, grow up and die in slavery, to know that your grandfather was a slave and you will be one too. You grow up gradually being weakened by fear, under-nourishment, illiteracy and poverty in a system that eventually grinds you down, and makes you believe that you are inferior. You are never free of constant fears about your security, about your future in the hands of tyrants and despots. No, you could not possibly understand. There are unbridgeable gaps between black and white that are a way of life. You see it from afar but we are living it every day."

Matthew continued after a pause, as Andreas stared at him surprised by his sudden outburst.

"And it cannot be otherwise, not while this white government separates us from our families and denies us the right to vote and the right of free speech. We're not allowed to own property, or to go to school. Something like 700,000 blacks get arrested and jailed every year because they're working in the wrong area or haven't got a passbook. In the meantime, a white immigrant arrives from Europe and he can work anywhere he likes. Add to this that the secret police can arrest us at any time that they want. They can lock you up; put you in solitary confinement and torture you for anything from ninety to three hundred and sixty nine days, with no trial and without letting anyone know where you are or what's happening to you."

Andreas interrupted him caustically, "Matthew, when are you going to stop whining about your troubles? When are you going to develop a national awareness, stand on your own feet and be ready to shed your blood for liberty? When will you learn that there are no social changes without struggle, sweat and blood?"

After another long pause, Matthew finally looked at Andreas with contempt and anger. With some effort, he suppressed his rage enough to reply.

"Baas, you remind me of a little cock crowing and strutting to show off its new comb."

"For God's sake don't ever use that stupid way of addressing me again. I do not want to be your baas. It makes me sick! What can I say? I hate the way that things are here and I really want them to change. I want to help make things change!"

"Baas Andreas, I am sorry, very sorry but I have nothing to say. You would not understand, and it would make no difference to tell you anything more. Please Baas, I don't need any more trouble, let me be. I beg you; please let me keep my job."

Andreas suddenly felt sad, tired and disappointed.

"I understand Matthew, I'm sorry that I bothered you, maybe I expected too much."

Andreas shook Mathew's hand, mostly in an attempt to reassure him that their conversation was to be kept private, and returned to his room.

Once again he felt very alone, depressed and disillusioned. Over the next few days, he turned to his diary to express his inner feelings while he played records of Greek music that helped him to recall happier moments in his life. Late one morning, the door opened and Linda rushed in, beautiful, provocative, and full of youthful exuberance. She wrapped her arms round him, kissing him passionately. Andreas was bewildered and stared at her in astonishment.

"Don't look at me like that," she laughed, "your mother sent me to get you out of this stuffy bedroom. She said that you have been lying here for days. Why haven't you called me?"

"Look, Linda, I'm sorry but I've been in a hole, hibernating. I have not been feeling well."

She got up and pulled his arm with all the force she could muster.

"Get up, lazybones. Philip and Maureen are downstairs waiting for us to go for a swim."

Andreas felt that he had no other choice and he reluctantly got dressed and followed her.

"We're going in Philip's car. You'll like him, he's a marvelous character. You always wanted to meet him didn't you?"

"Yes, I've seen him at a lot of meetings at the university. He's a good speaker."

Andreas's mother was glad to see them leave. She worried about the way her son had kept himself shut indoors for the last few days.

The car radio played a new Beatles song at full blast. Philip's finger beat rhythmically to the music. Maureen, not yet acquainted with the lyrics, hummed cheerfully.

"Andreas, let me introduce my best friends, Maureen and Philip."

"Hi. I've wanted to get to know you for some time, Philip. I'm glad of the opportunity."

Philip smiled pleasantly. "They tell me you've just got back from Greece. I can't tell you how envious I am. I'd give anything for a few days on some deserted Greek island. Anyway, hop in and we'll be on our way. We'll be able to talk at leisure later."

Andreas and Linda sat in the back seat where she curled up in his embrace like an affectionate cat. Andreas had to admit that the touch of her against him felt good.

"Where are we going?" she asked Philip

"If you've no objections, Santa Barbara in the Magaliesberg Mountains," Philip shouted to make himself heard above the loud music on the radio.

"Do whatever you like darling," answered Linda, "I'm a very contented lady!"

They soon left the city behind and Philip sped along the highway.

The abundant summer rain had watered and softened the ground and wildflowers bloomed everywhere in the countryside. Andreas enjoyed the vista of rugged blue mountains which seemed to move slowly in the distance, their sharp cliffs etched against the African sky. The road crossed over Hartebeespoort Dam where sailboats sauntered on the large lake.

Their destination was tucked away in a thickly wooded valley where a brown muddy stream murmured gently as it slowly wound its way around huge granite boulders. Set among the hills, a series of round thatched-roof rondavels, built African-style, with large windows and stone embedded walls beckoned the weary traveler to stay overnight, to eat and rest. Wide green lawns, red hot pokers, cacti and proteas added to the air of colonial luxury. At their rondavel, Philip and Linda plunged into the crystal clear water of the pool. Maureen, wearing a minuscule bikini, stretched out in a deck chair and enjoyed the warmth of the sun. Andreas downed a large glass of beer and lay down on the freshly cut lawn. Far in the distance he could hear the beat of drums. He closed his eyes and concentrated on the sound. The rhythm swelled, filling the air with its conviction that life still had much to offer. Suddenly, it became calmer and more melodious. A tenor voice began to sing with power and pride, and later he was joined by a sizeable chorus. Andreas strained his ears, enjoying the distant music.

"Ever since I was a little girl," said Maureen, "native drums have had a curious effect on me. Do you like them, Andreas?"

Andreas nodded assent.

"Every day, I find out something new about the Africans. Perhaps it's because I know them better now. Honestly, I really admire them. They deserve a much better place in life."

Andreas looked at her with interest.

"How did you get to know them better?" he asked.

"I work with them. I'm a school teacher. I teach night school in the Boksburg ghetto. I've got forty students, most of them a lot older than I am, but they treat me with respect. They work hard and really do very well. It's terrible the way they're so anxious to learn, and we've got so little to offer them."

"Is it a government school?" asked Andreas.

"You've got to be joking, Andreas. No, it's a mission school run by an old nun and a priest. It is supported entirely by voluntary donations."

Philip and Linda emerged dripping wet and came to sit down beside them.

"What they've accomplished is amazing," Maureen went on, "they work like mad without asking for any kind of reward and they're always trying harder to create something better still."

"You're always talking about those priests of yours, Maureen," interrupted Philip. "I'm sorry, but I've got to disagree with you once again. Don't take any notice of her, Andreas; they're not as remarkable as she likes to make out. In my opinion they're playing a propaganda role with the blessing of the police. They do nothing useful and they don't offer anything at all that the people really need."

"You're getting aggressive, Philip. You're carried away with fanaticism and you can't judge things properly any more. According to you everyone should be an activist, shouting slogans and stirring the passive mob. It would be a damn good thing if there were a lot more people like those priests. They offer what little they can."

"Maureen, when you use compromise and subterfuge, you do more harm than good to the people. You confuse them. You just prolong a state of wretchedness that corrupts and dampens their enthusiasm and their revolutionary ideals."

"Philip! You're out of your mind. You seem to think you're living in a free country!" Maureen warned, casting uneasy glances around her.

"I'm not scared of anyone. I'm a free man even if I do live in a dictatorship. No one can rob me of that right, and I'm not crazy because I talk about justice. Man has a right to be free. Free from other men and their gods!"

Andreas looked at him with a mixture of amazement and respect. This small young man with his skinny body and unkempt hair had the gift of magnetizing his listeners with his blazing blue eyes and lyric tongue. He admired him as a fighter in the cause as well as a man. He was one of the few students with the courage to raise his voice against the crushing power of the totalitarian regime.

"Maureen," said Andreas, "I'd very much like to visit this place of yours. I want to see how the blacks really live. I want to sort out my own impressions so that I can take an intelligent part in the conversation next time it comes up. Can I go with you some time?"

"Of course, Andreas. I'll get a permit for you. They're not likely to refuse it. I'll give you a ring when it's ready."

The rest of the day passed pleasantly. They swam, ate, and played tennis, chatted about everything under the sun. Andreas and Philip were quickly becoming friends.

On the way back, Linda invited them to her flat for a cup of coffee. They all accepted, so as to extend the enjoyment of each other's company. They drank coffee and French brandy. Eventually, Philip and Maureen left, leaving Linda and Andreas on their own.

"Excuse me for a moment. I just want to freshen up and then I'll drive you home."

Andreas poured a little cognac into his glass and smiled at her, "I'll wait for you. Don't worry about me, I'm in good company!" He pointed to his glass.

She soon came back, refreshed and strikingly beautiful, looking exotic and sexy in a filmy white negligee, slit at the sides, which allowed her superb body and lacy black underwear to be clearly seen. Her long slender arms entwined around him and her red sweet lips pressed moistly against his, taking his breath away. French perfume with the scent of opium lay heavy in the air and the touch of her flesh, aflame with passion, swiftly ignited his desires.

"What about Rena?" he asked himself. Linda was something different, a temporary means of mutual enjoyment. He was lonely and she was beautiful and pleasure-loving, like a spring of sparkling water in the midst of a burning desert, ready to give life abundantly. He was only too ready to fasten his parched lips to hers and drink insatiably. The hours passed slowly, abandoned to sensuality.

"Andreas, you're superb. You make me feel so…," she paused as if trying to find the correct word, "so different."

On return home, Andreas felt confidant, more like his old self, with an increased certainty that he would find the course that he wanted to follow. Two days later, Maureen phoned to say that she had got the permit and would come by to collect him the next morning. Andreas felt impatient and excited without knowing why. What after all was the purpose of this trip to the ghetto? What, he asked himself, was his real objective? Was it just to relieve his boredom by seeing the misery of others? Did he hope that somehow in all that degradation he would find the courage to make a decision? Or did he just want to see whether Philip was in any way accurate in his judgments?

The heat was intolerable and Maureen's small Mini jolted and bounced crazily over the appallingly corrugated road. Maureen slowed down and turned into a small, wire-fenced yard.

"Here we are," she said, as she parked in the shade of a solitary pine tree. There were workmen hard at it, knee deep in muddy water and surrounded by building materials. Amid all this turmoil, a statue of St. Augustine stood unnaturally calm and peaceful on his plinth. Maureen pushed her way confidently through the work zone, opened a door, and went into an old single-story building. A pure white, freshly painted statue of the Virgin and Child confronted them.

"This is our classroom, Andreas. As you can see it's very small even for the forty pupils I've got. With the new building of course all that will change and we'll be in a position to take more students."

She showed him around enthusiastically, explaining every detail in her characteristic warm and pleasant tone. Andreas followed her with increasing interest. Even though the building was small and ramshackle, it was well cared for. It had a little chapel, a music room, and a huge library packed with educational books, antiques and comfortable furniture. There were some original oil paintings on the walls, and Andreas recognized a few, thinking that they must be worth a small fortune. Maureen noticed the frown of disapproval on Andreas's face and hastened to explain.

"Those are all gifts and legacies from individuals. Of course, they don't mean much to our parishioners but..."

She stopped and silently from behind her a middle-aged woman appeared, dressed in white with a large cross hanging from a long chain around her neck. She greeted them warmly and hospitably. Andreas looked her over carefully. She was stout, of middle height, and her dead white skin contrasted with the black of her intelligent eyes. Her voice was soft and well-modulated.

After the initial introductions, Sister Mary said, "it's nice to see new people taking an interest in our work, Andreas. We'll need a lot of volunteers once the new building is finished. Unfortunately,

Father MacGregor is very busy just at the moment, but he'll meet us later for tea."

"In that case we'll go for a look around the community and see you later, Sister," said Maureen.

"No, dear, I think it would be better if I came with you into the ghetto. Although you have a permit, people here are suspicious. It would be less dangerous if I am with you. They don't take kindly to strangers. Besides, you could run into trouble with the police. I've got to invite various dignitaries to our party tomorrow, so that'll give us the excuse to go into a few houses. Then Andreas can see what kind of conditions these people have to live in."

The mission had been built in the middle of a bare, dry valley, stony and inhospitable, and in no way attractive or picturesque. The heat was stifling and the little car was like an oven as it struggled over a non-existent road, raising clouds of dust. The nun managed with some difficulty to extricate her portly body from the back seat. They had stopped at an isolated little house surrounded by a cane fence. The house had been cobbled together out of the most peculiar and amazing materials; thick sheets of cardboard, rusty corrugated iron and wooden boxes that still bore the name of the factory they had come from. Three young children, sweaty and dirty and with swollen bellies, were playing listlessly in the heat of the yard. The nun led the way and Andreas, feeling both out of place and appalled, stuck close to her.

"My God," he whispered as he looked around, "what ghastly misery. It's enough to break your heart."

The door was low and he had to stoop to go in. The gloom enveloped him and he could make out nothing in the darkness. The air was heavy and foul with a stale smell of dank coal. He stood there unmoving, opening and shutting his eyes to get used to the darkness.

"Hello, Sister, come in. Meisie is in the front room," a man's voice called out.

Andreas groped his way forward with short, uncertain steps, following Maureen and the Sister, leaving the door open behind him. The light streamed in and the man could be seen lying to one side on a shallow stretcher.

When he saw Andreas, he said, "Baas, have you got a fag for me?"

Andreas looked round and discovered that he was in a small, narrow and windowless corridor with a floor made of dry, compacted earth. The stranger's gaze was firmly fixed on him. A shiver ran down Andreas's spine and his ears hummed as if he were short of oxygen. He wanted to run away or disappear from the scene, but felt he had neither the strength nor the courage.

"Have you got any fags, Baas?" the man repeated.

Andreas's hand shook as he fished out a packet of cigarettes and gave him one.

"Thanks, Baas, thanks."

The man's breath reeked of alcohol and Andreas turned his head away in disgust as he offered him a light.

"Terrible hot, Baas, especially when a bloke can't get out of this bloody bed."

As he spoke, his toothless mouth gaped unpleasantly. Andreas noticed for the first time that he had his leg in plaster.

"How did that happen?" he asked sympathetically.

"Car accident. I'm a driver, but now I've been out of work for three months."

"When will you get the plaster off?"

"I wish I knew. They put a new lot on yesterday for the third time. The bone hasn't knit, you see."

Maureen called him from the front room and Andreas backed away apologetically.

"Andreas, meet Mrs. Viljoen. She's a hundred and two years old and still as lively as a cricket. Isn't that marvelous?"

Andreas could not share Maureen's enthusiasm. He stared vacantly at the room. It was squalid, chaotic, filthy, and cluttered with tattered furniture. A small child lay in a cot sucking his thumb. His little face was pinched and yellow and his eyes were clouded with fever. After briefly greeting the elderly grandmother, his attention was caught by a fierce looking woman standing behind a low table. Mrs. Meisie Potgieter, aged before her time, stirred some food in an aluminum pot that looked worn out from scrubbing. From time to time, she would bang on a gas pipe in order to get a spurt of feeble flame from her small gas cooker. Sister Mary, with blissful dignity, was chatting tenderly to the grandmother, who seemed to be listening hard, leaning forward with her wrinkled face on one side as though trying to understand her. Suddenly, the nun, as if she had just remembered something more interesting, turned impulsively toward the woman who was now beating potatoes in the pot with evident annoyance.

"Mrs. Potgieter, I heard the police again arrested your eldest son for stealing copper telephone wire. I think it's high time you did something about putting him straight before it's too late. The first thing to do is come to the mission and ask Father MacGregor to use his influence and get the boy into a young people's shelter before he turns into a common criminal."

The woman's eyes flashed with anger. She stopped her continual stirring and clenched her fists in a fighting stance.

"My son's not going downhill and he doesn't need your mission. As you know my husband has been incapable of working for weeks. What we need is money for bread, groceries and medicine and my son helps with the only way we can get any. I don't expect you to understand but when you are starving, stealing isn't a crime or a sin. So keep your moralizing for Sunday school kids and people who've got plenty to eat!"

She stared at them with violent anger. Her eyes gleamed with hatred. She was the only being in that household that showed any signs of life.

They left hurriedly, like fugitives. Andreas's curiosity about human misery was fully satisfied and he emerged in a daze, gulping down the fresh air. Sister Mary was used to such scenes and had lost none of her religious serenity. Maureen was pale.

The township gave the appearance of a collection of deserted ruins. There were sheds, hovels and improvised shacks, all leaning closely on one another, as if they needed the mutual support in order to avoid collapsing into heaps of useless junk. Labyrinths of narrow alleys revealed faces racked and distorted by cheap booze, drugs, lack of vitamins, constant violence, the nightmare of fear and the oppression of hunger. Rubbish was piled everywhere in heaps that stank appallingly and flies swarmed in their thousands.

"It's hard to imagine, but there are at least two families in every house you see," said the nun. "Also crime here rivals that of Soweto. One wouldn't dream of walking these streets after dark. We're coming to the center of the ghetto now and, as you can see, the surroundings are improving a bit. The homes may be small, but they're well-built and each one has a little garden. This ghetto was originally built by the government to house blacks. The families that were selected to live here have always hoped that they could get established here and put down roots. They used to call it Jerusalem, the promised land. But their dreams came to nothing. For some unknown reason, the government shifted them all to another area, but the coloreds liked the name and it stuck. You realize Andreas that this ghetto is mainly for people of mixed race."

Andreas was scarcely listening anymore to what the nun was saying. He was too preoccupied with what he could see.

"Sister, let's stop and see Mr. Patterson? I like him. He's such an eccentric!" said Maureen.

"I've no objection," smiled the nun.

They entered the ghetto's one and only supermarket, an attractively clean and contemporary shop. Two women with tired faces were serving the customers without pausing. A swarthy man of about forty came out of his little office to greet them. The nun performed the introductions.

"This is Mr. Patterson. He used to be a teacher but now he's a businessman and secretary of our community."

She turned to him and rebuked him in a friendly way. "Your wife looks worn out and you're not paying enough attention to your business."

"Don't be so hard on me, Sister. You know there are much more serious matters to keep us busy. Somebody has to deal with them! I've just finished an open letter to the Prime Minister complaining about the new law they want to pass to divide us Coloreds into four nationalities. We were born and bred in this country. We're the bastards, the offspring of the white man's lust. Like it or not, that's the truth. You lot are our ancestors regardless of whether you treat us the same way as you treat the blacks. Where's the logic in trying to make distinctions between us?"

"Patterson, you just go round looking for trouble," commented the nun caustically, "Whenever you see me with strange people, you like to unleash your political views. We came to pay you a visit not to talk politics."

"Oh, I see," he replied bitterly, "so our job is to stay shut up in our shells while you justify the wretched status quo. That's what you believe, isn't it, Sister? But don't worry, I may be a gas bag but I'm just a coward really. I haven't got the guts to raise my voice where it can be heard. I ought to be shouting my protests right in their faces. I ought to be screaming at them!"

Mr. Patterson turned towards Andreas gesticulating with his hands to emphasize his points. "Racism; is when you wait for your pension until the end of the month, and then when you eventually get it to pay your rent, you realize there's not enough money left to buy bread. Apartheid is when one white school produces more graduates than all of ours put together. It's when you stand on the platform for hours waiting for a train and when it turns up it's so full you can't squeeze in anywhere. Meanwhile, the dozens of empty carriages tease you with that maddening label 'Whites Only'. Apartheid is when the government spends countless millions on military hardware in times of peace, and can't spare a cent for the poor! Apartheid's when they won't let Christ get near his followers."

"Stop, for goodness sake. You're making us dizzy," interrupted the nun, impatiently. "Who are we and what can we do about it? You'll have to excuse us now, Mr. Patterson. We're running late and we have to visit the clinic."

Maureen and Andreas were so astonished at the turn the conversation had taken that when Patterson shook hands they did not know how to express their feelings. The people out in the square stared at them with a mixture of curiosity and hostility. A swarm of children surrounded the nun and jumped up and down demanding sweets. She smiled at them, plunged her hands into the deep pockets of her habit, and started handing out candies. Mr. Patterson stood and watched morosely from in front of his shop. Shaken by their experience, they walked to the clinic in silence. Andreas felt exhausted. He wanted to run away and be on his own. He had seen all he wanted, but tagged along with the others not knowing how to make his escape.

Like all government buildings in the ghetto, there was nothing attractive about the clinic. They went up a curved staircase and entered the foyer. The smell of antiseptic hit them immediately and Andreas felt even less comfortable. A nurse told them respectfully that the matron was waiting for them in her office. The nun knew her way around and led the others to a door on which she tapped discreetly. She opened it and entered, revealing the matron who was completely absorbed in studying some yellow cards.

"Well, at least there's one person who works hard in this place!" laughed the nun. The matron looked up with a smile.

"Do come in. I've been waiting for you for ages. Please, sit down."

"I hope we're not interrupting your work, Magda," said Maureen.

"No. Every now and then we get a quiet spot and I've found time to finish some research I've been doing."

"What research is that, Magda?"

She showed them a local street map covered with large, red-tipped pins.

"Every rectangle you see represents a house and every pin represents a TB case. The results are so depressing. There's hardly a house without two or three people with tuberculosis."

"Excuse me, but I thought, well, hasn't it been wiped out?" stammered Andreas.

The nurse looked at him oddly, "In other parts of the world perhaps, but not in South Africa's slums. Undernourishment, substandard housing and sketchy medical care allow plenty of room for disease."

She went on, quietly, "There is not much we can do to treat those that are ill and the government does nothing to help us take preventative measures. My God, when you think about it, you have to be lucky to live in conditions like these and not fall victim to all kinds of problems. Earlier today, I came across two little kids who were sniffing model airplane glue. They said it gives them visions. I can't blame them. Unfortunately, it is not unlike the work we do here. We are all in the thrall of temporary illusions."

"Oh, excuse me!" She forced a smile at her visitors. "I got carried away, I'm afraid. As a journalist however," she spoke to Andreas and tipped her head quizzically, "please write about all that you are seeing today. It is so important for people to learn how we live. Now you must excuse my rudeness, can I offer you some coffee or tea?"

"Thank you, another time, Matron. Father MacGregor is expecting us back at the mission. We're already late" said the nun.

Father MacGregor, tall and rosy-cheeked, stood in front of the building with a look of childish expectation on his genial face. He greeted them warmly and shook Andreas's hand in his own huge paw.

"You look very happy, Father. You must have had good news."

"Yes, Sister; God has helped me to persuade them. They're going to give us enough money to finish the building."

"Father, I know you're dying to show Andreas round the new center of the mission. I'll go and get the tea ready."

The priest proudly showed Andreas the modern architecture of the chapel, the recreation room, the lecture rooms for foreign language instruction, and the coffee bar. Maureen joined in and shared his enthusiasm, but Andreas followed him around only out of politeness, and with little real interest. He felt drained and found it difficult to concentrate on the priest's plans for the future of the mission. He was quietly relieved when he and Maureen finally made their way back home to the northern suburbs of Johannesburg.

CHAPTER 8 Conflict with Parents

Andreas returned from the Boxburg slums feeling ill and confused. Nevertheless, he continued to believe with all his might in the need for change. He was not sure if the mission school was the cause he was looking for, but he was determined to find a way of throwing himself into the struggle. When he arrived home, he was surprised and delighted to find a letter from Rena and he grabbed it and hurried to his room. It was the first letter he had had from her in months and he opened it impatiently:

My Darling,

Do you still remember me? For me, the thought of you has kept me sane. It gave me the courage to stand up to the torment of being imprisoned in the camp on Yaros. Well, I'm finally free but living in a country that's enslaved, groaning under this bleak dictatorship. These people don't hesitate to use every possible means to force us to conform, but they've met their match. I feel stronger now than ever before and it makes me proud to see the way that our people refuse to submit. Instead, they're waiting, getting ready for the day when they can punish these betrayers of freedom, these puppets of capitalism. During my months in exile, I came to the reality that people like us are a danger and hindrance to their schemes and they would wipe us out at the first chance, without compunction. So take care, dearest. How are things with you? I feel sure you'll have found your way by now. I long for you. I love you and I miss you.

Big hugs and kisses,
Rena.

He scarcely slept at all that night, tossing and turning in his bed, as voices and images tormented him. He awoke early, in a foul mood and went into the dining room. His father, ensconced behind the newspaper, was eating his breakfast.

"Good morning, Dad."

Frixos Magdalos noticed with some alarm how pale his son was looking.

"Good morning Andreas. How come you're up so early? Has something happened?" he asked with concern, folding up the paper.

"No, Dad. I just couldn't sleep."

"What's the news from Rena? What did she have to tell you?" Andreas's father inquired and Andreas gave him a brief summary of the letter.

"I'm so sorry about what happened to that poor girl. Please sit down and we'll have breakfast together. We seem to have drifted apart lately, but I do want you to see me as your friend. I'd like us to share our problems and worries."

Andreas filled his cup with strong black coffee and lit a cigarette.

"Oh, by the way son, that business with Cornelius has been sorted out," his father continued. "My legal adviser has got the court's decision reversed, so he can stay in Johannesburg without fear. I've given him a responsible job in the factory and he seems pleased. You should come and see him this morning, he's a different man."

"Thanks, Dad that was good of you. I'd like to see the old man again."

"Well, come to the factory with me, and then I'll take you to a good restaurant for lunch."

Matthew, polite and smiling, opened the back door of the car for them and they settled in for the journey. At that time of day, the roads were mostly empty and Matthew drove skillfully. It was the first time that Andreas had been to the new factory and he stared in amazement at the huge neon sign, 'Magdalos & Son Pty. Ltd., Textile Manufacturing'. A large number of Africans were standing outside the factory gate, blocking the road. Matthew sounded the horn repeatedly and forced a way through. The guard on the gate, with a big cudgel in his hand, ran to open the heavy doors for them.

"Is there some sort of trouble, Dad?" asked Andreas curiously, "What are all these people doing here?"

"They're looking for work" said his father. "Every day it is the same."

The enormous yard inside was a scene of feverish activity. The roar of machinery, trucks loading and unloading large bales of material and cotton ribbons, were accented by the shouts and curses of indiscriminate workers. Andreas was most startled by the change that came over his father. He seemed a completely different man to him. He had shed his face of familial softness, suddenly transforming into a hard-driven, dynamic businessman. In a voice laden with authority, he gave his foremen their instructions for the day, asked for information, and then gave new orders. Only when he was certain that he had gathered all the strings into his own hands, did he return his attention to Andreas.

"Well, now it's time I showed you our factory since you're a legal partner. It's completely up to date. I've worked hard to keep up with the latest technological advances. With this plant and our factories in Cape Town and Port Elizabeth, we're the largest manufacturers in our field in the country. You can't imagine, Andreas, how long I've waited for the moment when we could tour the factory side by side, and I could show you what I've built up for us, for our dynasty!"

Andreas listened to him in silent admiration. He loved his father. He was a born leader with the ability to attract others. He made people trust him and was able to pass on his own energy and enthusiasm to others. He liked the feeling of security and strength that he still had when he was with his father.

The textile factory was enormous with an army of workers and technicians organized on highly productive lines. They went into one of the production workshops where a row of machines pounded rhythmically back and forth in seemingly endless and monotonous motion. There was a pandemonium of noise as bales of materials rolled out in differing colors and textures. They then entered a large room where female workers with tired eyes followed every movement of smaller machines that were producing reams of cotton ribbons. White foremen patrolled continuously, keeping an eye on the quantity and quality of production.

At the piercing shriek of a siren, the machinery stopped. Suddenly, the dry, expressionless faces of the workers livened. The room filled with cheerful voices; their shift had finished. In a mass, they poured toward the exits. Four doors opened and the fresh air flowed onto the work floor. A black guard was stationed at each exit. Tall and well built, each man carried a red baton under his arm as his symbol of office. Guards were employed by the company to search the workers for petty theft, the white man's faithful servants. The female workers formed four queues and as each woman reached the guard, she stood to attention with her arms in the air. Then the guard's heavy hands started a shameless search of the female body, even into its most intimate parts and if the worker was young and attractive, the search lingered somewhat attentively. The others waited stoically and without complaint, accustomed to it all. Andreas was outraged, unable to believe his eyes.

"Dad," he yelled in a fury, "what the hell are those fellows doing?"

"It's just a routine job that's carried out independently and to the letter by every factory in the country. These people are dreadful thieves and this is the only way we can keep their thieving within limits."

"But Dad, searching like that is inhuman, degrading. It should be illegal. It's time you took your blinders off and looked at life as it really is. If these people steal, they do it because they're hungry. They pinch crumbs from us because we've been robbing them blind all their lives. I would never have expected anything like this from you. I am so ashamed and frustrated that you allow these things to happen in your own factory."

Mr. Magdalos looked at his son in anger and disbelief. He could not tolerate his lack of respect in front of his foremen.

"How dare you point your finger at me? I have nothing to be

ashamed of! You, on the other hand, are being stupid and childish. Let me tell you that in all your life you have had everything easy and rosy and you think life is, or rather should be a Garden of Eden. The world is a dirty place and you have to fight hard to survive. It has no space for fainthearted romantics like you. When you carry on with quixotic ideas like that, I can only feel sorry for you. I'm trying to understand where I went wrong in bringing you up. You have to learn that life's a jungle, and you've got to fight hard if you aim to survive."

Back at the office, Frixos Magdalos opened the door and slammed it behind them. He sat in his armchair and lit a cigar, filling the room with smoke. He was pale and visibly on edge.

"I can't think who taught you such ideas. As for me, my conscience is clear"

"Dad, how can you have a clear conscience when you know there are people living like pigs in a sty? They're hungry and oppressed. We pay them a tenth of the wages that's due to them. One in three of their children suffer from TB. Who would stop you doubling their wages so they've got a chance to live?

His father replied, "I always work within the confines of the law. I've worked extremely hard to earn what I own and I'll keep it at whatever cost."

"But of course, that is always the easy solution, just obey the one-sided laws of the country that are passed solely for the benefit of the white minority," Andreas said, "the laws that say the majority has to work and suffer so that the chosen rulers can live in opulence. As for me, you've offered me a great deal and I'm grateful, but I can't accept anything else from you. I'll fight my own battles and find my own way from now on. I don't believe in dynasties."

Mr. Magdalos sat motionless. The ash from his cigar fell and broke into powder on the glass surface of his desk.

"Excuse me, Dad. I have to go. Goodbye."

Andreas got up, opened the door and went out. He left the factory and for hours he wandered aimlessly in the streets of Johannesburg as conflicting thoughts bombarded his mind. He knew that he had reached a crossroads and that he would have to choose which route to follow. At last, he managed to catch a bus home, and on his arrival he felt a degree of relief at the normality and familiarity of it all. He sat in the half-dark of the veranda, gazing out over the beautiful array of flowers. He even enjoyed sipping at the cocktail that had been mixed for him. But he could not get rid of the bitter taste in his mouth.

"What a marvelous idealist I am, how big-hearted, what pity I feel for the downtrodden!" he thought sarcastically as the alcohol took effect.

When his father retuned from work, Andreas was still sitting there lost in thought. He got up and offered his father a chair, and made him a drink. Mr. Magdalos was obviously upset and seemed distant and distressed. For a while they sat without speaking.

It was a fine, warm evening, totally peaceful; the stars appeared shyly and trembled in the velvet sky. Night had tenderly covered the entire city's ugliness as it brought rest to the living world. A gentle breeze blew softly, a breath of coolness, and the leaves of the trees began to dance lightly. The beauty of the night and the pale gold light of the moon could do nothing to touch their spirits. Each of them was living in his own earthbound worry.

The silence affected Andreas's nerves and he tried to break the ice.

"Dad, I'm sorry about this morning. I did not mean to be disrespectful. I love you very much and I think very highly of you. After getting Rena's letter, I felt very edgy, confused and powerless to change anything, and I'm sorry."

His father stared at him steadily. "Andreas, we're both grown men and we ought to be able to speak up and make no secret of what we're really feeling. I'm very sorry too. It's heart breaking when you hurt people that you love. Please, forgive me for what I said to you this morning. I didn't mean it. I was angry. But you must understand, Andreas. I'm an intelligent man and I can see ahead. I started off in the gutter and life's taught me a lot of hard lessons. But you haven't had to suffer yet. You don't know how crude, hypocritical and cruel men can be toward each other. You're still like a piece of unshaped clay. You've got a lot of humanity in you and a lot of scruples, but you don't yet know how to put them together. I'll just ask one thing of you. Try and get through this difficult period by looking at life and the world as they really are, not the way you imagine they should be.

You're a dreamer and an idealist, and real idealists never get very far, or aren't allowed to. You asked for my friendship and I've never denied you anything. Everything I have belongs to you. If you've got problems, let's talk them over and help each other. You're in love with that girl in Greece, aren't you? She's just got out of prison and she needs you. Why don't you go back to Greece and when everything's sorted out, we'll come and celebrate your wedding day?"

His face had become calm and mild and his voice warm and enthusiastic. He no longer resembled the tough businessman. The way he spoke was heartwarming to Andreas. This was the father he knew. His cheeks glowed with excitement and his eyes shone with expectation at the thought of going back to Rena and being liberated from the troubles of South Africa.

"Yes, Dad, I would like to go. This land is not for me. This is a land of fear and hate. I can't stand this way of life. I can't stand meeting cruelty and injustice every day. I feel hunted, guilty and depressed. Haven't you had enough? How have you taken it for so many years? Isn't it time for you to go back home to Greece?"

"Yes, son, we'll go. We'll fix up a house on an island somewhere. That was always a dream of mine; a small village house perched on a hill with the waves at our feet and day and night, to hear the murmur of the sea. We'll buy a sail boat and travel from island to island like Odysseus. We'll make up for all the years we've lost. You know, son, you make me feel strong again; you make me recall all the dreams I had, when I was a youngster. You can leave when you're ready. I'll have to stay back for a bit because I'll have a lot of arrangements to make."

The breeze had stopped blowing and the heat had become stifling. Andreas's breath was coming in short gasps and he thought he would faint. He was soaked in sweat and there was a pounding at his temples. His father's face seemed to be transformed, its features distorted into one huge mouth. He thought of Rena and the way that she had held onto her courage even in that island prison. He longed to be with her. He wanted to leave, and yet, a familiar voice something like that of Mr. Patterson began to sound within his head. It became louder until it was shouting and ringing in Andreas's ears.

"Apartheid is when a teenage boy, with a pair of clippers in hand, steals wire to buy food and medicine for his family. That's apartheid, that's apartheid!"

The voice continued, on and on.

"Apartheid is when old men and women are discarded at the side of the road like human rags with no pension!"

The mouth was shrinking, becoming sharp and cynical as it began to whine in desperate tones.

"Apartheid is that everyone should have an equal share in the wealth of the country, except for the huge majority who do not have the right to vote!"

Andreas felt a call from a deep, internal need that would not leave him for an instant. His heart was breaking; for the pain, fear and misery of all those people, for that town, for all the other towns and villages, for all those desperate, hopeless eyes. How much time and how much degradation had it taken for South Africa to end up in this misery?

"No, I can't desert my country again," he murmured.

Mr. Magdalos got up, looking anxiously at his son.

"What's the matter, son? Are you all right? Don't worry, I'm here. Look, I'll organize your passport, your ticket and your money. Everything will be ready for you."

"I'm so sorry, Dad. I was carried away. But the die's cast. It's too late for me to leave. There's no way I can desert now. This country, this country of hatred and apartheid, is my homeland. Please try to understand. A lot of things have got to change here. We've got to change; too many people are suffering."

His father looked at him with contempt and fury.

"The way you think is just plain mad. I'm sorry for you with your half-baked philosophies. Do what the hell you like. But let me just make one thing quite clear, you're playing a dangerous game and you'll play it on your own. If you ever create problems for me or get me blamed for anything, you'd better know that you have no place here and your name will be a pure coincidence. Good night and I hope you'll take in what I've said."

Andreas, alone now, strolled around the garden. His head had stopped pounding and his thoughts were clear of taunts and hallucinations. For the first time since he had come back from Greece, he felt free.

The rhythm of life at home changed radically after the row with his father. Their relationship became formal and impersonal, with each ensuring that he kept out of the other's way. Andreas understood the disappointment and hurt that he had caused his father. He felt that the time had come for him to leave home. He did not know how to accomplish this goal as he could not afford to live on his own and continue at the university. He enjoyed being among the restless, youthful faces, all bearing the same signs of hope, idealism and eager inquiry. Of particular importance to him was his friendship with Philip, who was general secretary of the Student Union, and one of its most militant members. Philip helped him to build up a circle of acquaintances with people who shared his ideals and interests.

Among the student population, Andreas discovered that there was widespread disquiet about the political situation of the country and many had reached the conclusion that change had to come soon. The general feeling was that a democratic system was needed; one that would curb the suffering, and allow blacks and whites to work together to build a new and multiracial nation. It was perhaps the first time that the English-speaking universities had come together in brotherhood. They used their limited powers toward the goal of democratic change, and for the first time they came into serious confrontation with the all-powerful apparatus of the state. The architect of this union was William Pretorius, the fiery revolutionary president of the National Union of South African Students.

Andreas envied and admired the leaders of the student organizations. With unshakable determination, they fired off their accusations. They risked imprisonment, exile, the loss of their civil rights and possibly their lives. Absolutely nothing could terrify these youngsters, who were so completely dedicated to the struggle. Andreas felt however, that in comparison, he was a non-participant. He felt angry and guilty at his lack of contribution. He threw off his hesitations and spoke to Philip decisively.

"Philip, I feel that I'm ready for recruitment now. I want to be an active member of NUSAS. I want to do whatever I can, and join you in the struggle to put an end to racial discrimination and the oppression of the black population that underpins the present establishment."

Philip looked at him carefully as though he wanted to penetrate his mind.

"Andreas, the government's trying to pin a label on us. They claim that we're recruiting members to overthrow lawful authority. They say that we are anarchist terrorists or Communist stooges. They say that we are aiming to recruit militant members, in order to meet force with force, and create pointless bloodshed. They believe that we are enrolled members of the African National Congress. I wish we were, but that organization does not think that we white liberals are really serious about change. All the government's grandiose plans for separate states in the homelands have failed, despite all their efforts, simply because those efforts have been immoral and evil. We resist because we can't tolerate the sight of injustice and because we resent the blame, the abuse and the scorn which the rest of the world quite rightly directs against us. We're protesting because we ourselves aren't free either; we can't talk and express our opinions or exchange ideas without being afraid. They compel us to talk together in whispers like conspirators, so anyone who shares our views is welcome."

Andreas listened without interruption, impressed by Philip's clarity and sincerity.

"Also Andreas, I want to brief you on certain problems that you'll encounter every day while being a member of NUSAS. From the moment you join us, you need to be aware that a file will be opened on you in the records of the secret police. Once a member, if they arrest you, they can use anti-terrorism legislation against you. They'll drop it on you like a ton of bricks, with its ninety days imprisonment without trial. They have lots of spies and they work in an organized and conscientious way. They're everywhere, in all classes. They could even be friends of ours who are biding their time and passing on what they hear to their masters. I don't want to discourage you, but I have to tell you this. Now it's up to you to make your decision."

Andreas said nothing. He simply held out his hand to Philip, who shook it warmly. From then on the two of them worked together as members, participating in every protest, throwing themselves heart and soul into the effort to undermine the machinery of the state.

One afternoon, Andreas was summoned by phone, somewhat belatedly, to an extraordinary meeting of the Student Union. Thoughts concerning what the students hoped to accomplish were churning around in Andreas's head, as he drove through the heavy afternoon traffic to the university. The heat was still oppressive, even though it was nearing sunset. He parked his car and ran toward the ceremonial hall, his body soon soaked in sweat. He sighed with relief as he realized that he had arrived in time. The hall was filled with hundreds of students. The excitement and enthusiasm was pervasive. He found he knew most of the faces, friends who had worked with him on various projects. Exchanging jokes and greetings, he forced his way through to the stage curtain. When he eventually reached the front, he saw Philip mounting the steps to the stage. Andreas waited there, standing among the packed crowd of students.

Philip's voice, amplified by the loudspeakers, could be heard clearly. Immediately, all the chatter stopped and every eye was fixed on him. He was as untidy as ever, but obviously likeable and the object of everyone's affection.

"University staff members and student colleagues, as general secretary of NUSAS, I welcome you and thank you all for making the effort to get here. Colleagues, it's both moving and encouraging that in this land of degraded values and inhumanity, there are still young people who have not been infected by the horrible fanaticism of racism. I don't intend to bore you with a lot of pointless words on matters you know very well. Our aim is to secure the shallow foundations of our country. To work towards the day when blacks and whites respect each other, and have equal shares in the riches that our country has to offer. I doubt whether there have ever been richer people in the history of the world, who lived in such a scandalous society and yet enjoyed life so thoroughly. I imagine even the nobility of Tsarist Russia would have envied us South African whites. In the midst of all this intoxicating prosperity, do we ever wonder how our black compatriots live, those well-known unknowns? I'm going to call on Mark Stevens who urged us to hold this extraordinary meeting, so that he can tell us the results of his research. As you all know, Mark Stevens is one of the few competent journalists who has attempted to combat the totalitarianism of the extreme right with his powerful articles."

A young man of medium height and athletic build got up from his seat and, under the concerted gaze of everyone present, made his way to the stage. Philip greeted him warmly and offered him the microphone. Mark Stevens looked at his audience, waiting for the excited hubbub among the students to die down.

"Dear friends," he began, "I find it very moving to be here in this hall and to feel around me the pure ideals and the high convictions of you, the leaders of tomorrow. It is a great honor for me to be in this sacred place, one of the few remaining bastions of individual freedom in South Africa. As you know, I have been invited here today to share with you the results of my research. I lived for five months in the township of Soweto, to find out for myself how black people live today. I had a deep need to solve the riddle that had been nagging at me since my student days. Namely, how is it possible for these people to survive, to bring up families on the pitifully small wages they earn? A weekly wage is equivalent to two days' wages for a similarly skilled white worker. Apart from rent and travel costs, which are subsidized, all other goods offered to black workers in the townships are the same price as they are in wealthy white communities.

For many years, I have wanted to find out what it was like to live in Soweto. Nonetheless, I admit to being afraid at the consequences of such action. It's only recently that I've found the courage to dare and satisfy my curiosity. Thankfully, I have the support of my editor, and two black colleagues. Without their help, I'd never have been able to succeed. It was a difficult project. We had to change my color, which we barely accomplished using dyes, makeup and even boot polish. I also had to obtain forged papers and a passbook. What I hadn't anticipated as a major hurdle was finding accommodation! I then learnt for the first time that every home in Soweto houses two or three families. I discovered that hundreds of families are waiting for housing, that thousands of homes have been derelict for years. The municipal authorities don't repair or build any houses although the population keeps growing, because the belief is held that people will be returning to their so-called homelands.

After a lot of trouble and a bit of bribery, my friends managed to find me a bed in a filthy room which I had to share with four others. It cost me thirteen Rand a month with the arrangement that I was to try to live on fifty Rand per month; the average wage. I was transported to another world, one that was totally new to me. A lively imagination could scarcely dream up all that I witnessed. In the past, I'd read or heard many times about the circumstanccs that prevail in the ghetto, and about the way people live in fear of the police and under the tyranny of the passbook. But believe me, nothing, absolutely nothing can approach the horror of the reality.

The memory of it all is enough to make me weep. Along with my rent, I paid another four Rand to get my clothes washed. My travel expenses came to seven Rand a month. So I was left with twenty-six Rand for food, clothing, entertainment and tobacco. Never in my life have I been so hungry, never have I had such a longing for food, never have I eaten a piece of bread with such appetite or found a plate of mealie-meal with sauce so tasty. In the first month, I lost six kilos. By the second month I had lost ten. My money got dangerously low toward the end of each month, so I stopped buying cigarettes and started rolling my own, using cheap tobacco and pieces of newspaper. By the third month, I had become a shadow of my former self. I was living on bread and water and I began to feel incredibly feeble. Before the month was out, I hadn't a shilling in my pocket, so I had to borrow against my wages. What a treat, I ate mealie-meal with meat and smoked real cigarettes.

By the fourth week of the fourth month, I had fallen ill. My editor forced me to see a doctor friend of mine; a luxury not available to all those who live in the townships. After he'd examined me, he ordered me to stop my research because my health had deteriorated so severely. He suspected that I had the early stages of tuberculosis. My curiosity had been satisfied, and I followed his advice. With considerable relief, I called an end to my research. I completed my reporting task, but the memories of the experience are such that now I feel all the more ashamed about my privileged white status. We're all guilty: we're jointly responsible. The time of change must come soon and those of us with a shred of humanity in us must take up the fight. I'm appealing to you and to every freedom-loving and sane thinking citizen of our country. It's time we stopped worrying about trifles, time we clothed ourselves in a little courage. Let's make ourselves the nucleus of change. If we can't seek liberty for the majority, let us at least work toward making sure that all our people have at least some bread to fill their bellies. They're dying of starvation in the townships and it's our fault and our responsibility!"

In the same quiet, unassuming way as he had stood up to speak, he went back to his seat. The total silence of the vast auditorium was shattered by applause.

The audience was further invigorated by the magnetic personality of the student leader, Willy Pretorius. He was tall and well built, with blue eyes, handsome features. His well-proportioned head was sheltered under a cataract of blond hair. Willy had all the gifts of a shrewd leader. He was energetic, intelligent, and he exuded integrity and personality. He captivated his fellow students and roused them to their feet. His face was lit by an attractive smile as he raised his arms in greeting, and took over the microphone.

"Greetings, colleagues. I think we've all been shaken more than we had imagined by Mark's revelations. But I wonder why we're amazed when somebody drags us away from our illusions and takes us back to simple reality? How often have we had the experience, after a rich meal, of seeing black children sitting on the pavement and satisfying their hunger with a Coca-Cola and a crust of bread? Don't we ever notice the difference, don't we ever feel sorry, and don't we ever feel guilty? The question confronts us again: where do we stand, we who are young, we who are sane thinkers as Mark Stevens called us? How far are we willing to go? Have we got the courage? Are we mentally prepared for a new confrontation with the government over its indifference to change? Do we realize that our struggle will be difficult, long drawn out and dangerous? Are we willing to have a go? That's the question I'm putting to you, and I'll wait for you to vote by raising your hands."

The silence shattered. The atmosphere became electric with shouts of enthusiasm. Youthful faces lit up with eagerness for the fight. Without exception they all raised their hands. Andreas watched hopefully as representatives from other universities filed up on to the stage. William greeted them and shook their hands and soon the great hall was alive again, as the students applauded the leaders. The applause reached its peak when all the student leaders had voted in favor of continuing the struggle.

The student council withdrew for a brief consultation. The students waited patiently in their places, chatting to each other. After a short while the committee returned to the hall and Philip, his face suffused with joy, read to them the announcement from NUSAS.

"Colleagues, after the unanimous vote of our members, we rule as follows:

First: a general strike of all the English-speaking universities in the country, and a boycott of lectures by all students until further notice. We also need to reach out to more of our colleagues at the racially segregated universities so that we can join forces.

Second: occupation of all campuses.

Third: submission to the municipal authorities of demands for the conduct of peaceful demonstrations.

Fourth: collection of signatures from those citizens of our country who share the ideals of change.

Fifth: the besieging of multinational companies to demand an increase in the wages of their black employees.

Sixth: the completion and distribution of proclamations expounding our aims.

Seventh: the secretary of our union is to write to and seek the support of other universities abroad. We will petition them to support the boycott of all international companies with branches in this country.

Eighth: the propagation of our slogans both on and off university campuses.

Colleagues, let us all now throw ourselves into the struggle for change."

CHAPTER 9 Student Protests

The student movement gained significant attention in a very short time. The University campuses swelled with thousands of protestors, enthusiastically shouting their slogans. They lined the main entrances, the footpaths, and all along the university frontages where academic privilege protected them from police retaliation. Posters, which challenged, and or branded the racist establishment, were plastered on hundreds of billboards. Small campus presses churned ceaselessly, and teams of students distributed inflammatory leaflets from street to street. Tension and fear were clearly written on the participant's faces as police cars surrounded the universities. Police dogs, excited by the students' shouts, growled uneasily. The appearance of uniforms raised a storm of protest and the students shouted even more furiously:

"A living wage! Freedom! Down with Fascism! Equal treatment for all!"

Journalists and photographers were everywhere, asking questions, taking notes and photographs. What had started as an unexpected headache for the government was quickly becoming a serious problem, as the cities of Johannesburg, Cape Town, Durban and Port Elizabeth all caught ablaze with revolutionary fervor spread by their young people. The student leader, William Pretorius, traveled up and down the country tirelessly, flying from city to city, coordinating and encouraging the students. The student protesters anxiously awaited the decision of their city councils, as to whether they would be given permission for the demonstrations that had been planned.

Andreas was very proud of the trust NUSAS had placed in him. They had appointed him to lead the campaign to bring pressure on multinational companies, requesting that they increase the wages of their black employees in the Johannesburg region. His colleagues had accepted him without hesitation and Andreas felt the weight of his responsibility. He selected the most militant and the most determined from among countless volunteers, and he designated them in charge of various small groups. Each group was given the name of a company from the list that Andreas had prepared in advance. He gathered the groups and explained to them how they were to go about their task. Andreas, though excited, methodically gave his final orders to various groups who took the materials they needed and set off on their missions. Andreas stayed behind with the handful of students he had picked for his own group. There were seven of them and he looked at them one by one.

"The time's arrived," he said, "but before we set off I want to say that there's still time if any of you have changed your minds."

"You needn't have any doubts about us, Andreas. Every one of us is determined. Let's go," said Helen, a fellow student, speaking on behalf of all of them.

Without further discussion they set off towards their group's target. They stopped in front of a huge building on which was written in enormous letters POLARFILMS. They left their cars in the parking area and marched up the great, broad steps into a vast entrance hall. It was adorned with glass showcases filled with cameras, lenses, films and artsy photographs. Andreas told his group to sit on the plush leather armchairs, while he made his way to the receptionist.

"Good morning, Miss. My friends and I have been sent by WITS University and we would like to see the managing director of POLARFILMS on serious business."

The receptionist smiled politely with a touch of irony and said,

"I'm sorry, young man, my authority doesn't reach as high as that. I think it would be better if you saw his private secretary who may be able to help you. Her office is at the end of the corridor, number 25."

Andreas thanked her and strode swiftly down the corridor. The door was closed and Andreas felt a momentary qualm. He pulled himself together, knocked firmly on the door, opened it and went in. A well-groomed, attractive young woman was sitting behind a large desk that was covered with papers and a typewriter. She raised her eyes and threw a puzzled glance at Andreas.

"How can I be of assistance to you?" she asked, without offering him a seat.

Andreas sat anyway, produced his student card and held it in front of her, explaining that he wanted to see the managing director.

"I am sorry, sir, that's quite impossible. The general manager is extremely busy. If your business is as serious as you say it is, why didn't you phone for an appointment? Are you sure there's no one else who can help you?"

"Quite sure, Miss. As I told you, we have to see him immediately."

"You're wasting your time, sir. Excuse me, I'm very busy." She took a letter from the pile in front of her and began reading it.

"Believe me, Miss, we came here on a most serious mission and we're not going to leave until your extremely busy boss spares us a little of his valuable time. At this particular moment, we students are representing the black workers of South Africa, and since they're not allowed by law to strike, we're on strike ourselves. My colleagues, who are waiting in the front foyer, and we are prepared to hunger strike until your director grants us an interview. We demand for the sake of our country that your company cut back a little on its colossal profits, in order to give a respectable wage rise to those who are making you rich."

The executive assistant did not even glance up from her work. After a few moments of being totally ignored, Andreas retreated and left the room.

"Unfortunately he can't possibly receive us," he said sarcastically to his colleagues.

The students went outside, took out their placards and sat on the hot, sun baked granite steps. They attracted immediate attention as a crowd of curious people gathered around reading the slogans. The numerous customers of the business had to force their way through, voicing their annoyance as they stumbled over legs, bodies and placards. A head appeared out of a window above them and before long all the windows were occupied by the inquisitive faces of the firm's employees. Some of them took it as a joke and jeered at the protesters. Others began spitting in fury. The private secretary came down the steps. She was practically foaming with rage as she stood in front of Andreas.

"Take your friends and get out of here right away! If you want to play the demagogue, do it at home or at your stupid university. You're trespassers, on private property without permission and if you don't leave immediately, I'll send for the police. They know just how to deal with people like you."

"Miss, you're wasting your time. I've already told you that we're not leaving until we've seen your boss. As for your threats, we're used to them and they don't scare us. Go and send for the cops right away, that'll be the best possible publicity for your company. Your customers all over the world will get really enthusiastic when the police lay into us with their clubs, and even more so when they hear about the princely wages you offer your employees."

Her eyes flashed with rage. She turned on her heels and left as quickly as she had come.

"Don't leave, Miss," Andreas called after her. "Hang on a minute. The reporters have just arrived. Maybe they'll want an interview, and then you can be the heroine of the hour."

The journalists sat down next to them, cracking jokes, getting their story and taking photos. Andreas was surprised that the journalists truly seemed to be encouraging the protestors. During the interview, Andreas described the solemn nature of their cause. He stressed that they had made a decision to go on a hunger strike, until they were assured of the wage rise they were seeking for the workers. The journalists also sought to get an interview with the managing director, but even for them it proved impossible. As they left, they promised Andreas that they would give the students all the publicity they could, not only in South Africa but worldwide.

Eventually, the gawkers drifted away and the clerks went back to their work. The hours passed desperately slowly and monotonously, uninterrupted. Andreas hoped that he had correctly surmised that these multinational companies would do anything to avoid adverse publicity.

"You know," said Andreas to his friends, "if we can make a start here, a lot of other multinational companies will follow suit."

One of the group, Garry, opened a thermos and offered everyone tea.

"Are you all keeping your spirits up? Feeling hungry?" he asked cheerfully.

"You've got to be joking, Garry," answered Helen. "You don't know how long I've been trying to force myself to go on a diet. By the time I've finished here, I'll have the slimmest figure in the whole university!"

The streets became active once more, suddenly filled with pedestrians and vehicles. Teeming crowds poured hurriedly from the various buildings as the employees rushed homewards after the day's work. The besieged employees of POLARFILMS left as well. A deathly quiet settled over the district of Braamfontein which contained mainly offices. The students planted their banners to one side and stretched out as comfortably as they could on the hard steps. Pangs of hunger were beginning to invade their thoughts, but they remained determined. The sun set, the street lights came on, and the students started talking, first about political issues, then about more personal matters. They were getting to know each other in a way that might never have been possible under normal circumstances. The silence of the night was broken by the motor of a car which stopped outside the company offices. The students sat up in curiosity. Andreas leapt to his feet, recognizing Philip's car in the half light. The hunger strikers greeted Philip, Maureen and Linda, who also emerged from the car. The hours of restless waiting had tired them, and it felt as though they had spent centuries cut off from the rest of the world.

"Linda, Maureen, Philip, what fair wind blows you down here?" asked Andreas.

"We've brought you some blankets, orangeade, water and cigarettes, just to show you that we're thinking of you," answered Linda brightly.

The new arrivals handed out the blankets and cigarettes and then joined the others on the steps.

"Well, friends," Philip told them, "our members' enthusiasm for raising the basic wage is unprecedented. The universities are shaking the foundations of totalitarianism and building the bridges for change."

"Philip, have you any news from other groups?"

"Everything's going fine so far, Andreas. We haven't had any serious incidents or friction with the police. All the NUSAS members are proud of the job that's being done, and especially of your group which had the guts to get stuck into a hunger strike."

"Take a look at the evening paper," Linda added. "Just about the whole page is given over to you. You've become the heroes of the day!"

"Philip," asked Frank "is there any news from the Town Hall? Are they going to give us a permit for the marches?"

"Not yet, but I think it's too early to get worried. Personally, I'm very optimistic this time. Our efforts will get good results. People are starting to see what we stand for more clearly. Just imagine, today alone we've collected more than twenty thousand signatures of protest in Johannesburg. I reckon that by the time we call on the Minister for Labor, we'll have more than two hundred thousand. We'll make them see that people want change."

A beautifully clear moon was shining high in a cloudless sky. Linda and Philip went on their way, leaving behind them a sense of hope, and the assurance that the hunger strikers were not alone. One by one, the students pulled up their blankets and sought refuge in sleep. Andreas quietly picked up the paper that Philip had left. He carried it to the bright light that framed the entrance. He opened the paper and immersed himself in studying the news. Linda was not exaggerating; the entire front page was dedicated to the students' activities in protest. Placed between a two-column spread, there was a large photo of Andreas and his group. Involuntarily, his thoughts strayed to his parents, and he pondered their reactions bitterly. He tried to put aside such sentimental thoughts, and went on reading the headlines.

WHOLE COUNTRY IN UPROAR AFTER UNANIMOUS DECISION OF ENGLISH-SPEAKING UNIVERSITIES FOR GENERAL STRIKE!

OPPOSITION LEADERS CONGRATULATE STUDENTS AND HOPE

GOVERNMENT WILL MEET THEIR JUST DEMANDS

POLICE ON GENERAL ALERT SINCE DAWN...
SO FAR NO COMMENT FROM THE GOVERNMENT

With some consternation, he noticed that there had been a number of small incidents of confrontation, involving students and police during the course of the day. The newspaper reported that a young student had been arrested by the police and was being held under general detention in John Vorster Square. The imprisoned youth had been handing out leaflets at Johannesburg railway station, in a corridor demarcated blacks only. Andreas folded up the paper, went back to his position, wrapped himself in his blanket and allowed his gaze to focus on the star-filled sky. The POLARFILMS employees found them there the next morning, still half asleep. Once again, the hours dragged by with hopeless sluggishness. A journalist visited them, sat with them for a while and passed on the latest news. The pangs of hunger were becoming more acute, and the strikers had little to add to the previous day's interviews. The second day went by without any police entanglements and the students watched with relief as the employees finally went home.

Linda arrived in the evening and Andreas could see from her expression that she hadn't brought them pleasant news. He sat her down next to him and asked her anxiously, "Linda, why hasn't Philip come? What's going on? You look very upset!"

"Philip is caught up at a meeting, so he sent me. But I'm sorry to say, I haven't got very good news. The Council refused our request to allow a peaceful march in the city. Furthermore, the Prime Minister has been voicing some very serious accusations. He has openly stated that the university has become a nuisance; that we're a nest of communists, and that if we go on, he promises to close the universities down. He's stated that we are undermining the foundations of the state. Accordingly, the chief of police has been ordered to crack down on us, without mercy, if we don't fall in line. The news has forced William back from Cape Town. Tonight, they'll decide whether we go on with our walk-out, and our demonstrations."

Andreas and his group listened to her in silence, their lips pouted in an open display of their disgust.

"Linda, please go and tell them that we'll carry on with what we've started, even if it's on our own," snapped Andreas. "It's time we taught our Prime Minister that he isn't dealing with a bunch of under-age kids, but with mature, free citizens. We won't bow in to his threats. What do you say, do you agree with me?"

"Yes!" the group shouted in unison.

"The only way we'll leave here is on stretchers!" Helen added defiantly.

None of them managed to sleep that night. They drank tea or orange juice, and smoked one cigarette after another in an attempt to dissuade their hunger. They were all thinking about the Prime Minister's announcement. The third day without food was the most painful. Doubt began to undermine their resolve. The enthusiasm of the previous night had worn off, tarnished by hunger and fear. Andreas spoke to his colleagues encouragingly. He was anxiously waiting for the results of the student meeting with Willy Pretorius. He looked at his watch; it was three in the afternoon.

"Excuse me, sir."

Annoyed, Andreas turned toward the irritating, high pitched voice of the private secretary. He surveyed her with a look of unbridled hostility.

"The general manager will see you in his office, alone."

Andreas wiped the sweat from his unshaven face with his sleeve. To say he was surprised was an understatement. The secretary even had to repeat herself. The look of lethargy vanished from the students' faces, replaced now by hope as they got to their feet. Andreas followed the woman. The general manager proved to be a very serious little man. Even his posture exuded arrogance. He sat on a leather easy chair behind a luxurious desk, full of his own importance.

"Young man," he said in a commanding voice, "your impudence exceeds all limits. I still can't understand why I didn't call the police. And quite honestly, I still fail to understand the attitude of a government that allows you extremists so much latitude."

Andreas was blazing with anger, "I'm guided by moral convictions.

If you've anything interesting to say to me, I'm ready to listen. If not, I prefer the fresh air to the suffocating stench of this office."

The general manager angrily hurled the latest edition of the afternoon paper at Andreas, "Read it. My company's given its colored workers a thirty percent raise, and it'll soon give them more increases. But don't think you've influenced us in any way; it was already in our program. Now take that mob of yours and clear off!"

Andreas grabbed the paper and read the article. He felt like bursting with joy.

"Forgive me," he said ironically. "I misunderstood you. You're obviously a very generous man."

He turned and deliberately slammed the door behind him. Andreas's blood was coursing and he felt short of breath. He ran out the building like a madman, clutching the paper. He was dying to pass the news on to the others.

"We've won! They've granted the raise!"

Their hunger forgotten, the students hurled themselves into each other's arms, yelling with excitement. They had taken their first crucial step, and they each recognized the importance of the moment. They had succeeded in making an impression on a powerful multinational company. By the time they arrived on campus, the news had already reached the university. William and his fellow students welcomed them with demonstrations of affection that left Andreas and his group speechless. Nothing had changed on the university scene, except that the school was now fully surrounded by police. The students, untouched by threats, carried on with the same ardor and conviction.

Philip had gone to Pretoria with three other students, in order to hand over the petitions personally to the Minister of Labor. The whole student body was waiting anxiously for their return. Andreas and his colleagues gulped down a few sandwiches in the canteen then ran to hear William's speech, on the front steps of the Great Hall.

"Fellow students; brothers and sisters; this struggle of ours, this long barren tree, has at last born its first fruit. Those who achieved this miracle deserve the congratulations of all of us. Day by day, South Africa's blacks are beginning to recognize their immense strength. After all, they are the ones who drive the gears of our economy. Let's imagine what will happen when they're ready to exploit this strength. On that day, we will be the ones that are their helpless pawns. Our country's situation is not yet hopeless, and that's why I stress again that the time for change has arrived..."

He stopped suddenly and stared in disbelief at the entrance of the university grounds.

There was not a murmur of conversation now, as they all stood with mouths agape. William dropped his microphone, leapt down from the rostrum, and ran toward Philip. The mass of students parted convulsively, leaving a clear path to the central gate.

"Philip! My God!" wailed William, "what happened?"

The secretary-general of NUSAS dragged himself forward, his face unrecognizably bloody. He stretched out his arms for support and crumpled in a heap. William, trembling with shock, knelt down and anxiously checked for a pulse.

"Quick," he called, his voice breaking. "Send for an ambulance."

The crowd's whispers spread and mounted into a cacophony of furious shouts. Andreas forced his way through and knelt next to William, who was transfixed in his anguish. He pulled back the blanket they had draped over his unconscious friend. Philip's head had been shaved, and painted with red oil paint which was mixing with his blood. His face was totally disfigured. His shirt had been ripped to pieces and his body was a mass of cuts and bruises. His trouser legs were cut up to his thighs and his feet had been painted with the same red paint. Andreas stared in horror, unable to believe his eyes. At that moment, a group of students carried in Philip's companions, all in the same dreadful condition. They laid them down carefully next to him. One of them had regained consciousness and was groaning pitifully.

Andreas turned and cradled the wounded man in his arms. "Keith, Keith, for God's sake tell us what happened?" he urged.

Keith's body jerked. His mouth twisted involuntarily from pain and he started to weep. Andreas held him tenderly and spoke gently into his ear.

"I'm sorry to ask questions but we must find out who did this."

The young student looked at him through swollen, blackened eyes and realized what was being asked of him. He struggled to overcome his pain and emotion. A dribble of saliva and blood was running from his swelling lips. He spoke with difficulty, and indistinctly through his broken front teeth. Andreas curled in towards the wounded man, placing his ear close to his friend's bloodied mouth. Keith spoke erratically, loud then soft, with spurts of coherency. Bodies towered around them, awaiting Andreas's translation of their companion's whelps, yells and tears. Keith's face was distorted with spasms of pain. The ambulances arrived, their sirens screaming. Andreas helped with the stretchers, and William went along with the injured. The ambulances rushed away howling, as the students yelled and gestured their outrage. Fury gripped at Andreas and he felt its delicate caress as the blood grew warm in his ears and cheeks. Determinedly, he strode up onto the platform and seized the microphone.

"They waited all morning for the Minister to receive them," he started slowly, allowing his anger to seep slowly into his voice. "Finally, after they'd given the Minister our petition and our demands, he ordered them thrown out of his ministry. A whole platoon of men forced them into an army lorry. They were taken to the Afrikaans university in Pretoria. On arrival they were beaten, shaved and painted. The ruffians then continued to hit and kick our friends until they could no longer maintain consciousness. Every time they awoke, they were beaten back into the darkness. Their fun finally at an end, the fascists dumped our broken comrades at our central gate."

Anger had grasped Andreas by the throat now and threatened to rob him of every last trace of reason.

"Brothers and sisters! Fellow students!" he shouted with passion. "We don't need any more tears. What we do need is fresh effort to help put an end to this Nazi regime," he gestured toward the police assembled outside the gates. "Remember Germany in '39. Let's make it clear at the top of our voices that we don't want any more Hitlers, or any more holocausts. Let's pour out into the streets and shout aloud that we're not afraid of them. They have given us no choice now, but to fight them with their own weapons. We don't need any permission to march, only guts! Let's go, comrades. Onwards, into the struggle!"

Andreas led the way and the other students followed excitedly.

They poured through the entrance gates out on to the wide avenue, waving their placards. Traffic came to a halt and the perturbed drivers sounded their horns furiously in concert. The students advanced without hindrance toward the city center and one student in a hoarse voice began to sing "Nkosi sikelel'i Afrika." Thousands of student voices picked up the tune of this legendary song to the astonishment of the city workers. The song chorused as if it were being sung by the voices of angels. Andreas looked back proudly down the street at the mass of militant youth, ablaze with anger. Suddenly, the march was forced to a halt as a posse of police, with huge dogs, blockaded the end of the street. The barking momentarily stilled the student voices.

"What do we do now, Andreas?" asked one student.

"Who can stop us?" shouted Andreas as loudly as he could. "Who can silence the voice of truth? Democracy! Justice! Freedom!"

Once more the air shook with the shouts of the students as they began once more to proceed. Nearer and nearer, they marched toward the armed police. A police officer broke away from the mass and harangued them in a voice, powerfully magnified by a loudspeaker.

"Attention, attention! In the name of the law I order you to disperse immediately and quietly go home. You are contravening the law. If you do not comply, you alone will be responsible for what follows. Attention, attention! You have five minutes to disperse."

For a minute, the students were daunted. Would they dare to attack them? Would they really set their dogs on peaceful, unarmed demonstrators? The policeman's diatribe had inflamed the students even more and now they took up the refrain that Andreas was shouting indignantly:

"No more Sharpevilles! Protect us from our own police!"

The dogs excited by the voices, barked furiously and ceaselessly, tugging at the thick chains that restrained them. Those who passed by threw quick and curious glances as they hurried to get away from the scene. Andreas felt a cold stream of sweat running down his spine. He watched with a mixture of astonishment, fear and guilt as the police set free the huge, hairy beasts. The attack dogs launched themselves zealously, like barking bullets, at the crowd.

"My God," he screamed, "this can't be real!"

Quick as lightning, the cries of enthusiasm changed to screams of pain and fear. Panic-stricken youngsters pushed and shoved each other in their eagerness to escape. One dreadful scene followed another. In their haste, the demonstrators trampled on their fallen fellows. The dogs howled unceasingly; ripping into living flesh with their razor-sharp teeth. Policemen, screaming sadistically, hit indiscriminately with their long riot clubs. Spectators ran to get away. Shopkeepers stolidly closed the doors of their shops, refusing to offer sanctuary to anyone. Fresh police trucks arrived, packed with reserves. They leapt down and joined the apocalyptic melee. Ambulance sirens began to wail, adding to the confusion.

Andreas was stricken with fear as he tried to protect himself. Blows were landing from all directions without a moment's relief. Suddenly one of the dogs lurched at him. Instinctively, he brought his left arm round in front of his face as a shield. The beast's jaws closed around his arm above the wrist, its teeth sinking into his flesh, as far as the bone. The force of the bite was so heavy that it threw Andreas down on to the bitumen road. The pain was excruciating and he let out a bellow of pain. The sound was lost among thousands of similar shouts and screams. His eyes flooded as his blood poured on to the hot surface of the road. Finally, he managed to extricate his free arm. He was panting with effort as he sank his fingers into the dog's hairy throat, and furiously began to choke it. The grip of the jaws started to relax and now it was the animal that was fighting for its life. The beast's legs stretched out, trembled, and then stopped. A swarm of police surrounded him and began lashing him mercilessly. Blood poured down his face. A thousand gongs and bells sounded in his ears and the light faded out, as Andreas began a slow descent into a bottomless abyss.

Andreas had no idea how long it had been since they had carried him unconscious to the first aid post and then, with many others, to police headquarters. Endless hours of questions, statements, fingerprinting, humiliation and terror followed. When they finally released him, pending his trial, he felt his strength had completely drained away. The streets were empty as he surveyed the scene. It was a lovely peaceful night, with a clear sky and a huge full moon. A cool breeze was blowing. The pale stars shone down as indifferently they observed his predicament. He was a lone pedestrian and he shivered as he staggered and tripped with a heavy tread. A grotesque shadow followed him constantly as he struggled to walk on, doubled over and pausing now and then to rest his back against filthy walls. Each time he stopped, he heaved a deep and painful breath, and then with a mighty effort, he continued on his way. He was in a terrible state, with his head and his left arm wrapped in white bandages. As time passed, his movements became more difficult, his progress more unsteady, but he pressed on up the hill from the central police station in John Vorster Square. A taxi passed in front of him and by waving his legs and good arm like a lunatic, he managed to stop it. He opened the door with unprecedented relief and collapsed onto the back seat. With effort, he gave the driver his address. The taxi driver glanced at him in the mirror with unmasked curiosity.

"Here we are, Sir," he said when they arrived at the given address. He turned on the interior light and stared at his motionless passenger in horror. The passenger was pale as death and his white bandages were stained with fresh blood. Cursing nervously, the driver emerged from the taxi, looked around him uneasily at the house in total darkness.

"Just my bloody luck!" he cursed in a whisper.

In the darkness of the garden, he thought he could make out silhouettes that dived into hiding.

"Hey, do you work here?" he shouted loudly.

A black man wearing a cassock approached from behind a fence.

"What's going on Baas?" Matthew asked.

"I have a passenger who asked me to bring him to this address but now he has totally passed out. I just hope that he is not dead."

Matthew approached the taxi cautiously, with some anxiety. As he opened the door, the feeble interior light illuminated the unconscious form of Andreas.

The taxi driver, irritated and annoyed, demanded. "Who is going to pay my fare?"

Matthew took ten rand out of his pocket to pay off the driver. Roused by his urgent calls, other staff members ran out to assist him to carry Andreas into the house. They placed him on his bed and

Matthew felt for his pulse. With some relief, he phoned the family doctor who came quickly and disturbed by Andreas's condition, ordered him to be taken straight away to the clinic.

"Where's your master?" the doctor asked Matthew.

"They went away to Lourenco Marques for a few days' vacation."

Three days passed while Andreas remained in the clinic. He had been in a coma, with high fevers and incomprehensible rambling. When he came to his senses, he was in severe pain. As he lay in hospital, he recalled all the scenes that he had witnessed at the demonstration. He felt guilty because he had misled many innocent people into a bitter confrontation with the police, through his misguided spontaneity.

It was with mixed feelings of pleasure and remorse that he received a visit from Linda, Maureen and Philip, who descended on him laden with flowers. Linda kissed him tenderly, sat down on the bed beside him and gently stroked his sweating forehead. Andreas looked closely at Philip and felt his anger boil up again. Even after so many days, his friend was still in a pitiful state, his face dreadfully disfigured by the savage clubbing.

"First my turn, then yours, comrade," Philip teased him, "Those are the fruits of our efforts, bitter but unavoidable."

"Tell me, what's new, Philip? What's happening? Were there many victims? How could I have been so thoughtless?"

"Calm down, Andreas." Philip took a chair and sat down next to the bed. "What you did wasn't thoughtless; it was heroic, grand! You've been endowed with a fiery temperament, and you are decisive with great courage. Yes, we have had many victims. I'm not going to hide that from you, but when was there ever a war without casualties? We got a lot out of it too. The main thing is that we made the establishment show their real faces though their violent actions. Believe me, it was ugly, repulsive. Millions of TV viewers throughout the world saw what happened witnessed the police brutality and your self-sacrifice. Thousands of telegrams of support and donations are coming in from every part of the country and the world. Furthermore, all our universities are going on with the strike. The government of course, is threatening damnation, and coming out with the most ridiculous penalties and intimidations. What's more, they've banned and threatened the only black professor at Cape Town University, just because he's black. His students raised a storm of protest, seized the central hall of the university, barricaded themselves in and have declared a hunger strike. They're demanding the reinstatement of the professor, and free education for all scholars up to the age of sixteen, regardless of color. Andreas, the fire's spreading. Tomorrow afternoon, William and I and a crowd of students are setting off for Cape Town, to offer our support and join them in the struggle."

His pain forgotten and his doubts put to rest; Andreas felt his strength and fervor for the battle returning.

"Philip, I'd like to go as well."

"Andreas, you're crazy! You need rest. Don't you realize what a state you're in?

"I'm feeling fine. Anyway, do you think you're in any better condition than I am? Don't worry, Philip. This isn't the time for us to lick our wounds. Now's the time to fight with whatever we have."

The two girls followed their conversation intently.

"You poor deluded boys! Always in the battle!" said Maureen bitterly. "When are you going to understand that whatever you do it's a lost cause? Do you think you've got some magic power that'll enable you to make the slightest impression on the colossus that rules us? You're simply ruining your health and destroying your future by provoking the government. One of these days they'll send the goons of the secret police to arrest you. They'll come at dawn, cart you off in handcuffs and throw you into their dungeons, without anyone knowing where you are. The sort of change that you want can only come about with armed combat and lots of blood. Rivers of it! I don't think you've got many people in your classes who're ready to shed their blood for the sake of change. In any case, what makes you think that the wind is in your favor?"

Andreas and Philip stayed silent for a while. Andreas was the first to answer her.

"Maybe you're right. But the struggle has to start somewhere. In any case, in the position we're in, we can't retreat. It would have all been in vain. We would have to label ourselves cowards for giving up at the first hint of trouble!"

"Well, I have had enough of this madness. I am only going to stay involved with my teaching in Boksburg. At least that achieves something. You can leave me out of your plans. I'm out. I will not be able to bear watching your destruction. So cut me out."

Maureen got up to leave the room.

She turned to Linda, "Are you coming with me?"

"No, I would rather stay," Linda replied. "See you around."

Andreas and Phillip shocked and speechless watched Maureen depart. Visiting time ended soon after and Phillip and Linda departed, leaving Andreas sad and pensive.

The next day after some hesitation, the doctor signed Andreas's discharge and he went happily if not gingerly home. The staff greeted him with cheers and laughter.

"Andreas," said Matthew, "I'm glad to see you, but are you alright? I think you were in a bit too much of a hurry to get home. A little while ago your father phoned and I told him your news. They're very worried about you and they are on their way home."

Andreas smiled at him affectionately, "Thanks, Matthew, you really saved me. You're a good friend."

Andreas felt weak and sick after he got home. His various pains showed no sign of abating and in addition, he still continued to feel the inner agony of guilt and responsibility. He wondered how many other students, like Maureen, would opt out from the movement

"I am crazy even to think about going to Cape Town, when we are so ill-prepared and we do not even know what we are up against. We are so naïve and romantic. May be we are just little white heroes," he thought in disgust.

The telephone shrilled and Andreas hurried over to pick it up.

"Hi Andreas. Are you joining us? I reckon you must be crazy if you have not yet changed your mind?" It was Philip.

"When are we leaving?"

"Five o'clock tomorrow morning. Do you want me to stop by and pick you up on my way to the airport?"

"No, Philip. I'll get Matthew to take me."

He went off to his bedroom after asking Matthew to wake him at four am to take him to the airport. He swallowed down some pain pills and stretched out on his bed.

"Matthew," he asked on the following morning while been driven to the airport, "I'd like you to do another favor for me. As you know, I'm leaving for Cape Town and I want you to reassure my parents that I'll be OK, and that I will be back in a few days."

Matthew nodded calmly. At the airport, Matthew dropped off his passenger with a brief farewell.

"Have a good trip and be careful!"

"Thanks Matthew. See you soon."

Andreas walked into the noisy airport with his overnight bag in hand. On the plane trip to Cape Town, he recovered his courage amid the warm, friendly companionship of his fellow-activists. He sprawled out onto the uncomfortable seat, peering through the plane window at the boundless stretches of countryside racing past beneath them. The greater part of the vast land was still virgin and completely undeveloped. He calculated that under different circumstances, without prejudice and one-sided interest, South Africa could have fed twice its population. Moreover, it would be able to export food and primary produce to millions of other people in the world. The lights of the city of Cape Town shone ahead in the distant night. The jet circled in wide sweeps above the city, waiting its turn, then floated safely down to earth. In the arrivals hall, Norman Sharp was waiting for them. He was president of the University of Cape Town branch of the students' union. With him was a small group of activists who welcomed them enthusiastically.

"Congratulations Philip and Andreas, although looking at the state you are in, I'm surprised you are here. You should both be home resting," said Norman. "Nevertheless, you did an outstanding job with Polarfilms and the demonstration. We just hope we can match up to you."

"Norman," asked William, "have the other representatives showed up?"

"Most of them are here, and we expect the others any minute."

"Where's the meeting taking place?"

"Philip, our university is surrounded by police day and night. So I thought it best if we gathered at my house," said Norman. "It's not a very suitable time for us to be showing them our plans."

Norman's house was a pleasant cottage, set in a large park. Leaders from some of the other universities were waiting for them.

Without wasting time, they got straight to work. Philip and Andreas were too exhausted to keep up with them for long, and they stretched out on sofas and fell into a weary sleep. The others worked tirelessly through most of the day and into the night. They sketched out and then reshaped their program for the following days. They all knew that the upcoming hours would be significant and decisive. They anticipated that the police would launch sudden attacks on the universities in an effort to break up groups of protestors, including hunger strikers who had taken refuge in these institutions. Coordination was needed so that one group followed another throughout the country, thus prolonging official disruption and evading police efforts to stamp out the dissidents. They decided to send coordinators to ensure that all the English-speaking universities adhered to the NUSAS timetable. The opening movement of the new front would be right there in Cape Town. William immediately nominated Philip and Andreas for Witwatersrand, primarily because of their leadership, and secondly because he hoped that they would have some time to recover before facing another police onslaught.

As soon as the two students woke up, they were scheduled to return to Johannesburg. Once home again, they acted quickly, contacted the leaders of the various working parties, and divided the work. In a few hours, the first proclamations were being printed and placards were being painted. Philip volunteered to go to the municipal authorities and he came back a few hours later, delightedly waving a permit for a peaceful march that was planned for that Thursday. This permit rekindled their morale and removed the last misgivings of the students.

CHAPTER 10 Doctor of Soweto

The following day, Matthew set off again for the airport to fetch his employers on return from their vacation. His boss was nervous and upset.

"Hello, Matthew. How is Baas Andreas?"

"Baas, he is in Cape Town. I took him to the airport yesterday morning. He told me to tell you that he is well and that he'll be back in a few days."

"What do you mean he is well?" exclaimed Mr. Frixos Magdalos. "We thought he was badly injured and in hospital. We cut our vacation short especially for him and now he has gone off again!"

Mrs. Magdalos followed the conversation in astonishment.

"In Cape Town? You must know why he's gone to Cape Town," she snapped at her husband. "He's gone to join all those communist, anarchists who are on strike at the university. It's time to stop this nonsense of his before we find ourselves in serious trouble."

"I've told you, stop being so unrealistic," answered Mr. Magdalos. "Do you think Andreas is a little boy that I can put over my knee and spank?"

"That's your problem," she screamed at him. "You're his father!" She slammed the door behind her as she got into the back seat of the car.

Mr. Magdalos climbed into the front seat next to Matthew, who drove them home in silence. He had never before witnessed such a scene between his employers.

"Even with all their money, they also have their troubles," he thought

"Be ready to take me to the factory," Mr. Magdalos said to

Matthew when they reached home. "I may as well go to work. No point in staying here."

He followed his wife into the house, visibly shaken.

On the return journey from the factory that evening, Mr. Magdalos was still disturbed and upset. All throughout that day he had called Matthew into his office with further questions about Andreas. He had asked Matthew to describe how badly beaten up and in what shape his son had been.

Matthew looked at his watch as he went to his room. He was running late and he rushed to quickly change out of his chauffeur's uniform into an ecclesiastical cassock. He picked up his tall staff surmounted by a cross, and strode off into the night, which falls unusually early in the Transvaal. He made his way quickly to the river, and stepped carefully over rocks as he approached its bed. His mind was still preoccupied by the events of the past few days. He had to admit that was puzzled by Andreas's behavior.

"Who are you?" a voice challenged him from behind the bushes.

"The Prodigal Son," Matthew answered immediately.

"The service will start soon. Hurry up, sinner, or you'll be late!"

"Thank you, brother."

Matthew hurried along. He could hear the gentle murmur of the small stream nearby. The silence of the night was broken by the rhythmical beat of drums. A chorus of harmonized voices accompanied the drums. The white cassocks gleamed in the light of the newly risen moon.

A figure clad in white stepped out in front of Matthew.

"Late again, my son?"

"Sorry, father," said Matthew.

"Follow me, brother. He is waiting for you," the guard answered.

He led him into a recess, well hidden behind thick bushes and trees. A candle was burning in the middle of the cave, lighting up a man sitting inside on the rocks. Matthew greeted him with zest. They exchanged warm handshakes. The man sat back down and the guard returned to his post. The hymns outside, full of religious intensity and entreaty, rose up to God.

Matthew looked at the man who had given his life direction and purpose. He was the father that he had always wished to have, the patriot who had offered everything for the love of his country and his people. He was around fifty, of medium height and build. By all means a man of average appearance, but if you looked closely into his eyes you could see his intelligence and the strength of his soul. He was no ordinary man; a visionary who opened the road to possibilities. It was said that he could heal wounds with his compassion. He was a living legend; the Doctor of Soweto.

"Matthew, how are you doing? I am so pleased to see you again. I called this urgent meeting because I need you to take a group of young men over the border to be trained. I think, you should prepare yourself to undertake further training yourself. A special course is going to be held for team leaders. This time, I intend to join you myself. We have to meet with one of the leaders from the ANC who, as you know, has been in exile. He will brief us on what is happening out there, and advise us how we can coordinate our operations here. Do you think that you will be able to get a few days off anytime soon? "

Matthew thought for a minute and then replied, "I will try for next week and I will let you know the date as soon as possible. The problem is that my Baas is anxious and upset at the moment. He is having a lot of trouble with his son getting involved in all those university demonstrations. He may not be so willing to let me go so easily this time."

"Well do your best. Now with regard to our plans, where should we meet and what car are we going to use?"

"I think in the same place Doctor, and I will try to borrow a van from my work. It is much safer to use one of those vans."

"I will leave it in your good hands Matthew."

"Doctor, what do you think about the white student uprisings?"

"I think that what the students are doing is very heroic. They bring attention to what is going on here and reveal to the world how unjust this system of apartheid is."

"Sure, I agree. It's just that I'm sick and tired of attending meetings and waiting to take action. It's ironic, but I am jealous of the white students. Even in protest they are treated more humanely than we are. Could you just imagine if blacks took to the city streets? They'd slaughter us without a moment's hesitation."

Doctor Erickson looked at him and smiled, "Do you really believe that these students are doing anything that we have not done before? We have been down the path they are taking, with no real impact. And as you say, we pay too a high cost for the effort. It only makes it worse for us. In my opinion, the only effective alternative is armed struggle, but we have to be properly prepared and ready."

"What do you mean we have been down that path before?" Matthew enquired.

Doctor replied, "We have been protesting ever since the founding of the African National Congress by President John Dube in 1912. We protested after the 1913 Land Act when black people were evicted from their lands. Leaders of the ANC like Joseph T. Gumede continued the struggle in the 1920's. In 1944, the Youth League consisting of Walter Sisulu, Oliver Tambo, Nelson Mandela and Anton Lambede was formed. Mandela himself organized a boycott of the buses in 1943, after they raised the fares. Ten thousand blacks marched and the buses were empty for nine days until they lowered their ticket prices. Mandela was then studying law at Witwatersrand University. At that same time, I was studying medicine."

Doctor Erickson drifted into his recollections of past events. He recounted all the various protests that had taken place in the past, many of which had ended in violence. He told Matthew about the black mineworkers strike in 1946 that was broken within a week by police brutality that was sanctioned by Smut's government. The struggle continued after apartheid was legalized in 1948, when the Population Registration Act classified every man, woman and child according to race and divided races into urban and rural areas. This act caused great suffering as it empowered the government to forcefully remove black people from the so-called white areas. Three thousand delegates from many differing groups gathered at Kliptown in 1955. The Freedom Charter, which called for equal rights for all national groups, was enacted. Later that year, the Federation of South

African Woman marched on Pretoria with one hundred thousand anti-pass petitions.

"Since then things have got much worse. We have been suppressed in our own land by the white man's laws, arrogance and deadly weapons," Doctor continued. "The only light that shone for us was Chief Albert Luthuli. More than our leader, he became symbol of our defiance."

"I was surprised to find out that Andreas knew about Luthuli," Matthew told Doctor. "He said that he had read Luthuli in the university library."

"Who is Andreas?"

"The son of my Baas, the one I told you about. He was one of the leaders in the student demonstrations."

"Oh yes, now I know who you are talking about. I saw him on the news, leading the students into a clash with the police. I have some admiration for people like him because they could be useful to our cause. He also reinforces my belief that not all whites are the same. Some are willing to learn more about what is going on and even disrupt their comfortable lives. As for the majority, most of them know very little about us," Doctor replied. "None of this history is taught in their schools and black students have been banned from attending white universities since 1959. Most of these white students have never even seen where black people live. They only know us only as maids and servants. Actually, it might be a good idea to bring Andreas for a visit to Soweto one day. Make him a little more aware of what is going on with our people. You must decide if he can be trusted."

Matthew left the meeting with Doctor Erickson encouraged by the plans for future training and hope that he would soon be involved in further steps towards the struggle for freedom. When he reached home, he saw Andreas strolling aimlessly in the garden.

"Is that you, Andreas?" Matthew asked.

"Yeah, it's me," Andreas answered reluctantly. He was worried about the march that was planned for the next day. The tranquility of the night could not calm the tautness of his nerves. In the moonlight, he had seen the figure of Matthew, wearing his cassock, entering from the servant's gate. His first thought was to avoid him. He was still concerned that he could never gain Matthew's trust or overcome the differences between them

"Your parents, especially your father, were very worried and upset with you."

"They worry too much about me. I'm not a boy anymore. Have you just been to church?" he enquired.

Matthew ignored the question and asked in turn, "When did you come back?"

"This morning," Andreas replied.

"You look terrible tired! What about a cup of coffee?"

Andreas looked keenly at Matthew, his face momentarily betraying his sense of disbelief.

"That would be nice," he heard himself say, the words escaping of their own volition.

"What news? What is happening in Cape Town?" Matthew asked the question with intensity, punctuated by a pause in the preparation of the coffee.

"At long last you are showing some interest in what is happening? Well I'll tell you. I'm happy! I believe that I've found my direction. I feel as though I am not just living for myself anymore; as though a cloud of well-deserved guilt is finally threatening to clear. I know it's hard for you to believe, impossible for you to accept, but we are going to bring change."

Matthew looked at him thoughtfully, but the pale light of mockery shone in his eyes.

"So, Andreas," he interrupted unable to restrain himself, "now you and your fellow students are going to do away with injustice and convert this country into a Garden of Eden. Three cheers for you!" he added teasingly.

"Don't grin like an idiot! Yes, we're the ones who'll bring about change, because your people lost their guts. You should be demonstrating along with us."

"Leave me alone with your nonsense!" Matthew said in a strained voice, "I told you before, I don't want any trouble, Baas Andreas."

"And as I've told you before, don't use that stupid way of addressing me!"

"I don't know why you are trying so hard to provoke me. Do you think it is easy to get rid of a habit of speech that has been imposed and rooted in me since birth? In any case, what the hell do you know about our days of struggle? For that matter, what do you even know about where and how my people live?" Matthew continued sarcastically.

"I know nothing," Andreas admitted freely, without pause, "that is the problem. I wish that you could help me understand a little better. I was so moved when Cornelius told me his story. I knew nothing of people like him and it caused me to realize that even familiar people, people like your mother are for all purposes little more than familiar faced strangers. Matthew, you do realize that I know nothing of her life and yet, there she is in all of my earliest memories?"

"That's true," said Matthew. "What do you really know about Sharpeville, about Nelson Mandela, Robert Sebukwe and other leaders of the ANC? What do you know about the people who at this very moment are being tortured and killed by the secret police? In fact, what do you know about us blacks at all?"

"I don't know a damned thing," Andreas admitted. "I would really like to know. For example, what exactly happened at Sharpeville? Tell me what you know. I'm listening!"

Matthew responded cautiously and then gradually expanded:

"A great step was taken at Sharpeville. At Luthuli's request, the inhabitants of the ghetto poured out into the streets, laughing and smiling in anticipation. They gathered singing patriotic songs. They lit a huge fire and sang the anthem 'Nkosi Sikelel' i Africa' (God bless Africa!) as they threw those shameful passbooks into the flames. The load fell from their backs and they stood straight and tall, recalling the pride of our ancestors. Scenes like that will never be forgotten. The freedom fighters danced and sang until the storm inevitably broke. The ghetto was surrounded by heavily armed troops. Machine guns chattered, scattering death steadily and without mercy into the fleeing backs of the unarmed population. The shouts of joy turned to screams of pain and despair. The square filled with the wreckage of dead and wounded bodies. The blood flowed in an unbroken red stream down ghetto gutters. Sharpeville became a hell on earth. Scattered screams and shouts continued amongst thick clouds of rising smoke and dust. No one was left standing in the square. Everyone who had escaped the slaughter ran to safety. Yet, it is said that one wounded and dying man crawled on all fours over the corpses, struggling to get to the fire and with an enormous final effort; he flung his passbook into the flames. We will never know how many victims there were at Sharpeville because as soon as the slaughter stopped, the bulldozers moved in, burying everything and wiping the carnage off the map."

"So what happened to the movement after that?" asked Andreas.

"Luthuli was exiled to his homeland and soon after died mysteriously, in a so-called train accident. The passbooks continued to rule our lives. Strikes were banned. With increasingly repressive government bans, the Youth League or Young Turks as they were called became restless. They were convinced the time had come for action and change. Mandela formed 'Umkhonte We Sizwe" (the Spear of the Nation) with the purpose to organize acts of sabotage against the apartheid government. The ANC was reborn with the mandate that freedom could not be attained without bloodshed, One act of sabotage followed another and struck panic into the white population. Foreign investment slowed and the big companies transferred their assets to the safety of Swiss banks. As the movement grew, the economy came near to bankruptcy and many of the whites left, realizing their privileged position was in danger. In 1962, Mandela was arrested as was Walter Sizulu and Govan Mbeki and all were eventually sent to Robben Island for treason. Many other members of the ANC and known anti-apartheid activists were arrested or detained after that. The ANC was banned and the people's dreams were dashed. Those who were able to escape went abroad to carry on the struggle from there."

"What a history! Thank you for telling me. So what is going on now? Is everything dead? What's left of the warriors of your tribe?" Andreas exclaimed.

Matthew recalled Doctor's suggestion to bring Andreas to visit Soweto. He was not really sure whether he could trust Andreas but felt that Andreas had pushed him enough to test his resolve. He decided that now was the moment to show Andreas the true face of the struggle. He was faintly aware that his choice might mean the eventual imprisonment or death of his friend.

"Very well, do you really want to know what is going on now? I'll show you what's left of the Zulu warriors. You come with me! We will visit Soweto. Come on let's go. Right now! Get up!" he said, so assertively that Andreas was on his feet before Matthew had finished.

He strode out of the door to his car, an ancient beat-up Opel, got in behind the wheel and started it up. Andreas ran to catch up with him, opened the door and jumped into the passenger seat. Neither of them spoke and the only sounds were the alarming rattles of the tortured vehicle, which gave the impression that it would fall to pieces at any moment. They traveled for about an hour until they arrived without incident in Soweto.

A deathly silence blanketed the township. In the total darkness, the stink of fumes from kerosene heaters and charcoal, covered the whole district like a shroud; making it hard to breathe. The stars shone high in the sky, but the beauty of their light was unable to penetrate the acrid smoke of three million charcoal fires hanging like an asphyxiating mantle above the miserable city of five million people. It stretched as far as the eye can reach in any direction over a flat plain. It did not appear on any existing map. It was a ghetto that had risen up from the veld, a slum city with water supplied from street faucets. There were no amenities, not even sewage. There were no title deeds for the makeshift homes, put together using cement bricks, pieces of zinc, wooden crates and cardboard. Countless flies competed in size and color with rats, mice and cockroaches. All around dogs scrounged for food.

People lived there, as they do in all cities. They thrived despite the squalor and ugliness. They were determined to survive. In fact, Soweto continued to develop against the wishes of Pretoria, and in spite of the forced deportation of her people to the so-called homelands.

Matthew told Andreas, "as you can see, there is no electricity in this part of Soweto. The unpaved roads are home to children of every age. The 'children of the pipes', they are called and they survive in the sewage tunnels that were intended to meet the clamoring demands of the growing city. They exist on garbage, fighting with the dogs for the best scraps. Whatever money they find or steal, is spent on glue and benzene."

"Like the kids in Boksburg," Andreas murmured.

"This entire scene you see around you," Matthew continued bitterly, "is one of the mass graves of our warriors. Hardly anyone moves around at night, and those who do, do so on the run like hunted animals, with their hearts in their mouths, desperate to avoid notice. They shy away at the smallest sound. They never walk; they run to find refuge in their filthy burrows. The tsotsis (thugs) lie in wait everywhere, ready to kill, to steal and rape. They have no use for mercy. Like a new breed of carnivorous beast, bred in this great melting-pot of misery, malnutrition and fear, they hunt with unbridled hatred. The citizens here were never free of the watchful eyes of the police or the tsotsis."

Andreas listened, curled up in his seat, perplexed and inexplicably afraid. The car, groaning and pitching like a boat, made its way through the dark channels of Soweto streets. Andreas's heart beat faster; shivers ran up and down his body. He felt afraid in this enormous living cemetery, where the vampires roamed free, thirsting for blood. Matthew parked the car in front of a low-roofed house, made sure it was safe, then opened the door and told Andreas to follow him. He knocked hard on a shanty door. Something heavy was audibly pushed aside behind the entrance and it opened. Andreas looked around him in puzzlement, and numerous pairs of curious, inquiring eyes fixed themselves on him. Matthew signaled him to come further in, and pointed him toward a dark corner of the room where a man was lying on a wooden bed.

"See this man? He's my friend, Thomas. Actually, he's more like my brother. We grew up together in my so-called homeland. His older sister, Rosa, used to take care of us. She is more like a mother to me than my real mother. She insisted that we go to the mission school. Rosa now runs a shabeen (illegal beer bar) in the back of this house. A few weeks ago, Thomas was a strong, healthy young man. Now look at him, he's paralyzed for the rest of his life. He was on the train; the tsotsis thrust an umbrella rib into his spinal column, so that they could steal his wages. These woman and children all live here, sharing the rent for this house. Now they all help to take care of him."

Matthew smiling approached Thomas and hugged him warmly as they exchanged greetings in the Sotho language. He lit two cigarettes, stuck one in the mouth of the paralyzed man, sat down next to him and started to talk. The sick man's face came to life and every now and then he let out a hearty laugh. A lighted candle on a table cast its feeble light on various women of indeterminate ages. A baby cried and a woman picked it up in her arms, opened her blouse and offered it milk. The infant seized on the nipple and sucked contentedly. The women and children, all sprawled out on blankets on the floor, carried on with their chatter.

A back door opened and Rosa came into the room from the adjoining shabeen. She was a large, powerful woman and she listened to Matthew's jokes and joined in the laughter with great zest. Andreas felt himself an outsider and he recoiled from the laughter. He watched Matthew with astonishment. It was the first time since they were children, that Andreas had seen him unbound from his subservience. Matthew loudly called Andreas to come nearer. He introduced him to Rosa and the other women.

The rear door opened again and a stocky, big-bellied man with an angry face called out for them to be quiet. But as soon as he recognized Matthew, his drunken features lit up. Staggering, he pushed his way through the crowd to Matthew and threw his arms around him.

"Why do you bring a white man here?" he asked in Zulu. "Is he a spy?" he continued laughing derisively.

"No," Matthew replied in English. "Andreas is a revolutionary. He organized the student protests."

The large man ignored Andreas and grabbed Matthew by the arm, dragging him toward the room he had just emerged from. Andreas followed him into a long, narrow, low-ceilinged room, containing a number of men sitting on plastic crates round a rickety table covered with red and white cartons of local beer. There was an antiquated record player with records scattered around. The air was stuffy and foul with the stink of tswala beer and dagga. Andreas's eyes watered from the smoke, his nostrils dilated and inflated, gasping for air.

"Ha, good!" The large man bellowed. "Baas is a freedom fighter come to liberate us! I saw his photograph in the newspaper. Freedom fighting is difficult work, Baas," the man continued as he laughed. "First you have to drink and smoke with us and then you can save us from this devil's place."

The men around them broke out in laughter. Matthew made the introductions and Andreas was vaguely aware of names and faces. The men made room for them to sit down, but Matthew soon left the room after being beckoned by Rosa, leaving Andreas alone. The man next to him was patiently rolling a thick cigarette in newspaper. He liked it, stuck it down, and tapped one end on the table to pack it down. He inspected it and with a satisfied glance stuck it between his lips. He struck a match, lit it, and took several deep drags on the smoke. Andreas was engulfed in the pungent smell of dagga and found it hard to breathe. He looked around eagerly for Matthew to return. The man yawned and passed him the cigarette.

Andreas did not have the courage to refuse. He put the wet end of the cigarette in his mouth and drew in. His chest heaved, his eyes watered and his head felt immediately heavy. He took another few drags and soon a silly smile played on his lips. The room grew bigger, the music was beautiful and the deep shadows had gone off for a walk. Thirsty, he grabbed a bottle of beer from the case, and eagerly swallowed the liquid.

After some time, Matthew returned to the room. Andreas was still smoking, passing the dagga back and forth between himself and the master who had rolled it. Suddenly, Matthew snatched the cigarette from his mouth. He looked at Andreas disapprovingly and ground the joint angrily under his foot.

"What the hell are you doing, man?"

"Having fun," Andreas said stupidly. Matthew gave him a cup of coffee and sat down beside him. The room became depressing again with drunken men lying all around and the heavy smell of marijuana and tswala beer.

"I think you've seen enough of this place," Matthew stated. "Let's get out of here."

They made their way out carefully around the sprawled bodies.

The relatively fresh air of the ghetto washed over them and Andreas inhaled gratefully.

"Matthew, I apologize for being so arrogant and stupid. I was goading you," Andreas said simply.

"Never mind, Andreas, although you have been provoking me for quite a while. Nevertheless, I would like to speak to you freely and to get off my chest what I think about the student efforts. But you have to tell me first, how are you and your fellow academics are going to change all this?"

Andreas fell silent. How could he answer?

"What? Nothing to say? Well, listen to me while I tell you something. I don't know about you, but I feel that most of your friends are playing liberator to amuse themselves and become heroes to their mates. All those democratic ideals of theirs last until they've finished their studies. Then they take a warm drink of capitalism, and turn into regular law-abiding citizens in their ideas and beliefs. I'm afraid that change, Andreas, will only come about through bullets, guns and blood!"

They had forgotten their caution and were wandering about the empty streets of Soweto. Matthew slowed down and pointed.

"See that house? Doesn't it surprise you to see such a fine house among the slums? I'll tell you why. They call it the house of Tokoloshi (an evil African spirit). It is now deserted and haunted. Buried in there are the dreams and desires of a man; perhaps of all black people. A friend of mine built it. Perhaps he was the hero you were hoping to find. He had determination and patience. He used to work and study at the same time. In the end he managed to get his law degree. He married a girl who was a nursing sister, and shared his vision. They both worked hard to put up a house on a block of land they didn't own, just so that they could be an example. Just to prove that the South African blacks are quite capable of creating something beautiful on this otherwise barren land."

"I helped him to build this house myself. From that time, we became very close friends. He was my teacher, and this house became an educational center in Soweto. The couple had just had their third child, when one evening the secret police paid them a visit and arrested him under the anti-terrorism law. Every day I used to come and keep his wife company and play with the children. For four months we waited anxiously, not knowing if he was alive. One day, the police brought him back, but he was in such a state that there was no joy for us in his return."

"It took him some time to recover physically but even after that he avoided talking about what had happened to him. Time passed and proved to be the best healer. Little by little, he regained his courage and began to talk to us about the loss of freedom and human dignity. One evening, he told me the story of what they had done to him and those revelations horrified me so much that I couldn't bring myself to visit him for several weeks. Then one night, as we all feared, they came to arrest him once more. But this time they brought him back more quickly, in a nailed down coffin with a doctor's certificate that said he'd died of natural causes. His wife and I took him out of the coffin and undressed the corpse. We saw for ourselves the real cause of his death. His body was distorted from the beatings he had received and his genitals were blackened from electric shocks."

"I helped his wife and children escape across the border. She went to find the resistance fighters, to join them in the battle. Ever since then the house has been dead, haunted, decaying in the wind and the rain. It the nicest house here and it is empty. No one will go inside. It's become a symbol of the struggle for freedom, and yet none dare enter it because they say that the undying spirit of Tokoloshi (evil spirit) protects it. To me, Andreas, it is a temple of hope and courage."

Andreas had listened to all this without a word.

"Matthew, I'm sorry. I can understand your fury and your righteous hatred. Believe me, I don't have much strength, but the flame burns bright inside me. I swear to you, you can trust me. I would do anything to fight side by side with you. Here's my hand; give me yours and let's make a start."

Matthew, moved by the strange young white man, stared at the hand that was offered to him. He then put his own hands into his pockets ignoring the gesture.

"Give me a bit of time to think about it Andreas, and then I'll answer you."

With that they got into the car and set off home. They arrived in the early hours of the morning, neither saying a word.

CHAPTER 11 Power of Fear

Andreas woke up much later than usual, still dizzy from his night with Matthew. His brain was befuddled, his head ached intolerably and his stomach was bloated and flatulent. He looked at his watch and when he realized the time, he leapt out of his bed, dressed quickly and ran down the stairs. His mother appeared in the doorway of the family room holding a newspaper.

"Andreas," she said aggressively, "I've got to talk to you; right away! How involved are you in all this?"

"Mother, I'm really sorry to upset you, but I can't talk now. I am running very late."

"I never see you to talk to you. And now this!" she said shaking the newspaper. "My God, have you gone completely mad, Andreas? And look at the state you are in. It's disgusting. I'm ashamed of you! If you don't change the way you are living, and get rid of these stupid ideas of yours, you needn't bother to come home anymore."

Andreas wiped his face with his handkerchief and looked patiently at his mother, "You don't understand me and I know I disappoint you, but I can't change my way of thinking. I would only disappoint myself. We're at odds, in two totally opposing camps, and I know we can't ever agree."

His mother responded, "What rubbish you talk! When are you going to wake up to reality? If we were not supporting you, you would not be able to get up to all your misguided student antics. You would be too busy out there earning a living. I am sick and tired of worrying about you. Either settle down and stick to your studies or get out!"

"Oh, Mom, stop worrying so much. What's in the newspaper that upset you so much anyway?"

She said in disgust, "Look! Is this what you were up to in Cape Town?"

The front page of the morning paper was filled with bold headlines and photos of violent encounters between police and students.

'BLOODY EPISODES IN CAPE TOWN. Vicious encounters between police and students in the city streets. Bishop and his wife arrested on the Cathedral steps. Prime Minister orders the police to crush the student movement at any cost. Sadistic violence on the part of police. Prime Minister congratulates the security forces. Large groups of students arrested.'

Andreas said, "Mom, this is horrible. Those bastards are out to get us! I have to go! I should be at school already! I'm so late."

He brushed by his mother, ignoring her outcry, and soon he was in his car, speeding away. He found total chaos in the streets around the university. The police had blocked all surrounding roads isolating the university. A huge traffic jam prevented Andreas's efforts to penetrate the blockade. Police barriers were everywhere. He left his car at a curb a few blocks away and approached the university on foot, hoping to find a way. Solid ranks of police had filled the university campus and the surrounding areas. Nobody was allowed either in or out. The police and ambulance sirens intensified, adding their sounds to the atmosphere of fear. The air was thick with tear-gas and smoke. Students were running in all directions as the police chased them and beat them without mercy. The wounded youth were then handcuffed and thrown into waiting vans.

Andreas's efforts were in vain and he found it impossible to penetrate the solid ranks of police who had completely surrounded the university campus. He could clearly hear the growling of the dogs, audible amid the shrieks of hysteria, pain and fear. Paddy wagons packed with arrested students roared off to security headquarters. It was a total nightmare. Andreas cursed out loud for once more for sleeping in so late.

"What kind of a fighter am I? I should be in there with them. I let everybody down," Andreas thought. He stood there helpless and motionless, no more than a mere bystander. He was witnessing vicious violence being unhesitatingly visited on the university, violating its identity as a sanctuary. Agonizing hours passed as Andreas continued to watch the unfolding tragedy from afar. He felt heartbroken and guilty, impotently unable to offer any support. He walked aimlessly in the empty streets. Activity around the university eventually died down, but still police maintained their barricades holding their control of the university. It began to drizzle and Andreas welcomed the cool rain on his face. He found himself in a nearby park, not knowing how he got there. He picked up one of the numerous leaflets that were lying around. He sat down on a bench and read:

SOUTH AFRICA

You have all by now heard of the police attack on unprotected students and members of the public at St George's Cathedral, Cape Town, on Friday.

Surely all just men must be shocked at this use of violence: but let us not forget that violence occurs every day in South Africa.

* Hundreds of families are broken up; husbands, wives and children are separated by Law.

IS NOT THIS VIOLENCE?

* In the Homelands, one in five children dies of starvation before reaching the age of five.

IS NOT THIS VIOLENCE?

* Most Black parents cannot afford to educate their children. While they slave for pennies, their children wander the streets.

DOES THIS NOT BREED VIOLENCE?

*All Black students at Turfloop were thrown out of their University.

WHY? WITHOUT EDUCATION WHAT WILL THEY BECOME?

Students are beaten; for saying that we want an end to violence in our country.

We want food, family life, free education and decent living wages for ALL South Africans.

SUPPORT OUR PLEA FOR A JUST SOUTH AFRICA.

Issued by
Student's Representative Council
University of Witwatersrand University

Soaked to the bone, Andreas headed home. His parents were talking in the lounge. Andreas tried to dodge them, but his mother's strident voice called out to him.

"Andreas, we want to talk to you!"

"Mom, do you mind leaving it for tomorrow? I have a headache, and I am feeling very tired."

His mother stood up and she rushed into the hallway after him. She then noticed puddles of water and mud on the expensive hallway carpet, and she looked at her son in dismay. He was sopping wet dripping with water from head to toe.

"Oh, my God! You have finally gone totally crazy! Do you have any respect left for us and our home?"

Andreas turned and looked at the mud on the floor. "I'm sorry Mom. I didn't realize. I will clean it right away"

His father loomed large in the doorway. "Never mind about cleaning the carpet. We have servants to do that job. We want to clear up some things with you now!"

"What do you want from me?" Andreas replied. "Let me live my life the way that I want."

"No my friend!" his father said condescendingly. "While you live in this house you live the way that we want, on our conditions. You have created so much trouble between me and your mother, and you make me ashamed seeing you as you are. Not to mention the weird way you have been acting lately. If you don't come to your senses and change, there is no room for you in this house. I have worked very hard all my life to create a name for myself, and I will not permit you to destroy it."

His mother continued, "If you were focused on what you should be doing, like your studies or even if you had a job, you would not have time for all this nonsense. We have thoroughly spoiled you and you in turn, have taken advantage of our love and caring."

"Go and change," his father said, "then come down so that we can make it clear to you what we expect."

Andreas went to his bedroom. He threw a few clothes into a suitcase and went back to the lounge. He took the keys to the house and the car from his pocket, and put them on the table.

"I'm sorry to have disappointed you. I think it would be best that I leave. Goodnight."

His parents stood motionless, staring at him. Andreas closed the door quietly behind him and looked back at his home for the last time. He felt an overwhelming pain of despair in his chest. The streets were deserted. The rain had lost its gentleness and was beating down hard and mercilessly into his face. He stopped at the first corner under a street light and counted his money. He didn't have much, not enough to pay for a night in a hotel. A car's headlights shone from the end of the street. He stepped out and signaled that he wanted a lift. The car sped up and roared past, throwing a torrent of water over him. His suitcase was heavy in his hand. He was cold, hungry and exhausted.

Panic seized him. "Where am I going to go? What the hell do I think I'm doing? Does progress matter?"

Two familiar voices replied, "You're not yet educated and without money, home or car, you will never survive on your own."

"Be brave, have courage and you'll manage. Think how many millions of people are doing just what you have to do now. Learn to survive on your own. Of course you can make it!"

"But you're not a hero. Heroes are born, not made. You're just a piece of chaff blowing this way and that in the wind; you'll be blown away without any roots."

"Wrong! You're a human being. You have firm beliefs. You won't stand for injustice and the exploitation of man. Go on! Fear not!"

"Just think! You've no experience. You've never been hungry; you've never had to suffer. You've always had everything easy, and plenty of it. You've only got one life. Enjoy it while you can."

"You're not a yellowbelly. You can't be the sort of turd that's content only with making yourself comfortable."

"Oh, come off it! Is this your problem? Are you black?"

"No I'm not black, but I have a conscience. Humanity has no color!"

It was a long walk in the pouring rain but Andreas barely noticed, preoccupied with thoughts about his predicament. He reached a large suburban intersection; the light was red and the traffic was heavy. As he put his suitcase down for a rest, a child's voice broke into his thoughts: "Paper! Paper!" On the street corner a young black boy, half naked and soaked through, had taken refuge under the awning of a nearby building. He was calling out in a weary and mournful voice, stamping on the footpath at the same time to warm his feet. Without thinking, Andreas opened his suitcase, took out his overcoat and a pair of shoes and handed them to the boy. The boy grabbed them and looked at him perplexed.

The light changed and Andreas crossed the street. He walked a few blocks, and found himself in Hillbrow. The multitude of lights and the ceaseless traffic brought him back to reality. He stopped at the first telephone booth and phoned Philip's flat. He was curious to get the latest news about what he had missed that morning. He also wanted to ask Philip to put him up for a few nights. The phone rang, but no one answered. He tried again and again. The rain was heavier, without a break. After some hesitation, he decided to make his way to Linda's. He hoped that she was home and not in jail. The door opened immediately and Linda appeared beautifully smart in her red raincoat, with an umbrella in her hand.

"Andreas! What's happened to you? Come in."

"Linda, I didn't want to burden you with my problems. Were you going out?"

"I was going to get some take-out, but come in. You'd better get out of those wet clothes or you'll catch a chill."

"Linda, I've decided to leave home. Can I stay here until I can get in touch with Philip and William?"

"What a question! Of course! You can stay as long as you want."

"What happened this morning at school? How did you manage?" Andreas asked.

"I was plain lucky, I missed school today. I had to visit my mother who is ill."

"What about you? I heard it was terrible!"

'I missed it too. I overslept. Can you believe it?"

"Yes, you are probably not fully recovered yet."

Filled with concern, she quickly ran him a hot bath and helped him to pull off the wet clothes that had stuck to his body.

"Take a bath, Andreas, and I'll make us something to eat."

The hot water relieved his frozen body and from the kitchen came the tantalizing smell of bacon and eggs. He put on the dressing gown Linda had given him. They ate with gusto, and a glass of strong red wine calmed and helped to revive him. They talked about morning's events at the university and Linda filled him in on all the information that she had obtained about the others. Andreas was reluctant to share many details about why he had left home. They both tried repeatedly to phone Philip, but with no result.

Uneasily, he asked Linda again, "Are you sure the police haven't arrested him?"

"Of course, Andreas. Philip's injuries were too bad for him to take part in today's demonstration. He specifically told me that he'd wait at the airport to meet William who was coming back from Cape Town. Stop worrying, Andreas. You look worn out. Go and lie down. My bed's big enough for us both. We'll manage until you decide what you want to do."

Andreas lay down in Linda's bed, and she turned off the light as she made her way to the bathroom.

"Good night Andreas," she said.

"Good night."

He tried to sleep, but his thoughts kept whirling round and round in his weary brain.

"You're all upset, Andreas, Take it easy. Try and calm your nerves."

She cuddled up to him, her warm body pressed tightly against him.

"Make love to me," she whispered softly in his ear, "it'll be good for you."

The doorbell rang loudly, insistently, again and again. Andreas was jolted from his deep sleep. A sense of foreboding clutched his heart. Linda opened her eyes and clung to him. He looked at his luminous watch and saw that it was four thirty-five. The clamour at the door became more insistent. Andreas got up, put on his dressing gown and went to the door.

"Who do you think it could be at this time? Perhaps we should ignore it?" Linda asked anxiously.

"It might be serious. Let me go and have a look," Andreas replied.

"Who is it?" he called out, gluing his eye to the peep-hole. He stood petrified for a few moments, then quickly recovered himself and flung the door open. Philip, black and blue, with red, swollen eyes, fell into his arms.

"Philip! In God's name, what happened?"

Philip burst into nervous sobbing, trembling from head to foot, and tears poured from his puffed-up eyes. Andreas, astonished, supported him tenderly and laid him down on the couch. Linda, worried and frightened, got out of bed and covered him with a blanket. She quickly opened a bottle of brandy, poured a generous portion into a glass. She put it to Philip's broken lips and forced him to take several sips. Andreas watched Philip anxiously, wondering what could have turned this self-confident young man into a nervous wreck.

The strong spirits restored a little colour to his pale cheeks. Andreas lit a cigarette and put it in Philip's mouth. His reddened eyes held Andreas's for a moment, and then he covered them with his hands as he burst into a fresh bout of sobbing. He started to speak, but his words were unintelligible through his moans. She cradled his head in her arms and stroked his hair. Philip pulled away from her and stared at Andreas, his face swollen from crying and his eyes gleaming with desperation.

"I'm a traitor! I've betrayed you all to save my own hide. Don't look at me like that, Andreas. I was scared, so scared that they managed to break my resistance."

"Philip, I still don't understand you. Who broke your resistance? Don't tell us now if you like. You are too upset. We've got plenty of time ahead of us. Drink your brandy; it'll make you feel better."

As his body warmed and he grew accustomed safety, Philip calmed down. He gained the courage to loosen his tongue and unburden himself.

"We were coming back from the airport and we found them, the security police, waiting for us in my apartment. They pushed us into a corner, handcuffed us, and started a systematic interrogation as though they knew exactly what they wanted to find out. They gathered up all the papers and books they needed, before arresting us under the anti-terrorism law. We were stunned and helpless. We didn't know what was going to happen to us. They loaded us into a car and without another word, took us to the tenth floor of the security building in John Vorster Square."

As Philip described those terrible moments, the fear and anguish on his face showed that he was reliving them. Andreas listened with bulging eyes and a thundering heart.

"Shoving and swearing, they put us in two adjoining offices and left the connecting door open. They forced me into a steel chair and tied my hands and feet. Then they rigged up a powerful spotlight in front of me. It was blinding, and they left me alone like that for I don't know how many hours. The waiting was horrible and the damned light was so strong it pierced my eyelids. From the next room, I could hear furious shouting, and after a while I heard William screaming desperately. His broken screams made me forget my own pain. I only wanted to get at them, and I struggled with all my might to break my bonds. It was hopeless. They tortured him furiously and ceaselessly. His screams of pain became continuous until they lost any resemblance to human noises, and turned into nightmarish croaks of agony that tore at my ears. I wanted to scream with him, but I couldn't. My throat was too dry."

Philip raised a trembling hand and wiped the streaming tears from his eyes. Andreas gave him a little more brandy and lit another cigarette for him.

"Then the screams stopped and I heard them dragging William down the corridor. There was a terrible silence. I was so thirsty and my guts were on fire. My hair was sticking up like a thorn bush in fear. They didn't leave me alone for long after that. It was my turn. I wanted to open my eyes to see what was happening but that light, that bloody light was blinding me.

One of them said, 'Did you hear the party we had with your friend? Pity he didn't put up much resistance. Let's hope you'll prove better. Open your eyes, you bastard! Look me in the eyes when I'm talking to you!'

'I can't', I wailed, 'the light! Turn it off please!'

A strong hand grabbed my hair and another started punching me in the face.

'Open your eyes!' yelled a furious voice.

They kept pulling my head back by the hair and then they ripped open my shirt and stuck a lighted cigarette onto my chest. I screamed with pain and opened my eyes, but couldn't make anything out. I was a limp rag, with no will, no pride, cursing the moment I'd got involved in politics.

The torture stopped immediately when a fresh voice was heard: 'What the hell's got into you today, Shorty?'

Shorty answered, 'Let me get on with my work, Captain.'

'Leave him alone. He looks like a decent guy. I'll deal with him.'

'You'll get nowhere by being polite with people of his kind, Captain.'

'That's my business,' the captain answered coldly.

He switched off the spotlight, sat down next to me and put a glass of water to my parched lips, helping me gently to drink it. My eyes filled with tears of gratitude.

'You look like a decent sort of kid. I'm sorry for you,' he said, 'I'd like to help you.'

"At that moment, I forgot William, our cause, everybody. Only one thing mattered to me, to escape, to be saved. I told them everything

I knew. I betrayed all of you. I agreed with them that from now on, I would work for them. I have to keep them informed every day about what's going on in the university. That's why they let me go, but when I found myself outside on the pavement, I felt defeated. William's shrieks of anguish followed me every step of the way. I couldn't go to our flat. I wanted to find someone I could talk to, and I'm glad I found you two here. Please don't kick me out. I know I'm disgusting, but I was so afraid. I'm no hero, just a coward."

Philip covered his face with his hands and cried like a baby. Andreas thought that he was living through a bad dream. He closed his eyes but when he opened them, he still saw Philip's desperate and weary look gazing at him beseechingly. He felt sorry for him as he thought of the tempest of remorse that had battered him the previous morning when he had overslept. On the other hand this was different. He did not expect that Philip would crack so easily and reveal all their names and plans. He made an effort and smiled at him.

"Believe me, I don't despise you. I might have done the same in your position, Philip. I'm in no position to judge you because I don't know whether, if I were in your shoes, I wouldn't crack myself. Everyone has his limits. You did what you could, and to my mind that's enough. Also, you're not responsible for William's arrest. You can be sure they knew all about us already. In any case, what is there to know? It is great that you told us about being forced to be an informer. You could have kept it to yourself. The trouble is that they are going to expect more information from you. How are we going to deal with that? They probably have someone following you already, so they also probably know that you are here."

"I am so ashamed of myself. I don't even know how I will be able to go on at all," Philip said in low whisper as though the energy had completely drained out of him.

Exhausted, he closed his eyes and a vast sigh shook his whole body as he surrendered to a restless sleep. Linda went back to her warm bed and was soon sleeping peacefully. Andreas sat next to Philip for a long time, smoking one cigarette after another, his thoughts buzzing in his brain like angry wasps. He had no illusions. He saw clearly how dark and uncertain his future was.

Feeling suffocated in the tiny apartment, Andreas quietly got dressed and went outside.

The rain had stopped, but the dampness penetrated his bones. Dawn had not yet broken. The streets were filled with black workers, men and women, some wrapped in multi-coloured blankets, about to earn their daily wage in the factories. He wandered aimlessly through the streets, gazing blankly about him, heavy hearted. The sound of singing voices woke him from his daze. An iron-barred truck, the black people's cage of destiny, passed in front of him fully laden, and the song disappeared into the distance. The police scavengers had made an early start in collecting their day's quota. He recalled bitterly the tragic events that had taken place a few days before when a similar cage, laden with prisoners broke down on the way to the jail. It stood motionless for several hours, waiting for the repair truck. The prisoners shouted to be let out as they had not enough air to breathe. Nobody took them seriously. When the prison-truck finally reached its destination, three of the eighty-five prisoners had died of asphyxiation and many others were taken to hospital in a terrible state. Articles were written in the opposition papers demanding explanations from the Ministry of Justice. But the cages were obviously continuing their dreadful rounds, carting human beings like animals. His anxiety and concerns seemed to him paltry when placed in comparison to the courage and passion that the singing prisoners had shown.

"That is pure bravery," Andreas thought, "singing so early in the morning, on the way to jail. Matthew's right, we are just rich white kids who crack easily under pressure."

He whispered aloud to himself, "I hope I will be able to prove him wrong when my time comes."

He felt liberated by the challenge, more confident that he would not betray his ideals.

CHAPTER 12 Deepening Involvements

On the following morning, the front page of the *Rand Daily Mail*, a more liberal newspaper declared in large print the simultaneous arrests of NUSAS leaders, William Pretorius and Norman Sharp. The arrest of student leaders was described as yet another step in a negative direction. The article proclaimed that democratic institutions did not exist in South Africa and denounced the anti-terrorism law that placed an invisible noose around the neck of every democratic citizen, encouraging suspicion and insecurity to infiltrate into every relationship. It criticized the sweeping powers given to any policeman, at the rank of sergeant and above, to enter any house, on the slightest pretext, at any time. An article on the second page described the reactions of William Pretorius's parents to his arrest. With a blind fanaticism, they cruelly condemned their own son as a traitor and an enemy of the nation.

Andreas hurled the paper to the floor in disgust. He decided to continue his stay with Linda who had told him that he could stay with her as long as he needed. He returned to his classes where the last traces of the recent attack on the University were evident in the whispered fears expressed by his fellow students. He saw Philip moving about like a ghostly shadow with a pale face and dead, dull eyes. The atmosphere of the school had surely changed. The all-powerful state had conquered once more. The lofty sentiments of students in favor of change had died. He felt choked by despair. He could not believe that after so much effort, after so many sacrifices, they had seemingly failed.

An unexpected source of hope for Andreas and his fellow protestors was that the detention of two leaders of the student movement raised a storm of protest among the academic staff in all the English speaking universities. For the first time, the Vice Chancellor of Witwatersrand University called for a three-day strike and urged students to attend various protest meetings. He also called on the government to produce the arrested students before the court, to determine whether or not they were guilty. Once again the students took up their banners. They sent messages to the United Nations and to the offices of human rights organizations. Many of the more ardent protesters had spilled blood on the streets. The police dispersed them violently, chasing them into the University grounds, once more violating traditional asylum. Three days of protest passed in pain, anguish and distress, until the routine of university lectures and seminars recommenced and the students immersed themselves in their studies.

A few days later, in expectation of a revival of the movement, Andreas had hurried to a NUSAS committee meeting, specially arranged to elect a new president. Andreas was one of the first to arrive. He found himself consumed with impatience. He sat on a chair and studied each of the members, one by one, as they arrived from all across the country. Philip was a nervous parody of his former self. He bustled about ceaselessly greeting the new arrivals, while carefully keeping a safe distance from Andreas. The hall filled up. The meeting began and Andreas was both worried and amazed to see Philip taking part. He had hoped that his friend, albeit belatedly, would find the courage and the dignity to tender his resignation. As the secretary, Philip brought the meeting to order and read aloud the latest minutes.

"Colleagues, the oppression we've encountered over the last weeks, as you all know, has been very painful to all of us. We are still mourning the arrest of our beloved friend and president, and that of Norman Sharp. We also mourn for all those who at this very moment are in hospital or in prison. I ask you, what have we gained from all this? Don't you think the price we've paid is too high? My friends, I've always been one who called for action, but now I'm pleading with you for moderation, and common sense. I don't want us to mourn any more victims! The government has proven itself all-powerful. Now I beg you, friends and colleagues, let's use good sense as we vote for our new president."

Philip announced the names of the candidates, but Andreas was so distracted that he scarcely heard his own name among the others.

The voting took place smoothly. The committee collected the ballot papers and retired to count them. Linda, graceful as always, came in and sat down next to Andreas.

"I'm incorrigible," she said, "as usual I turned up late, and was only just in time to vote for you."

"For me? Well, you've wasted your vote for sure."

"Why, darling? I think you're by far the best candidate. Anyway, I like you."

He smiled at her. "Well, I don't have very much experience."

"Come on darling," she said, "who does? They have arrested all our leaders. Anyway so far you have not being doing too bad a job."

The election results came out quicker than anyone had expected. Philip, beaming with pleasure, mounted the rostrum and asked everyone to take their seats. Andreas stared in astonishment at the miraculous change in Philip's face and movements. They reminded him of happier days.

"Silence, ladies and gentlemen, please!" he called. "Dear friends, it is with great pleasure and pride that I announce to you the new president of NUSAS, one who will, I'm certain, tread with success in the footsteps of his predecessors. It is none other than our beloved Andreas Magdalos!"

The students burst into applause and shouting that mounted almost to hysteria. Linda threw herself into his arms and kissed him ecstatically. Philip stepped down from the rostrum and approached. There were tears in his eyes.

"Congratulations, Andreas. Electing you was really important at this difficult time. You're the most suitable man there is for this demanding job."

Andreas stood still as if he had turned to stone. He could scarcely acknowledge the fact of his election, the demonstrations of his colleagues, and the lightning change in Philip. Phillip took him by the hand and together they mounted the rostrum where someone pushed the microphone in front of him. The wild demonstration rose to a climax as Andreas stood there stunned, trying to compose himself.

"Speech! Speech! Speech!" yelled the crowd.

With trembling hands he lifted the microphone to his mouth, looked around the audience, cleared his throat, drew a deep breath and took the plunge.

"Colleagues! Brothers and sisters!" he finally managed to stammer in a voice trembling with emotion. "This is a great honor, and at the same time an intolerable burden that you've loaded on my shoulders. It's very difficult for me to replace such a charismatic leader, one whose face still seems to be present wherever we look. But I promise to try my best, and I hope I will match him in value. There is question that I want to put to you now that we're all present here. Are we any less guilty than William or Norman? I use the word 'guilt', and I feel like breaking out into uncontrollable laughter, because our activities have never included anything illegal. The truth is very simple. The government is afraid of the voice of truth. That's why it attacks us mercilessly, so as to intimidate us into shutting up. If it had the courage and the evidence, it would drag every one of us into court. I for one would like to see the legal arguments that would convict us there! For that reason, with the mandate you've given me, with your votes, I have decided to shout NO! That's right! NO! No! To moderation! YES! To the continuing struggle! Otherwise we and we alone will have betrayed our ideals, and our persecuted colleagues."

"We're with you! We're with you!" the students shouted enthusiastically.

"NUSAS will need to explore new directions and we'll talk about that at our first meeting. Colleagues, in conclusion I want to thank you once again for the trust you've placed in me. Thank you all."

What followed was a celebration, a festival of joy where new relationships were cemented, ideas were exchanged and lost morale threatened restored. Andreas circulated among the throng of students, accepting their congratulations and good wishes.

At one stage, Philip was alone with Andreas and mouthed at him, "Andreas, I want to speak with you in private."

Andreas looked at him curiously. "I'm always willing to speak with you, Philip"

Linda, bright and cheerful, came by interrupting them. "This is a great event," she said enthusiastically, "we've got to celebrate."

"Well, that would be a great idea, Linda, although we've plenty of work to do. Philip has to fill me in on the administrative side of things, and then we ought to lay the foundations for our future plans. Still, you're right; we ought to have some kind of party."

"Agreed! I'll leave you to finish your work, while I go back to my apartment and get some food ready. Oh, I'll get champagne too. Just don't be late!"

"You're terrific, Linda," said Andreas tenderly, "we'll be with you as soon as possible."

They were left alone in the meeting hall. Philip was nervous and worried.

"Ready then, Philip. I'm listening."

"I'd rather talk outside, in the garden."

Andreas, puzzled by Philip's attitude, shrugged his shoulders and followed him out.

"Don't get me wrong, Andreas, but I don't feel at all safe in the University. I'm sure they've bugged the place. They're listening in to everything we say."

"You've got to be joking, Philip," answered Andreas.

"You've got to believe me. They know everything, at any given moment. They insist on meeting with me twice a day. One time, I mustered up some courage and gave them some false information. They let me finish then looked at me coldly and said that the next time I tried to fool them would be my last. Don't look so doubtful, Andreas. You think I've gone crazy with fright, that I'm just talking nonsense. I only wish you were right. I'd leave here laughing. I'm very much afraid, that sooner or later, you'll find out for yourself. Anyway, that's not why I wanted to talk to you. I've wanted to speak to you for days, but I lost my nerve. I can't help but notice the contempt in your eyes. Don't try to deny it. I watched you all evening. You're wondering how I had the cheek to remain secretary of NUSAS, after I'd told you myself that I was one of the ones who betrayed them. If you don't yet understand the reason, I'll tell you myself! I don't have any choice! They're forcing me to stay on. Andreas, I've wanted to tell you all this for some time, but I was afraid and ashamed. That's why I wanted the movement to die out, so that I wouldn't be forced to betray it. My conscience gnaws at me. But I want you to know that all their bullying hasn't succeeded in destroying the other Philip, the part of me that you used to know. He's still alive and well, and carrying on the battle. He's the one who disobeyed their orders, and proposed that you should be president. He's the one who voted for you. He's the one who can't stand being a wretched traitor. It's him who's asking you to help him to escape from this land of hatred. You're the only friend I can trust, so that's why I'm asking you to help me."

Andreas stood still as a statue, looking with horror at Philip's tear-swollen eyes. Andreas suddenly felt tortured by remorse. Amid the labyrinth of his own insecurities and desires, he had not stopped for one moment to look at the drama, the tension in which his friend was living. He took him by the shoulders and hugged him.

"Philip, I've misunderstood you and misjudged you. You were all alone during this terrible time. I didn't respect you as you deserved. I made a big mistake and I should have known you better. Please forgive me. I promise I'll try to do what I can to help you. Do you think that you should try to get across the border?"

"It'll be terribly difficult, Andreas. They follow me all the time, and what's more I have to report to them twice a day. Do you think that it could be managed?"

"Believe me, Philip; we'll make every effort to get you out. I don't know how yet, but somehow I think we'll manage it. What I ask you to do is to go back to your apartment and carry on your normal daily work. But I want you to be ready at any moment."

Philip stopped trembling. He wiped his eyes and looked Andreas in the eyes, seeing an assurance that gave him courage and hope.

Later on that evening, the flames of two red candles gave a festive air to the table. The polished glasses gleamed. The lounge room was filled with the cheerful voices of the guests. They ate heartily and the bottles of champagne soon emptied, one after the other. There was widespread good cheer, but Andreas, behind his mask of cheerfulness, was trying to think of a way of getting Philip out of the country. When their friends had departed, Linda went to bed but Andreas was unable to sleep. He looked at his watch. It was past two. He strode up and down the room several times, tense and nervous. He made up his mind, dressed quickly and shut the door quietly behind him. Linda's car was parked in the same spot. He took out the key Linda had given him and started the motor. There was little traffic on the road at this hour. He drove around aimlessly for a while until he was sure that no one was following him, and then he stepped on the gas and headed for Parktown. He left the car in a side street and walked quickly to the back of the family property. With an easy movement he vaulted the high fence and found himself in the familiar environment of his garden. Silently, avoiding the lights, he made his way to Matthew's hut and knocked gently but insistently on the door.

Matthew was startled out of his sleep, his imagination racing wildly at the unexpected summons. Could it be the police? His half-asleep mind wondered whether he should open the door. The knocking went on unrelentingly.

"Who is it?" he asked at last.

"It's me, Andreas. Open the door."

He gasped in bewilderment. Andreas came in and closed the door.

"Andreas, you've gone off your head! Do you know what time it is?"

"Yes, Matthew, I know. But it's urgent. I need your help."

"Oh, I see. You want me to intervene for you so you can go back to the security of the family home."

"Matthew, this is no time for wisecracks. I'm sorry to disturb you at such an hour, but you're the only person who can help me."

Matthew looked at him sullenly, told him to sit down, put the kettle on the stove and got two coffee cups ready. The water started to simmer and Matthew lit a cigarette. They both sat down on the end of his bed.

"OK, I'm listening."

"Matthew, a friend of mine is in a fix. He has to get out of the country as soon as possible. I want you to tell me how."

"And what makes you think I know how to get him out?"

"You told me that you've done it in the past. Matthew, the secret police are involved. He's likely to be arrested under the anti-terrorism law. You've got to help us!"

"I told you to leave me alone, you and your grand ideas. I've no taste for getting mixed up in adventures and dealings with the secret police. My life's hard enough as it is, without any more complications."

Andreas hung his head in contrition. He stood up.

"Sorry, Matthew, it was stupid of me. I had no right to involve you in matters that don't concern you. Good night."

"Andreas! Come back, damn you."

Andreas paused and turned toward Matthew.

"Shut the bloody door. The water's boiled so we can have a cup of coffee while you tell me the whole story. Start from the beginning, with no short cuts!"

Matthew listened attentively without interrupting. Only when Andreas had finished did he ask, "Andreas, are you sure Philip told you the truth and this isn't some sort of trap laid by the secret police?"

"I'm certain, Matthew. I think the guy is very sincere. That's one thing you don't have to worry about."

"OK. Let me think about it. You must phone me on Thursday, at one-thirty precisely, at the phone booth in the factory. Meanwhile I want you to promise you'll say absolutely nothing to anyone, not even to Linda or Philip."

"I promise."

They drank their coffee in silence and then Andreas left. He felt paranoid and hoped that he had not been observed.

Back in the apartment, Linda was still asleep. He undressed and flopped down beside her, dead tired.

Andreas woke in a cheerful mood and whistled as he was getting ready to go to the university in his a new capacity as President of NUSAS. University students, who had learnt about the election of the new president through the student news, greeted Andreas with a grand showing of warmth and affection. He retreated to his new office and threw himself into the work of sketching programs for a new direction of the NUSAS movement. He worked day and night, putting off his social life as well as his academic duties. He trudged endlessly from one philanthropic organization to another, from diocese to diocese, hoping to obtain the co-operation of various institutions. He was sure the institutions would be willing to forge a powerful alliance with the students, and moreover that they could open the doors of the ghettoes, so that he and his fellow students could meet and get closer to the black population. His efforts were not in vain and he found that many religious leaders were keen to co-operate. Andreas also created avenues for students to increase their involvement in early childhood education programs and youth groups in the various townships.

On the prearranged Thursday afternoon, he was sitting in a cafeteria near the university, listlessly eating an omelet. He could not tear his eyes away from the big clock on the wall. He was consumed with anxiety as to whether Matthew would help him with Philip's escape. At one-thirty exactly, he snatched up the phone and rang the number. After the first ring, a receiver was lifted at the other end.

"Hello." He heard Matthew's bass voice.

"Good day. How are you?"

"Fine, thanks."

"What have you decided?"

"I think your lunacy must be catching. I'll help you, but on one condition, you'll have to do exactly as I say."

Andreas was so overcome with joy and relief that it took him several seconds to reply.

"Hello?" said Matthew's voice impatiently.

"OK. I agree."

"Listen carefully, then, because I can't spare much time."

Andreas concentrated, and listened without interrupting.

"You understand?"

"Yes, Matthew. I'll do what you want, don't worry."

"Goodbye then. Just as we've agreed."

Andreas stared for a while at the lifeless telephone then put it back on its rest. He went back excitedly to his office. Philip was already at the typewriter, working quickly. Andreas, with difficulty, restrained his desire to tell him the good news.

"Philip, aren't you going to eat?" he asked with concern.

"No, I'm not hungry. I'd much rather get finished, and

then afterward we can discuss when to call our first committee meeting."

"Let me think about it first, Philip, and I'll let you know tomorrow morning."

"As you wish."

The next morning, Andreas went about the business of following Matthew's instructions precisely. He made a detailed reconnaissance of the building and the neighborhood, before finally returning to knock on Philip's door. His brain was working quickly as he noted every detail. All the while, he was plotting his course of action.

"Matthew was right!" he muttered to himself. "Reconnaissance is indispensable."

He was sure now, that they would be able to slip away undetected. He knocked on the outer door more loudly with sense of satisfied confidence. Philip, half asleep, opened the door. His eyes lit up with expectation the moment he saw his friend.

"I'm ready, Andreas."

"You'd better be ready! The time's growing near. I came for a cup of coffee, Philip, and to tell you that our first committee meeting will take place this coming Wednesday. That is, if you agree, of course."

"I've no objection," Philip called from the kitchen.

Andreas did not reply. He swiftly detached one of the two front door keys from the key ring that was lying on the sideboard, and hid it quickly in his pocket. Philip soon returned with two big cups of fragrant, steaming coffee.

As Saturday dawned, a solitary night time pedestrian, alone and cautious, crossed the pitch dark, dusty by-lane which connected the buildings to their rear service gates. He paused at an iron gate, and when he was sure no one was looking, he opened it silently and slipped into the concrete yard. Knowing the surroundings, he moved quickly forward and began to climb the iron service stairs. He stopped at the second floor, and placed a key in the lock. The darkness inside the flat was complete. He stopped for a while, just behind the door, until his eyes adjusted. He then crept to the window that overlooked the main street and imperceptibly pulled the curtain aside. At the entrance, he could see a man seated behind the wheel of a black car.

"Maybe it's a coincidence, or maybe it's the secret police," Andreas thought. Philip woke up with a start. He got dressed in the dark, and from under his bed he dragged the suitcase that he had pre-packed.

"Let's go, Andreas and God be with us!" he whispered.

They reached Linda's car without incident. Andreas had parked it earlier in a distant car park. He drove swiftly and carefully for two hours, covering more than a hundred and fifty kilometers. He looked at his watch. It was a quarter past two. In five minutes or so, he was due to meet Matthew. Beyond a bend he saw the garage where they were to meet. He switched off the lights and parked on the far side of the garage. He was pleased because he was sure that no one had noticed them.

"Why have you stopped, Andreas?" asked Philip uneasily.

"Don't worry old man. This is where we'll meet the man who'll get us across the border."

"Who is he, Andreas? Do I know him?"

"I don't think so, Philip, but he's certainly worth knowing."

A car drew up beside them. Andreas's worries vanished immediately when he saw it was his own car, with Matthew sitting behind the wheel. Matthew was smartly dressed in his driver's uniform. They hurriedly locked Linda's car. Matthew stepped on the gas and the sports car roared off. He drove surely and expertly, piling on the speed without creating any impression of danger.

Andreas tried repeatedly to start a conversation, but got no response from Matthew who was totally absorbed in what he was doing. They arrived at the border area without mishap. In the east, the sky was starting to turn pink. Matthew had turned off the main road and was driving carefully along a rough dirt road. From the corner of his eye, Andreas constantly watched Matthew's expression. He was completely composed and professional. At that moment Andreas realized that Matthew had made this journey many times. Matthew was involved in much more than he had let on about. The car slowed down and stopped behind a grove of trees.

"Here we are, gentlemen!" he announced. "We have to finish

the trip on foot, and as quickly as possible before it gets light. You, Andreas, stay here and wait. I'll go ahead with Philip." Without waiting for an answer he picked up Philip's suitcase and disappeared into the high grass.

Philip threw his arms round Andreas.

"I'll never forget you, Andreas. I'll soon be myself again and I'll carry on the struggle from abroad. But you take care of yourself. Don't trust anyone."

"Good luck, Philip. I'll wait to hear from you."

"Goodbye, Andreas."

Philip ran after Matthew and disappeared into the undergrowth.

Andreas sat down to wait, gazing at the countryside. A band of monkeys passed by, staring at him suspiciously. He spotted antelope, guinea hens and wild rabbits down by the nearby river. In other circumstances, he would have run to admire them. His impatience and concern grew by the minute. He kept looking at his watch and wondering whether Matthew would make it. A whole hour must have gone by before Matthew silently and suddenly appeared at his side without his even noticing. Andreas sighed with relief.

"All over, Matthew?"

"Yes, Andreas, your friend is free. Let's get out of here. I fear we've started something!"

Without waiting for an answer, he got behind the wheel and they sped off.

"Don't you want me to take the wheel for a while, Matthew?"

"No, Andreas, I feel fine. In any case, Baas, I'm the chauffeur."

"Matthew, I don't know how to thank you. What you did was unbelievably courageous. I shall be forever in your debt."

"Forget it, Andreas. In fact, you've got to forget it! We had absolutely nothing to do with Philip's escape."

Andreas looked at him in amazement. "OK, that's a promise, Matthew. How are my parents?" he asked, to change the subject.

"They seem to be all right, Andreas, though I think they're very worried about you. They're afraid for your safety. Since you left they've gone away every weekend; like they can't bear the loneliness of a quiet house. They miss you much. Don't you think it's time you went back?"

"I'd love to, Matthew, but you must understand that it's too late. I have too many obligations."

"I read that you are the new president of NUSAS."

"It's something I never went after."

"It's a tough job. I hope you have better luck than your predecessor."

"Matthew, I've been asking you for weeks whether you wanted to work with us. I need you now more than ever before. Have you changed your mind by any chance?"

"Not yet, Andreas. But I'd like you to come around one evening for a discussion."

"I'd be happy to. I will call on you very soon."

Matthew smiled, "I hope it won't be at dawn again!"

It was almost afternoon when they arrived back in their district. Weariness and lack of sleep had started to show on their faces. Andreas said goodbye to Matthew, got into Linda's car and made for home as fast as he could. Fortunately Linda was out.

CHAPTER 13 Detention without Trial

Philip's absence was noticed immediately. Fear ran through the ranks of students, as many believed that he had been arrested by the secret police. Andreas dared not tell them the truth. Instead, he followed his instructions. He made a phone search of the hospitals, and then reported Philip's disappearance to the local police. Finally, he called the major newspapers and complained about his friend's obvious and illegal detention. It had been his own idea to involve the press, and he took some satisfaction in falsely blaming the government. In response, the Central Security Bureau in John Vorster Square was forced to announce that it had no knowledge or involvement in Philip's disappearance. Sometime later, Philip's parents told the newspapers that Philip had called them from overseas, and that he was well and safe. They added that they did not know what had pushed their son to leave the country so unexpectedly and illegally.

The atmosphere was chilly at the first committee meeting. The nervous members chatted with each other about the fate of their mutual friends. Finally, Andreas called the committee to order.

"Colleagues, we gain nothing crying for the fate of our leaders. What we will do instead, is to demand their release and to continue their struggle. I share your worries so I won't weary you with pointless arguments. Quite honestly, I would ask for the adjournment of this meeting, except that we need to intervene in the celebration of Republic Day. Unfortunately, time is short, but I think that we who are fighting for freedom ought to express our displeasure to our leaders. We must remind people that this 'republic' has created nothing worth celebrating! I don't intend to ask you for more sacrifices. We shan't undertake any more mass marches in the city centers. We've all had terrible experiences and we've mourned enough victims. I suggest that instead, we change our tactics. We will restrict speeches, marches and protest banners to university grounds. Nonetheless, we must spread our view. We shall produce a proclamation, which we shall distribute as widely as possible, on and off campus. It will describe what this shameful celebration means to us.

In general, then, from now on, our strategy will be to adopt directions aimed mainly at social service goals. We shall work in the townships and schools for change. With luck, it should bring us into less direct conflict with the system. The first objective is to organize events and functions that will allow us to collect money. With the help of church organizations, we can develop programs to assist those in the ghettoes and rural areas. These people need medicine, books, clothing, and academic support for black students. Secondly, under the aegis of the churches, volunteer students will be involved in early childhood education and in giving lessons to children whose parents can't afford to send them to school. Colleagues, this is the direction I'd like our movement to follow. I think in this way we can offer more appropriate services, as well as get closer to our fellow citizens in the townships. I'm not sure if you all agree with me? However, as I see it, we can preach politics and die on our city's streets, or we can work to affect real change for people who are in dreadful need."

The discussion went on around the table for hours. Andreas's ideas were accepted mostly with enthusiasm. Some members wanted to pursue more militant action. Many wanted a charter that lay down a firm basis, for the new directions of the movement. Working parties were formed to put ideas into practice. Plans were formulated as to how everyone would take part in the protest against the proclamation of Republic Day. Some students took responsibility for compiling a list of those who were prepared to volunteer for the Head Start teaching program in the townships. When Andreas finally left the meeting, he felt that there was hope that the foundations of a powerful new movement were being laid; a movement of students who would reach out to thousands of illiterate children, who were growing up without hope in the ghettoes.

Andreas went down to the university printer. The working parties were already hard at it, feverishly compiling the material they needed for Republic Day. Andreas looked with satisfaction at the first copies of the proclamation. He picked one up, its ink still wet and fragrant. He sat on a bench and started to read carefully:

WHAT DOES REPUBLIC DAY MEAN?

According to international statistics, our country of South Africa has more people in prison than anywhere in the world. Moreover we hold the record among western nations for the highest number of executions.

Is this a sign for celebration?

We spend millions of Rand for weapons in times of peace. As a matter of fact, more than any other country on the African continent. All the while, the great majority of our people struggle. Why?

In our Republic, people are imprisoned without trial, and without their families' knowledge.
Should we be celebrating?

No, our only course is to mourn!

Issued by
Student's Representative Council
University of Witwatersrand University

Satisfied, Andreas folded the proclamation and put it in his pocket. Back in his office, he spread out a street-map on his desk, and marked strategic spots where students could distribute the leaflets. He spent some time looking at the Soweto and Alexandra township maps. He drew two large question marks.

"That's the problem," he muttered to himself. "How can I get in there when the police are on guard day and night?"

The thought occurred to him that only Matthew could do it. Would he agree, though? He decided that he would visit him that evening. Taking every possible precaution, he arrived late at Matthew's room. Before he could knock, the door opened and Matthew pulled him inside.

"Andreas! I wasn't expecting you so soon. Is there any trouble over Philip?"

"No, my friend, don't worry. I've come for a different reason."

Matthew looked at him inquiringly. Andreas pulled the proclamation out of his pocket and gave it to him.

"What have we got this time, Andreas?" he asked suspiciously.

"Something that concerns us all. Read it carefully, please, and if you think it's worth the effort, I want you to help me undertake what I think might be a very difficult and dangerous job."

Matthew sat on his only chair, his face devoid of expression. Slowly, he unfolded the piece of paper and studied it thoughtfully.

"What do you think of it, Matthew?"

Matthew looked at him taking his time to answer. "Andreas, I know what you've got in mind. Come hell or high water, you want to involve me in trouble."

"Yes, Matthew, you're absolutely right. If you are not involved, then I intend to place you in harm's way! On the other hand if you're already involved, I think it's time you dropped your mask and we put our cards on the table."

Matthew shook his head but Andreas pressed on, "However much you try to deny it, I don't believe you. I'm quite sure you've carried out tasks for some secret organization with its own purposes. We are on the same side, but using different weapons."

"What do you want of me?"

"I want you to distribute these leaflets in the ghetto."

"Why don't you and your students do it?"

"Because, as you know very well, that would be virtual suicide for us. We simply can't get in there unobserved."

"Tell me, Andreas, what will you gain if these leaflets do get into the townships? I've told you before and I'll tell you again, there's no prospect of change without bloodshed."

"You're wrong, my friend, very wrong. If these proclamations achieve their objective, then first of all it will shake the power of the police by showing that they're not as powerful as they think they are. Then secondly, it'll show the people in the ghettoes that they're not alone, that there are many whites who stand beside them, and who don't agree with the government."

Matthew shook his head, "Andreas, you're still just a big kid. When are you ever going to learn that you can't make omelets without breaking eggs? Oh, well, don't look at me like that. I won't let you down. I'll distribute your proclamations. They're printed on nice soft paper, so I'm sure they'll come in handy for rolling cigarettes, or perhaps they will even be used as toilet paper."

Andreas replied, "Well never mind. You and I will never think alike. But thank you for your trouble. At least it will serve some good cause even if just one person gets enlightened."

After a long pause, Matthew responded, "I behave so stupidly with you around, just like the subservient black man you think I am! When am I going to set myself free? When am I going to be able to say no to you? Why else would you always get your way with me? Oh yes, you've certainly taken the easy way out once again, getting me to do you dirty work. And have you yet thought about what my position would be if they arrest you? Rather, when they arrest you; you will be forced to tell them about me, Philip and now these pamphlets?"

Andreas looked at him sternly. "What are you saying, Matthew? Have you changed your mind? If you have second thoughts don't do it. But one thing is for sure, I will never betray you."

Matthew continued, "no, don't worry. I never go back on my word. All the same, I'm wondering why I said yes to you! Anyway, where are the proclamations? It's getting late and I have to work tomorrow."

Quickly, in silence, the packets were transferred from Andreas's car and hidden in the trunk of Matthew's car.

"Good night, Matthew. I'll wait for you to phone." He nodded farewell and set off for home, thoughtfully.

The following days passed quickly. Many times Andreas would gaze into space and ponder Matthew's political attitudes. "Maybe he's right," he would muse, "and maybe I am just a big kid. Only time will tell."

On Saturday, the phone woke him. Half asleep he grabbed the receiver. "Hello," he whispered so as not to wake Linda.

"Everything's OK, Andreas. Your wishes will be carried out."

He was suddenly wide awake. "Many thanks, my friend. You're tremendous!"

"Andreas, I've got a few letters for you from Greece, but I'll be away for a few days. Come and pick them up in the middle of the week."

Andreas was itching to ask him for details. He was also dying to know whether at he had got a letter from Rena after so many months, but Matthew, suspicious and in a hurry as always, had hung up.

"Who was that, darling?" asked Linda.

"Just a friend of mine," he answered vaguely, and put the phone down.

He could not get back to sleep. At last, he thought, we've made a start, a small one perhaps, but a start all the same. He lit a cigarette and imagined with pleasure, the astonishment and embarrassment of the police when they found the proclamations.

"What are you up to, Andreas?" Linda asked again. Her naked body clambered over him. "That phone call got you excited. Who was it at such an hour?"

"It's nothing, Linda. Go back to sleep. I have to go to the university. The others are expecting me."

"Why don't you tell me the truth, Andreas?"

He got out of bed and started to dress hurriedly. Linda was sitting up and staring at him in curiosity.

"Linda, stop imagining things that don't exist. I've got to go now. Tomorrow's Republic Day and we've got a lot of work ahead of us. Don't forget you've got to be there yourself at eight."

As soon as he got to the student office, he made it his first task to open the street-map and, with a hand shaking from emotion, to rub out the two big question marks. Soon the committee members arrived. Each one went to his allotted task. Andreas, constantly on the go, supervised the plan for distribution of the proclamations. He went out into the university foyer which was packed with banners and enthusiastic students chanting their slogans. Satisfied with the overall organization, he seized a packet of leaflets and hurried to take up his own position at the 'Blacks Only' exit from the railway station. His arms were tired from handing out the proclamations, but his face beamed with joy when he saw the astonished faces of some of the black pedestrians. When his own pamphlets ran out, he hurried back to the university. As he expected, all the distributors had returned with empty hands. For the first time, there had not been a single violent incident. The shops closed their doors, the streets grew quiet, and the students, tired but happy, went home.

Andreas arrived at the apartment in a state of euphoria, only to find Linda agitated and frantic.

"What on earth's happened, Linda?" he asked anxiously.

"Andreas, we're in great danger," she screamed hysterically.

He took her in his arms and stroked her hair.

"Please, Linda, calm down and try to tell me what is going on?"

"They've only just left, three of them. They give me the creeps. They asked me what I knew about Philip's disappearance and who took him over the border. When I told them I didn't know anything about Philip, they got nasty. They threatened me. They said that next time they'd interrogate me at the Central Security Bureau! It was awful! Andreas, I'm scared!"

"I understand how you feel, Linda, but I don't think you need to be afraid. You've nothing to do with Philip's disappearance, and they know it. I'm sure they won't trouble you again."

She pulled away from him in a fury. "How can you be so damn sure?" she yelled.

"I'm just assuming, Linda..." he was cut off in his reply.

"You don't know what the hell you're talking about. They said quite plainly that they'd come back. Not just for me, for you, too. Doesn't that scare you?"

"Why should I be? I don't know anything about Philip."

"Don't try and convince me, because I won't be convinced!" she shouted in a frenzy.

"Where were you that weekend, Andreas?"

Andreas stared at her in dismay. This was a new side to Linda that he had never expected might lurk under that tender exterior.

"I went fishing, as you very well know."

"Lies, lies! Where are the fish you caught? Where's your fishing gear? Philip vanished, and I'm sure you had something to do with it!" Suddenly she covered her face with her hands and broke into hysterical tears.

Andreas, thunderstruck, sat and stared at her without moving. Linda cried and sobbed for some time. He went over to her and brought her into his arms. In response, she pressed kiss after kiss on him, with lips that tasted salty from her tears. She raised her head and looked at him with reddened eyes.

"Darling, you must tell them where Philip is hiding. I don't want us to fall into the hands of the secret police. Can't you understand?"

"Linda, I think you've had such a scare that you can't think straight any more. What gives you the idea that I know where Philip is, or how he crossed the border?"

She wiped away her eyes with the back of her hand, and looked him square. "Are you sure?"

"Of course I am!" he replied.

She stared into his eyes, "Forgive me, darling. I feel crazy, crazy with fear of those horrible men. My God!" she burst out, "How could I say such stupid things?"

Andreas just watched her silently, in an attempt to appraise her mental state.

"Andreas, talk to me please. Forgive me; I am so sorry for what I said"

Lost in thought, he stroked her hair mechanically. "

"I suppose you were very frightened."

"Yes darling. I have never been so frightened in all my life."

Andreas's sleep that night was filled with nightmares. Every sound, every footstep outside in the corridor acted like an electric shock on his nervous system. He expected the secret police to fling open the door and storm in at any minute. At the same time doubts were forming in his mind as he asked himself again and again whether he really knew Linda. It was a relief to see the dawn of a new day. Linda got up later than he did. She did not in any way resemble the other Linda he had seen the night before. They went to the university together and immersed themselves in work.

When they returned that evening, Linda was tired and irritable. She put on her apron and went into the kitchen to prepare the evening meal. Andreas sprawled out in the lounge with his eyes closed. He was chewing over the events of the day like a ruminant. His stomach rumbled, reminding him that nothing had passed his lips the whole day. The clatter of dishes stimulated his appetite. He got up, smiling, and went into the kitchen. Immediately he noticed Linda's drawn features and he felt sure that he was somehow responsible. He put his arms round her waist tenderly and pulled her toward him.

"Sweetheart, you've been working too hard and what's worse, I've been neglecting you lately, putting you to one side. Forgive me. Come on, forget the cooking. Tonight I'll take you to dinner in a quiet little restaurant I know. You'll like it. I'll tell you how much I appreciate everything you've done for me."

"Andreas?" He closed her lips with a forefinger.

"Ssh! I don't want to hear another word. We've had another big day and I want to follow it up with a splendid evening, dedicated just to you and me."

Without further discussion, she took off her apron, went into the bathroom to freshen up. She removed the scarf that bound her hair and a blonde cascade fell around her angular face. Andreas gazed at her in wonder.

"You're so beautiful, Linda. I'm so proud to be with you."

The restaurant was unusually full, and they were lucky to get a table. The atmosphere was lively and cheerful and the smell of the food tempting. Andreas picked up the menu and, with some style ordered without giving much consideration as to cost. Linda watched him in astonishment and as soon as they were alone she asked him nervously, "Andreas, how on earth do you intend to pay for all this?"

He looked at her jovially, took a wad of notes out of his wallet and showed them to her. "Don't worry, my sweet. As you can see, I've got enough. I won't embarrass you."

"Andreas," she insisted, "where did you get that money? As far as I knew, you had nothing."

"You forget that I am a rich guy. Believe it or not, my father still deposits money in my account even though we still have had no contact since I left." He frowned, considering the irony of his so-called independence.

"Why all the questions?" he continued puzzled, with some anxiety in his voice.

Her face softened. "Darling, don't get me wrong. You know how much I worry about you and care for you."

The waiter opened the bottle and champagne fizzed in the glasses. The candle flames shimmered and danced. He drained his glass, refilled it, and tried to shrug off the unpleasant suspicions she had put into his mind. His good cheer returned. He wanted to let go, to enjoy himself, to take his mind off things and set himself free from his worries. The food was superbly cooked and delicious. The third bottle popped open cheerfully and the chilled liquid slid pleasantly down his throat. His eyes shone with excitement. Not for a long time had he felt so relaxed, and under the influence of the drink, he did not notice Linda's cold and pensive mood.

"Andreas, did you read today's paper?" she asked unexpectedly.

"No, darling, I didn't find the time yet. But come on, what's got into you today? Something's bothering you, isn't it? I told you, this evening's just for us. Let's enjoy it, let's let it all slip away for a while!"

"Andreas," she interrupted, "this is serious. The papers say our proclamations have been circulating in huge numbers in Alexandra and Soweto. Now the police are investigating to find out who distributed them. Honestly, how did they get there, Andreas?"

"I don't know, Linda," he lied blithely. "All the same, I'm glad to hear about it. I hope the whole world reads them."

"If you don't know, then who does? I'm sure none of our crowd has the courage or the effrontery to distribute them without getting arrested. There must be a third party involved, perhaps whoever it was that rang you early this morning?"

Andreas looked at her grimly. "Linda, you've got me worried. Are you interrogating me? Honestly, I do not understand you."

"Don't jump to conclusions. There's no need to be cross with me. I just feel like you don't trust me anymore. You don't share your secrets with me these days, and that upsets me. You surely can't have any reason to think like that?"

"Linda, when are you going to stop worrying about me? Trust

me; I know what I'm doing. Now calm down and let's try and enjoy the evening."

She smiled, hugged and kissed him. "Andreas, I'm amazed you can put up with me. Come on, I want to dance. Then we'll go home and I'll show you how much I want you."

Later that evening, their naked bodies joined together and passion exploded in each of them. Weariness and drink sent Andreas off to an uneasy sleep. He dreamed that he was back in Greece, searching desperately from one prison after another, trying to find Rena and set her free. After entreaties, bribes and inquiries, he learned that she had been exiled to a small, deserted island in the Aegean. Hounded by the police, he dreamed that he eventually arrived at the island. Again in frenzy, he frantically searched cell after cell in dungeon after dungeon in a bid to find her. Out of breath, he heaved open a heavy door and found himself before a half-dead woman.

"Rena," he sobbed, and ran toward her. He bent down and took her in his arms. He looked at her with tender compassion as the tears streamed down his face. She was almost unrecognizable; her face covered in bruises and swelling, her hair disheveled, and her clothes merely dirty, torn rags.

"Rena," he managed to stammer, "How did the filthy beasts manage to reduce you to this?"

She opened her weary eyes which still burned with the flame of resistance, and suddenly recognized him.

"Andreas, my darling. I knew you'd come for me. I knew you'd never forget me," she said in an exhausted whisper.

"Don't try to talk, darling. You look so worn out. Be patient. I came to take you away, far away from this terrible place. And I swear I'll never leave you again."

"No, we can't escape, Andreas. There's nowhere else to go. We have to fight on. There's no way we can let those bastards win."

Savage blows battered at the door, threatening to dislodge it from its hinges. Andreas turned toward it anxiously.

"Listen to me, Rena. We've got to get away. We've got work to do."

"You leave, darling. I'm finished. You've got to escape and carry on the fight for both of us. Go, please go! Remember me; take the spark from within me. Keep it alive!"

The door groaned and crashed wide open. Linda, dressed in military uniform, appeared on the threshold, an automatic weapon steady in her hands. She was hardly recognizable, with her hair astray and her face distorted. She smiled maliciously and without a word squeezed the trigger again and again. The noise was appalling and deafening. With horror he saw dark holes appear in Rena's body and start to ooze thick, red blood.

"Linda," he shouted in hysterical hatred, "I'll kill you!"

He woke in terror and sat up in bed, his body trembling from the realism of the dream. He looked automatically at his watch. It was three forty-five. He cocked his ears. Was someone knocking at the door?

"My God," he whispered, "what a dream!"

Sleep weighed heavy on his eyelids, and he laid his head on the pillow and sighed with relief. The insistent knocking on the door grew louder, and in the silence of the night it sounded like a fearful portent of evil. Andreas did not know what to suppose. A vague fear gripped him and he felt as if a hand was surreptitiously tugging at his guts. The door was forced open suddenly and three shadowy figures rushed in, guns in hand. One of the three intruders found the light switch and turned it on. The room flooded with light and Andreas involuntarily closed his eyes.

Someone stepped forward and broke the tense silence as he snarled, "Andreas Magdalos, I am arresting you under the anti-terrorism act."

Andreas's eyes were now wide open and he stared at the man like an idiot, paralyzed by fear. The moment he had dreaded had arrived sooner than he had expected. Linda, next to him, woke startled, drew away from him, and silently watched the drama unfold. The two other policemen began a methodical search.

"You can stop searching," Linda called to them in a firm, authoritative voice. "What you're looking for is in a brown suitcase in the wardrobe."

Her voice brought Andreas back to reality. He looked at her

with contempt, unwillingly reminded of Philip's words, "Don't trust anyone."

The policeman nearest him grabbed him roughly by the arm and jerked hard. Forewarned, Andreas fell to the floor, pulling the sheets and blankets with him. He stared around him like a trapped animal with no means of escape. All that he had heard from time to time about the violence with which they treated their victims rushed back into his memory, and he broke out in a cold sweat. In panic and shame, he gathered his clothes and hastily dressed. Linda's naked body, curvaceous and feminine, stayed nude. She made no attempt to cover herself, but instead smiled coquettishly at the policemen, who in turn stared at her lasciviously. Andreas, dressed now, regained his composure. He grabbed a blanket and threw it over her in disgust. The policeman angrily seized his arms, twisted them behind his back, and snapped on a pair of handcuffs. They shoved him toward the door.

"Come on, we're leaving," he called to the others who were still ogling Linda.

They crowded around Andreas, pushing him in front of them and into the corridor.

"You've had a good run, you son of a bitch," remarked one of the two who were holding him, his voice laden with envy, "but from now on you'll find out what's in store for you."

"What are you muttering about, Shorty?" asked the leader of the group.

"I was thinking about her body, Sergeant. Gorgeous woman, but she doesn't condescend to notice us. She'd rather have young blood like this one."

"Well, you know, ours is a thankless task, Shorty."

"She made my mouth water," commented the third, "even if I am a married man." He turned to Andreas and asked him with interest, "tell us, is she as good as she looks? Is she good in bed?"

Shorty pricked up his ears waiting for the answer, but when he saw that the prisoner was taking no notice of them, he raised his muscular arm and drove his elbow hard into Andreas's ribs.

"Listen, you piece of shit. When you're asked something, you answer immediately. We of the secret police are very sensitive fellows, and we don't like people treating us snobbishly. You understand?"

Andreas doubled over with pain. He tried to catch his breath. Shorty cackled with pleasure and gave him a malicious shove. A car was double-parked in front of the entrance and the fourth member of the squad, waiting there, hurried to open the doors for them.

"Well done, boys," he enthused, "you got that over with quickly!"

"Hard luck on you, Nick," teased Shorty, "you missed a marvelous sight, the most beautiful naked body I've ever seen in my life."

Nick looked at him in confusion and then scurried to open the door for the sergeant, who had suddenly become grim and distant. His two colleagues squeezed the prisoner between them on the back seat. Andreas, his hands handcuffed behind his back, was forced to sit down. The pain in his right side was killing him.

Nick slipped behind the wheel and set off, giving his companion a sidelong glance.

"What's the matter, Sergeant, you look very gloomy."

"You're right, Nick. Sometimes I get fed up with this job. There's no interest in it, more especially when we have to arrest useless sods like him. They're all the same; full of piss and vinegar when they're free, braying like donkeys. But, when you arrest them they swallow their tongues and go broody like a bunch of pullets. I bet if you have a look at his underpants, you'll find he's shit himself."

"You're right, Sergeant. That's just like these communist rat bags. I can't stand them."

"Hey, Sergeant, our boy here looks like he's hungry. I say we feed him a bit?" interrupted Shorty. "At least let's have some fun!"

The driver objected. "Look, Shorty, he's not black. We could find ourselves in a heap of trouble."

"Bloody good idea of yours, Shorty," agreed the sergeant. "These little communists are more sickening than the kaffirs. Put your foot down Nick," he added to the driver. "You heard us. Our boy's hungry."

"Whatever you say, Sergeant!"

The car left the side streets and drove on to the major highway, which was almost deserted. The sergeant stubbed out his cigarette and knelt on his seat, glaring maliciously at the passenger. Slowly he took his big wooden truncheon from its sheath and examined it lovingly. 'Feeding' was his specialty, as the whole force knew. Suddenly Andreas realized he was planning something vile and he looked at him in contempt. His fear had left him and he felt at peace, ready to withstand everything with dignity. The car raced like a bullet. The sergeant steadied himself on the seat with one hand while he held the truncheon in front of him with the other. The heavy club had become an extension of his arm and he aimed it precisely at Andreas's mouth.

"Ready, Nick," he shouted excitedly.

The driver suddenly slammed the brakes on. The wheels skidded on the asphalt. Andreas's helpless body was flung violently back then forward again with twice the force. His mouth smashed into the thick truncheon. The muffled sound of the blow was sickening. The wood pulverized his lips and smashed his front teeth. His mangled mouth poured out a torrent of groans, blood, saliva and bone. He crumpled into the gap between the seats. The policemen burst into laughter and cheers.

"Well done, Sergeant. I'll bet that filled him up!" cried Shorty.

He switched on the overhead light. With the help of his colleagues, he pulled Andreas's body back and sat him in his original position. His face was a mask of fright and pain. The secret police gang found his state hilarious and burst out in fresh guffaws. Nick meanwhile, skillfully brought the car back under control.

"I've made your face unrecognizable, you poofter," crowed the sergeant. "If your girlfriend could see you now, she'd run away and hide."

Andreas fixed his tear-filled eyes on the sergeant. He gathered all his strength and, ignoring the intolerable pain, spat straight into the sergeant's face, spattering it with tooth chips and blood. The laughter stopped. The sergeant howled in amazement. His eyes darkened with fury as his raw-boned fist broke the prisoner's nose. Andreas was hurled backwards again. Like a maddened bull, the sergeant went on hitting him, cursing and swearing. Finally, worn out and panting, he stopped, took his handkerchief from his pocket to wipe his face, and glared at his men. None of them dared to return his gaze.

Satisfied he gave Andreas a final punch and said, "You son of a bitch, you'll pay dearly for that. There's no way you'll leave my hands alive, I promise you."

Without a word, Nick parked in the underground, beneath John Vorster Square. Shorty, with the help of his colleagues dragged out Andreas's motionless body. Andreas's legs did not have the strength to support him, and liquid streamed from his broken nose and mouth. Blood had drenched his clothes and was now dripping from them onto the ground. The two policemen grasped him under the armpits. The sergeant had summoned a lift and they all got in. The door closed behind them. He pressed a button and they swiftly rose to the twelfth floor.

The sergeant picked up his bag and said to them sternly, "I'm going to let the captain know we've arrived. You three take the prisoner to the interrogation room and wait till we get back there."

He glanced bleakly at Andreas and added, "Shorty, if this carcass keeps on bleeding; do something to stop it."

"OK Sergeant, don't worry. I'll try."

The door slid closed and Nick pressed the button for the thirteenth floor. "Phew, I've never seen Norman so furious," he whispered, "you poor sod. You'll be giving evidence against your mother's milk before you're finished!" he added, without sympathy to Andreas.

The interrogation room was large and looked like a doctor's surgical station. Shorty, with the help of his colleagues, took off the handcuffs and forced Andreas to sit on a steel chair, to which they bound his arms and legs with leather straps. They tried to clean up his face and stop the bleeding, but without success. Andreas groaned each time they touched him; the pain tore at his brain and made him giddy and faint. Norman opened the door for the captain and followed him in respectfully.

Captain Kolradie was the pride and terror of the force. He was one of the best interrogators, tough, laid back, effective and experienced. Worst of all, he was a true believer, totally dedicated to the government and to the philosophy of apartheid. As an anti-Communist, he had forged for himself one of the most respected names in BOSS, with contacts and influence that reached very high. Austere and restrained, but friendly to his subordinates when he wanted to be, he had become a role model for the younger men. He was about forty, but his arrogant bearing and the hardness of his large features made him look much older. He strode haughtily into the interrogation room and his subordinates greeted him with uneasy, obsequious smiles. As he stood beside the prisoner, his eyes turned cold and then lit up with a blaze of anger, as he saw the bloodied face. His unnaturally big hands moved quickly, first to switch off the powerful light that was directed at Andreas, and then to make a skillful palpation of his face. Andreas opened his red and swollen eyes with relief and looked at the captain. The captain stared at him for some time, and then in a voice like a whip-crack he snapped:

"Sergeant, I want you in my office. Go and wait there. The rest of you can leave. We'll talk tomorrow."

Alone now, he lit a cigarette, took several deep puffs, then picked up the internal telephone and asked for a doctor to be sent up. He shifted a chair and sat down facing Andreas.

"Listen, Magdalos, I want to tell you a few things and I want you to think about them very carefully. I know you're in pain, but what I have to say to you is a matter of life and death for you, so try to pull yourself together. I should tell you that most times I don't approve of the way certain elements in the police force go about their business, but it's hard to keep them under control all the time. I'm a police interrogator, but I don't like violence at all. I usually persuade prisoners to cooperate with me and that spares both of us unpleasantness. As a last resort, those who refuse to be reasonable compel me to take extreme measures. I'm very good at my job. Believe me, I've never failed yet; in one way or another, I always manage to find out what I want to know. You seem to be a smart lad. You come from a good family, and I still don't understand who led you astray or how they did it. What's happened to you so far is no more than a caress, and if you can't be sensible, you'll curse the day you were born. Believe me, there is no point in suffering. Try to be sensible, because either gently or by force we'll get out of you what we want to know. Strictly speaking, I ought to let the boys carry on with you, but as I said I'm a hopeless humanitarian, and I always like to give prisoners some guidance. I'll give you some time to think about it."

Andreas felt so exhausted that he allowed his eyes to close. The door opened and a man in a white jacket came in, carrying a leather bag. The captain got up and gently tapped Andreas on the shoulder.

"I want you to think carefully about what I've said."

The doctor opened his bag and took out his stethoscope.

"Doctor, I'll be in my office. Ring me when you get the opportunity."

Norman was sitting on hot coals in Captain Kolradie's office, smoking one cigarette after the other. He could not understand what Captain Kolradie enjoyed, in his love for opera. The strident sounds of the chorus burst his eardrums, increasing his anxiety, but he did not dare switch it off. Captain Kolradie stormed into his office and stood in front of him, his huge body like a mountain.

"Sergeant, I can't put up with you any longer. I'm fed up. You've driven me to distraction with your idiocies and your crazy moods."

"Captain, he offered us resistance. He spat in my face. You can ask the boys!"

"Shut up! I know the way you work. You're nothing but a psychopath."

"Sorry, Captain, I did go a bit far, but you know how I hate whites like him. Something goes snap in my brain, and I get this heavy feeling in my chest. I just have to do something."

"You fool, were you too stupid to think what would have happened if anyone had seen you, if this story got into the newspapers? Couldn't you work out how valuable this prisoner is to us? Aren't there any blacks left for you to try out your sick obsessions? Get the hell out of my office."

The telephone shrilled as the sergeant left the office. "Yes?" the captain snapped.

"Captain, I've examined the prisoner. There's nothing seriously wrong, but he's lost a lot of blood. He has a fracture of the lower mandible and rhinal…"

"I'm not interested in your bloody medical jargon," the captain interrupted impatiently, "when can I have him back?"

There was a moment's silence on the other end of the line and then the doctor's voice resumed coldly, "I think he'll be all right in a couple of days."

"Look after him as well as you can. This character's very important to us."

He put down the phone and foaming at the mouth, burst into a stream of swearing. He calmed down enough to pour himself a drink and he increased the volume on his music. The room filled with the high-pitched voice of a female singer, singing an aria with pathos. Captain Kolradie was transformed, absorbed by the music. Tears welled in his eyes. He leaned back in his chair and listened silently.

CHAPTER 14 Repercussions

As on every morning, Matthew woke at dawn, stretched to clear the sleep from his eyelids, and with an ill grace, began to dress. He did not like waking so early, but it was a condition of his employment and he had become used to it. He dressed quickly and went down to the big house. He unlocked the garage and began his routine, dusting and polishing the car. His hands were frozen and he rubbed them together for warmth. The morning cold was sharp and the grass outside was white with morning frost. He looked at his watch; it was six-thirty. In exactly ten minutes his boss would make his appearance. He strode quickly down the long, paved passage to open the heavy iron gate and, as usual, emptied the mail box. He unfolded the morning paper carefully and from force of habit cast a quick glance over the front page.

Mr. Frixos Magdalos had eaten his frugal breakfast, and his maid helped him with his overcoat. He picked up his briefcase and opened the door that connected directly with the garage. Usually Matthew was waiting to open the door for him. Mr. Magdalos did not at all enjoy pointless delays. But Matthew was standing in the middle of the passageway, his eyes bulging out of their sockets as he stared, unable to tear them away from the paper.

"Matthew, Matthew!" He heard the boss's impatient voice. He turned, and with trembling hands he closed and folded the paper, without yet having recovered from the shock. He tried to regain his composure and shake off his fear. He needed to think logically, and find a way out of the trouble that was surely headed his way.

"Matthew," called the boss, still louder.

"Sorry to keep you waiting Baas, but I went to collect the mail," he said apologetically as he opened the door and took his place behind the wheel.

Mr. Magdalos gave him a piercing look. "What's got into you, Matthew? You look upset today."

Matthew stumbled over his words,

"Baas, my mother is very sick. I've just heard about it," he answered convincingly.

"I'm sorry to hear that, Matthew. Selina is such a good woman. What do you intend to do?"

"I honestly don't know, Baas," he replied gloomily.

"I think you should go and see her. As soon as we get to the factory, go and find Samuel and tell him to take your place, then you can leave straight away."

"Thank you Baas. You've always been very good to us."

The forecourt of the factory was full of noisy workers, who had arrived for the morning shift. Mr. Magdalos surveyed the scene. His staff worked long, hard hours and although he used to take pride in what was being achieved, none of it now touched his heart. From the time that Andreas had left home, he could derive no satisfaction from work as he used to. The thought of his beloved son's rejection saddened him, and he felt unusually alone. He really ought to be angry with him, but instead, he found himself admiring his steadfast courage. It was stupid of him, he knew it, but recently he was more of the persuasion to abandon his pride and look for Andreas.

"Tell Samuel to wait in the garage because I have a lot of appointments today. If you need any money you can call the accounts office. I want you to keep me informed about how your mother is."

The office employees began work at the later hour of eight-thirty and during the interval, Mr. Magdalos took the opportunity to open the books and assess the financial state and development of the company. Someone knocked discreetly on his office door and Mr. Magdalos raised his head in annoyance from the ledger before him. He looked at his watch; it was just eight-twenty. This was unheard of, and it irritated him because everyone knew that he requested to be left undisturbed until nine o'clock.

"Come in!" he snapped.

His private secretary stood in the doorway with the paper in her hands.

"What is it, Maria?" he inquired coolly.

"Mr. Magdalos", she stammered, "it's terrible. Haven't you read the paper yet?"

"No! What the blazes is going on? Has a war started?"

"It's the police. They've arrested Andreas under the anti-terrorism act," she wailed.

The color left his face, his mouth dropped involuntarily and his heart started to thump irregularly. He felt his whole body broke out in a cold sweat.

"What did you say, Maria?" he whispered hoarsely.

She nodded sadly.

"My God, this is what I was afraid of. It's happened sooner than I expected. Maria, give me the paper. Take these books away and cancel all my appointments. And I don't want to be disturbed by anyone. You hear me? No one!"

"Very well, Mr. Magdalos."

He lapsed into a pathetic state, reading and rereading the brief front page article with bated breath:

> *Today at dawn, members of the secret police raided the apartment of the president of the students' organization, Andreas Magdalos, and arrested him. According to the city police authorities, the aforementioned Andreas Magdalos was arrested under the anti-terrorism act. Further details will be given in the next edition.*

His private telephone rang irritatingly. Mr. Magdalos cursed its inventor. Fretting and fuming, he picked up the receiver.

"Hello,"he growled.

"Frixos, have you heard the news?" asked his wife frantically.

"Yes," he responded curtly.

"Frixos, I'll go mad, I can't stand it." His grief-stricken wife sounded shrill and hysterical.

"I don't know what to say, Lanie. I'm at my wits end."

"My God, what a disaster for us all. That irresponsible, stupid boy!" she went on, bursting into loud sobs.

His wife's lamentations shocked Mr. Magdalos into recovering his spirit. He tried to calm her down and encourage her "Keep calm, Lanie. I'll try to do what I can to get him freed. Trust me. This time, I'll get him out of the country, for better or worse."

"Our poor boy! He's suffering! Frixos, I know he is! How could this happen to our child? She went on, "Think of the disgrace. Think about our relatives and friends!"

Mr.Magdalos became furiously angry. "I don't give a damn about our relatives and friends! They can all go to hell. What concerns me is how to get our son out of this mess."

His eyes welled up; full of dark despair, tears trickled down the side of his drawn face. He put the phone down and held his head in his hands.

"What to do?" he pleaded aloud. He pressed the button of the intercom.

His secretary answered immediately. "Yes, Mr. Magdalos?"

"Maria, I want you to get me our solicitor on the phone, please."

In a few moments the lawyer was on the line.

"Frixos, I'm terribly sorry about Andreas."

"There's no time to be sorry, Stanley. There's got to be some way out. My son is white not black," he urged.

"Frixos, these affairs aren't my specialty. We'd do better to go and see your compatriot, the barrister George Bakos. He may have some advice to give us."

"You're right, Stanley. From what I've heard, he's the best in these political cases."

"Wait in your office, Frixos, and I'll try to get in touch with him. As soon as he has the opportunity to see us, I'll come and get you."

"Thanks, Stanley. I'll wait to hear from you."

Later that morning, Mr. Magdalos and his lawyer crossed the busy central thoroughfare that led to the courthouse. Mr. Magdalos was so impatient that he could not wait for the elevator. Instead, he took the staircase at a run. His lawyer followed in tow, puffing and panting up the marble steps.

George Bakos's office was on the fourth floor. Bakos greeted them without ceremony and asked them to sit down. He was a heavily built man, of few words. Magdalos summed him up doubtfully.

"Mr. Magdalos," he said in his stern bass voice, "I'm sincerely sorry for your son, as I am for anyone who falls into the merciless hands of the secret police. I must tell you plainly, that at this moment we have nothing to offer your unfortunate boy. The only thing we can do, is to petition for a regular trial. I'll put a request to the court but, as has happened to me so often in the past, the request will probably end up in their waste paper basket."

"But that's unheard of!" stammered Magdalos. "Surely there's some other way? My son's not some ordinary black!"

"Your son's no ordinary man, Mr. Magdalos. He's a young man who's had the guts to contradict them. BOSS doesn't forgive that."

"Mr. Bakos," shouted Magdalos angrily, "I too have a great deal of power. I have close ties with many ministers. They always ask for my financial support at election time. I'm sure they'll help me now."

Bakos looked at him frostily. "You'd do well to go to them, Mr. Magdalos, rather than to me. But first ask yourself whether these friends of yours are not the very people who profit most from the BOSS?"

* * *

Matthew had left the factory as fast as he could, after first making a quick phone call. He went home, hastily threw a few clothes in a suitcase, and said farewell to the rest of the staff, telling them that he was off to see his sick mother. Only when he found himself in the city, crowded with people, did he feel a degree safer. He knew he had been panicking and tried to compose himself. He wondered whether he was acting wisely in leaving, or whether it was just his fear that was driving him to run. As he walked he realized that he had no other course. Naturally, everything depended on the resistance of the hapless Andreas. As soon as he gave way to psychological terror and the pain of torture, he would talk, and then the security people would come. Nothing could be more certain.

How long, then, could Andreas resist? Matthew cursed himself again for the lightheartedness with which he had twice now agreed to play Andreas's stupid, childish game. The road to Soweto seemed endless, and fear gnawed at his guts. Would he be able to hide before they started the hunt for him? Kerosene and charcoal smoke was burning his eyes, and he gazed absentmindedly at the ragged children who were playing on the dirt road. He arrived without mishap at Dube, a suburb inhabited by a few privileged blacks who, by their wits or by considerable effort had managed to become moderately successful. The owners of these houses had built them with their own money, on land that did not belong to them. Of course, the law forbad African people from buying land. Matthew paused, looked around, and when he was sure that no one was taking any notice of him, he crossed a well-kept garden and knocked on the door of a modern house. A woman of about thirty-five, clad in a multi-colored blanket, opened the door and let him in.

"Good morning, Matthew. You're late and we were getting very worried about you."

"Good morning, Sylvia. I'm still OK. Sorry I'm late. Is Doctor home?"

"Yes, he's waiting for you in the kitchen."

Matthew, who was familiar with the house, went ahead confidently, crossed the corridor and walked into the spacious kitchen. Doctor Erickson was seated comfortably in a large armchair, sipping at a large cup of coffee. When he saw Matthew he jumped to his feet and embraced him warmly.

"Glad to see you, Matthew. Sit down and tell me what's going on. I've been on tenterhooks ever since you rang."

Matthew looked at Doctor's ample features with love and respect. Despite his fifty years, his youthful stance spoke of a young man's energy. He sat down next to him and recounted the whole story of Andreas's unexpected arrest. Doctor Erickson listened to him in silence until he had finished.

"Matthew, it's a bit late to ask you to explain why you helped Andreas before letting us know. Inwardly, I know that whatever you've done, you did because you thought it would further our cause and I don't blame you for that. The curious thing is that, strange as it may seem to you, we would not have said no. On the contrary, we'd probably have asked more of you. That boy has proven himself a real fighter, and people like him are indispensable to our struggle.

Matthew, I can understand your fears. They're our fears too, but despite all that, they don't help us. We've got to think logically and calmly about whether we should take it for granted that Andreas will break. If he does, then you surely will be arrested. Then, if you in turn can't stand the torture, it'll be catastrophic because a whole string of our agents will follow you into the security service dungeons. The work of years will be lost. Naturally, that's the last thing we want to happen. Then again, suppose we were able to get you out of the country today, and Andreas doesn't talk. We'd have made a big mistake, and it would be impossible for you to come back and explain your disappearance. There is, of course, an alternative. We can hide you here temporarily, until the storm blows over. That way, if Andreas breaks, we'll still have a chance get you out of the country, where you can join the rest of our exiled freedom fighters. Hopefully, he doesn't talk. His loyalty to you is evident. Then, after a time, you can go back to your job. More so, you can continue the struggle here. You know how important you are to us."

"Doctor, I think you're forgetting something very important," Matthew interrupted. "Andreas's imprisonment could last three or four months. If I stay hidden for as long as that, it'll be equally difficult to explain my disappearance. As you'll understand, my mother's illness can't be extended indefinitely."

Doctor Erickson shook his head. "I don't agree with you. From my own experience, and from what others have told me, the first weeks are the most difficult. If the prisoner can withstand the tortures of the first few weeks, he's not likely to break later. After a time, they get used to the fear, and even the pain. Hatred and the need for revenge take root in them. These feelings help to steel their resolve. The torturers know this very well. That's why they hurry to get confessions. If he survives, we won't have to worry after the first few weeks."

"I guess you may be right, Doctor. I sure hope so," said Matthew thoughtfully.

"Right, then give me a hand to shift the table. The cellar you helped dig is going to come in useful now."

Matthew lit a kerosene lamp, and the pale flame lit up his spacious hiding place. The cellar was complete with two beds, a heap of prohibited books, and a little table. He calculated the months of hard work they had put in, to dig it out.

"I'll have to go now, Matthew. I'm already late, and they're waiting for me at the hospital. I'll see you early this evening when I've finished." He smiled encouragingly.

"Don't worry about me, I won't be bored. The only thing is, I'll have to read all these books. Ironic that finally, I have all the time in the world to read."

The trapdoor closed gently and Matthew heard the scrapes of the table, as it was pulled back into place. He chose a book, Che Guevara's handbook on resistance fighting. He lay on the bed to read, but his thoughts kept wandering back to Andreas. He felt almost ashamed that he hadn't shown him much trust.

"Courage, brother, courage. I hope you'll emerge victorious from your Golgotha," he murmured as if in prayer.

* * *

Captain Kolradie was listening attentively to Linda's report.

"Well done," he said finally, "you've done a good job. But you'll have to go on. Once and for all, I want to wipe out every communist element in the university."

"Captain, you must surely know that WITS University hasn't created any problems for us in quite a while. The panic that took hold of them in reaction to the news of Andreas's arrest defies description. Besides, in my opinion, there is at the moment, no leader with any spirit to carry on."

"I hope that you're right, Linda, but I repeat that I want you to keep me informed about what's going on. OK, you can go now."

"Captain, haven't you got anything for me?" she asked beseechingly, using all of her generous feminine charm.

With evident displeasure, the captain opened a drawer, took out a small packet and threw it to her. She caught it in mid-air and pressed it longingly to her nose.

"Thank you, Captain; you treat me so well."

She pushed the packet into her handbag and got up. "Goodbye, and don't worry. I'll keep you informed about what's happening, as before."

His nostrils were full of her provocative scent. He liked this woman and desired her, but he lived by a strict rule never to mix business with pleasure. He opened the window and the chill night air washed over him. He breathed in slowly. When he had no interrogation to perform, the captain felt bored and lonely. In a foul mood, he took out a bottle of brandy, poured a generous helping into his glass. He swallowed it at a gulp. He picked up the phone and asked to be connected with the clinic.

"I want to speak to the doctor," he said abruptly.

The nurse who answered the phone recognized his voice. With the revulsion, fear and respect accorded to everyone in John Vorster Square, she called the doctor.

"How's our patient, doctor?" he asked with disinterest.

"Remarkably well. As I told you, he'll be at your disposal tomorrow."

"All right, I'll send for him tomorrow."

He refilled his glass, picked up Andreas's suitcase and emptied it onto his desk. He began a monotonous and detailed examination, writing down all the items he would use as evidence in his indictment. Most of the items consisted of forbidden books with communist content. He had seen so many of them during his lengthy career, that they no longer made any impression on him. In an envelope, he found a batch of manuscripts among which he discovered the original of the latest proclamation. He continued his search with undiminished interest, and from a small leather bag he pulled out a bundle of photographs and letters. At last, he produced a hard-bound exercise book on the cover of which was written: Personal Diary of Andreas Magdalos.

"Ah, ha!" he exclaimed with unrestrained enthusiasm. His eyes lit up with expectation. His look of triumph soon turned to disappointment. The diary was written in a foreign language. He drank another mouthful from his glass.

"Sergeant!" he called.

The connecting door opened almost immediately, and the sergeant entered smartly.

"Norman, take this diary to the interpretation department. Tell them I want it translated word for word and as quickly as possible. Understand?"

"Certainly, Captain."

He emptied the rest of his glass; feeling pleased.

"Norman, have you anything to do this evening?"

"No, Captain" the sergeant replied hastily, looking at him expectantly, since he knew this was an invitation. After an uncomfortable pause, the sergeant continued

"Captain, I've discovered a superb little model. What say we whoop it up a bit tonight?"

"Not a bad idea, Norman. Where?"

"At my place, in a couple of hours."

Norman's farmhouse was well out of the way. They would take out the day's frustration on the black girl Norman had already eyed. Norman knew how to pick them.

"OK, I'll see you there, you pick her up. And Norman, try not to be late."

He went back to his armchair with a smile and lit a cigarette. He deserved a reward. This time he had caught a big fish; he was sure. He had a nose for such things.

* * *

Andreas woke feeling better. He even felt grateful for yesterday's painful experience, and the hospital stay it had granted him. The BOSS butchers had given him time to think, to prepare psychologically. He knew he had to get used to the idea that he was now in their hands. He was single-mindedly determined about one thing though, he would not break; he did not want to give them the pleasure of an easy victory. He knew they would stop at nothing, that these people knew no bounds. He would have to surpass himself; since there was no way he would let them turn him into a frightened, psychological wreck. But the thought of such men brought shivers to his spine, and his sensitive nature could not accept that there was such medieval barbarity among human beings in the twentieth century. In particular, the honeyed politeness of the captain scared him and filled him with disgust. During their short encounter, he had been able to discern the temporary disguise. Under the lamb's skin lurked an unhesitatingly bloodthirsty wolf. But why were they taking their time? The waiting was worse than the reality, but Andreas was determined to be ready for them.

Their footsteps sounded hollow and menacing in the clinic. The moment had come. Andreas recognized Sergeant and Shorty. He got up and even dared to smile at them.

"Here you are, boys! You're late and I was getting worried. Where are the others? Or are you going to manage it on your own?" he asked them facetiously.

"Sergeant, the corpse has come to life! Cheer up, he's pulling our legs!"

"I hope he'll keep it up, Shorty. I hope he'll provide us with a bit of interest."

They led the way, and Andreas followed them obediently, aware that there was no way of escape.

The interrogation began by seating him in the same metal chair and tying him up. Shorty arranged the spotlight and Andreas's deformed face was bathed once more in light. It was a peculiar pale yellow light, gentle at first, but after a little while it pierced even his closed eyelids. It seemed to grow stronger in his mind, and grated on his nerves. Andreas made a brief, urgent prayer, before repeating passionately, again and again his internal mantra:

"I will resist! I will resist!!"

The interrogation room door opened softly and Captain Kolradie came in, genial and animated. He nodded to his men and stood in front of the prisoner. His huge body blocked out the light, and Andreas opened his eyes and looked directly at the captain. Andreas did his best to hide his fear. The captain wore a wreath of smiles.

"Magdalos, I can see from your attitude that you haven't taken my advice seriously. I can see quite clearly in your eyes the steadfastness of the hero. I think it's probably unnecessary, but I'll tell you anyway; no hero has ever escaped from here! I have to admit that once or twice we've had a hero or two here, but none of them has ever left here alive to boast about it."

The smile had left his face, which now become as hard as granite.

"I hope I've made myself clear. I'll make you a proposal for the last time. If you answer what I want to know and co-operate with us, I'll give you my word that in a few hours you'll be free and back home again. If you want to play the hero, you'll curse the hour and the moment you were born. That said, I want to draw your attention to the way I work. Every time I put a question to prisoners, I expect an answer. But if they don't answer, or they tell me lies, I turn into a wild animal. I'll leave you to think about that for a while, and I hope you'll see sense."

Andreas had no doubts at all, about the genuineness of what he had heard. There was no bluff in it, just the naked truth. With the cleverness of experience, the interrogator had planted the psychological seed of fear and doubt, which had quickly started to germinate in Andreas's mind. The captain's words echoed grimly and mournfully in his ears. He took a deep breath, "God help me," he pleaded.

"Be brave," he muttered to himself, "fear is the poison of the mind. You don't have to give in. Better an honorable death, than a future full of shame. You can resist!"

"Shorty, fix us three black coffees, and let's have a game of darts. We've all the time in the world. We still have the day and the night is long," called the captain.

Shorty quickly made the coffees and put them on the table. The captain opened a cupboard, took out a bottle of brandy and poured a liberal measure into each glass.

"The darts are ready, Captain," called Norman, "we can start."

The captain switched on his tape recorder and his beloved opera music reverberated in the large room. He weighed a dart in the palm of his hand, took his stance, concentrated and with his forefingers threw one at the board. He smiled in satisfaction. Norman took a few swigs and wrote down the score. Time passed slowly and the dull, monotonous plop, plop, plop of the darts as well as the raucous strains of music sounded hollow and irritating in Andreas's ears. Norman uncorked the bottle and filled the empty glasses. One game followed another and the contents of the bottle were getting steadily lower.

Andreas's face was flushed; his eyes were swollen and full of pus. The way he was tied restricted his circulation, and he felt as though a thousand ants were crawling over his body. He was thirsty, but no one paid him any attention. His head was aching and the light shone like the devil's eye. The plop, plop, of the darts, the screeching wail of the singer, and the imaginary infestation of ants, all worked together threatening to drive him crazy. When the bottle was empty, the game lost interest and they gathered the darts and put them back in their box. The captain yawned and lit a cigarette. The brandy had made him drowsy. He yawned again and stretched his arms to waken himself up. He went up to the prisoner, glanced at him. He looked pleased. He lit another cigarette and stuck it in Andreas's mouth.

"Perhaps you'd like a drink before we start?" he asked.

"Yes, please."

He drank the water greedily, all the while trying to keep his eyes open.

The captain took a few more draws at his cigarette, then asked him quietly: "Do you want to co-operate with us?"

"No!" said Andreas firmly.

"Very well. To tell you the truth, I don't like traitors. What's your name?"

"Andreas Magdalos."

"How long have you been a member of the ANC, the African National Congress?"

"I've never been a member," answered Andreas resolutely.

"Where and when were you trained?"

"If you mean military training, I've never had any."

"Who sent you here from Greece, and what is your mission?"

"No one. I came back of my own accord. My mission was to come home to my family and my native land."

"If that was the reason, why have you betrayed your native land?"

"You're wrong. I love my country very much and I've never betrayed it. I simply don't agree with the way it's being governed. You're the ones who are endangering our country and unless you make a radical change to bridge the chasm of hatred you've created, it will lead inevitably to revolution."

"You've got the cheek of the devil, Magdalos. You're quite an orator. Is that what you've been teaching the blacks? Listen, boys," he added jokingly to his helpers, "he talks so nicely that if we let him go on, he'll change our ideas for sure."

"Captain, this little boy's far too smart. We don't need politeness and beating about the bush. Leave him to me for a while and I'll make him swallow his tongue," answered Norman.

"Norman, I'm trying to avoid giving you the opportunity to play your part, but I think you're right. He leaves us no other course."

He turned back to Andreas and asked, "Do you know a Philip Wells?"

"Of course. He's a friend of mine."

"Do you know where he is now?"

"No, I haven't seen him for several weeks.

"You're a liar, Magdalos. You and your comrades got him out of the country! Tell me, Magdalos, do you know what this paper is?" he asked, shoving one of the proclamations in front of Andreas.

"Yes, it's the proclamation we had printed for Republic Day."

"Who wrote it?

"I did."

"Tell me now, how did these proclamations get into the ghettoes?"

"I don't know," asserted Andreas.

"You're telling lies, lots of lies. But never mind, I'll hide my impatience," he said, smiling ironically.

"He's playing with me like a cat with a mouse," thought Andreas.

"Who paid you and where did the money come from?"

"No one. I've never accepted money from anywhere."

"Tell me, Magdalos, you are a rich man. What made you turn against your country?"

"Human feelings and a sense of pity for the oppressed people whom the damnable establishment you represent has treated worse than animals."

The captain's eyes flashed with anger, but he restrained himself.

"So you're a communist, then?"

"If you call common humanity, communism, then yes, I am!"

The captain's fist lashed out and punched Andreas hard in the face. His head jerked back and a stream of blood started to trickle from his nose. Shorty took a piece of cotton wool, wet it, and pushed it into his nostril.

"Magdalos, we've finished playing games. You'd better realize you're as good as dead," roared the captain. "How did Philip Wells get out of the country?" he asked again.

Andreas looked at him in contempt. The captain shook the ash from his cigarette, observed the red glow for a moment, then jammed the lighted cigarette on Andreas's arm and held it there firmly. Andreas reeled as the room filled with the smell of burnt flesh. Andreas screamed in agony, his bloodshot eyes filled with tears, and his fingers turned white as they gripped the arms of the chair. Without expression, the captain took the cigarette away and gazed at the deep, red-black wound. He grabbed Andreas's hair, in his huge fist and pulled it hard. With a look of disgust, the captain wiped the tuft of Andreas's hair from his palm.

"Heroics aren't an easy thing, as you can see. Well, now, where were we? Ah yes, who organized Philip's escape?"

"I don't know," answered Andreas stubbornly.

The cigarette made another orbit and implanted itself a few inches away from the first burn.

"I told you, you bastard, I'm not playing games. I'll break your bones one by one; I'll kill you if you don't tell me what I want to know."

The cigarette came down again and again on Andreas's body, with the horrible sound of fire meeting flesh.

"Talk, you son of a bitch! Talk!"

Andreas gritted his teeth frantically to restrain himself. The burns were abominably painful, his eyes streamed; but his interior voice called to him imperatively: You can resist!

The cigarette had almost burnt down to the filter and the captain dropped it on the floor and crushed it with his heel. He looked at the prisoner's stubborn face and became enraged.

"Shorty, get the beater," he ordered.

Norman pressed a button, and the chair collapsed into a horizontal position. The captain nodded. Shorty started skillfully beating Andreas's bare soles, laying on one stroke after another. It took some time for the results of the 'phalange' to be felt. At first, Andreas's feet grew numb and swelled up. After a few seconds, an unbearably sharp pain reached his brain. Andreas choked, his mouth stretched wide open in agony, his eyes bulged from their sockets, and a cold sweat drenched his body. His screams of pain filled the well-insulated room. Shorty continued the methodical beating, his pale skin flushed to the color of singed raw meat. The captain's face had assumed a diabolical expression as he bent over Andreas.

"Are you ready to talk now, you shit?"

Andreas did not hear him. Bells, gongs and cymbals were clanging too loudly in his ears. The light of the spotlight had unexpectedly become multicolored and attractive. Unseen hands were dragging him down into a dark, distant world.

"Stop, Shorty," snapped the captain angrily, "the bastard's fainted."

"Shall I wake him up, Captain?" asked Norman.

"No, that'll do for today. He's had his first lesson. That'll give him something to think about. In any case, we don't want to exhaust him. He knows a lot and we need him. Lock him up."

Without further discussion, the two assistants dragged the unconscious man by the armpits into a nearby cell, and left him on the concrete floor. Norman turned the heavy key with a scraping noise.

The first rays of the sun made their appearance. Night gave way to the light and the stars went out. Captain Kolradie went back to his office and looked at his watch. It was close to six.

"He's a hard nut" he said to himself, "but I'll crack him like all the others."

CHAPTER 15 Enduring Torture

Andreas recovered consciousness. He was still in the same position in which they had left him. His head buzzed as though a whole beehive was trapped in it. His breathing was rapid and shallow and his heart-beat was irregular. As the haze in his head began to dissipate, he became aware that his body was freezing. He quivered uncontrollably causing his teeth to chatter as his jaws rattled against each other. He tried to figure how long he had been lying there, but he could not. He groaned in despair. In the half light of the cell, he could just make out a bed adorned with bedclothes. It was so inviting that his sense of self-preservation was powerfully aroused. He gathered all his strength and crawled like a worm toward it. It was impossible to walk, and both his legs and feet were numb from the beatings. Sweat poured from his body and his watery eyes distended with pain as he stared hopefully at the bed. He finally reached it and managed after a few feeble attempts to clamber up onto it. He covered himself in the provided blanket and soon started to feel a little warmer. Exhausted, he fell into deep unconsciousness. The noisy and violent opening of the door woke him. He shot up like a hunted deer, his whole body trembling with fear.

"Not again, please," he stammered feeling at his lowest point, "not again!"

An unknown man came in without looking at him, left a plate of food and went out without a word, locking the door behind him. A sigh of relief escaped Andreas's lips. If Captain Kolradie had chanced to come into the cell instead of the unknown warder, Andreas was sure he would have told him everything. The thought made him ashamed and he covered his face with his hands and burst into a bout of poignant weeping. The sobbing racked his tortured body, but he was powerless to curb it. Strangely, the weeping fit actually gave him some relief; his brain cleared and began to work again. As if in a vision, the faces of his torturers appeared before his eyes mouthing hideous sounds. He clenched his fists; his agonized body recoiled as his whole being filled with anger and hatred. His interior voice came alive and resounded agonizingly in his head:

"Don't blame yourself for wilting in a moment of weakness. It's natural to be afraid. You should feel proud instead. You stood firm. You beat them. The first, difficult round is over and you were the victor. You faced them four-square and taught them a good lesson. No whips or other tortures can hold back freedom. Don't let them corrupt your spirit! You are strong, Andreas, you can grind them down! You can!"

They came that same evening, took him away upright and brought him back unconscious. The days passed filled with pain and suffering. Nothing further interested Andreas except that he had to stand firm and die on his feet. He now welcomed death. When the torture went too far, they would leave him alone for several days. The doctor would come to see him, tend his wounds, and then they would come again.

On occasion, the captain was in a good mood and went into his workshop, as he liked to call it. He approached his prisoner and studied him with interest, smiling inanely.

"I've been feeling sorry for you. I've missed you all this time." Andreas stared at him with hate.

"Well, have you decided to talk?"

"I know nothing about what you keep asking me," he replied calmly.

"One of these days I'll lose my patience and throw you out of the window."

"Like you did with Ahmet Timol?"

The captain stood for several moments thunderstruck at Andreas's courage and impudence. But he soon recovered and his fist shot out and smashed hard into the prisoner's face.

"You son of a bitch, I'll teach you to play the smart arse with me!"

He went on punching him mercilessly in the face, chest, belly and genitals. The sight of blood had turned him into a raging bull, and he continued punching as hard as he could without even looking at the result. Andreas collapsed, screaming with pain. The captain stopped, grabbed a large cloth, soaked it in water and stuffed into Andreas's bloodied mouth. Andreas's bound legs started to kick spasmodically, his fists opened and his features showed his state of extremity. The captain tore the cloth from Andreas's face, which had turned black from lack of oxygen. He watched without expression; the cloth, a constant threat in his hand. Each time the prisoner seemed to get a good breath, back in went the cloth. This dreadful game went on for some time.

"Now tell me the names of your accomplices, you bastard. You won't talk, eh? Shorty, bring a hot egg."

Norman grabbed Andreas and turned him on his side. He took a pair of scissors and cut the clothes away from his armpit. Shorty was holding a steaming hot egg with a pair of tongs and carefully placed it in the hollow of Andreas's armpit. Norman seized Andreas's arm firmly and pressed it against his ribs. Andreas howled. The pain was unbearable. His broken body twitched nightmarishly. His voice had lost any resemblance to a human, but his torturers went on mercilessly.

"Will you talk now, you fucking bastard?"

Andreas bit hard on his upper lip.

"Shorty, bring another egg for the other armpit."

Andreas could not withstand the ordeal. Everything around him was dancing crazily. Darkness descended as he lost consciousness. Captain Kolradie went back to his office in a fury. He had never expected such resistance from this boy. He washed his bloody hands, filled a glass of brandy and downed it. Frustrated, he switched on his record player. The strong spirit, accompanied by music, always relaxed him.

"You're a hard nut all right, but I'll crack you, or else you'll leave here completely useless. That I promise you." And he raised his glass to seal his promise. He filled it again, picked up the telephone and asked to be connected with the translation unit.

"Special Translation Unit."

"I want to talk to Sergeant van Vuuren," the captain announced loudly. "Is that van Vuuren?"

"It is. Who's speaking?"

"Captain Kolradie."

"Hello, Captain. How are you?"

"To hell with me! Tell me what's going on with that diary I sent you."

"It's progressing; Captain, but we have a lot of work. You'll have to wait."

"To hell with your work," he interrupted. "I need that diary fast, van Vuuren. It's extremely important. Drop everything else you're doing and just concentrate on that. Understood?"

"Very well, Captain," the sergeant answered numbly.

Kolradie put down the phone, finished his drink and put on his overcoat. The boy could wait till tomorrow.

Back in his cell, Andreas was soon restored to consciousness by the unbearable pains that attacked him from every part of his body. Sleep had deserted him in this pitiful condition, and it never returned to relieve him or grant him a little peace. Thoughts, more thoughts, fleeting visions of the past, came and went in his clouded brain allowing him to escape for a moment from the tragedy of his reality. Then the pain would return even more acutely, and bring him back to his present truth. As time passed, he would awake in fits wrought with laughter. Perhaps this was the onset of madness. The pain did not diminish but rather somehow transformed. In his delirium, the whole scene became funny to him and through his crazed laughter he muttered;

"No, I am not afraid of them, they are harmless. Besides, I love the way they make me laugh."

The two henchmen came to get him again. He had no strength to resist, but he looked at them with sorrow and pity, for he had learned that these special interrogators had no feelings. They were human robots, chosen and thoroughly trained by the system. For them a traitor was a parasite, and you stamped on them without mercy. They only had one ambition, to make the prisoner talk, and the quicker the better. They were cunning, their inventive game had no rules; it was furious, heartless and without a hint of mercy. The pitiful screams of the parasites gave them pleasure, strengthened them, and sounded as music to their ears.

When the captain saw the state Andreas was in, he changed his tactics. He put violence aside for the time being and switched to psychological warfare, which he knew could prove equally painful and fruitful. He did not leave Andreas in peace for a minute; day and night he was nearby. Frequently they would pull him, half asleep, like a dog into the workshop. They stood him upright, bound him hand and foot with chains and forced him to remain standing for hours. Other times they would lay him down in an armchair and keep him awake for whole nights; whenever his weary eyelids drooped, they would drench him with freezing cold water and keep him awake with threats of further torture. On yet other occasions, they would fit a nylon bag over his head and squirt water over it from a hose. The plastic would stick to his mouth and nostrils, and Andreas would quiver like a fish from lack of oxygen. Over and over again, they would revive him just to put the bag back on. Their ingenuity knew no limits; the tradition of the middle ages was carried on in the name of civilization. And all these ruses were accompanied by the same continuous, insistent questioning.

"How long have you been a member of the ANC?"

"Who is your leader here?"

"How many members do you know?"

"Is the Dean of the Anglican cathedral a member of the ANC?"

"How does the money get here, and where does it come from?"

On the last occasion they used the bag, Andreas could hold out no longer. Something snapped in his brain and again all seemed like a joke, so absurd that he broke out into peals of nervous laughter. He laughed and laughed and his body shook with spasms; his eyes had turned glassy and ran continuously; his face contorted into a hideous grimace. He looked at these human fleas, the pawns of totalitarianism and he laughed and laughed.

The torturers were worried, debilitated. They stood and stared at him speechlessly. His crazy, hysterical laughter frightened them. Norman rushed at him and punched him in the mouth where he lay.

"Shut up, you fucking bastard! Shut up or I'll shut your mouth for good!"

The captain regained his self-control, stopped Norman and ordered him to take Andreas to his cell.He sent in the doctor who gave the prisoner a sedative. After his fit, Andreas was transferred to another cell which, as he was later to learn, was an isolation cell.

He found himself in total darkness and silence for endless hours. Never before had he felt so keenly the need for the company of another human being, for communication. He craved a friendly hand, a comforting word, a ray of sunlight, a breath of air, a smile, a friendly voice, the tic-tac of a clock, or even the sound of the captain's music. He talked to himself aloud and his voice sounded alien to his ears. He knew that the deathly silence, the complete insulation was making him mad. He shouted and wailed to prove to himself that he was still alive and that his senses were working properly. Time stood still as he marched up and down within the narrow confines of his cell like a puppet. He tried to dream up ways of occupying his mind so as not to go insane. He fell into reveries and philosophical thoughts. He calculated the size of all the armies of innocent people who had passed through here before him and all the armies of those who would follow him. Grief choked him and his emotions were torn to shreds by the anguish of such thoughts.

At some point, Andreas wiped his sweating face with the back of his hand. He had a high fever and his bowels were on fire. The insecurity of waiting was driving him mad. He never knew what their next step would be. He trembled with shivers; he was hungry; he was all alone. The cell door opened and Andreas jumped up expectantly. A guard with a rubber hose in his hand came in. Without a word he turned the faucet and a stream of high pressure water gushed out and drenched him. Before he was properly aware of what was happening, the door closed as silently as it had opened. It was a new ordeal that was repeated many times, night and day, at irregular intervals. Every time the door opened, Andreas jumped up and tried to find some way of protecting himself from the cold deluge, but there was no escape. Each time, wet and shivering, he would tell himself through clenched teeth,

"I can resist. The bastards won't get me down!"

Captain Kolradie, disgusted and disillusioned, angrily threw the translation of Andreas's diary onto his desk, cursing and swearing.

It was all about thoughts, ideals, and philosophy; and his personal affairs. His eyes gleamed dementedly. He had built so many hopes on the translation of the diary and now he saw all his hopes crumbling into a heap of ashes.

"I should have realized," he muttered, "That bastard's too smart, too well trained. He'd never leave written evidence lying about." Frowning with worry, he lit a cigarette and tried to think what his next step should be. He knew time was getting away from him. His grandiose ego could never accept defeat. Moreover, for the first time he had been under pressure from the ministry. They now demanded daily reports and information about the condition of the suspect and the conduct of the interrogation. On the other side, the opposition newspapers, those communist shit-sheets were publishing stories about Andreas's work and personality. They openly expressed concern about his safety, stirring up public opinion at home and abroad. His family must have some powerful friends.

"Damn it all," he growled, "they're tying my hands. But I'll go on. I don't give a damn for anyone. I'm sure he's a danger to the security of the state. He knows a hell of a lot and he's got to talk!"

Andreas had become a small bundle, wrapped in blankets lying on the end of his bed in his isolation cell; his whole body shivering. Shorty, cheerful as ever, came in and stood over him. He looked at him without pity, silently comparing him with the carefree student they had arrested a few weeks ago. He smiled with pleasure.

"You've had enough rest. Come on, get ready. The team's waiting for you."

The sergeant appeared in the doorway.

"Need any help, Shorty?"

"No, Norman. Our young hero's fine. We're on the way."

Andreas gathered all his strength and tried to follow them with dignity. The captain was enthroned in his chair waiting for them. Norman stood to attention in front of him, awaiting instructions.

"Undress him and lay him down on the bed," the captain ordered.

The two assistant moved quickly and tore all his clothes off. Andreas felt even more helpless and undignified; instinctively he tried to cover his genitals with his hands. The sergeant grabbed him roughly and threw him on to the low, wooden bed, to which he tied him with stout leather straps. The captain watched the procedure with a fierce and watchful eye, and when they had finished he stood up and went over to the prisoner.

"Our battle is nearly over. We've reached the last round. As a man I want to tell you you've stood firm, like a rock, and I congratulate you. I'd rather have you as an ally than an enemy, but you're a danger to the state and to everything I believe in. What I do, I do for love and security of my country. We don't need traitors, fucking Greeks like you and Tsafendas. Your diary shows that you obviously admire him. Ungrateful shits. We bring you to this country so you can reap all its benefits and this is how you repay us! I'm giving you your last chance to talk and co-operate with us. If you refuse, you'd better know that you'll either die, or leave here a vegetable."

Andreas wanted to tell him all the things he had been thinking about, but did not have the strength. Wearily he closed his eyes.

"Norman, he's all yours," said the captain colorlessly.

The sergeant squeezed the small tube he was holding and a thick ointment like Vaseline came out of it. Expertly, he picked out the parts of Andreas's lower extremities and smeared them with the substance. Shorty had brought a trolley laden with equipment and wheeled it up next to him. He took a thick rubber spatula and thrust it roughly into the mouth of the helpless prisoner, telling him to bite down on it. Norman attached electrodes to the greased patches, and cast a fleeting glance at the captain who nodded decisively. Norman flicked the switch. Andreas's tormented body twitched wildly as his teeth bit down savagely on the rubber. Froth was forming and sliding out the side of his mouth. The torturer, unmoved by the horrifying sight, turned off the switch.

"Will you talk now, you fucking Greek? Talk, you son of a bitch! Talk or I'll burn your balls off!"

Andreas just screamed. He was overwhelmed by the unbearable pain. The sergeant, infuriated by his failure, quickly smeared more ointment on his victim's testicles, which had shrunk to two wrinkled pellets. He flicked the switch again. Andreas's pathetic body arched and stretched like a bow-string. His face was distorted by the incessant clenching of his jaws, and saliva trickled from the sides of his compressed lips. His breath whistled in bursts, his eyes rolled into the back of head as he collapsed completely.

"Stop, Norman! Stop! You'll kill him," the captain roared in fury. Anxiously, he tried to find his pulse.

"Quick, Shorty, call the doctor." He pressed down hard on Andreas's heart with the palms of his hands to try to make it work again.

The doctor arrived immediately holding a syringe with a long needle and without hesitation injected it into Andreas's heart. The bell for the last round had sounded.

The captain returned to his office. It was one of the few times he had been beaten. With a frown, Captain Kolradie grimly reread the urgent letter he had just received from Pretoria. It was from the Minister of Justice himself, the powerful and important Kruger. In a few brief words, it demanded that he either release Andreas Magdalos or bring him up for trial. The ninety days without trial, allowed under the anti-terrorism law, had expired and the Minister could no longer resist the pressure from public and press. The Minister's letter added that since Kolradie had not collected enough evidence to justify Magdalos's arrest, he would have to be let go. He reminded the captain that he was not dealing with some ordinary man, but with the son of a very influential and wealthy family who were staunch supporters of the National party.

"Fuck them! Fuck them all, they've tied my hands again," exclaimed the captain angrily, "they won't let me do my job."

He took a deep breath and tried to suppress the deep fury he felt. Then he calmed down and tried to look at the situation pragmatically.

"Damn it all, the bloody bastard's guilty, but I'll be the laughing stock of all the lawyers if I bring him to court without his confession. I haven't even got any written proof. Oh well, I'll have to obey orders; I haven't any other choice. We'll have to let him go!"

The office door opened and the sergeant came in.

"What is it, Norman?"

"Captain, Magdalos is out of danger. The doctor's positive."

The captain sighed with relief. "Lucky not to have a corpse on my hands," he thought to himself.

"Norman, tell Shorty to bring Magdalos here immediately."

The sergeant gave his superior a puzzled look, but hurried off without comment to carry out his orders.

Andreas felt weak and completely exhausted. Often he had thought that he had reached his end. His tenacity had been maintained by a spirit of revenge, hatred and a determination to wage merciless war against the pillars of apartheid.

"I've just got to get out of here alive," he told himself again and again.

Shorty brought Andreas his clothes and told him to get dressed. Andreas's mouth was dry with fear, his imagination ran riot, anticipating whatever torture was to come next. He tried to control himself and get up, but he collapsed on the soaking wet blankets, groaning. They had deprived him of every ounce of his strength.

"Bloody hell, you bastard, move! We've no time to lose, the captain's waiting."

Shorty looked at him and realized that he was wasting his time. The prisoner's face was as yellow as a corpse, his eyes dull and surrounded by black rings. His appearance reminded him of some ascetic in a religious painting. Lacking finesse but with plenty of foul swearing, he dressed him, lifted him up and just managed to drag him to the captain's office. A wild, sick panic seized Andreas's genitals and spread up to his stomach, deadening his whole body as he saw gathered before him the terrible faces of his tormenters. The captain looked at him fiercely and then suddenly his expression changed. Blank faced, he tossed Andreas a parcel of his personal belongings.

"You're free, Magdalos. The boys will take you home, but until you get a decision from the public prosecutor's office you'll be under house arrest. That means you're forbidden to have any contact whatever with anyone at all, except the immediate members of your family. But at the same time I want to give you a final piece of advice. Keep well away from me, because if our paths cross again, I'll tell you now, you'll never escape from my hands again! Shorty, take him away."

* * *

Matthew was closing the garage door, when out of the corner of his eye he saw the black limousine, which had stopped silently some thirty meters from the entrance to the house. He felt his legs tremble. He knew it was the secret police. His heart beat irregularly, but he carried on with his work. He heard a door opened and shut.

"It's my turn now?" he thought.

He locked the door and put the key in his pocket, then walked away as naturally as he could. He saw a man doubled up and trying to stand, while the black car backed out. The sun was in his eyes and he shaded them with his hand, to get a look at the newcomer. With difficulty he restrained himself from running toward him immediately.

"They've brought Andreas back!" he whispered joyfully, and when the black car was out of sight, he ran toward him.

"Andreas!" shouted Matthew. He had just managed to prevent him from collapsing on to the paving. He lifted the emaciated body into his arms and gazed with agony at his friend's half-closed eyes. He had seen this picture before.

"Andreas, what have those swine done to you?"

But there was no reply.

"Master, Baas. Master!" he shouted as loud as he could in his deep bass voice. The heavy door opened and his worried boss appeared. Suddenly he understood and ran toward them, wide awake.

"Master, they've brought Baas Andreas back!" called Matthew.

Mrs. Magdalos appeared, distraught. "My boy," she sobbed, and her tears poured onto her son's face. Mr. Magdalos was deeply moved but tried to bring his emotions under control.

"Matthew, put him on his bed. I'll ring for the doctor."

After all those years, Matthew went into Andreas's bedroom for the second time. He still remembered every detail; everything seemed so familiar, so like the memories that he had harbored all those years. He laid Andreas carefully on the bed and discreetly removed himself to a corner of the room.

Mrs. Magdalos, sobbing and crying continuously, laid her son's head on her lap and stroked it tenderly. Mr. Magdalos, wild with fury, looked lovingly at his son and his eyes blazed with the desire for revenge. The doctor soon arrived, undressed the patient without a word and examined him thoroughly. He gently administered an intravenous injection which calmed Andreas.

"There's no immediate cause for alarm," he said to the parents, who were hanging on his every word, "He's terribly exhausted and in shock. I don't recommend hospitalization. I think he'll recover more quickly in a familiar environment. He needs rest, quiet, and nourishment. I'll send a nurse immediately. I'll return tonight."

Matthew left without a sound, his eyes taking in Andreas's injuries.

"I'll never let them take me alive," he whispered to himself. "Death would be better!"

The first days were filled with worry and anxiety for Andreas's parents. Andreas had neither the strength nor the inclination to talk. Most of the time, he slept a wretched slumber, consumed by terrible nightmares which made him jump up in his bed. Often he would awake to the sound of his own piercing screams. The memory of his unforgettable days of imprisonment and the faces of his torturers constantly plagued him, leaving him not a single moment to relax. The doctor tried to encourage the family, by telling them that the difficult stage would soon pass, but in truth, even he was unsure whether Andreas would fully recover. His parents devoted themselves utterly to looking after their son, and during this time of suffering, the ruins of their family relationships were rebuilt. They became the most important instruments to Andreas's recovery. After the first few weeks, Andreas's progress became evident on his face. Good food, undivided attention and time itself gave him the strength he needed. The pain and the terror went away and his mind became clearer. Nevertheless, those appalling days had left an indelible mark in his expression and his face had become more mature, older and grimmer.

As the month went by, Andreas became more distant and less inclined to talk. The imprisonment to the confines of his house was getting on his nerves and he felt stifled. He tried to read to divert himself from his persistent thoughts, but it was impossible. Periodically, he would clench his fists and wander from room to room. His father understood the unspoken restlessness that plagued his son, and knew that he and his wife could not fulfill all the needs of their disturbed child. He tried to find ways to help him, to lead him out of the impasse, to show him new avenues. He tried to get the house arrest lifted, but despite all his connections in higher places, he was unable to shake the power of BOSS. Mr. Magdalos waited helpless and anguished for the decision of the public prosecutor. It was within the depths of his despair that he took his son's correspondence out of his office drawer and looked at the letters thoughtfully.

"If I could only persuade him to go back to Greece, even if it means that we are apart," he reasoned with himself.

Mr.Magdalos found his family in the drawing room. Andreas was stretched in an armchair, politely trying to follow his mother's gossip.

"Hello," said Mr. Magdalos heartily, "what are you two talking about?"

Mrs. Magdalos put down her knitting and smiled at him tenderly.

"Hello darling. I'm glad you've come because I'm sending our poor boy crazy with all my chattering. Will you have a cup of tea with us?"

"That's not a bad idea. Thank you," he replied, and turned to his son. "How do you feel today, Andreas?"

"Better, thanks, Dad."

"Andreas, I've brought you your letters. With all the recent upset, I forgot I had them in my drawer."

Andreas took the letters without enthusiasm, but when he began to leaf through them his eyes sparkled and his face lit up with a broad smile. He felt released from his mental anguish when he thought of Rena. Mr. Magdalos watched him from the corner of his eye, and felt a glow of satisfaction. For the first time since his son had been released, Mr. Magdalos saw that his spirit had not been broken, that he was still alive and going to get better. Yet inside, he felt an unexpected twinge of fear. Andreas's face softened and grew calm. He fell into a reverie, forgetful of himself. His whole being had changed in a moment. The thoughts of Rena had reawakened his thirst for life. At once he longed to leave South Africa forever, to be with Rena and forget the horrors of this terrible place. He was startled when he heard his father calling, "Andreas! Andreas!!" He turned toward his father's voice. His body tensed and his eyes darkened with suspicion, as he saw the stranger who was standing next to his father.

"Andreas, Mr. van Rjker is from the public prosecutor's office."

The newcomer had put his briefcase on the table and took an envelope from it.

"Mr. Andreas Magdalos," he said formally, "on behalf of the public prosecutor I present you with these documents and I wish you to sign that you have received them."

The renewed life in Andreas's face quickly drained as he slowly took the sealed envelope and signed the receipt.

"Thank you, Mr. Magdalos. It will naturally be unnecessary to tell you that you must comply precisely with the public prosecutor's instructions." He closed his briefcase, made his farewells, and Mr. Frixos Magdalos hurried to see him to the door.

Andreas stood in the middle of the room looking at the bulky envelope and trying to guess what was in it. He wiped his sweating palms and opened the package with trembling hands. Mr. Magdalos hurried back followed by his wife. Anxiety was plainly written on all their faces. He saw how pale his son was, and his mind involuntarily flooded with ugly premonitions.

"What do they say, Andreas?" he asked uneasily.

Andreas's face was bitter and angry. Without a word, he handed his father the papers. Mr. Magdalos sat down heavily in an armchair and started to read, It was his turn to pale.

"This is unheard of, it's illegal," he shouted angrily and leaped to his feet. "These bastards have gone too far!"

"For God's sake, you're driving me crazy, the two of you," stammered Mrs. Magdalos plaintively, "will you please tell me what's going on!"

Mr. Magdalos tried to swallow his anger. He replied flatly,

"They're stripping him of his South African citizenship, and ordering him to leave the country within eight days."

"How can they do a thing like that?" she demanded, "what's their excuse?"

"It's because he has dual passports."

"Frixos, I don't understand what you mean. He was born here."

"Damned if I understand either. I'm going straight to our lawyer, and by God I'll stir the whole country up. Our son belongs here and nobody has the right to expel him."

He gathered up the papers feverishly and rushed out of the house.

Mrs. Magdalos in despair, burst into tears, "Oh, my God. What have we got to go through now?" she wailed through her sobbing.

Andreas's mouth was as dry as leather. There was a dangerous light in his eyes, "Oh no, the bastards won't get rid of me that easily. He laughs best who laughs last!" His thoughts of Rena were gone and the peace within him was replaced by rage.

His mother stopped crying and looked at him with even more confusion than before. Then in a flash she thought, "Perhaps this decision will be our salvation. Perhaps when he's far away from South Africa, Andreas will start a normal life."

She clutched at the thought like a life vest, calming her down.

Andreas, still deeply disturbed, simply needed to be alone. His fury subsided as his mood settled into one of despair. Trembling from head to foot, he shut himself in his room. His gaze was troubled and in his mind, he could not tear his eyes off the official paper from the prosecutor's office. It had become for him a revolting, greasy mouth, mocking him, incessantly shouting and callously trumpeting its victory. The injuries to his body were suddenly renewed and an unbearable pain speared through him. The sarcastic voices of his tormentors echoed in his head, loud as Sunday bells. Now, as never before, he knew that he ought to struggle to get out of the deadly trap that they had laid for him.

"Yes," he thought, "I have no other way out. I shall have to make a run for it. I'll have to stake everything on escape."

As each day passed, his yearning to get out of the house became even more insistent. He wanted to show his contempt for the order of house arrest and to walk the streets again among other people. He wanted to see his friends and fellow students. He needed to incite them to carry on the struggle that had fallen into inertia since his arrest. Suddenly, he made up his mind, opened the door and ran like a madman down the stairs. He crossed the garden and found himself at the main gate.

The sight of a stationary black limousine with smoked windows parked across the street acted like a tranquilizer dart. Behind the windows, he could just make out, like fleeting shadows, the faces of Shorty and Norman, grinning at him sardonically. A shudder of rage shook his body and he automatically turned back.

"No," he murmured, "I'm not voluntarily going to give them the opportunity they're waiting for. No unconditional surrender!"

Agitatedly, he stumbled around the garden. The beauty of the well-kept grounds did nothing to calm his storm-swept mind. In the heat of the sun, Matthew, half naked and sweating, was listlessly digging the vegetable patch. He heard the heavy, whistling breath before he saw Andreas, frowning and dragging his feet. He put down his spade and went over to him.

"Andreas, come to my room."

Once inside, they sat down opposite each other.

"Andreas, you've no idea how much I've wanted to get together with you."

Andreas wondered how it could be that the thought of this young black man was one of the factors that had given him the strength to withstand the torturous interrogation. He gazed around the little room.

"Matthew, do you remember an evening many years ago, when two little boys in all their childish innocence tried to break down the system of apartheid?"

Matthew's eyes suddenly widened with disbelief. "Honestly, Andreas, you can't still remember that night?"

"Huh, do I remember it? I think that night was a watershed in my life; it was as though I had been granted an appointment with destiny," answered Andreas gloomily.

Matthew lit a cigarette and sank into a reverie. "Yes, it was a beautiful, warm night. Something important was going on at the boss's house because it was all lit up and full of people. I was all alone. It was a long time since I had eaten and I was thirsty. My mother had too much work to do to be able to come and see me. I'd crawled into a corner and was waiting every moment for the evil spirit to appear in the half darkness. The door opened taking my breath away, but instead of the tokolosi, the boss's son appeared. I was disconcerted but glad. I followed you confidently. You took the first step to reach out to me when I was a child and I'm grateful to you for that. Yes, Andreas, it was an unforgettably beautiful night. It was a small incident, but it was big enough to make a mark on my life."

The kettle whistle shrilled insistently. Matthew got up and made coffee.

"Andreas, is it true they will expel you from South Africa?"

Andreas went into a spasm of agony at the recollection of his plight.

"It is true, my friend," he stammered bitterly. "They've squeezed me dry like a lemon; crippled my body and now they want to toss me out of the country I was born in, as though I were a piece of rubbish."

"You have the wrong attitude, Andreas. You should feel proud that they're throwing you out. Don't you see? They're afraid of you! Sure, they've tried to break your body, but they haven't been able to defile your mind. That's why you're so dangerous. They're terrified of people like you."

"Matthew, if you believe what you say, prove it to me in practice. Help me to escape from the country, to deprive them of the satisfaction of an easy victory."

"I can understand how you feel, Andreas and I sympathize with you, but you've got to look at things realistically. We can't do it. We can't give them the opportunity they're waiting for. Your house is watched day and night. As soon as we stick our noses outside they'll have us arrested, and this time it'll be the end for both of us."

"Damn your logic, Matthew, I know all that," he shouted furiously, "I know, but I can't forget what they did to me and what they'll do to thousands of others. What they're doing to the whole nation. I've got to fight them. Matthew, please help me. We might be able to make it if we're careful. I beg you; help me stand up to them!"

"Calm down, Andreas. Think coolly and rationally. They're the ones who are giving you an opportunity without realizing it. From the moment they put you on the plane, you're free. And believe me, there are ways of getting back here! Do you follow me?"

Andreas stared at him confounded, still unable to grasp what Matthew meant. "Speak plainly, Matthew, for God's sake."

"Andreas, I think the time has come to confess a few things that have been on my mind for some time. I've never laid down my cards for you, never taken you seriously. I thought you were a silly rich boy with stupid dreams. When you ridiculed me for not taking a stand, I wanted to disembowel you; to drink your blood! I wanted to shout at you with pride that I am a freedom fighter for the ANC, fighting actively for the things you could only babble about."

Andreas listened, hardly able to believe his ears.

"All that came to a head when they arrested you. I felt remorse and fear. I cursed the day that I got Philip out of the country because I'd responded to your taunts. I hid in a cellar, expecting the vultures from BOSS to come crashing in at any moment. But at the same time, I felt sorry for you and prayed that you would resist and emerge once more as a man, so that I could come and tell you what I've just said. I wanted to shake your hand, to beg your forgiveness and tell you how much I admire you. I also want to tell you, for the first time, you have given me faith in a white man. We're not fighting a racial war. Our enemy is the system, the establishment, the corrupt people with their rotten values."

Deeply moved, Matthew held out his hand, "Comrade, late as it is, I'm offering you my hand, and with it, my friendship."

Andreas got up and hugged him. They sat next to each other like brothers, talking late into the night about the present and the future.

CHAPTER 16 Polytechneio Calling

The airplane was now flying high, leaving far behind the lights of the City of Gold. The attempts made by his lawyers had failed. Even his father's efforts had been in vain to shake the decision of the public prosecutor. Andreas was once more saddened by the pain of separation. He had never seen his parents so demoralized. He settled down in his seat and tried to sleep. When this attempt failed, he took Rena's letters out of his pocket and read them again. He felt a warm glow of happiness and his thoughts ran free; he was setting out for a new life. He needed rest, and time to think about which direction his life should take. Eventually, pale and tired from lack of sleep, he passed through the Greek customs formalities into the noisy arrivals hall. Bewildered and pulling his suitcases behind him, he searched the crowd wildly, looking for someone from his family.

"Andreas! Andreas!!"

He heard his name being called above the hubbub of the throng. He turned hopefully and encountered his Uncle Pericles, who was waiting to greet him with open arms and tears in his eyes.

"Andreas, my boy, you don't know how much we've missed you. I'm so glad to see you back. I want to tell you how sorry and how proud I am, for what you had to go through back there. When you feel ready, you'll tell me about it."

After a warm embrace, Andreas, puzzled, inquired as to the whereabouts of Rena and his cousins. Uncle Pericles looked around conspiratorially.

"I'll explain when we get into the car, my boy," he said it softly.

With his eyes he pointed out the armed men spread out around them.

For the first time, Andreas noticed the soldiers with automatic weapons that were scattered around the airport. He nodded as a sign of understanding. Uncle Pericles grabbed a suitcase and hurried through the crowd. In his haste to keep up with him, Andreas bumped into an elderly lady and almost knocked her down. Upset, he begged her pardon and ran to catch up. They put the bags in the trunk and he looked in bewilderment at his apprehensive uncle.

"Uncle, tell me exactly what's going on."

"Son, you've had the bad luck to come back at a nasty moment. Greece is going through difficult times. Our country is not much better than yours at the moment. Once more, the altar of liberty needs sacrifices."

He sat down heavily behind the wheel and wiped the sweat from his face with his handkerchief.

"There are several thousand young people, Nikos, Stathis and Rena among them, who've taken over the Polytechneio. They have been there since Wednesday. They have started up illegal radio broadcasts, and are making constant appeals for support. They're asking the people and the army to join them in overthrowing the dictatorship. Those in power have gone mad. They've threatened to move heaven and earth to get to them. They've set siege to the Polytechneio with tanks and machine guns. If the students don't leave the school by this evening, then the government has promised to remove them by force. But threats have not made any impression on those youngsters. They say that they've made an appointment with history. I'm proud of them, but I fear for them also."

Andreas was moved by his uncle's words and immediately anxious for Rena, his cousins and the other students. He patted his uncle on the back.

"You're a remarkable man, Uncle Pericles, and I admire you. If only my own father were like you."

His uncle stared at him reprovingly, "You don't know what you're saying, Andreas. Your father was always our hero, the pride of our family. As a boy of fifteen, he took part in the resistance against the Germans!"

"Who? My father?" he asked in astonishment.

"Yes, your father" his uncle replied firmly, "hasn't he ever told you about his achievements?"

"Never, Uncle."

"Well, as soon as this mess is over, I'll tell you myself. You ought to know about it."

Andreas was dumbfounded. He was hesitant to reassess his impression of his father.

"The scum have surrounded the whole of Athens."

Andreas stared at the tanks, the heavily armed troops and the swarms of police. The nearer they traveled to the center of Athens, the more their numbers increased.

His portly aunt greeted him joyfully, but she could not hide her worry. She burst into tears when she saw the scars on his face.

"Andreas, my boy. What have they done to you? You must have suffered a lot!" she cried.

"I have been on a difficult journey Aunt, but I have survived. But never mind about me. Have you had any news from Rena, Stathis and Nikos?"

"Absolutely nothing. I am very worried about them. I have just been listening to the radio station. I think that they are too marvelous, so heroic. May God protect them."

"Any new developments, Penelope?" Uncle Pericles asked.

"They are appealing for help. They are in need of doctors and medicine," she replied.

"I'd like to hear their radio broadcasts too, Auntie. Is it possible?"

"Oh, my boy, you look so tired. You'd do better to go and lie down for a bit. You have had your fair share of trouble."

"You're joking, my dear. He's a young man and his blood's boiling. If he'd come sooner, I'm quite sure he'd be in there with them," interrupted his uncle.

Andreas continued, "I'm fine and I would really like to find out what is going on."

Aunt Penelope turned on the radio and the room filled with the uncompromising female voice of the announcer. They gathered and listened intently.

"Polytechneio here! Polytechneio here! This is the Radio Station of the free fighting students, the free fighting Greeks. Down with the Junta, down with Papadopoulos. Americans out! Down with fascism! The Junta will fall to the people! People of Greece, come out on the streets, come and stand by us, reclaim your freedom. The struggle is a universal anti-dictatorial, anti-Junta. Only you can fight in this struggle. Greece is governed by foreign interests! The dictator Papadopoulos is trying to hide behind a mask of democracy, with the fake government of Markezinis. Go to the streets! Condemn the false elections which empowered the fascists."

When the announcement was over, Aunt Penelope wiped her streaming eyes, blew her nose, and in a voice that shook with emotion said, "Bravo, my girl! Well said! God bless you all."

Equally moved, Andreas watched his uncle straighten himself, his eyes gleamed with the fire of resistance.

"Penelope, there's going to be a massacre down there. I'm going down, they'll need help."

Andreas, flushed with enthusiasm, got up and said, "Uncle Pericles, you're needed here. Someone has to look after the house. You did your duty when you were young, now its other people's turn. I'll go."

Pericles eventually agreed to stay home after his wife insisted. He nodded sadly at Andreas.

"You're right, son. These matters need youth and strength. Take care!"

"Don't worry, Uncle. I know how to look after myself."

The streets were almost deserted, but through every closed window Andreas could hear the young woman's warm voice becoming hoarse from calling.

"Polytechneio here! Polytechneio here!"

The breeze was blowing cold and fresh from the surrounding hills and it cooled his overheated body. The distance was fairly long and had to be covered on foot because taxis and buses had disappeared from the streets. Andreas pushed on quickly and carefully, avoiding the main, busy streets where large parties of police had set up roadblocks at strategic points. The closer he got, the more insistent became his longing to join his fellow students. He wanted to fight at their side. He also longed to see Rena again and to hold her in his arms, if only for a moment.

As they approached the school, he could hear the music of Xylouris. The refrain echoed, 'When will the sky be clear again.' A bell from a nearby church rang out with a deathly knell, such as that heard at a funeral. The sound filled him with shudders of foreboding. He took courage however, from the small groups of people heading in the same direction. Somewhere nearby they must have fired teargas and a light breeze blew it toward them. His eyes smarted and began to tear. A young man took out a little jar of Vaseline and smeared it around his eyes. He then handed it to Andreas who copied him. Without realizing it, he found himself caught up in a crowd of people moving toward Alexandra Avenue. Four enormous barricades had been erected by the students in an attempt to repel a large force of police. Stories and rumors were circulating through the crowd as more people gathered. In Chalkokondili Street, the police tried to disperse a huge group of people who stood outside the Polytechneio. They stood firm and refused to budge. At last, it seemed that the populace had been aroused, and that they were finally ready to stand up to the monstrous Junta. The crowd began to chant passionate slogans.

"Down with Fascism! Long Live Popular Rule! Long Live Democracy!"

Andreas's progress was cut off by the crowd. He forced his way into the narrow side streets again. He had to get there at any cost. He lengthened his stride and soon found himself running. With his heart in his mouth and dripping with sweat, he reached Patission Road. In front of him, unreal in the moment, stood the neoclassical building of the university. He hid in the dark recess of a doorway and let his gaze rove admiringly over the ranks of the 'free besieged.' The Polytechneio building was abundantly lit and it resembled a large beehive in which the students were hard at work. There were hundreds on the roof. The halls, the grounds, the staircases, the railings of the main gate and the gardens were all crowded with people. From each end of the road and from every side-street there came more groups of young people in a continuous stream to join them. Every bit of wall carried slogans; 'Papadopoulos, you fascist!

Take your washerwoman wife, take Despina and go! The people don't want you.' Andreas's favorites were 'Bread, Education, Freedom!' and 'Today Fascism dies!'

The radio station loud speakers blared constantly.

"Polytechneio here! Polytechneio here! Here is Radio Free Greece. We are unarmed. We are unarmed. Our only weapon is our faith in liberty. Our only defenses are our bare chests. So if the usurpers come with tanks or machine guns, we shall oppose them with bare breasts. We believe that our soldiers will not shoot their brothers and sisters, will not shed their brother's blood."

The broad boulevard was crowded with police and soldiers with automatic weapons. Far in the distance, Andreas could hear the roar of approaching tanks. Throughout the length of the street, fights and clashes with police had already begun to break out. The chatter of machine guns mixed with cries of pain, curses, the shouting of slogans and the revolutionary music of Mikis Theodorakis; all creating a Dali-esque canvas.

The radio station loudspeakers were intoxicating. They had turned into mythological sirens, inviting the people of Athens to give their lives for liberty.

"Polytechneio calling! Polytechneio calling! People of Greece, this is the moment for you to learn. You need to know what is going on in this Greece of ours, what exploits! And you should be here beside us. How can you sleep at such a moment? How can you sleep when armed forces have stationed themselves in front of the Polytechneio gates and are aiming at your children? We are not afraid to die! We die as free people! People of Greece, learn the truth. Know that your children were born free. Know that your children will live and die in freedom…"

Andreas took a deep breath, clenched his teeth, and ran like a maniac to try and get across the street. He found himself in the middle of a melee; his eyebrow was split open by a police club. Next to him, a young man fell groaning and bleeding from bullet wounds. Andreas bent down, picked him up in his arms and went on running. He reached the barred front gate and stared, gasping, at the youngsters who had climbed up. The students clung to the gates, singing the national anthem and calling to the soldiers, "We are brothers."

"Come in by the side door, comrade," they called down to him.

His knees were trembling with exhaustion, and he was drenched with the blood of the unknown boy. The students opened the side door for him immediately and helped him with his burden. Two first aid workers laid the wounded boy carefully on a stretcher and carried him to an improvised hospital. Out of breath, Andreas leaned against the wall to gather his strength. They showed him a tap where he could wash up and someone gave him plaster for his eyebrow. The drama that was unfolding in the Polytechneio was difficult for even the most fevered imagination to comprehend. Young men and women, their eyes streaming, their throats hoarse, their eyes ablaze remained filled with conviction and faith in what they were doing. Seized by their enthusiasm, Andreas shouted and sang along with them, while constantly searching for the friends he longed to find.

"Polytechneio calling! We are asking for representatives of the International Red Cross to come to our aid. The state of some of the wounded is serious. We also ask the Red Cross to send ambulances to transport the wounded. Polytechneio here! Polytechneio calling! Please send us morphine, antibiotics and tourniquets. We urge doctors to rush to our aid. Gas masks have already arrived and we need more, please. Thank you for all the tinned food you've sent. Thanks to the housewives who have sent us meals. Long live the fighters."

The ringing of machine-gun fire grew deafening. More and more skirmishes broke out, and the stalwart columns amplified the screams of the wounded. Andreas searched from room to room.

"Dear listeners... All of you in Athens who are with us right now...forgive us for being so emotional...forgive us for asking you to stand with us. Forgive our tears...we are crying for joy. The joy of liberty. Polytechneio calling! Don't be afraid of the tanks! Down with fascism! Soldiers, we are your brothers. Don't become murderers."

Among the crowd in one room, Andreas discovered a former fellow student. He fought his way through to him and shouting to make himself heard, asked whether he had seen Rena, Stathis or Nikos.

"Yes, I saw them earlier near the main gate, Andreas."

With difficulty, but hopeful, Andreas made his way through the crowd. He heard the army loudspeakers blaring. They were warning the students that they had twenty minutes to get out. He saw a tank take up a position near the main gate. It was 2.50 am on Saturday, 17 November, 1973.

"Polytechneio calling! Polytechneio calling! I must inform you that at this moment two tanks are at the gates of the Polytechneio. The muzzles of their guns are pointing straight at us. There is no need for them to attack the Polytechneio. They are going to kill young Greeks, the hope of Greece's future. They're coming in!! They're coming in!!"

Andreas stood speechless, his mouth agape with awe as he saw the steel monster crashing into the gate, onto which the youngsters had clambered. The iron gate collapsed under the impact, bringing down and scattering the marble columns. Iron, marble and bodies were crushed to rubble under the tank tracks. Wails and shrieks of horror broke in unison from a thousand throats. The radio announcer started to sing the national anthem as security forces and Special Commandos poured in. Suddenly the lights went out and in the darkness, chaos reigned.

The darkness and the firing of automatic weapons created panic among the unarmed youngsters, who ran in all directions in search of safety. Their onrush was like a river that carried Andreas with it. In the dark, police waited to pounce. They had no respect for the wounded; they finished them off sadistically, with boots and pistol butts. The breaking of glass, ambulance sirens, and the wails of those who had been struck down echoed in the dark. The ambulances tried to get through the police cordon, but the soldiers instead of making way, flung the doors open, dragged out the wounded and murdered them. Confused and panic-stricken, the students ran to find a safe place to hide. The doors of nearby houses and units opened and total strangers hid them in their homes; their rooms were filled with weary bodies, tears and sobs.

Andreas had no idea how long it all lasted, but gradually the firing, the shouts and the running subsided. A hushed silence followed. Before dawn, Andreas with a bowed head went out onto the streets of a changed and distant world. He eventually arrived at his relatives' house. His uncle and aunt were crying, and Nikos was standing, scratched and bleeding with his head bandaged.

"What happened, Nikos? Where are Rena and Stathis?"

Nikos clenched his teeth in anguish and bravely held back his sobs.

"Stathis is in hospital, seriously injured. Rena ... Rena is dead. The tanks killed her."

Days of mourning followed with the whole country crying for its lost youth. Andreas, heartbroken and disillusioned, decided that he had no further reason to remain in Greece. He made contact with the ANC in London and planned his return to South Africa. It was hard to get his aunt and uncle to accept his departure given that they were numb with grief and worried for his future.

The cypress trees in the cemetery with their slim but sturdy trunks and their somber wilting foliage, created a peaceful air of strength and tranquility. Andreas felt anguish as he looked with lusterless eyes at the cold white tombstone. It was all that remained of the woman he had loved. She had offered up her love, her youth and her life for the ideal of freedom and human dignity. He wanted to lie down on the cold stone and weep, but he knew she would not have wanted that. Lines from the poet Ritsos, that she had liked so much, came into his mind:

"No more tears, fresh struggles; the first among our dead, are the leaders of hope."

He brushed his tears away with the back of his hand. He reverently laid down the red carnation he had brought for her; the symbol of uprising. He looked down and bade a silent farewell. The thousands of memorials, the funereal columns and crosses all cried in one voice: 'Life is death'.

The taxi, with his few personal belongings, was waiting. He opened the door, got in and took his seat.

"Western airport, please" he said firmly.

CHAPTER 17 Training Camp

The great African continent was drawing him in like a huge and powerful magnet. The seatbelt and no smoking signs lit up simultaneously.

"Ladies and gentlemen, in a few minutes we shall be landing at Luanda airport. Please fasten your seatbelts and extinguish your cigarettes. To those who are disembarking here, we say thank you for flying with us."

After a detailed customs examination and endless questions in Portuguese and broken English, they let him through. As he entered the large, vaulted hall of the airport building, Andreas was bemused to see the tough-looking military security guards. The sun-burnt, heavily armed soldiers stared suspiciously in all directions.

"All pigs have the same face," he thought, "the same brutal features, as though they had all been cast in the same mold."

Leaving the airport building, he felt as though he had stepped into a blazing oven. The heat and humidity were so intense that within a few minutes his suit was sticking to his sweating body. He tried to form an impression of Luanda from the taxi. It was a handsome modern city; the seafront boulevard, with its hotels and its tall, slender palm trees flanking the tranquil ocean, could compare with any European city. The hotel, in contemporary style, was air conditioned and his room was comfortable. He revived himself with a shower and drank with deep enjoyment the scotch and soda he had ordered.

Yet once again he reviewed the instructions that he had received in Greece from the ANC office in London. He was so very pleased and astonished to get a message, enclosed in the package, from Philip who was based at the London headquarters. He studied the map of Luanda and was pleased to discover that the address he wanted was only a few blocks from his hotel. He switched off the light and for what seemed the first time in a long while, fell asleep immediately.

The rest revitalized him and he had the appetite for a substantial breakfast before going out. The heat was still stifling, yet nonetheless, the streets were filled with people. Andreas strolled into a residential area and felt almost at home. Naturally there were differences. Blacks and whites used the same buses, shopped at the same shops, and ate at the same restaurants. There was no apartheid in Portuguese Africa, but there were still armed soldiers at every corner. Their presence illustrated the conflict in relations between the black and white citizens. He was searching for the Black Tulip, a shop that sold antiques and curiosities, hand-made by anonymous black craftsmen. He located the store and entered confidently. A short, middle-aged man with a dark skin and quick, darting eyes approached him with a friendly smile.

"Good morning, sir. How can I be of assistance?"

"Good morning," answered Andreas, "I want to buy a good quality rug."

"I'm sorry, sir, you've made a mistake. As you can see, our business does not deal in rugs."

"That's odd," Andreas persisted, "a fellow countryman of mine recommended that I come here."

"He must surely have made a mistake, my dear sir," the other replied somewhat coldly.

"I'm a tourist here. Perhaps you could recommend somewhere where I could buy a black rug?"

The shopkeeper continued to look at him without expression.

"You say you want to buy a black rug? How strange. That's the first time in my life I've ever heard such a thing."

Andreas started to get rattled for the first time.

"Have I made a mistake?" he wondered, but he pressed on. "But you know, sir, that black is a very nice color.

The shopkeeper's attitude suddenly changed.

"Come into my office, please."

Andreas sighed with relief and followed him into the back of the shop.

"Sorry, my friend, but things have got much more difficult and we have to be very careful. Besides, I wasn't expecting you so soon. Can I offer you some refreshment?"

"I won't say no. It's very hot outside."

The man sat opposite Andreas, where he could maintain a good view of his shop. Andreas felt apprehensive. He did not like the man very much. He knew nothing about him and yet, he felt as though he were locked in a dark maze with no way out. His companion divined his fears and tried to reassure him,

"Comrade, I can understand your worry, but for security reasons we have to go our own way."

"Alright, well what's my next step?" he asked impatiently.

"You're in too much of a hurry, my friend, like all the new fellows. But unfortunately, it is not as easy as you think. I need time to organize your transport. Things are a lot tighter these days and Luanda's full of BOSS agents. The best thing you can do is go back to your hotel and wait till I contact you."

Andreas realized it was pointless to ask any more questions. He would have to comply with the man's suggestion.

"Best not to go too far away," the stranger added, "I'll want to find you straight away when I need you."

"Don't worry, you'll find me round here. I've no intention of going anywhere."

Loneliness and boredom brought with them memories of his lost love. The long, hot days seemed the most miserable of his life. The beauty of the African town with its gloriously lush, green vegetation could do nothing to ease his mind. The image of Rena's broken body was constantly in his head and in his imagination he tried to relive every happy moment he had spent with her. How he loved her, and how he missed her! The anguish of her loss filled his eyes with tears and his heart with longing. He even started to wonder whether it was worth living any longer.

On the fifth day, a telephone call from the stranger at the Black Tulip, reminded him of the obligations he had undertaken.

"Hello."

"Good morning, sir. I'm the man from the antique shop. Do you remember me?"

"Certainly," answered Andreas, somewhat taken aback.

"You must be a very lucky person, sir, because I've managed to organize your safari, but you'll have to leave immediately. Can you be ready in half an hour?"

"Of course. I'm ready right now."

"Excellent. Then wait outside your hotel. A red Land Rover will come and collect you. Is that alright?"

"Yes. Thank you very much."

The car was there waiting for him. The driver opened the door and Andreas threw his few possessions on to the back seat and sat in the front passenger seat. The car immediately set off. Andreas tried to strike up a conversation with the driver but without success. He knew no Portuguese and the driver spoke no English. Twilight was falling as they left the city and entered the suburbs. The driver hunched over the wheel and stepped on the gas. The speedometer needle hovered nervously above the 100 kilometers per hour mark. The countryside was a verdant green, tropical and teemed with people walking. Soon the sky became completely dark, so that nothing was visible. Andreas's mind was preoccupied and tired and he soon fell into an uneasy sleep. A sudden swerve woke him, as the car dodged a couple of antelopes crossing the road. He looked at his watch. They had been traveling for more than three hours. The driver turned off the main road and, without slowing down, took to a dirt road. The car became lost in a thick dust cloud. It filled Andreas's nostrils and stuck to his damp clothes adding to his discomfort in the stifling heat. Finally, they passed through an iron, arched gateway and drew up in front of a large stone mansion.

The man from the Black Tulip came out to meet them and led them into the house.

"Well, comrade, the time has arrived. Within a few hours you'll be at your destination."

He led the way into a sitting room decorated with various animal skins and horns, where five other men were waiting, talking among themselves amiably. They were all black and about the same age. The man from the Black Tulip made the introductions, but they greeted the newcomer coldly and with evident suspicion. Andreas was not in the mood to try and win them over. In any case, he knew it would be a waste of effort. Instead he asked their host, "What time do we leave?"

"In a few minutes my friend, in a few minutes. So if you're hungry, grab a sandwich from that plate, because you've still got a few hours of travel ahead of you. As for where you're going, that's something I can't tell you. In any case, you'll find out for yourself."

Andreas was hungrily finishing a sandwich when the driver who had brought him came in and said something in Portuguese. Their host's face lit up with a wide grin,

"It's time, comrades. We can go."

Two men, holding torches, led them out into the open air and down a pathway toward what appeared to be a small landing strip. A buzzing cloud of mosquitoes fell upon them greedily and within a few moments, Andreas could feel his skin prickling and itching. In the dark, he heard the roar of engines and then managed to make out the silhouette of the Cessna that would take them to their destination. The man from the Black Tulip shook their hands, as one by one they clambered aboard the plane. In no time, they were flying over the totally dark jungle. The flight lasted more than three and a half hours and Andreas felt stiff and cramped from the lack of movement. In stark contrast to the surrounding darkness, the pilot spotted a scattering of lights on the ground. Accustomed to the conditions, he skillfully landed the plane on a small patch of macadam carved out of the bush.

Through the plane window, Andreas could make out a few people holding lamps. The door of the aircraft was opened from outside by a man of about thirty-five, in a camouflage uniform. He greeted them amiably as he cradled a Russian Kalashnikov automatic rifle:

"Comrades, on behalf of the ANC, welcome to our camp. Please pick up your gear and follow me."

One by one the passengers got out. The night was cool and the sky was brilliantly highlighted with thousands of points of light, like a huge chandelier. The coughing of a nearby hyena broke the silence. A tribe of monkeys, woken by the beast, began chattering and leaping from branch to branch in a neighboring tree. From a little further away, a family of jackals howled their response to the commotion. Night or not, the jungle was wide awake.

"Hurry up, comrades, we have to get to the camp before daylight," the commander shouted.

Andreas strode out and followed him. In the torchlight he could make out five or six men. They walked quickly for about twenty minutes, their guide calling out passwords every so often to unseen sentinels. Once inside the camp, it was totally dark, and all one could see were vague shadows. The commander led them to a wooden hut and lit a kerosene lamp.

"Comrades," he said quietly, "I know you're all tired from the journey. This is where you'll sleep for the time being. Tomorrow I'll sort you into squads. You can sleep where you like, because on the first day you're not on duty. I'll see you again when you wake up. Good night."

Andreas felt worn out and he lay down on a bunk as he was, with his clothes on. He must have slept for a few hours because when he woke he was hungry and felt sluggish from head to foot. He took a shower, put on the fatigues they had issued, and went to join the others. The camp, as he had correctly guessed, was built at the top of a rise. It was a primitive camp, with makeshift dwellings consisting of wood and mud huts, camouflaged under tall trees, and three raised lookout posts. A high barbed wire fence separated the camp from the jungle.

Training began the next day. It was tough and demanding, with little free time. Every muscle in his body ached tremendously. The coldness between him and the others dissipated as their survival depended upon a team spirit. They each helped one another and soon, Andreas felt reasonably accepted. As the days went by, life in the camp became even more exacting. Within a few weeks he felt transformed into a completely new man. He was now an obedient soldier with trained movements and numerous new skills. He learned to handle, strip and assemble every kind of weapon so well, that he could do it with his eyes closed. With each day that passed, he felt himself becoming stronger and more pragmatic, with little time for misgivings or sentiment. It was a case of kill or be killed. The rhythm of life in camp was unremitting, fast and furious. Gradually that which had been entirely unfamiliar, became second nature to him; to aim straight, to make bombs from readily available materials, to disguise him, to carry out sabotage, to pick his targets.

The pace of life was so rapid that he had lost all sense of time or of his past. It was as if he had been born again and had had to learn to live a new life. The confidence he felt in himself was a new experience. It was a differing perspective for him to feel physical assurance. At the same time, he felt more attentive, more cautious and more clear-sighted. Andreas knew that when the training was at an end, he would be thrown into battle. He would be asked to translate what he had learned into practice. His calculations were not wrong.

One morning Andreas was ordered to report to his commander. The moment he had been waiting for had come and he welcomed it. Filled with enthusiasm and excitement, he went into the simple little office and looked questioningly at the determined, sun burnt face of his commander. He was a man of average height, with bright intelligent eyes and a nose hooked like a vulture's. His face emitted forcefulness, an expression of liveliness and competence which Andreas had rarely come across. He had a natural smile and a way of looking people straight in the eyes that made one wonder if he was reading their minds.

"Sit down, comrade. We've got some serious business to talk about today. You may not know, but in the last few months there have been significant changes in the world which exceed our most optimistic expectations. The situation in Portugal, since the death of the dictator, Salazar, has been chaotic. The people, the army and the leadership are all at odds with each other. Many soldiers have been maimed in the wars of resistance in Angola and Mozambique, most of them working class boys. The people of Portugal, including quite a few of the officials, are demanding Portuguese withdrawal from the African colonies. They don't want any more dead or wounded, and in any case, they have realized that they have nothing to gain because the profits derived from the colonies never come their way. After the dictator's death, the troops who found the courage to stop fighting went home to their families, and now the freedom fighters are going from village to village and town to town, setting the slaves free.

"However, these unforeseen developments do not please the

powers in Pretoria. You see, they can't stomach the idea that after Angola, Mozambique and Rhodesia, it'll soon be their turn. So, with the support of the western imperialists and under the pretext that they're rushing to the aid of the UNITA resistance fighters led by that western-loving mercenary, Savimbi, they have unleashed a terror attack on Angola with every contemporary weapon available to military science. In the course of their attack, they're sweeping everything away, burning, destroying and killing the civilian population.

"Now that their attention has been diverted elsewhere, it's the best time to slip men and materials across the border. Moreover, if we extend our efforts, we can exploit the sensation stirred up by the Samora liberation movement. The mission we want you to go on is difficult, but of prime importance. If you succeed the profits we shall reap from it will be incalculable. We've chosen you because we have faith in you and because your white skin will make it easier for you to move around."

Andreas could hardly contain his joy, especially when his commander unveiled to him the details of the plan and the targets they were aiming at. The two men then worked systematically, eagerly studying maps and going over the plan of action again and again until Andreas had made it his own.

The two-seater aircraft landed in Zambia, at a small airstrip near the border with Zimbabwe. The ANC agent was waiting with car keys and a large package.

"You're on your own from here, comrade. Good luck!" he spoke to the plane's only passenger.

"Thanks, friend," Andreas replied.

Acting as though he were the owner, he climbed into the new station wagon and set off. After traveling for a few kilometers, he stopped in an isolated spot. He emptied the contents of the package onto the passenger seat and the black metal of a Browning gleamed up at him menacingly among various other documents and identity papers. He picked up the gun and examined it carefully checking the details and the number of the weapon with its license. They matched exactly. He gave it a final glance and pushed it into the holster at his waist. In the same way, he examined all his papers, driving license, registration papers for the car, identity cards, bank account and cheque book. He nodded with satisfaction and slid them carefully, one by one into his brief case.

Andreas lit a cigarette and gazed out at the dry savanna. Whistling to himself, between puffs, he started the car again. Only a few kilometers separated him from the border post. As he approached, he heard the increasing noise of rushing water. Then came towering vapor clouds which shroud the majesty of Victoria Falls, Even though he had seen them so many times in the past, he was still stunned by the grandeur of this magnificent site. His passage across the border over the Limpopo River was even easier than he had expected. His passport opened all doors effortlessly, together with his new Afrikaans name and his white skin.

"Have a good trip, Mr. De Villiers and drive carefully," the corporal on the border post said to him in perfect English. Andreas waved in reply, already moving away.

The road was long and seemingly endless. The African countryside that he loved so much, stretched endlessly to the horizon all round him. Perhaps, he reflected, this is the only continent where white invaders have managed to rob it of its wealth and enslave its people, without destroying or defiling the wild beauty of its nature. Tired as he was, Andreas drove carefully, thinking constantly about how he would be able to accomplish the difficult mission on which he had been sent. He avoided the city of Bulawayo, heading directly toward the southern border post. He reduced speed and eased through the Rhodesian border without a trace of nervousness. He brought the car to a gentle halt in front of the South African post. The radio, which Andreas had previously tuned to Springbok Radio, was playing a popular Afrikaans song. He left the radio on, stepped out of the car and walked toward the customs officials. He did his best to seem annoyed and arrogant. With a broad smile, he greeted them in Afrikaans. The guards were delighted with their congenial compatriot and made only a token inspection of the car. One youthful guard looked at him slyly and asked,

"Mr. De Villiers, I don't suppose you have any forbidden publications to declare?"

Andreas laughed cheerfully and replied, "You're joking, my

friend. What would I do with pornography when we have in our country the most beautiful women in the world? But I do have something else to declare."

He opened the trunk and took out two bottles of mature Portuguese brandy. "Here you are boys, if you'd like to drink to my health. I've done very well out of my dealings with the kaffirs."

One of the officers hastily stamped his passport and gave it back to him.

"Totsiens, Meneer De Villiers and baaie dankie."

"Totsiens," answered Andreas.

He had succeeded in taking his first step. He had finally returned to the soil of his native land. Weariness, hunger and a need for sleep suddenly overcame him and he stopped at the first motel he came to. The stress of the border crossing had affected him more than he was willing to admit and after a hot meal, he slipped into coma-like sleep.

In the afternoon of the following day, he arrived in the center of Johannesburg. The shops and offices were closed and the streets were almost deserted. He walked quickly and pushed open the door of the cathedral. The high vaulted nave echoed cheerfully to the sound of the organ and the psalms of the faithful. He well knew his way from his previous visits as a student. Andreas turned down a corridor and without knocking opened a door. A middle aged man in a cassock rose to his feet and his round face peered hard at Andreas.

"My son, I think you've taken the wrong way. The cathedral is right through there."

"Father, all roads lead to God."

The priest went to the door and bolted it.

"I've been expecting you," he said in a low voice.

He took a bunch of keys from an invisible pocket and some papers that included a lease agreement and gave them to Andreas. "Do you know how to get to the property?"

"Don't worry, Father, I'm a local."

"You'll have to be very careful, my son, especially when you come here. I think the security police have been following me lately."

"I don't think I shall have to trouble you again."

"God go with you."

The priest opened the door. The corridor was empty, and he nodded to Andreas who quickly and silently slipped out and mingled with the congregation. He was not afraid of being recognized; with his new look of long hair, thick moustache and glasses.

The small property which had been rented in the name of Jan De Villiers was chosen after a long search. It was in an ideal position somewhere between Johannesburg and Soweto. It would give Andreas ease of movement and the opportunity to communicate with the black national freedom fighters of Soweto. It was also remote and isolated enough to evade the curious eyes of any neighbors and the local community. He found no difficulty in locating the property because he saw the whole district firmly in his mind's eye, based on the map that he had studied in the camp.

The house was in total darkness, without a sign of life. He looked around for the man who should have been there waiting to meet him. Andreas stopped the car and got out without turning off the engine or the headlights. Suddenly he turned around, his hand going for the butt of his gun, as he heard an indistinct noise behind him. A gigantic black man approached him holding a stout club in his right hand.

"Are you the watchman?" asked Andreas.

"I am the child of the night, Baas."

"If I'm not mistaken, you must be Zulu."

"Yes, that's my name. And who are you?"

"I'm the new tenant. Tell me; is there anyone else on the farm apart from you?"

"No," answered Zulu's with his deep, rhythmical voice.

Zulu was a tall, fierce man with ebony black tones in his dark skin. He was obviously a warrior with a huge chest and arms balanced on sturdy strong legs. His shaved head emphasized large wooden discs in his ears, around which his earlobes were stretched, proudly distinguishing his tribal ancestry as a Zulu. People in the towns had called him Zulu for as long as he could remember; his real name seemed forgotten in the distant past of the rolling green hills of his childhood.

"I hardly need to tell you, Zulu; I don't want any friends and acquaintances on the farm. They'll cause us nothing but trouble. Turn the lights on, please, and open the garage door so I can put the car in. I want you to help me unload."

Zulu leapt forwards and grabbed Andreas. He had him by the neck of his shirt, before Andreas could even think of a response.

"Listen," he growled, "We'd better sort a few things out between us right from the start. You don't appeal to me at all. You're arrogant and rude, like all the fucking whites. I don't know how you got mixed up in the struggle or ever came to the training camps, or how I got landed with you, but I do know I'm not taking orders from you! You've got legs, haven't you? Go and open the door yourself. I'm here to assist you, not to serve you. Understood?"

Andreas stood speechless with astonishment. He stared in admiration after Zulu's retreating figure. He suddenly realized that he had seen him before on one of the training expeditions. He liked this fellow. He had character.

"Hey, Zulu, come back. No time for games. We've got serious work to do and, believe me; I haven't the slightest intention of bossing you around."

Without waiting for a reply, Andreas opened the garage and parked the car inside. Zulu appeared in the doorway glowering. Andreas shut the door, then took out a screwdriver and started to unscrew the car's secret compartments. He unloaded weapons, cartridges, fuses, plastic explosives and a variety of other weaponry. Zulu's face beamed with amazement.

"You've brought enough stuff with you, Jan. Do you know how to use it?"

"Well enough. The main thing is to pick the right targets."

The two men worked tirelessly for several hours, arranging, sorting out and hiding the valuable cargo. Only when they had finished, and every sign of their work had disappeared, did Andreas take out his cigarettes, light one, and toss the packet to Zulu. After a slight hesitation, Zulu took a cigarette and sat down near him. He still hadn't warmed to Andreas.

"My orders," he told Andreas, "are to establish a strong alibi here, so that we can stay for some time. The position's ideal and we don't need to arouse any suspicions."

"How do you think you'll manage that, Zulu?"

"Easy. We create the impression that you're a small farmer and you've come here to start making your living again from scratch, after being divorced."

"I don't object to that; it provides us with a perfectly reasonable explanation. The only problem is that I don't know the first thing about farming."

"You don't have to worry about that," answered Zulu. "I've spent my whole life working on farms."

"Well, we'd better get cracking on it tomorrow."

"Agreed, Jan. I'll find a few workers and we'll get on with it. Time's getting on. We'll see about it tomorrow. Goodnight," said Zulu as he got up to go.

"Aren't you going to stay in the house?"

"No, I live over there in the separate rooms, the servant's quarters. Don't forget I'm black!"

When Andreas woke the next morning, Zulu and a few farmhands had started work. A small tractor was puffing and panting, as it tore at the vitals of the virgin land. Andreas spent the next few days working on the farm. He even began to enjoy his new life. For the first time, he found himself working under the hot sun, in the fresh air.

One night Andreas was aroused from his sleep by the front door shaking under the heavy blows. He jumped out of bed, naked, and without thinking grabbed his gun. Through the half-drawn curtains, he saw the rotating blue light of a police car. The hair stood up on his neck and a shiver went through his whole body.

"My God," he murmured "not already!"

The knocking on the door became more insistent. Andreas took a deep breath and tried to concentrate and quell the panic that had seized him. A thousand thoughts flashed through his mind, but as the initial shock faded, his reason took over.

"They can't have come here for me," he mused, "the secret police don't come with flashing lights nor do they knock on doors; they break them down. Something else must have happened."

"What the devil's going on at this hour?" he shouted angrily, knowing that with Afrikaners, attack is the best defense. "Bleksem donder, I'll fuck you up good!"

Swearing all the time in Afrikaans, he opened the door and found himself face to face with a heavily built sergeant with a red face.

"What the hell's going on?"

"Goeie nag, meneer," the sergeant said formally.

"Is there no fucking respect for decent citizens in this country anymore?" yelled Andreas furiously.

"Obviously, since there are people who don't respect the laws of the land."

"What do you mean, man?" demanded Andreas, at the same time casting a swift glance behind the sergeant. He saw that about ten policemen, white and black, had rounded up and handcuffed Zulu and all his black workers.

"You talk to me about fucking respect, man? How about this country respecting me, since I fought for more than a year in the Strip killing fucking blacks?"

Andreas saw the sergeant's animosity fading.

"All right, man, but most of these blacks of yours are illegal. They're not allowed to be in the Transvaal."

"You fucking wake me up to tell me that? Arrest the bastards then, kill them for all I care. Don't fucking bother me with your problems."

"Calm down, meneer. I'm sorry we woke you like that, but how were we to know we were dealing with one of our own? Anyway, these blacks are illegals and I'll have to arrest them and send them back."

"And how the blazes am I going to get any work done tomorrow, tell me that? If I don't plant tomorrow, all my seedlings will be ruined and so will I!" yelled Andreas aggressively, knotting his fists.

"Look, man, fix me a coffee and I'm sure we can work something out."

Andreas thought about the proposition, then, in a quieter mood, invited the sergeant in. He offered him a chair, put the coffee-jug on, poured a glass of brandy and sat down with a deep sigh. The sergeant's eyes gleamed with greed.

"Maybe you'd like a stronger drink?" asked Andreas innocently.

"I'd prefer that, to tell you the truth."

Andreas passed him the glass and the half-empty bottle.

"I don't suppose you'd have any Coca-Cola?" the sergeant asked apologetically.

He took a bottle from the fridge and put it on the table. Then he hurriedly pulled on a pair of trousers and sat down. He knew he had won the first round.

"Sergeant, I know I must have done something wrong, but I need your help. I only just rented this farm a few days ago and I haven't had time to go and register at the pass office. You understand?"

The sergeant half-filled his glass, drained it in one gulp and smacked his lips in appreciation.

"I quite understand, my friend, but as you see I'm not alone. It's difficult to turn a blind eye. What would the others say?"

"I need some help, man. I'm new to this district. As you know, we don't have problems like this in the bush."

"Well, it's difficult, you know. I have to worry about what the others would think. They need their own cut otherwise they would think I was keeping it all to myself and that wouldn't be right, don't you think?"

"How much?" asked Andreas.

"Let's say fifty Rand a head. That's not much. They'd relieve you of three times as much in court."

"You must be crazy," answered Andreas indignantly. "Where the hell would I get money like that? I can give you twenty. Take it or leave it," he added laconically.

The sergeant refilled his glass. "You drive a hard bargain. Still, you're one of ours. OK. Twenty it is."

"Thanks, Sergeant. You're a friend," said Andreas as he counted out the money.

"My name's Johann van Wyk. If you ever need any help with the police, come and see me at the local police station."

He took the money, counted it and stuffed it in his pocket.

"If you want my advice, young fellow, you'll take them to the Bantu Affairs office and get them registered. You're not in the bush here. There are millions of them here, and we've got to know what's going on."

"You're right, Johann. I promise I'll take them as soon as the planting is finished."

They went outside and the sergeant shouted to his men. "He's one of us, so we'll let him off this first time. Let the kaffirs go, except that aggressive one. Although he is the only one that is registered, he is a cheeky bugger, a troublemaker. He's far too smart for a kaffir. I reckon he's some sort of provocateur."

He grabbed the handcuffed Zulu with his powerful hands and shoved him forcefully in the direction of the police wagon.

"I'll teach you a few things, kaffir."

Andreas hurled himself in front of them, grabbed Zulu by the throat with one hand and punched Zulu's thick lips as hard as he could, covering the man's face in blood.

"You fucking kaffir, I've told you before! I don't want any smart tricks on my property. If you weren't such a good worker, I'd cut your balls off and make you eat them!"

"Sorry, Baas. Sorry, makulu Baas, I won't do it again. Sorry, Baas, sorry," wailed Zulu.

Andreas gave him a final punch in the stomach. Zulu doubled up on the ground and lay motionless.

"Right, you cheeky kaffir, that'll teach you some respect for white men. Every white man!" raged Andreas.

"Well done, Jan," said the sergeant, "you know the black man's language and how he thinks!"

"Leave him with me, Sergeant, and I'll make him as meek as a lamb."

"Take the cuffs off him. We've got to go."

They got into the vans and left. The blacks shrank back, hanging their heads and waiting in silence.

"Go back to sleep. We've got work to do tomorrow."

"Thank you Baas," they said with one voice, and disappeared fearfully into the night.

Andreas waited till the police headlights had left the property and then bent over Zulu. With some difficulty he got him on his feet, helped him into the house and applied first aid.

Zulu opened his eyes and grinned. "Jan, you're pretty strong, but I'd advise you never to lift a hand against me again! At least you've got some guts and you fooled them nicely. Thanks for getting me out of their clutches."

"Zulu, I'll tell you something. I understand how angry you feel about everything that's going on. You and I, and a lot of other people are trying to change this state of affairs. But the job we've taken on is very important, and we mustn't make any more mistakes."

"Yes, Jan. It would have been better to obtain registered workers. Someone must have reported us to the police."

"Anyway, how are you feeling, Zulu? I'm sorry I had to hit you."

"I'm fine, Jan, you did just the right thing. That was clever of you, you know how they think. They're all the same."

Andreas looked at him thoughtfully. "I think we've been very lucky. We'll have to be better prepared in the future because, believe me Zulu, they're not all the same." He thought with hatred of Captain Kolradie and his gang in John Vorster Square.

"Jan, before I go to bed I want to tell you that I'm here to work with you at any time you need me. Just call and I'll be ready."

"Thanks, Zulu. I need your friendship. We've got some difficult times ahead of us, I think. I had better get all our workers registered in my name tomorrow. Could you collect their passbooks for me? We probably all need to go to the pass office tomorrow."

The building in Albert Street was a world of futile hopes and grave disappointments for every black man and woman who ever had to wait in its long, crowded queues for hours and days. It was a world of entreaty, degradation, fingerprinting and supplication until, if at all; one received the stamp allowing you to live in a white neighborhood for one year. The Bantu Affairs or Passbook Office was a new experience for Andreas because, although he had been born and had grown up in this country, he had never needed to go to this miserable place. Every door and every window, right up to the top floor, was covered with heavy steel safety mesh. Hundreds of black men and women of every age were scattered all round him. As he approached his destination a swarm of blacks literally fell upon him.

"Do you want workers, Baas?"

"Please give us a job, Baas, please!"

Dumbfounded, he shook his head in refusal. The crowd continued with their entreaties.

"Give me twenty cents, Baas. I'm hungry."

"A cigarette Baas!"

"I'm hungry, Baas!"

Andreas stopped seeing faces and features, only mouths with hungry lips, some with sharp white teeth, some with none, asking, beseeching and begging. Who could you help? Whose misery could you relieve? Without realizing he had arrived at the entrance on which was printed in large letters: WHITES ONLY. Two black policemen with thick wooden clubs in their hands spoke to him politely and obsequiously and pointed him in the direction he wanted to go. But at the same time, like janissaries, they pushed his followers away with a rough order to get into line. He entered a big hall and breathlessly sat down on a bench.

A woman approached him. "Can I help you, sir?"

He passed her the booklets, greasy with years of use and she took them, gave him a number, and told him to wait. He lit a cigarette and tried to shut out the voices and the visions of the embittered mouths. People were coming and going continuously, the numerous benches had filled to suffocation point with whites who had come on similar errands. He waited for nearly three hours before they called his number and told him to see Mr. Levine in room fifteen. A middle aged man with a long, thick nose lifted his glasses, gave him a casual glance and told him to sit down. He picked up the top booklet, opened it and started to leaf through it attentively. Then he turned to the policeman who was standing in the doorway and said, "Bring me Jacob Moleto."

"Jacob Moleto," the policeman bellowed, "Jacob Moleto."

Jacob entered the office, with his hat in his hands.

"Yes, master!"

Mr. Levine ignored him completely, and said to Andreas in a monotonous voice: "If you want this boy to work for you, you have to submit an application and explain the reasons why you want him to work on your property. Meanwhile, Jacob must return to his village. If your application is approved, then within about four weeks, Jacob will return and will be allowed to work exclusively for you for one year."

"What chance of success will my application have Mr. Levine?"

"That depends on the way you frame your application. If you can explain why this black is indispensable for your work, then your application will be approved."

"Very well, Mr. Levine, I'll complete my application right now."

The official handed him a sheet of paper without comment and turned to Jacob.

"Muna, you will take this form and as soon as you reach your village you will give it to your chief to sign. It will cost you ten Rand. You understand?"

"Yes, master."

Andreas cast his eyes over his application and handed it back. Mr. Levine took it, asked for twenty Rand, and gave him a receipt.

"Mr. De Villiers, as soon as Jacob returns, you will bring him here and we will enroll him on our register. Then we shall issue him with a work permit. Should you later dismiss him from your service before the expiry of the year, you will sign his book and write in the reasons why you have decided to dismiss him. Of course he will then be obliged to return immediately to his village."

Andreas nodded.

"Simon Tsombe"

"Simon Tsombe, Simon Tsombe," yelled his echo.

"We have no problem with this one. He was born in Soweto."

He took from a drawer a large square rubber stamp and stamped one of the pages. Then he opened a thick ledger, made the appropriate entry and sent Tsombe out. He then carried on the same routine with the following passbooks.

"Saniboy Mareto."

"Saniboy Maretooo!"

A frail man with a scanty moustache hurried in and bent in half, demonstrating his obedience.

"Muna, you're a permanent resident of the Transkei homeland. What the hell are you doing here?"

"Makulu Baas, there's no work in the Transkei. I have a wife and six children to support. If I don't work they'll all starve to death. Please, Makulu Baas, let me work here. I need it so bad."

"Our government has given you land and farms. If you're not prepared to work, it's better you should die."

"But Baas, that homeland was for twenty thousand people. There are more than two hundred thousand of us..."

"Oh, I see. You're some sort of a demagogue, are you?"

He signaled to the policeman waiting at the door and he rushed in, put the handcuffs on him and pushed him out of the door, kicking him as he went.

With difficulty, Andreas managed to keep his face impassive, though within himself, he was blazing with uncontrollable anger. He had always felt some reservation about armed struggle. Watching this scene gave him a taste for blood. He was sure that there was no other way to bring about change in South Africa. The rest of the workers met similar fates. The policeman took them away, and Andreas was sure he would never see them again. It took enormous effort but he managed to swallow his feelings.

"And now what do I do without workers, Mr. Levine?"

"I'm sorry, my friend, but the laws of the state say that all blacks who were not born in the Transvaal have to go back to the homelands set up for them. However, if you want workers, take this note, go to the ground floor, office number three, and ask for Mr. Kruger. He will fix you up immediately with as many workers as you want."

Mr. Kruger was a compact little man with small, glassy eyes. "How many workers do you want, Mr. De Villiers?"

"Five, please."

He slid open a wooden hatchway which looked out into a small internal hall. A sea of heads appeared in front of him. They were all shouting together.

"Me Baas."

"Me, me, me!"

"I want five boys who know how to do farm work."

Dozens of hands were raised in appeal. He chose five and told them to go into the office through a neighboring door. He enrolled them and stamped their passbooks. Andreas and Zulu took their new legal staff back to the property. It was four in the afternoon and they had wasted the whole day sitting in line, and now they were both exhausted.

CHAPTER 18 Drumbeat of Freedom

In the factory staff room, Matthew was asked to pick up the phone. He went to take the call with some annoyance. He did not like to be disturbed at work. His boss's temperament had changed considerably over recent months and had become irritable and short-tempered.

"Hello!"

"Sakubona inkosan, kunjani? Greetings Mister. How are you?"

Matthew's face lit up as he recognized Doctor's voice.

"Sikubona, nawena (Fine and you?)"

"I just happened to be in your area. Any chance to join me for a coffee at the corner restaurant?"

"Right, brother. I'll see you at lunch time. Goodbye."

As soon as the siren sounded Matthew hurried to the local blacks-only restaurant, which at this time was full. He spotted Doctor Erickson sitting in the rear with another man at a rickety table, drinking coffee from a tin mug. Matthew bought a dish of steaming mealie-meal with sauce and a little meat. He looked for an empty seat. When he approached Doctor's table, a man picked up his empty plate and left. Matthew sat down in his place. He cut a piece of bread and dipped it in the thick sauce.

"So nice to see you Doctor. What good wind brings you over here?" Matthew asked softly.

"I have very good news, Matthew. The high command has decided to quicken the pace and to exploit to the utmost the commotion caused by the liberation struggles in Angola and Mozambique. It has just sent two of our agents to extend our operations. The orders I have are definite; we must get in touch with them, support them and help them in their work as much as we possibly can. So make sure you're free this weekend because we're going to spend it with one of the agents, coordinating our activities."

"OK, Doctor, it is about time that something is happening. I'll be at your disposal. Where do you want us to meet?"

"Six o'clock on Saturday outside Central Station."

Matthew swallowed his mouthful and nodded his agreement.

The handful of tables had filled up and customers were standing with plates in their hands waiting hungrily for someone to get up so that they could grab their place. Doctor Ericson drank the last sip of his coffee and stood up. Immediately, a woman sat down heavily on his chair, her ample bottom hanging down all round the narrow seat. Matthew, finding the restaurant food quite tasty, finished his plateful with gusto.

On Saturday, as arranged, he hurried out of his room at five o'clock to keep his appointment with Doctor. He suddenly stopped and instinctively searched the inside pocket of his jacket, and then sighed with relief; his passbook was in its place. He would certainly not have wanted to be picked up today because he had left the wretched booklet in his other jacket. The police lay in wait everywhere. At exactly six, Doctor's car stopped in front of him. He opened the door and settled into the passenger seat.

"Where are we going, Doctor?"

"To a property a little way out of town."

Matthew frowned. "Don't you think it's a bit risky to spend the night on a property? You know the police often make raids and if they catch us they'll be asking things we can't explain."

"I've thought about all that, Matthew. There has to be some special reason. Our orders clearly state that we have to go there to meet the man we want."

"I don't know what to say to that, Doctor, but personally I'd prefer our meeting to take place in Soweto. At least there we'd have somewhere to hide. Anyway, let's just hope we're lucky."

Doctor Erickson, who knew the district well, found the road to the property. The car headlights fell on the shape of a man waving his arm. He was tall and well-built and his bald head was shining under the half-moon.

"That must be our man, Doctor."

Doctor, silent and with all his senses at the alert, stopped the vehicle near the stranger without turning the engine off.

"Good evening. I'm a doctor and I've been told to come here to see someone who's sick. Am I at the right place?"

"Sorry, Doctor, you're too late. The patient died a little while ago."

Doctor, relieved, tried to make out the face of the man he was talking to.

"Don't worry, comrade, you're in a safe place. Put your car in the garage."

Doctor Erickson drove the car into a garage attached to the house. He was alarmed to see a white man waiting for him there. Andreas immediately understood his fears and he smiled in an attempt to calm him down.

"Welcome, Doctor Ericson. Don't be alarmed. You are among allies."

Matthew's hair stood on end as he heard the stranger speak in so familiar a voice. He opened the window and looked at him carefully.

"Andreas," he gasped, unable to believe his eyes.

"That's right, Matthew, it's me. Back home again."

Matthew flung the door open and threw his arms round him. After the initial burst of excitement over the unexpected meeting, Matthew grabbed the arm of Doctor who was standing discreetly a little way from them.

"Andreas, I have the honor to introduce you to Doctor Erickson, the Doctor of Soweto."

The two men shook hands warmly.

"I've heard so much about you, Doctor. I'm delighted to be working with you."

Zulu noisily closed the garage doors behind them. He approached the group shaking both Doctor's and Matthew's hands, in traditional Zulu greeting, as he introduced himself. They all entered the house, closed the doors, windows and curtains and sat down at the table.

"I am very sorry to hear about Rena's death, Andreas."

"Thanks Matthew. How are my parents?"

"From a health point of view they're fine, but they're worried, nervous and anxious. They have no idea whether you are dead or alive."

"It must be very hard on them but for the moment, I have no other choice."

The conversation turned to the immediate problems that faced them. Matthew bombarded them with a torrent of questions in a tone of friendly aggressiveness that surprised Andreas. It was a new experience to hear his childhood friend expressing his concerns so firmly and clearly.

"Yes, comrades, I think the time has come for guns to speak so that we too, like our neighbors, can taste the fruits of freedom. I'm fed up; believe me, tired of hiding like conspirators and talking hopefully behind closed doors. I'm tired of having to carry that blasted passbook and of being jailed without reason. I'm tired of playing the role of the stupid black. Why, brothers, do we have to accept that our struggle is so sluggish and inflexible? We ought to get into action, fight and die, because I at any rate can't stomach any more the strategy of wait and see. We have nothing to lose!"

The other three men listened to him, nodding their heads to show their understanding.

"Matthew, there's no point in trying to run, when we're barely able to walk on our own two feet," Zulu said.

"Come on, Zulu, enough of that! I'm sick of hearing the same thing over and over again. I thought, that at least as a trained agent, you might think differently."

"Matthew, I don't think you should jump to conclusions. We mustn't be led astray by what's happened in our neighboring countries. The situation there is different and unique for several reasons. The enemy here is tough and implacable, all-powerful and fanatical. Furthermore, our geography doesn't offer us anywhere to hide. Unlike our neighbors we don't have mountains or jungles enough to hide us. Additionally, we cannot for the moment, ask them for help. They are very weak and won't let us construct bases there because they're afraid of retribution from Pretoria. If we ignore all that and start open rebellion, we'll be cut to pieces quickly and thoroughly. But that doesn't mean that we can't be more active; just that whatever we do has to be done intelligently."

"Intelligently and thoughtfully, of course," added Doctor Erickson. "In my view our struggle faces three major problems. The first is the traitors, those hired spies who'll sell out everything for a few Rand. When you think about it, every movement so far has been broken up because of them. Secondly, there's the local nationalism that the government skillfully excites under the motto of 'Divide and Rule'. They turn one tribe against another, dredging up old enmities and creating new ones, sending Zulu police into Xhosa lands, Sotho among the Venda and so on. Thirdly, there are the hot-headed youngsters who act impulsively with little thought. We've got to influence the student population to take the reins from the hands of their parents who've been beaten down by fear and have grown accustomed to simply hanging their heads. Then, Matthew, if we can overcome those problems, you'll see the results you dream of. Most difficult of all though, we have to plan and act despite the fact that they continue to imprison all our leaders."

"You're dead right, Doctor. That's the cold reality and I completely agree with you Andreas. What do the people abroad think about how we should proceed?"

"The main order that Zulu and I were given is concerned with how to deal with the traitors. We need to engage in merciless suppression of the traitors and those who collaborate with the present regime. We need lists of names and addresses from the whole of the Transvaal and no misgivings. We've got to deliver a merciless and impressive blow against them, as they deserve. Traitors have got to learn that we'll repay them with death! Maybe that way we can limit their dirty work."

"That's a decision I completely agree with. It's something we should have done a long time ago. But I'd like to know who's going to carry out these executions," said the doctor.

"Don't concern yourself with that, Doctor. Our squad will take care of the purges and punishments; we've got specially trained agents here waiting to work with us," said Andreas, closing the subject. "What I need from you are the lists of suspects."

Doctor Erickson looked at them skeptically for a moment, "It won't be easy, but we'll try to get them as soon as possible. I'll use all available resources, Andreas, you must be sure of that. We all know that this is a huge problem."

"Then we can proceed," continued Zulu, "and develop along the lines they want us to follow. Naturally I don't have to tell you that the ANC is relying heavily on you two, and of course on your network, which in their opinion, is one of the best organized groups they can call on in the whole country. There are plenty of arms and materials now, stored away in our neighboring friendly states. It is up to us to get them into South Africa and distribute them to our resistance fighters. This is my primary job."

Zulu continued, "Another task. We've got to maneuver our own people into key positions. We need trusted hands involved in everything including heavy industry, military installations, even in the police force and government services. Wherever we decide that they'll be useful. At the right moment, when we give the order, we'll need these plants to throw the enemy into confusion. And of course, we've still to throw our weight into recruiting as many new members as possible."

"Doctor, you must pass on these orders to every network in the Transvaal. Brothers, those are the most fundamental messages they told us to pass on to you. If you have any reservations or questions, we are ready to answer them," Andreas added.

"I think you've both been very clear about what they expect us to do, Zulu and Andreas," answered Matthew. "We shall all have to try to do whatever we can."

"Andreas, will you and your group be amalgamating with us?"

"No, Doctor, for reasons of security our group will be developing a completely independent course of action. However, I'll be in constant contact with you so that we can co-ordinate our activities."

"We'll have to work out some way of communicating because it's not easy for us to come here, and it'll be hard for you to get into Soweto."

"Don't worry, Doctor, it will be sufficient for me to get in touch by phone, and when necessary, Zulu can go to Soweto."

"Right, then all we have to do is get on with the job," Matthew concluded with satisfaction.

"Get me those lists and we can start right away. Also, Matthew, if you can, it would be great if you could stay with us here for a while. I need you to bring me up to date on certain matters, and we can use the time to draw up a plan of action. We have many things to talk about."

"Perhaps next week, Andreas, I have a couple of days off while your parents are away and I'll be happy to spend them with you guys."

Andreas refilled the glasses, opened the fridge, took out various plates with cold food on them and put them on the table. They enjoyed the meal and afterward, over coffee, Andreas asked Doctor Erickson:

"Doctor, what's your opinion about the government's latest move to reduce 'petty' apartheid? I gather they've abolished those WHITES ONLY signs in the parks and elevators. I hear that blacks are now allowed to visit the Zoo, the airports and even certain hotels."

Doctor's eyes gleamed with anger. He took a deep breath and laughed bitterly and sarcastically.

"Andreas, absolutely nothing has changed here.That's all a skillful smokescreen, a hypocritical strategy for the sake of international public opinion. They are trying to lure in foreign investors! The situation here is still the same. These changes are just soap-bubbles that only intellectual cripples can believe in."

"That's as I guessed," Andreas said.

They spent near the whole night planning, talking and generally enjoying each other's company.

* * *

The following Sunday, the rich harmonies of the organ and devout hymns of the congregation trembled in the air of the great Gothic church in Johannesburg, filling it with an air of mystery. Andreas, hymnal in hand, joined in song. As the service neared its end, the middle-aged priest stepped down to the communion rail. His kind face remained completely impassive when he saw Andreas, who had purposefully waited until last, approaching the rail with a bowed head. The priest paused as the previous communicant returned to his pew. He turned and asked Andreas.

"Have you made your confession, my son?"

"Yes, father, I'm prepared," answered Andreas.

The priest bent down to deliver the host into Andreas's outstretched hands.

"The Body and the Blood of Christ," he said aloud and then added in a whisper, "Tribal dance at Randfontein coal mine."

Andreas received Holy Communion, made the sign of the cross, and then quietly slipped out. His car was parked a little way down the street and as he started the engine, he realized that he was whistling a cheerful tune to himself. As soon as he was sure there was no one following him, he turned on to the A1 motorway and sped up. A few kilometers from the small town he saw the large advertisement. He read aloud;

RANDFONTEIN GOLD MINE CORPORATION. FREE ADMISSION TODAY. PERFORMANCE OF TRIBAL DANCES BY BLACK WORKERS.

He drove into the narrow private road for a few kilometers until he arrived at a large open space that was the visitors' car park. The mine's open-air amphitheater was divided into two sections, one for the white and the other, for the black spectators. It was almost full. Two coaches filled with American tourists arrived belatedly. The visitors emerged in a noisy throng, laden with movie cameras and photographic gear. Andreas grabbed the camera he always carried with him and mingled with the Americans. Policemen with dogs and automatic weapons had long since taken up their prearranged places to guard against any incidents that might occur among the thousands of miners.

These dance performances took place at regular intervals in almost all of the country's mines and they had become one of the popular attractions of the City of Gold, drawing hundreds of visitors. What had initially been a form of local entertainment for transient miners to offset a lonely Sunday afternoon; had been promoted into a large enterprise by the mine owners. The dances helped the miners to cope with the monotony and the ever-present sense of isolation that they suffered in their daily routines. It was free entertainment for which the mine owners did not have to pay, but which made the miners more amenable to their work and less susceptible to tribal fights. Andreas adjusted his camera and then cast a fleeting glance at the program leaflet handed out to him at the entrance. The show would begin in a few minutes. He bought a hot dog and a coffee, then took his seat comfortably on the soft cushion, enjoying yet another privilege to which he was entitled by virtue of his white skin.

The loudspeaker announced that the program would start with a bird dance performed by workers from the Matsagani tribe. The dancers rushed in groups, onto the earthen arena, whistling through reeds held in their mouths. They were beautifully dressed in multicolored feathers. Their bodies began to sway in time to the musical urging of the whistles, which alternated between quiet and loud. The powerful black bodies of the dancers were expressive, rhythmical and full of grace as they mimicked the flight of birds. The dance was intense. The self-taught dancers' energy, joy, yearning and dignity reflected in their steps. It was hard for Andreas to believe that these vibrant souls spent their long days hopelessly in the damp, sunless corridors of the mine. Although these miners undertook the most tiring, dangerous and dirty tasks underground, their pay was not even a tenth of that of their white colleagues. He knew that there was nothing romantic about this impressive dance. Andreas had no idea what it symbolized, which confirmed once again to him, his total ignorance about his fellow-countrymen. The white spectators watched with bated breath, while the blacks, even though squashed in one on top of another, shuddered in unison with the dancers. At the end of the dance, the spectators burst into applause. Many of the tourists ran forward to the open-air surrounds of the stage to obtain a better vantage point for photographs and Andreas followed them.

The dances continued. They were graphically expressive and so different from each other that the public watched them with undiminished interest. The show concluded with a war dance by Zulu men. The drums thundered, overwhelming, rhythmical, wild and loud. The air filled with ululation and loud war cries from the dancers who ran onto the arena raising a thick cloud of dust as their bare feet stamped the ground. The Zulus were clad in the traditional way, in animal skins, leather thongs and multicolored feathers. Their earlobes had been pierced at an early age and now displayed large, round, wooden rings painted in vivid colors. The men held leather shields, wooden spears and assegais in their muscular hands, beating them loudly together. Their movements were short, quick and threatening, proud and expressive of manly grace. The bone plaques, hung around their wrists and ankles rattled in their distinctive sound, in time with the warlike beat of the drums. This war dance was majestic and sent the black spectators into waves of appreciation for the dancers.

Andreas watched with admiration and also with despair for the vanquished order of the past. Their dance had such a powerful spiritual dimension that it seemed as though the dancers had left the twentieth century, to go back in time and become again, the fearless warriors; the conquerors of the South. They had been completely transformed and in no way resembled the dispossessed and unfortunate people forced to hurtle down into the bowels of the earth each day. Andreas marveled at the spirit within the men that could produce such vivid emotion in such desolate times.

The enthusiastic audience burst into cheers and the black spectators poured onto the arena, dancing and shouting enthusiastically. The police dogs strained at their leashes and growled. The police were always ready to intervene if they thought it necessary. Once more, Andreas joined the tourists from the coaches as they surged forward to capture the dancers on film. One of the dancers approached Andreas, gleaming feverishly, with sweat streaming from every pore of his body. Andreas recognized him immediately as fellow trainee from the camp. This was the man he was supposed to meet. He went up to him boldly.

"Umnumzane, can I take your picture?"

The black man's eyes flashed strangely as he looked at Andreas. He raised his assegai in the air as a greeting.

"Of course my Baas," he said and took up a proud pose.

Andreas took some pictures and gave the man five Rand.

"Ngiyabonga Umnumzane!" the dancer said clapping his hands in thanks in the traditional Zulu way and then murmured, "meet me at the public toilet in a half hour."

Andreas went to the bar, ordered a beer, and struck up a conversation with an American tourist, while the announcer declared that the boot dance by the Sotho tribe was about to begin. Andreas drank his beer slowly, an eye on his watch. When the time came, he stood up and followed the sign to the men's room. It was empty, but as he came back out, the Zulu dancer appeared in the doorway.

"Hello Jan! Good to see you again."

"Hi Patrick. How are you doing? Where are the others?"

"They are waiting. Let us go and meet them. Follow me."

Opposite the toilets, sporadic lights showed the numerous long buildings of the hostels where the miners lived. It was quiet there because nearly everyone, including security was at the dance arena. They entered a dark empty kitchen in the compound. In the dim candlelight, Andreas was able to distinguish three men waiting for them; Martin, Moses and David, men who made up the team and with whom he had trained in the camp. In the security of darkness, they exchanged warm handshakes.

"We have to be quick Jan. You must get out before the dances end," Patrick said. "How was your entry? Did you have any problems? Have you been able to establish yourself?"

"Comrades, the color of my skin made it easy to cross the border. I live on a farm and I was able to bring in all the hardware that we will need for our operations. I also bring good news. In a few days, I believe, we will have the list of known traitors from Soweto," Andreas said.

"That's the best news I've heard since I got back, Jan. About time too. I was getting fed up with waiting and working in the mine. It is no fun. The more I see how our people live and work here, the more impatient I get! On the other hand, it is a perfect place for us to meet and as they predicted in the camp, it is the best place for recruiting new members. Everybody here is fed up and everyone wants change."

"I can understand that brother; it's not the ideal place to work or live. That's one of the reasons why we're in this struggle. Anyway, let us hear how you guys have sorted yourselves out?" Andreas asked.

"To tell you the truth, I've had a lot of difficulties, but I'm ready now," David replied. "I am registered and I got a job working in a supermarket in Soweto. It's an advantageous location, and I am finally ready for action. By the way, what news from Zulu?"

"He is fine, he is with me. Actually at this moment, he is on his first mission."

"That's good to know. He is a great guy," David responded.

"I have a job as a cleaner at the Carlton Centre," Moses added, "as you all know it is one of the most prestigious buildings in the country. The right attack will send a powerful message when the time comes."

"As we had planned, I managed to get a job as a taxi driver serving Johannesburg to Soweto," Martin said. "I will be able to provide transportation for our missions. I must say Jan, you being a white is a great help. You can go just about anywhere in the white areas without suspicion."

"Thanks Martin. It is good to feel that I am part of this team! It seems that we are ready. They've promised me the list for Soweto within a few days."

"That's great!" said Patrick. "Our first priority is how to deal with these traitors. So let us work on our plan."

"We've gone over it so many times at the camp, Patrick. Let us not waste any more time. We need to get out of the compound as soon as possible. We don't need to take any more unnecessary risks," David interjected.

"OK," said Andreas. "We are all here and ready so let us go ahead as we planned. What is missing is the list of names, which I will soon have. Patrick, can you to ring me at this telephone booth on Thursday at exactly seven? If I'm ready, I'll arrange to meet Martin and give you the names."

Patrick committed the telephone number to memory, folded the paper in his gnarled fingers and pushed it into the ashtray where he set alight to it with a match

"OK, Jan. Thursday at seven."

"We must all be careful and not rush things," David said.

"There's no need to hurry. Time's on our side," Moses added.

"Don't worry, brother, we're all professionals. Anyway I want to live long enough to experience freedom," Patrick replied. "Jan, it's been great to see you. I'm glad we've started to move. Good luck, comrades."

"We'll see each other regularly, Patrick. Take care, and congratulations on the dancing, you were terrific." Andreas smiled as he returned in the dark to the car park.

He was lost in thought the whole ride home. He felt a sense of great satisfaction, that all the plans that they had prepared for so long, were finally starting to take on flesh and bone. Andreas suddenly felt his stomach complain that he was hungry. He made himself a few sandwiches, opened a beer and sat out in the cool of the veranda. He had only just started to eat when he saw Samuel, one of his workers, coming toward him, with his hat tucked under his arm. He was clapping his hands gently, in a sign of obedience.

"Excuse me, Master, for disturbing you at this hour, but you've been away all day."

"Come closer, Samuel, and tell me clearly what you want. Don't be afraid."

"Baas, I want to visit my wife who works in the city and I may be a little late. Would it be possible for you to give me a permit?"

"Of course, Samuel, hang on while I write you a note."

He wrote, 'Please permit my boy Samuel Ngobe to travel to Johannesburg after nine o'clock. He is a good boy and a reliable worker. Thank you. Jan de Villiers.' He shook his head in disgust, as he gave his worker the permit.

Early the next morning, Andreas called from a phone booth on the nearby highway to get news from Doctor. He was relieved and delighted to hear that Zulu and Matthew were back from a successful mission and he arranged to pick them up. Zulu had completed his first difficult trip to smuggle weapons from the border. Matthew had accompanied him on the trip, to show him safer routes on back roads. As soon as his trusted colleagues joined him back at the farm, they began planning. They studied the city map to determine possible strategic targets for sabotage. Andreas and Matthew discussed old times as well as new prospects for the future. Doctor had assured them, on the phone, that he would have the list of names by the end of the week at the latest. Andreas felt confident, knowing that before long, things would start to move in earnest.

One Thursday evening, Zulu, his knobby assegai in his hand, went off on his regular evening patrol. Andreas had already retuned from the phone booth, where he had received the arranged call from Patrick. They had agreed to continue the calls until Andreas had received the whole list of names. The night was particularly warm. Zulu strolled around the property with all his senses on high alert. He came to the barbed wire, external gate and set the alarm system which Andreas had installed after the unexpected visit by the police. Satisfied, he went back to the house and knocked on the door with their agreed signal. They sat down to eat their evening meal, which they had earlier prepared together.

"Andreas, I feel pleased that we are operating on several fronts and that we will strike as hard as we can," stated Matthew.

"All the same, Matthew, we can't ignore the likely consequences," countered Zulu. "The Afrikaners will strike back with a vengeance."

"I agree with you Zulu, but tell me what did a population like ours ever gain from passive resistance? Did we gain anything from the miners' uprising? Only corpses, plenty of corpses and packed prisons. And what happened as a result of peaceful insurrection in Sharpeville? Exactly the same! When have revolutionary goals ever been achieved without deaths? Never! Of course there'll be victims, of course we'll be mourning the dead, but without some deaths we'll never get our freedom."

"I'm afraid Matthew's right," added Andreas. "I'm sorry for the people, and I'm sorry that violence is the only way to justice."

The alarm bell rang interrupting their discussion. Zulu seized his assegai and hurried out. Andreas's face showed his anxiety as thousands of possibilities flashed through his mind. Matthew got up and began pacing up and down.

Zulu came back, panting, and called from the doorway, "Jan, we've got visitors!"

Andreas calmly collected the scattered papers from the table and hid them in a safe place.

"I'll have to hide you, Matthew. We can't risk you going out with the other workers. It'll be disastrous for all of us if they catch you here. Come with me."

They went through the inside connecting door to the garage where Andreas moved some boxes aside and opened the trapdoor to the hiding place where the armaments were.

"It's a bit cramped, my friend, but we haven't any other choice."

Matthew was experienced in coping with difficult situations. He squeezed himself in.

"Don't worry about me, Andreas. Just shut the trapdoor and get out fast."

The police van, its lights and headlights extinguished, approached quietly and stopped some fifty meters from the house. Two men jumped out and one went surreptitiously to the back of the house while the other walked up to the front door.

Zulu approached him, clapping his hands in servile greeting.

"Good evening, Makulu Baas."

The sergeant smiled in satisfaction at the black man's stance. "Is your master home, kaffir?"

"Yes, master, he's inside," he stammered.

Sergeant van Wyk strode arrogantly to the front door and knocked loudly. Andreas choked down his anxiety as he calmly opened the door.

"Good evening."

"Sergeant van Wyk! Don't tell me we've got problems again?"

"No, Jan, it's an off-duty visit tonight. I was just passing by and I thought I'd come and see how you'd managed with your blacks."

"Thanks for your interest, Johann. All my blacks are legal now. If you want I can call them so you can take a look at their passbooks."

"No need for that, Jan. I believe you. In any case I'm off duty, like I said."

"Then come in and have a drink and keep me company."

"Well, if you insist, I'll just come and have a quick one. But just give me a couple of minutes to call my colleague from the car to join us."

Andreas opened a bottle, put ice in the glasses and switched off the television.

"Nice house you've got, Jan."

"It's not bad, though it's a bit large for one person."

"You know, I have a great weakness for these old colonial houses. I like to study them."

"You should have been an architect, Johann, not a policeman."

"Ag, it's only my hobby, Jan."

Andreas had quickly formed the idea that this innocent visit was leading somewhere.

"Johann, if you don't mind a bachelor's disorder, perhaps you'd like to take a look round?"

Just please ignore the dishes in the sink. I have not had a chance to wash them for days"

Sergeant van Wyk jumped at the chance.

"Far from it, Jan. I'm a bachelor myself."

Andreas got up brazenly, and with feigned politeness led them from room to room, even opening the built-in wardrobes. When they got to the garage, he noticed a look of disappointment on their faces. But what on earth were they expecting to find? The bottle soon emptied and the atmosphere warmed up as their tongues were loosened and the ice of formal politeness thawed. The sergeant turned out to be a real blabbermouth, in love with the sound of his own voice. Andreas patiently endured the situation and tried to guess what it was all really about.

"I'm particularly pleased this evening, Jan."

"Why's that, Johann? What happened?"

"I went to the afternoon service and our pastor read us a passage. I must say, what he told us was amazing. It made me feel really proud."

"What did he say, Johann?"

"I'll tell you because you're a real Afrikaner and one of us. The Bible predicts that a nation from the north will overcome the omnipotence of America and bring darkness to the world. But it will not rule for long, because it will be overcome by the yellow races. Well the Bible goes on to say that a small nation from the Southern hemisphere, with the blessing and support of God, will overcome them and bring them back to the light of the world. But what's that nation going to be Australia, New Zealand or South Africa? Well, my friend, our pastor believes that we are the chosen people of God, and it will be up to us to liberate the world. That's why we've got to be stronger every day!"

"Well, that's terrific, Johann. You must tell me where this church is so that I can get to know this important teacher," said Andreas.

Fortunately the policemen were too drunk and too flattered to notice his ironic smile. Andreas opened another bottle. The good cheer increased, religious obsessions took a back seat, and the sergeant started to tell jokes.

"Have you heard the one about Mrs. van der Merwe, when she went to France on her own for a holiday? As soon as she set foot in Paris, she heard about the big international sex seminar that was taking place there. So she went straight along and enrolled, thinking she'd give her husband a surprise when she got home. Well, as soon as the seminar ended, Mrs. van der Merwe caught the first plane she could and flew back to South Africa. The minute she got home, she took van der Merwe by the hand and led him into the bedroom to give him his surprise. But while they were making love, van der Merwe jumped up in astonishment and said, 'ag man, wife, what's got into you? You're fucking like a bloody kaffir woman!'"

It took some time for the guffaws raised by this typical Afrikaner joke to die down.

"Honestly, Jan, how do you get on? How do you manage for a woman? I've never yet seen you with one of ours. You don't even have a servant to keep you place clean? "

Suddenly Andreas woke up to the real purpose of this visit; they had come to find out whether he had a black woman to sleep with, something strictly forbidden by law. Andreas gazed back at them seriously.

"Johann, it's still only a short time since I lost the wife I loved. Believe me; it'll take me some time before I start looking for another."

Johann gave him a friendly, patronizing pat on the back.

"Jan, now that we're friends, if you want to fix yourself up with a kaffir woman, my men and I will turn a blind eye."

"Thanks, Johann, but I don't need one for the moment."

"Hey, boys, I'm dying for a bit of action. Jan, let's go out, find some women and have some fun!"

"Bloody good idea, Johann," said Andreas, "but I'm too pissed for anything. Some other time, eh? Right now I'm going to bed."

"Well in that case give us a bottle of your excellent Portuguese brandy so that we can continue our party somewhere else."

Andreas grabbed a bottle and handed it to the Sergeant. After they had departed, he closed the door behind them and sighed with relief. Zulu emerged from the darkness.

"Oh, Zulu," Andreas said. "If only you could have heard what shit I had to listen to."

Zulu replied with a contemptuous smile, "I heard it all. I was standing by. God help us if He has chosen them! I need to make sure they have left and set the alarm, before we can get Matthew out."

CHAPTER 19 Uprising of Soweto Schoolchildren

Sweating under the blazing sun, Andreas tried to fix his punctured rear tire. An old taxi stopped right behind him and its driver, a black man with a round face in his early thirties, got out. He approached him with a broad smile on his face and he wiped the sweat from his shaven head with a handkerchief.

"Need any help, master?"

"Do you happen to have a wheel-brace? I can't unscrew the bolts on the wheel."

"I have, baas. Just a moment while I get it."

He opened the boot and soon came back with the tool. He knelt down next to Andreas and his powerful hands soon started to budge the lug nuts.

"Did you bring the names, Jan?"

"Yes, Martin. The next step is up to you."

"I'll let you know as soon as we're ready. You must be at your phone booth every day at seven."

"No problem my friend. I will be there."

Andreas took out a folded banknote and the list of names, and handed them to the taxi driver.

"That's for your trouble. Thanks for your help."

A traffic police car pulled up beside them.

"What happened?"

"Nothing serious. This boy is helping me to change my tire. I'm on my way right now."

Martin, still smiling, put the note in his pocket, got back into his taxi and left.

Andreas went back to the farm to meet with Zulu and Matthew. They worked for the rest of the day on topographical maps, marking entry routes from the neighboring states and ways to get essential weapons.

In the evening there was an unexpected visit from Doctor Erickson, whose face was beaming.

"What fair wind blows you here?" asked Andreas pleased to see him.

"I've brought the lists from the ghettoes of Tambiza, Alexandra, Boksburg and Lanseria!"

"That's marvelous, Doctor. How did you manage it so quickly?" Zulu asked.

Andreas took the invaluable lists and examined them carefully. They were complete in every detail with names, addresses and occupations. He looked at Doctor with admiration. How fortunate he was to be working with such men.

"It was a lot easier than I'd first expected," Doctor answered quietly and then he continued with building enthusiasm; "but not only that, comrades, I've got good news, really good news for us. I attended a meeting of young people and their dedication is deeply moving. I'm proud and happy to tell you that a new breed of youth is developing in those wretched ghettoes."

"It's obvious you've brought good news, Doctor. I've never seen you looking so optimistic," Andreas commented.

"Why are you so excited?' Zulu inquired.

"You guys have heard about Steve Biko and his movement of black consciousness? He is a medical student at the University of Natal who started the all-black South African Students' Organization, SASO. He would not accept that the white leadership of NUSAS could represent black interests because he believes strongly that black people must define themselves and escape from a sense of inferiority in relation to the white man. Our youth have identified with him and his movement. They are embracing his ideas and a sense of a new found pride is emerging. I believe they are getting ready to come face to face with their white oppressors. Simply, they are proud to be black. There are even posters saying, 'Black is Beautiful' being nailed all over the townships."

"It's about time that somebody has inspired and involved the younger generation," Zulu commented.

Doctor and Matthew departed as both had to return to work. The days went by and Andreas received no further phone calls from Patrick. Without news of the men in the squad, he became moody and impatient. He was anxious and the lull in the action made him dwell on the difficulties they would have to face. All the same he sketched out in his mind how the first phase should go. Travelling in his car, he paid visits to the places he had picked as the first targets. He wanted to leave nothing to chance. Everything had to occur with mathematical precision so as to create the maximum confusion. He had picked two targets about sixty kilometers apart, since he wanted to create the impression of an attack on several fronts. He carefully noted all the details on his map and went home satisfied.

On his return to the farm he stopped at the phone booth and waited for the appointed time. The phone rang exactly at seven and Andreas seized the receiver impatiently.

"Hello!"

"Good evening, Jan."

"Hello, Patrick. What's the news?"

"Very good. We're going hunting tomorrow. You'd better send me the parcel with the presents for your auntie."

"Right, Patrick. When do you want us to meet?"

"About nine in the evening so that we can set off straight away afterward."

"OK, my friend. I'll be there."

Andreas was trembling and sweating with excitement.

"At long last! We are ready for action. The lies are over!" he told Zulu.

Andreas and Zulu opened the secret crypt, reached inside and pulled out four Scorpio automatics. That examined them carefully one by one, filled the magazines and set the safety catches. They wrapped them in oilcloth and put them in a sack with some extra ammunition.

"My aunt will be very pleased with these presents," he said to Zulu.

"It is a fine present, Andreas. These bastards deserve every bullet in Shaka's name!"

Andreas arrived at the pre-arranged place at exactly nine and parked at the side of the dark, deserted street. Within a few minutes, Martin's taxi stopped next to him, its lights extinguished. Andreas passed over the heavy sack from the open window and the envelope with the new names. The taxi raced away immediately and disappeared round the corner. Andreas did a U-turn and went back to the property.

The next day, the two first executions shocked the public and stirred up great upheaval in Soweto. The morning papers seized on the murders, turning them into front-page news with bold headlines, photos and full stories.

Two police officers of the Soweto division, one of them a sergeant, were discovered in the early morning murdered on their way home after a duty period. There are no eyewitnesses. The assassinated bodies of these protectors of law and order were found riddled with large caliber bullets. The laconic notice found near the bodies upsets the initial theory that they were the victims of personal differences. The brief notice written in red ink reads: "In the future this will be the reward of every traitor. ANC"

Reinforcements were immediately sent to Soweto and the sordid ghetto filled with stern-faced police, carrying out extended and detailed inquiries. They took in suspects without discrimination, pushed them into paddy wagons and took them to the station for questioning.

Andreas sensed that his turn had come to divert the attention of the police in another direction. He set out at night by car and drove quickly but carefully for more than an hour until he stopped a considerable distance from the nearest inhabited area. He hid his car behind a clump of trees, opened the boot, took out his small haversack and pushed his way through the tall grass. He wriggled his way easily under the barbed wire fence and let himself roll gently down to the railway line. He worked calmly and silently, quickly placing a landmine under the rails. Then he swiftly taped the trip wire to the top of the rail with a piece of sticking plaster. He covered the bulk of the mine with pebbles and crawled up the low, slippery embankment on all fours. He retraced his steps, got back in his car and sped away from the area. Andreas had joined the main road among dozens of other cars when he heard the distant sound of the explosion. He knew that by the time the police had been alerted to close off the whole district, he would be well away.

The next target was much easier and had no particular significance. He had simply chosen it to scatter the police and create a psychological effect. The electricity substation was unguarded and he found no difficulty in slipping between the fence posts and placing a crude time-bomb on the condenser, setting it to explode in two hours' time. He got back to the property without mishap.

Andreas bought the papers of both the Afrikaans and English media. Zulu and he read the news as they watched the events unfold on a newly acquired TV that Andreas had bought. Television had just been introduced in South Africa and they were surprised by how much was being reported by both the English and Afrikaans channels. He felt an inner joy as he sensed the rising panic and perplexity of the general public. As a response to the blowing up of the train and the electricity substation, the police command had offered a reward of ten thousand Rand promising complete protection for informers. Numerous clergymen hastened to take up a position against the murderous terrorists. The newspapers continued their front-page coverage, resurrecting earlier accounts of ANC activity and in the process increasing the anxiety of their readers. The Transvaal police had been put on full alert sealed off sensitive areas and arresting thousands of citizens. Zulu said he was sure they had unleashed armies of paid informers with the promise of princely rewards. Two days of nervous tension went by as the events continued to be the sole topic of report.

Newspaper reports of sabotage and violence then receded into the past with the relative peace and quiet of the following days. Confident statements were made by the police that they were already on the track of the terrorists, whose arrests were imminent, merely a question of days. Before the echo of these episodes had died down however, another murder in Soweto and two more in Tambiza stirred up the muddy waters and revived public skepticism about the competence of the police force. Despite the watchful presence of the police, thousands of proclamations filled the streets, not only in black but also in the white areas, adding to the general disquiet. The climax to the events was an explosion of terrifying force that shook the center of the city, as a liquid fuel dump blew up.

Doubts about the infallibility of the powerful police force started to penetrate the minds of the well-to-do whites. Rumors began to multiply. Panic began to make its insidious presence felt. The opposition newspapers propagated a war of words against the government, stressing that the inhuman system of apartheid was increasing the hatred of the black population and driving it to the use of arms. Editors called for speedy change that would permit the various peoples of the country to coexist peacefully. In contrast, the nationalist papers criticized both the government and the police for their flexibility and moderation. They demanded the heads of the guilty. They demanded that the government should strike mercilessly to grind down the black population before it grew still more vociferous. The war of resistance continued undiminished, opening new fronts in Natal and Cape Town with fresh sabotage, new proclamations, and the further murders of traitors.

The National Guard was called out to undertake extensive searches and night-time blockades right into the central streets of the white cities. Every car was examined without any distinction concerning the color of the driver. These efforts added to the electric atmosphere and to the insecurity and worry of the population. As Doctor and Zulu had rightly predicted, the active resurgence of the struggle and the naked violence of the police toward the unarmed population produced the resistance they had been longing for. The ideas of the ANC found ready reception among hundreds of young people who organized themselves into groups. In contrast to this unique phenomenon of strong and youthful willpower, the older generation stood aside in bewilderment and fear, unable to believe what was happening and too frightened to follow suit.

The consequences of this upheaval among the youth were exacerbated by a strange injunction perpetrated by the government itself, adding to the mounting tension by enacting a provocative and poorly thought out law. It decreed that black and colored students should be taught in the Afrikaans language at the expense of their own language. The aim was to impose Afrikaans by force as the principal language of the state. The effect of this decree was like detonating an atomic bomb in the restless ghetto of Soweto. For the black youth, it was seen as an act of sheer provocation. The scholastic imposition fueled their hatred and incited general disorder, especially because Afrikaans was seen to be the language of the police. The student outcry mounted: "No to the Afrikaans language! No to racial separation! Black power! Black power!"

The majority of Black, Colored and Indian school children ignored both the admonitions and threats of their teachers, and the frightened pressure of their parents. They categorically refused to accept this law and as a sign of protest stopped attending their classes. With every day that passed, the number of absentees grew in proportion, and those teachers who remained faithful to the system had to give their lessons to almost empty classrooms. Every day, infuriated school children would gather in the assembly areas of their schools and exchange opinions. Then almost invariably, those who carried on with their classes would face the contempt and derision of their fellow students and inevitably the dissent would culminate in stone throwing at school buildings.

The Police Minister made the following statement on June 15, 1976:

> *The government stands firm by its views. Schoolchildren must go back to their schools and cease fantasizing with imported communist ideas. The police have been instructed not to show any leniency because you cannot fight communism with modern, civilized means or democratic principles. The only way to combat communism is to fight it with the weapons it uses itself! Tomorrow the schools will be operating normally and soldiers and police will guard the entrances to protect*

the overwhelming number of children who want to go on with their classes but are afraid."

Night settled heavily over Soweto. Suspicious shadows, tense and watchful figures, flitted from alley to alley. Bolted doors, secret gatherings, whispered conversations, anxious hopes and dreams reflected the tensions of the day. Secret meetings were held by the young leaders of school committees. At the same time, messages were sent throughout the country urging every school pupil not to go to school.

On the following day, 16 June 1976, the schoolchildren of Soweto set out for school without their school-bags. Dressed in their black and white school uniforms, thousands of children of all ages gathered in front of their closed schools ignoring the pleas of their terrified parents. They took occupation of their school, kicked the teachers out, locked the doors and threw the keys away. They raised their fists in the air and sang passionately:

"Black power! No to Afrikaans! Freedom! No, they won't get away with it!"

Pupils from each school, shouting continuously, made for the central square. On the way they joined up with other children from other schools, so that the volume of the procession kept increasing. Powerful police forces were immediately put in place. They were armed with semi-automatic shotguns, shields and staves, and they surrounded Soweto to prevent any chance excursion of schoolchildren toward Johannesburg.

The mass of striking children kept on growing and their defiant shouts could be heard several kilometers away. The nervous police could not believe their eyes when they saw this gathering and in perplexity they tightened the grasp of their sweating hands on their weapons. The front ranks of the children inevitably came face to face with the armed police. Ragged barefoot children with raised fists and impassioned faces glared at the police who were fully trained in the use of deadly weapons. The two extraordinarily contrasted groups stood gazing at each other, each assessing the other's intentions.

The commander of the police, with a megaphone in his hand, shouted in autocratic Afrikaans:

"In the name of the law, I order you to disperse and to go back to your schools."

Soweto resounded to the sound of children's voices as they shouted their answer to this police order:

"No to Afrikaans! Black power! Nkosi sikelel'i Afrika!!"

Suddenly, the police opened fire without warning. The cries of unbounded enthusiasm and exasperation turned into screams of pain, panic and despair. The dusty streets of Soweto filled with the bullet-riddled bodies of children. The stink of gunpowder mixed with the iron smell of fresh blood. The thunder of automatic fire and fierce, stony faces contrasted with the feeble, ragged children's faces now masks of terror. Soweto had transformed into a Dantean vision of hell.

The underage demonstrators quickly reorganized themselves, armed themselves with whatever weapons came to hand. Stones, pieces of wood, bottles, iron bars and petrol were grasped by children, who had become numb with a mad desire for revenge. They began to destroy whatever they could find that belonged to the hated white boss. Buses were quickly emptied of passengers and drivers, tipped on their sides to form street barriers, and then set on fire. The same fate befell all kinds of commercial vehicles bringing supplies to Soweto. First they plundered whatever they were carrying, and then they set fire to the vehicles, shouting incessantly:

"Bulala umlungu (kill the whites)! Amandla (strength!)"

The police used random machine-gun fire, teargas, clubs and sneezing machines. They hurled their poison gas at the demonstrators making it hard for them to breathe and subjecting them to uncontrollable sneezing. Flames, smoke, gas, fire-engine and ambulance sirens, shrieks of hysteria, wails of grief, death-rattles, the reek of burning oil, metal and rubber filled the air. The doors of the houses opened wide and mothers, their hair astray, barefoot, terrified and panic-stricken, with their hearts in their mouths, ignored the bullets and searched frantically for their children. Laments and the stench of ever-flowing fresh blood were added to the symphony of disaster in this new holocaust.

But the children did not stop running, fearless, suddenly grown up with the flame of the desire for freedom that burned inside them.

"Fire to the schools of shame!" someone shouted.

Molotov cocktails were quickly improvised and new flames burst against the blackened sky as one after another the school buildings went up in flames, only to collapse into shapeless, heaps of coal. The flames and clouds of black smoke could be seen as far away as the white city of Johannesburg. By midday, the dead and the wounded were multiplying constantly. The only hospital for blacks in the area was filled to over capacity with the wounded and dying. Doctors and nurses, exhausted by the influx, were only barely able to cope. They made constant appeals for blood, medicine, serum and medical assistance. The wards were at bursting point.

The police tried to force their way through the blocked streets, but a continuous shower of stones rained down on them. They replied by savagely firing at anyone they saw. Hunted groups of angry children arrived at the most hated building in Soweto, which housed the offices of the Department of Bantu Affairs and the government liquor stores. Black policemen in their dark uniforms poured out of the building to intercept them.

"Bulala umlungu inja! (Kill the white dogs) Bulala umlungu! Amandla!"

Molotov cocktails exploded with a deafening roar and flames started to lick at the brick walls. The black police suffered terrible deaths as they were literally hacked into pieces. The heavy doors crashed open. Howling children rushed into the buildings, setting on fire anything they could get their hands on. The white staff, pleading for mercy, were cruelly beaten to death. Millions of bottles and barrels of beer were smashed to pieces and the devouring flames rose higher and higher into the sky as the spirits caught. Fresh reinforcements of police and soldiers kept arriving by truck and helicopter. The nightmarish clatter of small arms fire could be heard continuously, and huge bulldozers cleared the streets of blockades.

The children, unable to oppose them, weary and crying with frustration, sought refuge in any house they could find and with clenched fists watched from half-open shutters, as the soldiers and police scoured the streets of Soweto with their fingers on their triggers. The men of Soweto, the fathers and elder brothers of the schoolchildren, working in the city, stared toward the ghetto from a distance in fear and anguish, unable to make contact with their families. The roads and the phones had been cut off by the army. Soweto was under siege and the white bosses, for the first time allowed their black workers to take refuge for the night in the forbidden white areas.

The mass media broke the news to the uneasy white population emphasizing police reports that the insurrection was under control. Rather than acting as a calming force, this information increased the general anxiety. All those who had guns took them out, cleaned them and loaded them. The gun shops were besieged by customers and the price of weapons rose to unprecedented levels. The night brought a frost to Soweto in the harsh highveld winter. The doors were bolted, but the residents, worn out and speechless, could not sleep. They sat in darkened rooms licking their wounds, choking back their pain and mourning their dead. In the heat of the next midday, the remains of a government school building presented a grim picture of burnt charcoal and dust, a reminder of the recent student uprising.

Young demonstrators had for the first time in history, taken the struggle into their own hands. They had provoked the establishment by refusing to be taught in the language of their white oppressors. They demanded to choose the language of their schools. The price was high. Police trucks spread out into the city, on every road. Heavily armored policemen fired haphazardly into any crowd of black students. In their desperate need to find the leaders of the school uprising, police violently entered homes at random, indiscriminately arresting schoolchildren, who were transported to John Vorster Square for interrogation with torture.

Although weeks had passed by, many of the dead were still unburied. The authorities had not given permission for the bodies to be moved from the mortuaries. They knew from the previous episodes, that emotions ran high, and that funeral services would lead to more uprisings. While underage children were binding their wounds, their elders looked on with astonishment and pride at what these young people had attempted. The heroic young inhabitants of Soweto had set an example to all Africa in their struggle for freedom. The children, now confined to the gravel backyards of their dwellings, looked at the police patrolling backwards and forwards down every street with hatred and contempt.

CHAPTER 20 Draconian Reprisals

Andreas and Zulu climbed to the top of a hill on the far end of the property and watched the condemned, flaming city of Soweto. In the distance, dark grey clouds of smoke rose into the air. Andreas's eyes filled with tears of sorrow. His feelings were strangely mixed. Sadness mingled and danced with admiration for the fallen heroes. They returned to the house and again watched the latest on the television news. It was obvious from TV reports that the entire world's attention was focused on Soweto. The heroic fight of the schoolchildren had touched people all over the planet.

Andreas commented to Zulu, "Soweto has become a nerve-center and if it is allowed to sink into inactivity, it will be the end of any movement for many years. I wish we could connect with Matthew and Doctor."

All means of communication with Soweto had been cut off. For days he had heard nothing from either Doctor or from Matthew. He tried desperately to reach them from the phone booth, but to no avail. Eventually Zulu suggested that he should to take the risk of going there. Andreas insisted that they should go together, although they both knew that it would be an act of sheer madness. Finally, Zulu convinced Andreas to listen to reason. After hours of thought and planning, Zulu subdued his misgivings, and tried his best to disguise himself. He put on some old, scruffy clothes and a battered balaclava hood that covered his face. He inspected with scrupulous care the forged papers that had been supplied him back in the camp. Satisfied, he put them into his inside pocket. Andreas drove him as far as he could. Alone, Zulu stepped out boldly into the dark night.

"Please try to call me. I will wait at the phone booth for your calls; make it a little later, eight o'clock if you can," Andreas shouted after him.

Zulu's journey was a veritable Odyssey; an experience that could only be understood by African people in South Africa. Several times he thought he was done for, as policemen loaded with weapons conducted numerous spot inspections. More than once, they pushed him against a wall and searched every part of his body. They examined his papers, swore at him, and then arrested some men that they had stood up next to him. They took all of what little money he and the other offenders had. It was only by sheer luck that he managed, hours later, to get into Soweto. The streets were deserted, full of rubbish, holes and burnt cars. The cold night was dark and wet. Zulu proceeded cautiously and quickly, continuing to avoid the patrols. Doctor Erickson's house was pitch dark and silent, and he wondered whether anyone was home. He circled round it twice. Only when he had made sure that nobody could see him did he press against the wall next to the front door and knock with the secret signal. He could hear a surreptitious sound behind the door. He waited a second, and then knocked again.

"Who on earth is it at this hour?" whispered Doctor's voice.

"I'm the singer," answered Zulu.

"What do you want to sing at night, man?"

" Nkosi sikelel'i Afrika!"

The door opened noiselessly and as soon as he was inside it closed quickly behind him. Doctor switched on the torch he was holding and shone it on Zulu.

"And who the devil may you be?" he gasped in alarm.

"Calm down, Doctor. It's me, Zulu. I had to see you at all costs, and find out what was happening. We thought that this was the only way we could get in touch with you."

"It's amazing that you got through all those barricades. Anyway, I'm very pleased you came because I need you. I wanted desperately to contact you. Matthew's in hospital, wounded."

"How serious is it, Doctor?" asked Zulu with concern.

"Serious enough, Zulu. They took two bullets out of his chest but he seems out of danger now. We need to get him out as soon as possible. The police have begun invading the hospitals. We had a lot of casualties. The struggle has taken on a new dimension."

"How can I get to him? Andreas will be very upset that Matthew has been wounded. We have to let him know somehow. The phones are down or damaged by the police,'" said Zulu alarmed.

"Visits are not very wise under the circumstances. The security police are questioning all the wounded in connection with the riots. Besides we have so much to do in order to extend our operations. As you have seen, the place is crawling with police and a lot of blood has been shed. They have also brought in the army. We still haven't really got the means to fight them," stated Doctor.

"I understand that it's going to be hard," replied Zulu. "The only way at the moment is with continued support from the youngsters."

"Don't you think we're expecting too much from these children? They are dying out there. My heart breaks every time I treat a child. How can we ask them to continue? What more can we expect from these kids?" There was a tone of desperation in Doctor's voice.

"It must be very disheartening for you, Doctor. Living it first hand and you see how much these kids are suffering. But I raise my assegai to their heroism; it is their struggle as well as ours. Besides, I don't see them stopping now. We have to encourage them so that lives lost will not be wasted."

Doctor Erickson paused for a while before he finally answered wearily,

"I guess you're right, Zulu. Actually they don't need our support, they have their own agenda. There is a meeting going on right now with some of the leaders of the school movement. Let's go and hear what they have to say."

Doctor led the way with his torch, lighting up the dark corridor, until they got to the kitchen where he opened the trapdoor and they both climbed down. The cellar was half lit by a kerosene lamp and Zulu stood next to Doctor, and tried to make out the people who were sitting on two wooden benches. Most of them were boys of about sixteen. They all looked sullen and defiant. Of the five men there, Zulu recognized two from the training camp; Martin, the taxi driver and David. The others were total strangers.

Doctor spoke to the group pointing at Zulu, "Brothers, the reason that this man is here, is to pass on to you the congratulations of the ANC and to give us orders from the leadership."

Zulu continued. "It is well recognized that what you have achieved so far is amazing and heroic. You've earned the interest and admiration of the whole democratic world. All black school students in the country have adopted your slogans. They have even put your words and acts into song. What's more, they've committed themselves to the struggle and are trying to prove themselves as commendable as you. You have endured the ferment of backlash. The whites of South Africa for the first time have tasted fear and insecurity."

Doctor then turned to the group gesticulating as though pleading with them, "But I feel that we need to find another way. Too many of our children are dying. Others are being tortured like adults in John Vorster Square. I turn to you and to all those who follow you, and say: let us carry on with this battle; let us widen the struggle and demand the support of your parents. That's indispensable; they've got to join our struggle, willingly or under duress, because it's time they learned that nothing is gained with bowed head and folded arms. After all, an honorable death is better than an exploited life."

Zulu interjected on Doctor's appeal. "Brothers, I don't believe we can stop at this point. The bloodshed should not discourage us, nor should our spilt blood be wasted. Just the opposite, it should give us the same courage and inspiration that it has produced across Africa."

Doctor agreed. "It is true. We can't betray those who died for the great ideal. On the contrary, we must be ready to offer our own lives for the sake of liberty. The ANC requires not only the continuation of the struggle which you started with such spontaneity, but also its extension to all ages and all classes of society. The struggle has to become generalized. Brothers, you have brought us a little closer to reality, to the dream that one day all men will be equal and free. You have done that without established leaders, without big names such as Luthuli, Mandela and Gandhi. Instead, you have harnessed the power of youth; young people who had the strength and courage to use their own bodies as barriers to the racist regime. But as we have seen, our children are dying like flies. Do we still need to stand on the dead bodies of our youth to enhance our cause?"

After a few minutes of tense silence, one of the young men got up, trembling slightly, and turned his gaze on his companions with large, shining eyes. Dlamini was very tall and frail with thick, curly hair and a determined expression.

"Brothers, we are proud to be black and we refuse to kneel down under the white man's yoke. Steve Biko has helped us to understand what it means to be proud. Our leaders, like Tokyo Sexwale and Nalede Tsiki, have shown us that we don't have to accept the white man's language, schools or any of his customs. We will keep fighting until we have our freedom. You think we have become demoralized by fear and disheartened by the fact that we're fighting automatic weapons with stones? Of course, we are shattered with grief for the youngsters who were riddled with bullets and shotgun pellets, and by the mourning of their mothers. We are also horrified by the naked terror on the faces of the children being hunted down and running for safety. All of us carry these images of horror with us constantly. But we've got to shut them out. We can't stop! Our struggle has to go on. Let's have done with words. What we need from you is guns to get on with the job. Then, we will show them what we can do!"

Soweto awoke, noisy but peaceful, with the air and the earth frozen from the overnight frost. Workers, male and female, wrapped in overcoats or blankets, set out in the dark of the night on their daily journey to the factories. They traveled in overcrowded, asphyxiating buses and trains. The deserted Johannesburg central station suddenly filled with scurrying workers, pouring out in their thousands from the third-class carriages labeled BLACKS ONLY. Muffled up against the morning chill, they emerged in teams from the station exits on to the empty streets, chatting vivaciously. Illegal street-vendors greeted them shouting and showing their wares. Hot bread, coffee and rolls mixed with the smell of people. Among the noisy throng, children of every age mingled to avoid giving target to the eyes of the watching police. As the white city woke up, the streets filled with traffic and became lively and colorful; the shops opened their doors, and the typewriters banged away quickly and rhythmically. Uniformed black people prepared steaming coffee for their white overlords. The huge, noisy city pulsed with life.

It was close to midday when the astonished pedestrians noticed isolated students getting together and forming groups. Within minutes, the groups had amalgamated into a mass of more than five thousand black schoolchildren and the number was growing continually. From threadbare jackets and overcoats they extracted and unfolded large white banners with black lettering. A forest of arms with clenched fists multiplied inexorably. The shouts of the young demonstrators smothered out every other noise, bringing traffic to a halt and causing a chaos that was unprecedented in South African history. Worried white pedestrians ran panic-stricken to hide in whatever doorway they could. Frightened shopkeepers hastily closed their shops. The typewriters stopped and the windows were crowded with astonished onlookers who took out their guns and loaded them. The mass of children kept on growing. Suddenly, the crowd began to take on a different form as hundreds of black workers joined the students. The huge procession poured down the streets like a storm tide, and the crowd erupted into shouting: "Amandla! Africa for the blacks! Black is beautiful! Justice and freedom! Nkosi sikelel'i Afrika."

Police stations were bombarded with phone calls from anxious, frightened citizens and the news traveled from one end of the city to the other. The peaceful procession met no resistance and crossed the central business district. They were headed toward the hated building that housed the main offices of the secret police in John Vorster Square. Screams of hatred flew from thousands of youthful throats and the shouting of slogans rose to a fever pitch. The vast structure remained mute and the small police force on duty within closed and barred the doors and windows. The instinctive fear of John Vorster Square, innate in every black heart was put aside as someone shouted:

"Fire! Let's set fire to it!"

The more daring forerunners approached the building threateningly. Hundreds of sirens could now be heard as police cars, followed by truck-loads of police, converged from every part of the city. The leaders of the march knew that a confrontation would mean sheer suicide. Their aim had been achieved. For the first time, they had brought the struggle to the white areas. The dread of future insecurity had rattled the nerves of the white minority. In an attempt to curb the oncoming bloodbath, orders were given for the crowd to break up. The success of the march acted like a tonic, rekindling the morale of the children and stirring up their determination to fight for a better future. For all the efforts of the authorities to damp down the effects of the triumphant demonstration, they remained helpless. The black parents proudly discussed their children‘s exploits while the anxieties and doubts of the white population intensified.

Zulu worked ceaselessly in Doctor's hot cellar preparing the next step. One evening, Zulu and Martin slipped quietly out of Doctor's house and melted into the night. Zulu carried a loaded rucksack on his back. With infinite care, checking out every shadow and every corner, they made their way toward the local police station, dodging the numerous patrols that wandered the ghetto day and night. They reached their destination without mishap and hid in a thicket of leafy bushes. Zulu ran an experienced eye over the bulk of the illuminated building. A guard was standing at the entrance holding an automatic weapon. Police cars arrived and departed. He silently circled round the building, sliding along on his belly like a snake. He smiled when he realized that he had correctly judged the lack of police preparation. They had obviously not taken serious security measures. He approached the back of the courtyard and pressed himself against the high surrounding wall. It was not difficult to clamber to the top of the wall and when he had made sure there was no one around, he jumped down and landed lightly inside. He wasted no time in choosing a suitable spot to put the explosives. His face was impassive, even though all his senses were on guard. With practiced, steady hands he attached the silent time fuse. At six in the morning, Soweto was rocked by a tremendous explosion and more than half the police station collapsed in on its foundations. Police in pajamas and uniforms ran fearfully about the shattered heaps. The screams of the injured, the mess of corpses, ambulances, the continuous arrivals of reinforcements and rescue teams, investigating teams, explosives experts, all combined to turn the area into bedlam.

* * *

Andreas remained on the farm unable to travel to Soweto. He

continued to follow the battle through the media. Zulu finally was able to get a message to Andreas through Martin, the taxi driver. Matthew's condition had deteriorated and he was again in a critical condition in the intensive care unit. Martin told Andreas that Zulu had warned him not to attempt to visit him. It would be a death sentence for both of them if he was caught and furthermore it would jeopardize their position. Nonetheless, Andreas was totally frustrated that he could not visit his friend in the intensive care unit at Baragawanath hospital.

"The situation in Soweto goes from bad to worse," Martin informed Andreas. "All the hospital beds are filled with wounded and the security police are trying to get information out of them, no matter how badly injured they are. The army and police do not have any fragment of concern for human rights. They are determined to destroy the student movement. They treat the children as though they are the worst criminals."

Tension in Soweto was further inflamed by the continued refusal of the authorities to hand over the children's bodies to their parents for burial, supposedly for fear of further disturbances. The widespread indignation and outcry that followed provoked fresh hostilities and despite police action, the authorities could not suppress the ferment in Soweto. Constant pressure from the people finally forced the local authorities to give in and hand over a number of the dead, with the proviso that each funeral must be limited to close family. But despite these regulations, large gatherings of people attended the funerals. Many were eager to show their respect for the young heroes. The funeral speeches, most given by fellow-students, raised the ire of the crowds and once more Soweto was subjected to the sneezing machines, teargas and the thunderous shock of automatic fire.

Soweto and every ghetto in the country filled with student proclamations demanding that their parents strike for three days as a sign of respect for the dead children. They even demanded that during those three days no black person should enter the white areas or buy any item from white shops. They added that anyone who failed to conform to these instructions would be regarded as a traitor and could expect death at the hands of his or her own children. The freedom fight was rekindled throughout the country and a frustrated government kept on calling up fresh military reinforcements to put down the youngsters who were willing to sacrifice themselves in the fight. The three-day strike met with almost one hundred percent success and endangered the country's already shaky economy, costing millions of dollars. For the first time, the black population realized what immense power they possessed while the whites saw how dependent they were.

The commercial center was edgy, traffic was minimal after sunset, and luxury restaurants were devoid of customers. Revolutionary sabotage was succeeding in its aims and the struggle had extended to all classes of society and to all age groups. Fires and skirmishes had become part of the daily routine. All indicators were that the racist oligarchy was nearing its end. The authorities tried to contain the news reports so as not to engender panic in the white population but they had little success. As upheaval continued, shares fell in value and bankruptcies reached a record level. Houses and buildings were on sale for less than half price, but still no one was buying. Whites who had dual nationality made preparations to leave the country; academics tried to arrange foreign visas for themselves; those who had no such resources scoured their past and remembered that their parents had come from England or France and pestered the embassies for passports. The crisis the government now faced was much worse than the one that had followed Sharpeville so it took draconian measures, mobilizing the army and every available reservist to restore order. The authorities knew that panic among the white population was the greatest threat to their existence. This unprecedented insurrection cracked the shallow foundations of the country's stability and threw its future into uncertainty.

The government, harassed and anxious to ease the strain, then proclaimed with fanfare, through the mass media, that it had repealed the previous language legislation affecting the schools. It called on the children and their parents to bury their animosities and to return to school. As a gesture of goodwill, it offered a general amnesty to all those who had come up against the law. This governmental withdrawal, the first in its history, caused a ripple of enthusiasm, joy and hope. It was the first reward for so many sacrifices and the result was that everyone threw themselves unhesitatingly and with renewed zeal into the battle for independence.

In response to the continued insurgence and the refusal of the students to accept their bargain, the government then intensified its response and issued strict orders to the police and the military: Strike mercilessly, use every method and every means. The black uprising must be brought quickly under control. Huge rewards were offered for information, followed by methodical mass arrests. Fully armed police burst into houses at all hours of the day and night, beating, breaking, wrecking impoverished households, seizing hostages of eight years old and above, deaf to the protests and entreaties of weeping mothers. They carried them out like carcasses to the paddy wagons and began them on their road to martyrdom, after a visit to the torture chambers in John Vorster Square. Experienced torturers conducted inhuman inquisitions. Confronted with this psychological and physical violence, children who had been snatched from their families were burnt, beaten, left hungry and thirsty and forced to stand upright for days. They finally gave names and addresses and these their torturers hastily scribbled down and passed on to the special squads which raced off to make more arrests.

Panic and fear began to take on enormous dimensions in the wretched townships which were becoming growing cemeteries. Zulu and Doctor watched in horror the spread of this new form of genocide. They suspended every other kind of action and rallied all their men in an attempt to save as many children as they could. Orders were given for the children to change their place of abode every day and every night. Black families willingly shed their fear and offered lodging to the children who were being hunted. They commandeered every available means of transport and under the very eyes of the butchers, began the enormous task of ferrying thousands of children out to rural areas or villages where distant relatives and friends worked or lived. Zulu was very active in helping hundreds of older children to secretly cross the borders, where ANC men then took them on to the safety of camps that had been set up inside neighboring friendly countries.

Police armed with lists continued their attacks on homes. When they failed to find the children they wanted, they would beat the parents ruthlessly and drag away mothers, grandmothers, grandfathers and fathers to security force dungeons. Every possible torture was used to force them to reveal where their children were until every spark of resistance was gradually extinguished in the ruined ghettoes. People were indiscriminately arrested without restriction by the hordes of police and military. Once again, the freedom fighters paid dearly for their bravery. All human rights organizations condemned the racist government of Pretoria. Their pleas made not even the slightest impression. The major western nations called for a boycott on all sorts of trade and stopped sending arms to South Africa. But democratic France, freedom-loving Britain and that international watchdog for the combat of communism, the United States of America made exceptions to the rule. A franchise was supplied for Mirage fighters; assistance was given for the construction of a nuclear power plant, as well as other forms of high technology.

CHAPTER 21 Incarceration and Trial

Andreas and the rest of the team continued to act, working fanatically spurred on by their successes. Police reprisals had failed to manifest in their camp, and they felt confident and relaxed. Meetings were now held with Patrick, on the property. Their plans were still mainly focused on continued sabotage in Johannesburg and traitor reprisals. Extended excursions were taken to possible targets in the white areas. As Andreas was driving home after one such venture, he heard a special announcement on the radio. The Minister of Security and the Interior issued the following statement:

> *This evening at 8.00 p.m. officers of our security police arrested the leaders and a number of members of the banned ANC, who have been active for some time in Soweto. Apart from the aforementioned, the police also discovered and seized a large quantity of up-to-date military weapons, ammunition, explosives and time fuses. We are all delighted with the great success of the officers and men of the security service who, risking their own lives, arrested these dangerous gangsters who for months have been disturbing the peace and security of the country.*
>
> *The names of the terrorists will be announced to the public after inquiries have taken place; when those responsible will be called on to account before the law for the series of frightful crimes they have committed.*

> *I wish to take this opportunity to stress to the people of South Africa that there is no question of an uprising in this country, because the safety net cast by our security police is so tightly knit that there is absolutely no possibility of organized insurrection. The recent terrorist activities in our country were the first steps of communist action intent on the overthrow of South Africa. They hoped that these criminal activities would incite revolution. Naturally we have learned a great deal in the past few months which will help us to organize ourselves and become even more efficient in the future in ensuring that no similar situation occurs again in this country.*

Andreas was shocked by the news. He wondered who had been arrested and what it would mean to the cause. He decided to stop at the phone booth, hoping by some miracle that Zulu would try to get in touch with him. The phone rang at the appointed time.

"Andreas, have you heard the news?" Zulu screamed on the other side of the line. "Doctor has been arrested. Thomas told me when I got back from the border. The police silently surrounded Doctor's house yesterday evening before they could offer even the slightest resistance. Doctor and the others found themselves thrown on the ground and handcuffed. They took them all away."

"Don't you think you should come here?" Andreas asked Zulu.

"No, I can't," he replied, "I have another large group of kids waiting for me to take them out. I will call when I get back. Good luck Andreas."

After Andreas returned home, he turned on the news desperately trying to get further information about the arrests. He was interrupted by the alarm and then again, a few moments later by knocking on the door. He opened it to the sight of Sergeant van Wyk. The sergeant had a huge smile on his face and was dressed in civilian clothes.

"Goeie aand, Meneer. Hoe gaan dit? (Good evening, Mister. How is it going?) I was passing by and I wondered whether you had any more of that brandy that you offered me last time?" said the Sergeant.

Andreas looked at him in resentment and confusion. "It is rather late and I have a terrible headache. Can we leave it for another time?"

The sergeant put his foot in the doorway, "I am not going to stay. Just a drink and then I will go."

"This is not a good time, but if you like I will give you a bottle to take with you."

"That will be fine," he said following Andreas into the room. Andreas took a bottle of brandy from the living room bar and he handed it to him.

"Thank you," said the sergeant taking the bottle in his hand. "You know, I wanted to mention that I have a terrific memory. I recall the first time I met you. I was puzzled because your face seemed so familiar to me. Then you got mixed up with that bit with your kaffir. You said you were one of us, but you didn't smell quite right did you? So, I decided to pay you visit. Tell you a holy story and watch your responses. That night, I knew there was something wrong about you, so I checked your fingerprints on the last bottle that you gave me. Did I mention that I have a terrific memory?"

How could he have been so stupid? The 'feeble minded sergeant', that is how he'd thought of van Wyk. But this man was no fool. He was the worst that the system could produce. He was smart, cunning and patient. Worse so, he was a true believer. Andreas knew that he could not bargain with this kind of man. He reached for his gun, but Sergeant van Wyk proved too quick. The policeman had been ready for Andreas's attack. As the young man went for his side arm, van Wyk raised the brandy bottle and smashed it across his head. Andreas stumbled backwards and felt his legs surrender beneath him. Within a split second, van Wyk was upon him. Andreas felt blindly around him for his weapon, but the sergeant already had it in his hand. He used the butt to split Andreas's lips against his teeth. Andreas was stunned by the pain and stopped moving. Sergeant van Wyk rose to his feet and looked at the bleeding man sprawled on the floor below him with an undisguised disgust.

"Mr. Andreas Magdalos. It is about time we really met. By the way, I have also brought some of your old friends along. They were so disappointed to hear that you were back in town, but didn't bother to say hello. They are anxious to see you again."

Though the half open door, Andreas saw Shorty and Norman followed by the shadow of Captain Kolradie.

Andreas was taken to John Vorster Square and again locked in a cell. His mind was engulfed by hair-raising memories from the past. He knew that his end was near. Although he had lived with the belief that he would soon die ever since the day of Rena's death, he realized he had not yet surmounted his fear of it. He was so scared. Photographs, fingerprints, the cold metal chair, the powerful light in the eyes, he anticipated all the same tactics of psychological and physical ill-treatment as during his previous incarceration. The experience was to be familiar and yet, he trembled and sweated involuntarily, at the thought of it.

The newspapers boasted photographs of the arrested leaders. They declared the total annihilation of the resistance movement. The Prime Minister proudly commended the officers and men of the police force on their outstanding success. He stated categorically that the country would never again experience such disturbances. Finding itself once more in a position of strength, the ruling government party returned even more determinedly to its old arrogance. The state announced that from now on it would be merciless in its punishment of any new outbreak of extremism and communism in the country. In an attempt to throw dust into the eyes of international public opinion, it professed its belief in the legal process of justice and stated categorically to representatives of foreign news agencies that by the end of the month, the guilty would answer to a court of law for their perverted crimes.

The government announcements and the endless pressure to bring the guilty before the bench led to increased hours of work and headaches for the security police. They were plainly at a disadvantage because the politicians had not given them enough time to properly do their job. They needed to conduct an interrogation in depth so that they could comb the country and arrest all those who had escaped their net. Their job required time, patience, secrecy and freedom of action. They did not give a damn about the outcry in the wider world. The problems of their country were theirs alone, and only they knew how to solve them. Until now, twenty-four hour interrogations had proved fruitless. The prisoners obstinately kept their mouths shut and the puzzle widened for the investigators. They had discovered that Jan De Villier's fingerprints, belonged to the former president of the student organization NUSAS, Andreas Magdalos. How did he fit into the picture? What had happened to him since his deportation? Where had he been trained and with whom was he linked? The papers opened their archives and republished the forgotten story, while journalists besieged the home of the mega industrialist Frixos Magdalos in search of interviews. They found him silent and unapproachable.

For six days and nights, Andreas had hung by his wrists from the ceiling. He was exhausted from lack of sleep, thirsty, his eyes, lips, hands and feet were now hideously swollen and covered in blood. Throughout the period of interrogation, his mind had constantly played strange tricks on him. In addition to the feeling that he was losing his faculties, he had also lost all feeling in his extremities.

"Magdalos! I told you once that our paths had better not cross again! You remember?"

The loud, imperative voice he knew so well reached Andreas's tormented brain like an evil omen. His body quivered and he tried to block it out. Small windows of memory opened one by one as scenes of torture flooded into his fevered brain. His head swam with recollections of all the agonies he had suffered at the hands of the owner of that voice. He forced himself to open his swollen eyelids and his eyes, full of tears, hatred and contempt, fixed on Captain Kolradie.

The captain bellowed, "So you do remember me, eh? Well done! You've got a good memory. Magdalos, from this moment you're mine, and believe me there's no power in the world that'll get you out of my hands."

Andreas closed his eyes and cursed to himself for not having turned his attention to this swine from the first day he arrived back in the country. The captain's huge hand grabbed Andreas's drooping head and shook it hard.

"When I'm in front of you, you bastard, you'll keep your eyes open and look at me!"

Andreas felt a compulsion to spit on him, but his mouth was too dry.

"Captain, I want to speak to you in private," commanded a middle-aged man at the back of the room.

Captain Kolradie turned and followed him.

"Captain Kolradie," he ordered when they were in his office, "I forbid you to mistreat the prisoner. His trial will start in a few weeks and it will be followed by dozens of journalists from all over the world. Moreover his father has got the services of the best barristers and has invited representatives of the UN organization for human rights. We don't want to give them the slightest excuse to demand a medical examination. The government is unequivocal: it does not want to face international outcry. In any case, the evidence we have is enough to send him to the gallows ten times over with the full blessing of the law."

"But, General," the captain protested, "this fellow knows a tremendous lot that we can't find out from anyone else. He was trained abroad and we've got to find out how he got here and who is behind him. It's not in our interests for this fellow to go to trial yet. His trial must be put off. He has to talk! If we learn all he knows, you can be sure we can wipe out every revolutionary movement for the next ten years."

"I know you're right, Captain, but unfortunately that's the government's order and I can't do anything else. On the one hand they are under pressure to reassure our people that we've got control again, and on the other, the fuss that's broken out internationally is very bad for them. Legal trials of proven terrorists are their only way out. The prisoner must be transferred to a cell and provided with every comfort and medical attention. I want him to be in first-class condition on the day of his trial."

"Forgive me, General, but it'll be very difficult for me to go through all those ceremonies with that bastard. I might strangle him by mistake. Hand him over to someone else."

"Very well, Captain, I know how you feel. Call Second Lieutenant Potgieter and you keep yourself well away from the prisoner."

Andreas looked again at the names on the walls of his cell, each one keeping watch on its own story. He stretched to relieve the numbness and yawned listlessly. His eyes, bloodshot from lack of sleep, were irritating him. He needed rest but knew that sleep could not conquer his strained nerves. He reached for a cigarette packet, but it was empty and he screwed it up and dropped in on the floor. His watch showed three minutes past midnight, a long time yet till dawn. He got off his bed and began monotonously pacing up and down the narrow confines of his cell. His mind turned over with agonizing worries about the crushing of the movement. Who was to blame?

Could it be that all those dead children, all that blood, all those efforts had been in vain? No, he could not believe that it was so. The seed had been sown; the enslaved black people would be freed. It would not be so easy to destroy the momentum for change now that there had been a brief glimpse of the power that could be wielded. What would his comrades do? Would they carry on? Perhaps they too had been captured as he and Doctor had? Matthew, Zulu, Martin, Moses, Patrick and so many others. How he longed to know! All these unanswerable questions were driving him crazy. Wearily, he lay down on the bed again. Sleep overcame him unexpectedly.

He was back on the island of Poros with Rena. The sun was hot and the sea was like smooth oil to the horizon. The gentle sea breeze blew life into them as they lay together on the warm sand. But suddenly, the sky darkened and ripped violently apart with peals of thunder. The storm was upon them. Rena began to vanish into the distance, a tiny vision with disheveled black hair. Her arms were stretched out in entreaty as she cried plaintively: "Come, come, I'm waiting for you." He woke in fright to the thunderous clang of the iron door. The bad-tempered, hostile guard had brought his breakfast.

Andreas sat up miserably on the bed and rubbed the sleep out of his eyes, looking at the food without appetite. As he tried eating the soft porridge, his teeth clamped down on a hard grain of uncooked corn. Instantly his mind turned to Cornelius and he smiled fondly at the memory of the old fellow. The warden came into the cell and told him that he had a visitor.

"Who is it?" Andreas asked.

"It is a lawyer. He told me that he has been instructed by your father to represent you in your court case. And he wants to you to prepare your defense."

Andreas laughed, "you must be joking. Do they still believe that justice can be done in this country? I don't think so. I don't need any lawyers. I know my fate. Tell him to go away."

At eight o'clock, they took him in a special van, under heavy police guard, to appear in the Supreme Court in central Johannesburg. Andreas looked longingly out of the little window at the fleeting images of a free world. It was a sunny spring day and the trees along the road were dressed in fresh greenery. The traffic was thick, but the police sirens forced a way through. To his surprise, he saw that the area surrounding the grounds of the court, were packed with spectators. As the van approached, the crowd erupted.

They shouted in rhythm, "Black Power! Black Power!"

Their faces shone with fierce determination. Armed police encircled the Supreme Court building. Trained police dogs were hard at work, snarling and snapping, keeping crowd at bay. People had been gathering there since early that morning. A political trial was about to begin. Morning newspapers had published special editions with reports, photographs and striking headlines:

ANDREAS MAGDALOS, SON OF INDUSTRIAL MAGNATE ON TRIALTODAY ON TERRORISM CHARGE FOREIGN TERRORIST, INSTIGATOR OF RIOTING IN SOWETO

> The accused is closely connected with the banned African National Congress. He planned political murders, the overthrow of lawful government, and the release of long-term prisoners from Robben Island.
>
> Informed sources have revealed that as the trial begins, police are continuing intense investigations into the full membership lists of the illegal ANC organization.

The Supreme Court was a graceless, looming building, blackened with age and pollution. The little garden surrounding it had just a few sickly, dusty trees and scanty grass that did nothing to alleviate its dingy appearance. Heavily armed police, posted in strategic positions, kept wary eyes on the neighborhood. Their fingers never left the triggers of their guns.

A mixed crowd of people of all races had gathered outside. Whites and blacks were talking about the trial and the recent bloody events that had begun in Soweto and spread like mushrooms throughout South Africa. Some were obviously fearful, others simply curious. Many, more than ever before, were worried about the future of their country and their livelihood. Television crews, journalists and photographers, both local and international waited impatiently for the arrival of the accused. The piercing wail of police sirens signaled that action was about to begin. The crowd pushed forward expectantly and police dogs growled in retaliation, threatening the bravest of onlookers. An armored van stopped at the entrance to the court. The back door opened and more armed police jumped out, looking suspiciously around them. One man banged the side of the van and immediately a tall, heavily built policeman emerged, pulling the accused behind him on a heavy chain attached at both their wrists.

The tumult rose to a crescendo, amid the continuous dazzle of flashbulbs, as the journalists tried to jostle their way forward to hurl questions at him. Angry police pushed them roughly aside. A man boldly raised his clenched fist and shouted in exultation:

"Amandla! Black power! Nkosi sikelel'i Afrika."

Others seized the slogan and repeated it loudly and passionately:

"Amandla, Black power! Black power! Nkosi sikelel'i Afrika (God save Africa)!"

The dogs, baring their white teeth, snarled viciously as saliva dripped from their jaws. Armed police tightened their grip on their guns, while plainclothes policemen photographed the crowd of mostly black demonstrators. The accused, Andreas Magdalos, looked grimly at the assembled crowd. Black fists punched the sky, and the shouting got louder:

"Amandla, Amandla. Black power! Black power!"

The police escort, enraged by the developing situation, shoved Andreas down, and vehemently pulled him forward with the chain. He angrily said to Andreas, "I'll fix you later you kaffir lover."

Undaunted, Andreas looked up at the two field guns, relics of the Second World War, which stood on either side of the entrance to the court. He had seen them before, but it was only now that he finally figured out why they had been put there. They were supposed to be there to remind the world of the millions who had fallen in war for a better future, for a free world.

"What fucking freedom is that?" he whispered to himself.

In reality, he postulated, they were there as a warning to those who go against the system.

"How quickly one can go from citizen to enemy," he thought.

The outburst among the crowd had reached a level of militant strength and it began to march slowly and menacingly toward the court. Dozens of long-barreled automatic weapons were trained on the leaders. The dogs went berserk, barking madly and trying to break the leashes that restrained them. One dog suddenly freed itself and attacked a young man. It pulled him to the ground with a savage hold on his arm; his terrified scream could be heard way above the chant of the crowd. The demonstrators backed off fearfully as the other dogs surged forward. The guards grabbed the accused and rushed him into the court building. The heavy iron doors slammed, leaving the crowd outside in disorganized retreat.

The large courtroom was filled with those who had been fortunate, or brave enough, to gain admission. Secret police would certainly already be investigating the nature and extent of their interest in the trial. The courtroom had been quiet shortly before the entry of the accused. Now the atmosphere ignited like a spark on tinder. All eyes were pinned on him and the whispering became an urgent murmur.

An angry voice shouted, "Traitor, you white kaffir, son of a bitch."

Other voices joined the anthem, "Kaffir lover, rot in hell. We hope they hang you." The expectation of a lynching was obvious in their expressions.

In the specially constructed bullet-proof dock, the binding chain was removed from Andreas's body. He was handcuffed to the dock, without any time to rub his numb and aching wrists. He looked around him at the typical picture of a South African court. Even here in this place of justice, apartheid had managed to separate the spectators according to the color of their skins. Rails divided the large theater-shaped room into two. The larger and more luxurious section, with large comfortable seats, offered hospitality to the elect of God, who had the privilege of being born with white skin. The smaller narrow section, with rough wooden benches closely pushed together to economize on space, was crowded with the larger audience of blacks.

The ashen faces of Andreas's parents suddenly caught his eye. The sight of their anguish brought home to him their suffering. He wondered whether they would ever be able to understand or forgive him for what he had done. A heavily built man in his forties, with lively brown eyes, spoke to the guards and showed them a card. They admitted him to the dock and he sat down next to Andreas with a sigh. Andreas looked at this stranger with perplexity and indifference.

"My name is George Bakos," he said without preamble. "I'm a barrister and your father has instructed me to defend you. It's a bit late of course, but if you'll have me as your lawyer I'll try to do what I can, naturally I can't make any promises."

When Andreas heard the name Bakos, his indifference subsided somewhat and he became interested in what this man might have to say. Andreas had heard the name Bakos many times over the years. He was one of the few competent lawyers who were prepared to defend people accused of political crimes. In particular, Andreas remembered a story he had often heard as a university student. During a lengthy political trial, a young and inexperienced prosecutor had gone to an old judge to seek his advice. The proceedings were extremely complicated and the guilt of the accused was doubtful. The old judge was tired and asked wearily:

"Who's the defending lawyer?"

"George Bakos," the young man replied, with obvious admiration.

"Then hang the bastard," the old judge shouted.

"Well, Andreas, what have you decided?" said Bakos.

"Look, I admire you and I do not doubt your ability or your intentions, but I think it's a waste of time," said Andreas. "You know as well as I do that this case has already been decided. Today's trial is just a farce. Anyway I'm tired and I have been through too much to be bothered with this nonsense."

"Sorry, but I can't agree with you, Andreas," said Bakos. "In its own fashion, justice does still manage to hang on by a thread in this country. Besides, I thought I was dealing with a freedom fighter, but obviously I am mistaken. There's a whole nation in the dock with you, Blacks, Asians, and Whites like myself who all still believe in change. You have a moral responsibility to put up a good fight, to get across the reasons and the motivations that made you rebel."

Andreas looked at the lawyer with disdain and said caustically: "Don't talk to me about obligations and moral responsibilities. You are only here because you are a famous Greek advocate and my parents are willing to pay you to defend me."

Bakos patiently continued his effort to convince Andreas to accept his help. "The press will be covering this trial so you've got to make the world understand that you're not just some anarchist, or that your actions were for personal ambition or for money. Also you do not want to be represented as crazy just as they portrayed Tsafendas. You protested because you were infuriated by the betrayal of your fellow man. Tell the world what it means to be arrested under the Terrorism Act."

He went on, more quietly, "Andreas, you've got to co-operate with me. I need your help because without you, I cannot do my work of fighting this system. But even more than me, they are the ones who need you to take a stand," and he gestured toward the black section of the gallery.

Andreas immediately replied bitterly, "The struggle will go on without me and all the other half-baked pink liberals like me."

Andreas pondered for a moment and then he glanced over to the black section of the gallery where Bakos had pointed. The tired and angry faces of those who sat there made him remember the forces that had led him here. Bakos shook his head, temporarily at a loss for words. Andreas sat quietly despondent for a while, and then he sighed in a milder tone of despair:

"Well, perhaps you're right. Maybe justice does still operate. I know it is worth the trouble of trying but it is getting really fucking hard to fight. You may represent me and do whatever you can, but I have no illusions about getting out of this alive."

The barrister's face showed no emotion. "Maybe that's true, but we still have to try. So I'll go ahead then?"

Andreas nodded his head, "I am grateful that you are willing to try."

"What I've got to do now," Bakos murmured to himself, "is to find grounds for postponing the case for a few days so we can prepare properly."

A court official announced the arrival of the presiding judge and Bakos hurried back to his own seat. As Mr. Justice Viljoen stepped up to take his place, the court fell silent. Everyone stood up and bowed to show respect for the man whom the State had appointed to administer justice. The judge settled himself comfortably in the high, formal armchair, surveyed his courtroom and declared the trial open. The clerk of the court read out the names of opposing counsel and then called on the Public Prosecutor, Mr. H.V. Lichtenberg, to read the charge against the accused, Andreas Magdalos. The public prosecutor was a tall, lean man with blue eyes. He had very fine, straight, fair hair that kept falling over his narrow forehead. With a dry expression and very deliberate movements he stood up, bowed to the judge and then turned to stare grimly at the accused.

"Your Honor, with the court's permission, I would like to make a small excursion into the past of Andreas Magdalos so that we can gain a rounded impression of the man who is to stand trial here today," his voice boomed in guttural tones, heavily accented with rolled r's.

"Objection, Your Honor," called Bakos, "the Prosecutor should get on with the charge and only the charge."

"Objection overruled, Mr. Bakos," said the judge, "Mr. Lichtenberg, please proceed as you have indicated."

"Your Honor, three years ago, Andreas Magdalos, who possesses two passports, returned to South Africa from a long stay in Greece. From the very first days following his return, and especially after his enrolment at Witwatersrand University, he started to engage in political activities that had as their intention, the overthrow of the lawful government. From official information that our secret service acquired, almost immediately after his arrival, it appears that the accused was an active member, with a considerable record, of various leftist organizations in Greece. He was an enthusiastic supporter of Marxist philosophy and an active member of the communist party as well. Moreover, he has been convicted several times in Greek courts for insurrection."

"Objection, Your Honor," Bakos interrupted indignantly, "there's no evidence about any of this. These are just smears concocted to implicate my client."

The prosecutor was annoyed by the interruption. "Your Honor," he demanded, "I do ask to be protected from these intrusions. Evidence exists and will be produced to the court later."

The judge banged his gavel to restore order.

"Mr. Bakos," he said caustically, "I will not permit you to interrupt the Prosecutor again."

The Prosecutor threw a contemptuous glance toward Bakos and went on.

"The secret police are certain that the accused returned to this country under orders to recruit new adherents and to prepare the ground for agitation on behalf of the expansionist programs of international communism. The accused was well trained and worked hard and skillfully, so that within a short time, he had become the leader of the university agitators."

"As president of the National Union of South African Students, he took part in many illegal meetings with illegal terrorist group, the African National Congress. During this time, he missed no opportunity to slander his country to the rest of the world. His activities expanded continuously, leading eventually to the provocation and incitement of people to armed rebellion."

The prosecutor was in his element now and he continued with a venomous confidence.

"Additionally, he organized an escape network for political suspects. He set up a printing press in a university basement with money he had received from abroad. I have here for the inspection of the court, copies of the illegal and provocative leaflets he produced."

"Eventually the police managed to infiltrate his organization with an agent of their own, who was able to collect enough evidence for the arrest of Mr. Andreas Magdalos under the Terrorism Act. After the expiry of his sentence, the Ministry of the Interior ordered his expulsion from South Africa."

The prosecutor took a sip of water and looked around to see what impression he was making on the spectators. He let his words weigh on the air, made eye contact with the angry crowd and continued:

"Before this honorable court, I charge Andreas Magdalos as follows:

> That during the year 1973, after he had been lawfully expelled from our beloved country, he did illegally reenter South Africa using a forged passport,
>
> That in recent years he has acted as a spy for an Eastern bloc country.
>
> That he has secretly recruited and trained a group of terrorists abroad for the purposes of sabotage and the overthrow of lawful authority,
>
> That he has engaged in acts of unparalleled sabotage and terrorism for political purposes,
>
> That he has murdered white and black police officers and innocent civilians,
>
> That he took part in anarchical student riots and instigated the arson of public buildings with damage amounting to millions of Rand,
>
> That he planned the murder of government officials,
>
> That he planned the escape of dangerous political prisoners from Robben Island.

Thank you, Your Honor," the Prosecutor concluded and resumed his seat amid the congratulations of his colleagues.

The judge angrily banged his gavel repeatedly to restore order after the pandemonium that followed the prosecutor's indictment.

"Andreas Magdalos, stand up. Has the prosecutor's office provided you with a copy of the indictment as the law requires?"

"Yes, Your Honor."

"Then, as presiding judge I ask you, in the name of the law, are you innocent or guilty of these charges?"

Andreas pulled himself up to his full height, raised his head and said in a loud, firm voice, "I am innocent on all counts, Your Honor."

Andreas's reply was followed by another spate of disorder in the crowded courtroom when a group of white spectators began shouting,

"Hang him, he's a traitor."

Bakos looked pleased and smiled for the first time. He got up quickly, holding his papers and hurried to hand them to the clerk of the court. The judge banged his gavel again and instructed the Prosecutor to proceed with the case.

"Your Honor," interrupted Bakos, "as you know, until recently the accused refused to be defended. I have had no time to prepare his defense. I have lodged an application for the adjournment of the trial and I ask the court to grant time for the preparation of a defense for this man, as the law prescribes."

"Objection, Your Honor," said the Prosecutor, "that is entirely unacceptable."

The judge examined Bakos's application in silence.

"The application by the defense is approved. This trial will be adjourned." He looked at his diary for a moment, and went on, "the trial will continue on the 27th of this month at 9.00 a.m."

He banged his gavel for the last time and got up from his seat.

Bakos grinned with pleasure, turned to Andreas and gave him the thumbs-up sign. Andreas's parents hurried from their seats to shake the lawyer's hand and to thank him.

"We'll try to get to see you in prison," Andreas's father shouted at his son as the court emptied. Andreas nodded reluctantly as he was again chained to a policeman who led him away through a small side door to avoid the crowd of people who were waiting for him outside.

Outside the court, the media waited to interview George Bakos and

Andreas's parents. Photographers surrounded them with flashbulbs firing as journalists zoned in like mosquitoes with blood-sucking questions. Bakos, realizing the distressed state of the elderly couple, began talking to draw the attention of the pressmen toward him. He signaled the parents to move away. Frixos Magdalos pushed his way through the crowd, pulling his wife along by the arm, as they ran down the concrete steps. According to a prearranged plan, their car was waiting at the curb with the engine running. They hurried into it and the driver pulled away at speed. The reporters ran after the car, but they were too late.

The sun had disappeared behind a heavy, leaden sky. The heat was oppressive. Ominous black clouds had gathered, thunder echoed and lightning flashed across from one horizon to the other. A storm was beginning, one of those well-known highveld summer storms. Rain and hail battered the car, increasing the nervous anxiety of the elderly couple inside. Lanie Magdalos, normally an attractive and well-groomed woman, looked drawn and shriveled. She looked much older than her fifty years, shrunken as though her body had been completely dehydrated. She wearily shook her head many times in disbelief at the events that had overtaken her. Frixos Magdalos smoked one cigarette after another, furiously puffing with each breath as though to extinguish his very life force. They did not exchange a single word, each living through the same misery, knowing from past experience that the other would not be able to offer any support.

At home, the house was empty, drab and inhospitable. Mrs. Magdalos fell exhausted on to the lounge sofa in the sitting room. The prosecutor's voice still echoed in her ears, terrifying and merciless. She covered them with her hands and broke into hysterical sobbing

"My son's a criminal," she wailed in despair. "My God, how could he have done all those terrible things? Didn't he think of us? He betrayed his country and us, too." Her sobs echoed in the empty house.

Helplessly, her husband brought her a glass of water and then tried to calm her down. He searched for words that would make her feel better.

"You're wrong, my dear," he said gently. He thought for a moment and then added, "We're the criminals. We're the traitors. We're the ones who closed our eyes and sold our souls, our ideals and our faith to money-making and our own selfish interests."

He nodded emphatically gathering strength, "At least Andreas didn't sell out to his God. He stayed a human being. He'll become a legend, you'll see, something for future generations to look up to."

Mrs. Magdalos stopped crying and turned on him with vehement hostility.

"It's you! Yes, it's you! It's your entire fault. You're the one who brainwashed him when he was a little boy with your talk about revolutions and your ideas about freedom and democracy. You're the one who fed him with all this rubbish."

"That's not true," her husband protested. "I was only trying to teach him what was right. How else was he supposed to know right from wrong in this god-forsaken country?"

"And I suppose your country knows what's right? All those years under Turkish rule, and you bloody Greeks didn't learn a thing. Killing each other off during the civil war like barbarians. Is that what you want here? Black and white killing each other? At least my country has given the blacks their own land."

"Yes but it is so bad that they can't possibly live on it," her husband replied.

"Listen to you," she said. "My father told me not to marry you, a rooinek and a foreigner on top of it. How could you understand this country? I should have married one of my people, a solid god-fearing Boer. Not you, with all your money and your stupid ideas about life. Look what it has brought me, I have lost my son," she wailed. "I am being punished. God is punishing me!"

Her husband looked at her in bewilderment. "Yes, perhaps you're right," he said weakly. "It is my money. Once I also stood by my moral convictions, just like him."

"I don't care," she screamed, "just bring me back my son. I want my son. I want my son," she repeated with loud and heartbreaking sobbing.

He left the room angry, unable to endure her misery and recriminations and without realizing it, found himself in his son's bedroom. It seemed strange and distant to him, yet he had spent some of the happiest hours of his life there. He looked at the pictures of Greek revolutionary heroes on the wall, at the paintings of the Parthenon, Pericles, Hercules, and Achilles. His face lightened, even became animated. A flood of memories streamed through his brain. It was as though he could hear Andreas's happy and affectionate voice in endless childhood stories and conversations. He recalled how much he had loved the boy even before his birth. What dreams he had held for his future, how much he had wanted to give him, everything that he himself had been deprived of.

His eyes filled with tears. "I'll make things right for you, my son," he whispered, "even if it costs me my very last cent."

He hurried into his study, picked up the phone and firmly dialed a number.

"Good afternoon," a voice answered, "Ministry of Justice. Can I help you?"

"I'd like to speak to the Minister," said Mr. Magdalos.

"I'm sorry sir, the Minister isn't here. Perhaps I can help you?"

"Magdalos is the name, Frixos Magdalos. Could you ask the Minister to phone me when he gets back?"

"Certainly, Mr. Magdalos, I'll tell him you rang."

Magdalos put down the phone and sank heavily into an armchair, struggling to overcome his sense of despair. Outside the rain continued to pour down. It seemed never ending.

CHAPTER 22 Necklace of Death

The heavy rain reverberated like a drum on the zinc roof in the nearby servant's quarters. Matthew seated at his table, unconsciously followed its rhythm on the wooden surface with his fingertips. Night seemed to have fallen early, and the storm had lost none of its initial force. He looked once more at his watch. He stood up and carefully uncovered a loose floor board and retrieved and automatic machine gun. The Kalashnikov rifle felt smooth and cold in his large calloused hands. With obvious experience, he quickly snapped in a fresh clip and then hung the gun strap over his shoulder. He put on his white church robe and pocketed two loaded magazines in the side pocket before he silently left the room. He avoided the large house, which was now in darkness except for a small light in the study. He pulled back the bolts of a small side gate and peered out. He scanned the street and was relieved to find it completely deserted.

"I like this rich neighborhood," he thought, "you can't see from one house to the next, and they're all too scared to walk outside anyway."

With all his senses on alert, he strode toward a nearby park and cautiously began climbing down into a small gorge. As he descended he heard the roar of the river in full flood. It was completely dark, but he walked with assurance on the familiar terrain. With great striding leaps, he hurried down the riverbank toward his destination. As he reached the river's edge, he heard the call of a night owl above the sound of rushing water. Instantly, he knew that he was being observed and with some satisfaction he echoed the call.

From the shadows, a silent figure appeared, unreal and ghostly, clad in the white robes of the church.

"You are again late my child," it said.

"Forgive me father, I am a sinner," Matthew replied.

"Then you may enter the eye of a needle, the brothers are waiting for you," the figure replied and directed the newcomer toward the side of the gorge.

Two men were sitting huddled over a candle, protected from the rain by a jutting rock formation carved out of the riverbed by centuries of passing water. One of them, noticing the newcomer, stood up with respect. The men grasped hands like compatriots and exchanged greetings.

"Dlamini! How are you doing?" inquired Matthew, "Have your wounds healed? Are you ready to fight again? We cannot do without you, you are missed."

"I am ready, Matthew." Dlamini replied. He was a young man, the sparse prickles on his chin indicating that he was barely seventeen years old. Yet his gaunt body with its burdened and haggard demeanor suggested that he had already lived through many years of harrowing experience. Even now, he showed evidence of a recent violent encounter. Large, blotchy, dried bloodstains were dimly visible in the flickering candlelight, on bandages around his chest and arm.

"How about you? When did you get out of hospital?"

"I was determined for them to let me go especially after I heard that Doctor and Andreas had been arrested. It was very difficult to get back here but Martin, as usual, was able to achieve miracles with his taxi. It must have been difficult for you guys to get here tonight?" asked Matthew. "The police are running fucking crazy in the townships."

"It was rather easy. Their attention was on all those coming into the townships, not those going out. They are all so crazy about what's happening with the court case. They don't want anybody coming in who could stir up trouble," said Mafuta, making a futile effort to keep the candle flame alight.

He was a large man with pale skin, and his khaki pants hung limply below his huge belly. He wore a black jacket over a dirty creased T-shirt that displayed the ANC slogan, a large fist holding a spear. He peered cautiously at Matthew as though trying to gauge his mood.

"Finally," he said anxiously, "after so many arrests, they say those grunting pigs are offering hundreds and thousands of rand to anyone who would give them information to have you arrested. You have become very valuable to them brother. You have to be bloody careful. There are informers who would be only too willing to betray the cause for a few rand as they did with Andreas, Doctor and so many others."

"Fuck them," Matthew said with contempt, "they don't have a goddamn hope in hell of catching me."

"Do you think that Doctor or Andreas would talk? Will they squeal under pressure? Should we get away for a while?" Mafuta persisted.

"Impossible, brother," replied a third man as he suddenly entered the group from the darkness.

"Damn it, Zulu. You scared the hell out of us." Mafuta said alarmed, 'you move like a fucking cheetah."

Ignoring his remark, Zulu sat beside Matthew. Martin, Moses, David and Patrick followed closely behind him. Matthew explained to Mafuta, "Those men are tested. The security police have arrested them before, in past days. They released them, half bloody dead, but they never talked."

"Stop worrying Mafuta!" said Dlamini, "you will be arrested more quickly for wearing that shirt, than you will because they talked!"

"Hah!" said Mafuta, "I will never take this top off. Never, not until we have a land free of these white rooinek bastards!"

"Comrades," interrupted Zulu in a harsh voice, "I bring bad news. Steve Biko was arrested by the security police."

The men groaned, some in defiance and others with contempt.

"Also, we have had more deaths. The police again opened fire in Soweto at the funeral service of one of the school kids. Five more students were killed, some as young as eight years old. Many more were wounded."

"The fucking bastards kill us even while we bury our dead," Mafuta cried in despair.

"We have other problems too. We cannot even get close to Andreas. The police have transported him to a high security jail in Pretoria," exclaimed Matthew, "It will be impossible to free him from there."

Zulu burst out, "They hem us in on all sides, like the horns of a bull, so that we cannot move. The rivers will run red with blood. We will not be defeated, even though they imprison our leaders and kill our children."

Matthew raised his hands, both fists clenched, determined to destroy the enemy. He took a deep breath, controlled his emotions and said with authority, "Our white masters are shitting themselves with fear and they act in desperation. We have to make them understand that as many as they arrest and kill, there will still be enough left to reclaim our country."

He turned to the wounded man, "Dlamini, I want you to regroup. The students must continue with the struggle."

He then directed his attention towards Mafuta, "We must demand of the people another four day general strike. Get the pickets out. No black man or woman must go to the white cities or do any buying from any white. Anyone who disobeys must be punished, even if it is our own mother."

"Patrick" he turned to the warrior, "I want you and the rest of your team to plan a bombing in Johannesburg. Choose two good targets, high-rise buildings or a busy parking lot. Create as much havoc and destruction as possible, so that they will see that we are not fucking scared or dead. David, you were right about the informers. They have caused us the most harm; we have to be very harsh with them. Their deaths have to be very painful, not even the necklace of death will be good enough for them. I especially want the names of those who turned in Doctor and Andreas. Also, contact Rosa and Thomas. And Mafuta," Matthew continued, "throw that fucking ANC shirt away! The last thing we need is for you to get arrested for shit like that."

Mafuta began to protest and Matthew shot him a fiery glance. Mafuta knew that it was futile to argue with him.

"Are there any more questions?" Matthew asked. No one replied. "So let us get on with what we have to do. There is no time to waste."

The meeting ended, the men embraced and one by one, they silently disappeared into the pouring rain.

A few days later, early Sunday afternoon, a crippled beggar could be seen walking the streets of Soweto. The beggar pulled his twisted leg along with the aid of a short stick. His stained and misshapen hat covered most of his face. Obviously drunk, talking and singing to himself, he passed the police road block.

"Dirty kaffir," he heard one policeman say, 'I wish I could kill them all with one bullet. They stain this country.'

The crippled man continued on his way down a dusty red road onto a well-trodden footpath that wound past a derelict huddle of burnt car wrecks. No one paid him much attention and he continued to walk at his own slow pace, finally stopping at the painted wooden door of a long ramshackle building. When he knocked, a small child opened the door. The boy's bare feet were hardly visible under his black potbelly that protruded uncovered below a skimpy grey vest. A blast of fetid air escaped the room, stinking of tswala beer, smoke and dagga. The room was filled with makeshift tables, wooden boxes and chairs. Men of every age sat about drinking, laughing and talking in loud voices. He sighed deeply, now less anxious than he had been on the street. He ordered the child to bring him a tin of beer and to tell the madam that he had come for the job. He sat down at an empty table and waited for his drink.

The beggar turned his eyes when a back door opened and a large woman in her forties, walked out. She was the owner of the shabeen, and as she maneuvered her enormous frame through the bar, she chatted and joked with the customers in a booming voice that matched her figure.

"Dumela, ousie!" she shouted toward him in greeting using the Sotho dialect.

She was assertive and sure of herself. Her large breasts and buttocks moved in waves as she walked toward the beggar. She wore a colorful cloth wrapped around her head that gave her the brash and carefree appearance of someone who had survived many close encounters with death. When she saw the boy scurrying around the shabeen, she reached out and pulled him onto her hip with one powerful hand.

"Haaibo, dumela Mama," the beggar answered as she planted herself in front of him.

"You have money?" she inquired, "Nobody drinks here for free."

"Asinamali (We have no money)," he replied in measured tones.

She gave him a curious look; half surprised and said, "Well, you lazy one, have you finally come then for a job. How else will you pay for that beer?"

He pulled out a few crushed rand from his pocket and she slapped a tin of tswala down before him on the table.

"Well, when you finish your beer, come and see me in the back," she said, nodding toward the back door. "You can start right away. There is a pile of cups that needs to be washed."

The beggar hurriedly finished his beer, put his tin cup down and pushed his way through the sprawling drinkers into the kitchen at the back of the house. The large woman was waiting behind the door.

"Haai, Matthew, you even fooled me. I didn't recognize you at first, hidden under all those ragged, smelly clothes and with that crazy hat. How you get about! I had to send Thomas out to check on you. Of course, these days, I know we have to be so careful, there are traitors all over the place, but you do look funny!" she exclaimed.

He took his hat off his head and she hugged him with a warm friendliness. She was a compatriot and they had known each other for a long time.

"Rosa, how are you?" he asked her and then he added with relief, "you look wonderful."

"Well despite difficult times, we live on," she threw back her head and shook her large body with a defiant toss of her shoulders.

Zulu appeared as they were talking, pocking his head out of a side door. He spoke to Mama Rosa with obvious respect.

"Sorry Mama Rosa. We have to hurry; the soccer match begins in less than two hours."

"I'm coming right now, Zulu," Matthew responded, "Rosa; I've missed you very much. One of these days when things quiet down, I'll pay you a visit."

She smiled at him with understanding, "first is the struggle. The rest will follow."

He looked at her with affection and followed Zulu into a small office at the back of the shebeen. He was sure that Rosa would not move from her position of guarding the door until the meeting was over. As he departed, Rosa looked at him with love, solicitude and pride. This man, Matthew, disguised in rags, was her cousin. He, and her brother, Thomas, now in a wheelchair, held special places in her heart. She pulled up a chair and sat down. Her memories returned to when she was a young girl growing up in the village. As was the custom, she, being the oldest, had assisted both Thomas's mother and Matthew's mother when they each gave birth to their sons. Later on, while their mothers were working far away in the white cities, she had helped her grandmother look after the young children. She loved them like her own. When they were little, they would come to her for advice and protection. Eventually they finished high school at the nearby missionary school then left for the big city to obtain jobs. Years later, she too had come to the city to join her brother, Thomas, after he had been stabbed in the back.

Thomas was waiting in the small room and he looked up as Matthew entered. He exclaimed with admiration, "I hardly know who you are!"

The two men hugged each other. Thomas's head was shaved like a peeled onion and his eyes glowed with intelligence behind his thick rimmed glasses. The structure of his face was homely, yet he was mysteriously very attractive and engaging. One could sense however, that this was not a man to antagonize or fool around with, despite the physical limitation of his wheelchair.

"How are you? How is your wife? Did you manage to hear anything from her," Matthew inquired.

"Well," Thomas paused, "you know how impossible it is to get any information from the security police about anyone arrested less than the ninety days."

"She is a tough woman. I believe she will make it," Matthew replied.

"Now, I have to be even more careful about where I go and who I meet, because I feel that they are watching my every move." Thomas continued, "the shebeen is a good place for us to get together, because so many men come and go from this place. Isn't it peculiar that I feel safest from the police when I am in an illegal drinking establishment?" His lips spread into more of a grimace than a smile and for a brief second, his pain was clearly visible to the other two.

"The bribes also help of course," he continued.

Zulu added, "well, it's good that we are becoming better organized, thanks to the efforts of yourself and Rosa here."

"That is very true," Matthew agreed, "but there is so much we still have to do. Thomas, how sure are you about the traitors?"

"As sure as I see you before me, Matthew. My informants come directly from the Soweto police. What more would you like to know? These men drive new cars. They recently bought new furniture and they dress up like lords. One of the men is a distant relative of Doctor and I am sure he is member of the ANC. Many times he was seen coming in and out of Doctor's house."

Zulu looked at his watch, "Compatriots, we have to make tracks if we want to finish this mission."

Matthew stood up and after sticking his head around the door to say goodbye to Rosa, he followed Thomas in his wheelchair out to the backyard. A handmade rickshaw was standing there loaded with cold drink bottles in crates. Toward the back of the rickshaw, three large barrels and several plastic bags of crushed ice were balanced on two old car tires. Matthew knelt down and shook Thomas's hand.

"You did wonderful work, brother. I hope I see you soon."

"Good luck and be careful," Thomas looked at them with envy, "Hell, I wish I could come with you. I always do the easy part."

'Matthew," Zulu said, "sit on top of the crates. I will pull." He went out in front, loaded it up and began pulling the rickshaw while Matthew hastily clambered aboard. Thomas waved goodbye as they rolled down the street.

Zulu's mind flowed back to when he was a young man, and he had pulled one of these carts to make a living. He had been dressed in full regalia, a young warrior adorned with skins, bone and feathers but instead of fighting for his chief, he had swallowed his pride to offer his services to tourists on the busy streets of the city of Durban. Although he now often missed his homeland, the time had come when he could no longer tolerate being the obedient 'boy' responding to the needs of the white man. He had left South Africa to cross the border to join the ANC. He had been determined to join in the struggle to liberate his country. 'Umkhonto we sizwe,' had become the motto of the liberation movement for which Zulu was prepared to dedicate his whole life and if necessary to die for. A police block jerked him out of his reverie and with mastery and strength; he stopped the carriage and said subserviently,

"Good afternoon, my Baas."

"Where do you think you're going, kaffir? Don't you know that there is a blockade?" the policeman said with hostility

"I have a permit my Baas."

"Show me your permit and your passbook, kaffir."

Zulu clapping his hands with a show of deference and respect took his passbook and permit out of a satchel tied around his neck and gave it to the policeman.

"My Baas, here is my passbook, we are going to Orlando to sell cold drinks at the soccer match."

The policeman opened the book and found the permit and thirty rand. He quickly put the money in his pocket.

"OK, kaffir, go!"

As they approached Orlando stadium, crowds of people were moving along toward the stadium. Police presence was again very obvious. Zulu jockeyed the rickshaw into the crowd going along with the flow, until he was able to maneuver to a position outside the main gate of the stadium. He and Matthew unloaded the cold drinks into each bucket, filled them with ice and began shouting, 'Cold drinks, cold drinks for sale,' competing with the cries of the other peddlers situated near them.

Patrick approached them and as he was buying a drink, he said to Zulu.

"Gate 6, Platform 11. Second row on the left."

Zulu gave him his change and waited for him to leave. He picked up a bucket with cold drinks, put it on his head and went into the stadium. He showed his permit to the attendant as he passed Gate 6, all the while shouting, "Cold drinks, cold drinks!"

The stadium was alive with thousands of spectators gesticulating and talking excitedly about their favorite teams. Zulu looked around until he saw Platform 11. David approached him and pointed out with his eyes a man sitting on a bench. Zulu took a careful note of him as he sold his drinks and went outside to get more. The teams entered the field and a huge cheer went up from the crowd.

Matthew was still waiting patiently outside, selling the drinks to the crowd. Time passed and the game progressed. Zulu went in and out of the stadium many times. Toward the end of the game, Zulu deviated from his normal round in the stadium and as he passed the media room he knocked on the door. A young man opened it and Zulu handed him a tape. Zulu descended the ramp and walked quickly toward the exit near Gate 6 where Matthew was now waiting with a much lighter rickshaw. At the end of the match, just as the spectators were making their way toward the exits, a metallic voice blared from the loudspeakers.

"People of Soweto, people of Azania. Amandla! The struggle has to go on. The students of Soweto declare a four-day general strike. You will all boycott every white store for the next four days."

Chaos and pandemonium ensued as police rushed to enter the stadium with weapons in hand and barking dogs at their side. The spectators were hurriedly trying to get out, fearing trouble in the confined space. Zulu and Matthew did not move as the chaos erupted around them. They heard a scream from nearby and could see flames flickering above the crowd.

A voice said, "We accuse you of being a traitor and traitors from now on will die with a parting gift; a necklace of death!"

People passing by looked anxiously in the direction of the voice, confused and fearful about what was happening. Suddenly the man Zulu had been watching was at the gate and before he could escape, Zulu caught hold of him with his powerful hands. The man let out a whimper as he knew what fate would befall him. With precision, Matthew took one of the spare rickshaw tires and placed it over the man's shoulders. The man screamed for help pleading with Matthew that he was innocent but the match was already lit. The instant it made contact with the gasoline filled tire, the man burst into flames. Matthew tasted bile in his mouth as the odor of burning flesh hit his nostrils. He was angry at the traitor for forcing him to commit such violence on a member of his own community. Zulu grabbed his shoulder and they could feel the heat on their backs as they disappeared into the crowd. The flames quickly engulfed the traitor and his cries of fear and pain echoed in the air. The rickshaw flowed with the crowd, moving around and past the police. By the time the police reached him, the informant had become a human torch. There were leaflets scattered around his smoldering corpse.

THIS IS HOW INFORMERS AND TRAITORS WILL BE TREATED FROM NOW ON.

They began rounding up and arresting people, but Matthew and Zulu, along with their rickshaw and their fellow conspirators were long gone.

CHAPTER 23 Ultimate Price

Andreas was once again locked up in a prison cell. He felt extremely tired and despondent. He wanted to just give up; close his eyes and let the world take him over. So much had happened over the past few months to exhaust him, so many exciting hopes and victories, disappointing sorrows and defeats, his arrest and now, finally, the trial. He thought of his courageous compatriots he had been forced to abandon so unwillingly. He was nagged with worry about them. Could they possibly have escaped the dragnet of the authorities? Were they carrying on with the tasks as planned? Bakos was right. The struggle had to go on.

"One certainty," he told himself, "one consolation is that the seed had been sown, the fire had been set. The struggle for freedom has not yet been lost."

Sadly he continued, "as for myself, I know that I have arrived at the end of the road. They will never let me go this time. I'm too dangerous for them. Perhaps it might even be a kind of deliverance, the final step toward total freedom."

He stretched out on his bed and tried to relax. Lighting a cigarette, he allowed his thoughts to wander freely. He would rather die than be imprisoned. He felt that he could not tolerate being shut up inside four walls with no communication with others. In his isolation, he feared the disintegration of his mind, his ideals, his emotions and even his will to live. He still experienced a great longing to be free, to fill his lungs with fresh air, to bake in the sun, to cleanse his body in the caressing waves of the sea. He saw with renewed clarity the liberty that freedom really is, and how oppressive it was to be subject to slavery and inequality.

"How can they say that God created man in his own image?" he said to himself. "Does God have a color? Is God a racist? Is he unjust, hard-hearted, bloodthirsty and arrogant? Surely not. But then, why do churches accept things the way they are? Why don't they raise their powerful voices? Why don't they put a stop to violence, poverty, slavery, warfare and the exploitation of others?'

"Here I go with my philosophical dreaming," thought Andreas, "the hard reality is that I am in jail."

He felt that his end was fast approaching. The silence was deathly; the only signs of life were the ill written names on the walls of the cell, names in various languages, each with its own story, its own unique drama.

"What about my life? How have I spent it?" he wondered. His mind drifted back to the past, to events that he thought had been completely expunged from his memory.

"Growing up in Johannesburg," he reflected, "most people in the world, and especially my father, would have said that I was unusually fortunate. Possessions that other people could only dream of were served up to me on a golden plate."

He was born with social status, power and wealth, all of which his parents had struggled to acquire.

"And yet, it was weird," he recognized with sudden insight in his prison cell, "the richer my parents became, the less I was able to talk to them and the more distance there was between us."

At precisely ten o'clock, two guards came in and lead him to a special cell where the barrister, George Bakos, was sitting at a steel table. The guards pushed Andreas inside and took up guard outside. Bakos's plump, expressive face lit up and his big, dark eyes looked Andreas up and down, affectionately, as he shook his hand.

"Andreas, I'm glad to see you again, even under circumstances like these. I'm not trying to flatter you, but you're a rare kind of person."

Andreas accepted a cigarette from Bakos's packet, lit it and inhaled with deep pleasure. He was encouraged by the sight of the lawyer's vigorous, almost clumsy figure, his sparkling eyes and his sharp brain. Bakos took from his pocket a typed sheet of paper and asked him to read it. Andreas looked at it unmoved for a moment, and then read what was written:

> *Andreas, I am certain the secret police have bugged this cell, so I am using this way to tell you a few things I do not want them to hear. As we both know, in this context, the likelihood of winning this case is small. As you said to me once, your fate has been decided. On the other hand, from a point of justice, I disagree. The police reports do not have any concrete evidence against you other than entering the country illegally. What is important now is that by means of this trial we can deliver a series of powerful blows which will act as a revolutionary strike. We have to expose them, to show everyone in the world how this insane and illegal racist regime really operates. I hope we are fortunate and that they do not find a way of stopping the trial. Finally, my friend, since I know how strong you are, I am sure this bitter truth is not going to scare you. Honestly, Andreas, I wish we had the opportunity to talk freely under very different conditions from these.*

Andreas nodded, looking at Bakos's serious face, and smiled his understanding. They worked for hours at a stretch in front of a small tape recorder, with dynamic Bakos constantly firing questions. These daily visits by Bakos over the next few weeks were an oasis of comradeship and relaxation for the imprisoned Andreas. When the appointed date came for the continuation of the trial, Andreas was transported with same high security to the Supreme Court. As on the previous occasion, the outside of the court was surrounded with people waiting impatiently for his arrival. Reporters, the press photographers and TV camera crews pushed forward to record the historic moments for posterity

Andreas ignored the pushing and shoving of his escorts and paused to look affectionately at the crowd. Then, clenching his fists, he raised his handcuffed arms above his head and shouted with all the force he could summon up: “Amandla! Amandla! (Strength!)” The shouts of the handcuffed terrorist sent the crowd into a delirium of enthusiastic pandemonium and Andreas's flushed face reflected his pride at being part of the movement.

"The tide against people of color has started to flow the other way. It was now merely a question of time," he thought with satisfaction.

The growls of the police dogs were lost among the cheers and shouts of the frenzied crowd. His escort picked him up bodily and hurried him to the entrance.

"Courage, brother, we're with you!" a familiar bass voice thundered near him. With an effort, Andreas turned his head and saw the giant form of Zulu among the crowd with Matthew at his side.

He managed a brief smile at them and called in a choked voice: "Keep up the struggle! Amandla! Amandla!"

Andreas felt content and his heart filled with courage at the knowledge that his sacrifice would not be in vain. The court was packed to suffocation point, divided into two sections which kept whites and blacks apart. Andreas's parents ran toward him, ignoring the objections of the police. First, his father opened his arms and, deeply moved, embraced him, his voice shaking with emotion.

"We're with you, Andreas, and we're proud of you!"

His mother held him longingly in her arms; speechless with tears. But the police, unmoved, broke the embrace and when they finally got him into the semi-circular dock, they breathed a sigh of relief and removed his handcuffs. Andreas looked toward his father, wanting desperately to hug him and thank him, late as it might be, for his understanding. Their glances met; they were both in the struggle together; the same flame burned in their eyes. His father raised his heavy, clenched fist in the air.

The clerk of the court announced the presiding judge and a deathly silence fell on the courtroom. The judge banged insistently with his gavel as he announced in a disdainful voice that the trial had begun. The prosecutor, imposing and arrogant, started to examine the prosecution witnesses. Andreas's unbridled imagination, set free, carried him outside to the courtyard with the people and with Matthew, Zulu, Martin, Patrick and so many others.

Bakos proved to be an extremely intelligent, clear-sighted, quick-witted and obstinate antagonist both toward the prosecution witnesses and toward the prosecutors themselves, fully justifying his reputation.

"Chuma Matolo!"

The calling of the name brought Andreas back to earth within the crowded courtroom and his eyes blazed with interest. A tall, slightly built man of about twenty came in with bowed head from the internal side-door from the witness room, his step nervous and unsteady. When he had taken the oath, the prosecutor stood up and smiled for the first time.

"Mr. Matolo," he asked politely, "How old are you?"

Andreas had difficulty in restraining himself from laughing at the prosecutor's courtesy.

"Witness, please speak clearly into the microphone so that we can all hear you," the lawyer insisted.

"Twenty-two, sir."

"Can you tell the court a few facts about your life?"

"Yes, Baas. I was born in Soweto and grew up without a father. My mother worked as a care-woman in Doctor Erickson's house and he gave me a lot of help to become a nurse."

"Witness, if I am not mistaken, the accused is connected with Dr. Erickson?"

"Yes, sir. I heard Dr. Erickson say many times that he had met with the accused."

"Tell us how Doctor Erickson made you become a member of the ANC and afterward an urban guerilla."

"Doctor started talking to me about communism, equality and the dissolution of the illegal white regime when I was quite young. But the pressure from him got stronger after my mother died and I was a student in the school of nursing."

"Explain what you mean, and please speak more loudly. You have nothing to fear in here."

"Doctor told me he had been a member of the ANC for years and that he had dozens of armed men at his disposal, and that from time to time would carry out the war against the whites. He was always talking to me about wars, heroes, beautiful white women, about lots of money, official positions and glory and so he persuaded me to become a member of the ANC. One night he summoned me to his house and told me the reason he was so helpful to me was that he wanted to send me abroad for training so that I could become a leader of the struggle. I accepted. With another four boys, I crossed in secret over the Lesotho border where men of the ANC were waiting for us. They took us to the training camp."

"What nationality were the people who trained you?"

"Mostly Russians and Cubans."

"What did they teach you there?"

With trembling hands the witness took out a large handkerchief and wiped his sweating face.

"First we learned the theory of communism and they fostered in us a hatred for the whites. Then they taught us how to kill without scruples, how to undertake sabotage and the art of guerilla warfare."

"Witness, before we go on, I want you to tell us whether there is anyone in this courtroom today who trained with you in that camp?"

The witness cleared his throat nervously.

"Yes, master, there is," he said pointing at the accused.

"Witness, I want you to look at the accused carefully and to repeat whether Andreas Magdalos trained with you?"

Trembling from head to foot, the witness raised his bowed head and his eyes met those of Andreas who was looking at him only with pity.

Bakos's cross examination was relentless. He focused mostly on days, times and places. His questions pushed the witness to correct himself continuously. It became painfully obvious to everyone in the court room that the witness was wholly unreliable. Then the witness did the unthinkable. Even Bakos could not hide his surprise as the informant suddenly stood bolt upright, and with pitiful sobs seized the edges of his shirt and ripped them open. The buttons popped, exposing the inflamed skin of his chest.

"I couldn't stand the pain of the electric wires, brother. They beat me! They gave me what I had to say today in writing. But I'm not a traitor! I don't even know the accused. This is the first time I have ever seen him. What I said today is lies! All lies!"

Court officials and the public alike sat shocked, their mouths agape. The public prosecutor blushed, paled, and then went as yellow as a lemon. The judge's gavel kept banging without anyone hearing it. Black policemen hurled themselves on the witness, threw him to the ground and forcefully dragged him from the court.

"It's all lies! I'm not a traitor!"

Then silence. The judge stood up angrily, banged his gavel and he adjourned the court until the following Monday. He demanded that the prosecutor meet with him in his quarters. Then he hastily vanished. Later in his quarters, he addressed the prosecutor:

"Mr. Lichtenberg, today you made a laughing stock of my court. You made the whole justice system and the country look bad. I told you from the beginning that you had a very poor case that would not stand, more especially with Bakos on the other the side. I am not going to tolerate you or of any of the people that stand behind you any longer. By God at the next hearing, if you don't bring me solid evidence I will dismiss this case. Do I make myself understood?"

* * *

The twin skyscrapers at the Carlton Center were the new pride of the city of Johannesburg. Elegant, tall, and modern with glass and red granite structures, it represented the best that technology had to offer. The economy was doing well for the whites and they were reinvesting their capital in properties. They were very proud of their city and they nicknamed her the New York of Africa.

Matthew was driving the Rolls Royce with confidence through the streets of Johannesburg. He had returned to his work as a chauffeur although he was still feeling weak after having being wounded. He was lonely and melancholic following the arrest of his friends. His employers were sitting silently hidden in the rear of the car. He was astonished by how they had aged, following the recent capture of Andreas and the current court case. As he observed them through the driver's mirror, he felt sympathy and compassion for them. He never thought that he could have such feelings for white people and strangely he felt perplexed and betrayed by his own emotions. These people were like his second parents as he had worked for them since he had left missionary school at age fourteen. He had known of them in his childhood years because his mother worked for them before even he had been born. He felt as though they were his people.

They had been mostly kind to him and he had always treated them with respect. But at the same time there were memories of rejection and humiliation such as that fateful day when Ms. Magdalos had screamed at him in Andreas's room. He felt that if they were able to understand him, he would like to talk to them; to tell them how much he understood their misery and anxiety, and that if it were possible, he would do anything to free their son. But he said nothing; the barriers were too high.

Heavily armed policemen wearing yellow and green phosphoric bullet proof jackets brought him back to reality as they signaled him to stop. They were checking every car passing by. Frixos Magdalos with a weary gesture lowered his window and showed his invitation card. They were allowed entrance to the building. A large fund raising celebration, a ballroom dance for the National Party of the Transvaal was being held in the newly built Carlton Center Hotel. From what Matthew had read in the newspaper, all the top leaders of the National party would be there. Matthew surmised that his boss was attending so that he could make a deal to bargain for his son's life. Matthew felt angry because a proud man like Mr. Magdalos was forced to grovel in these circumstances. At this moment, he felt the urge to blow up this new Center and with it all the architects of apartheid who had polluted his country with their sick ideas. It was no longer simply a matter of black against white, but rather in his soul he knew, that the struggle was about good versus evil.

He was told to park the car at the fifth level of underground parking. He opened the door for the elderly couple,

"Matthew," Frixos said, "please don't go far away because we will be leaving shortly."

Matthew decided that he really needed to explore this new building. He took the elevator to the ground floor. He found himself among hundreds of well-dressed white people and he had no doubt in his mind that it was only his uniform that permitted him to wander about among the noisy throng. The whites were busy marveling at the elegant stores and huge ice rink in the new shopping center. Matthew with an observant eye noticed a garbage truck reflected in the thick panels of shop front glass. The men wearing municipal uniforms ran about collecting and exchanging the garbage bins. Suddenly he knew exactly how the Carlton Center could be successfully bombed.

* * *

Andreas's cell door opened interrupting his continued lapses into recollections of the past. The warder entered the cell.

"Come with me," he snapped; "your lawyer wants to talk to you."

Bakos was striding up and down the little office, his face creased with worry. When he saw Andreas he tried to smile and shook hands with him.

"I came sooner than you expected, Andreas, or rather they sent me to see you."

Andreas looked at him in surprise.

Bakos threw himself on to the chair and stared at the floor, "Andreas, I've tried everything I could to get you out on bail, but it can't be done. They're determined to treat you as an enemy of the State."

"Who sent you?" asked Andreas suspiciously.

"A senior government official from the Ministry of Public Order and I think your father had something to do with it. I bring you a proposition that I don't like, but it's my duty to deliver it to you since your life is at stake. They'll treat you very leniently, a few years of jail followed by exile, if you'll co-operate with them and betray the whole movement."

Andreas went red with anger. Bakos went on: "Before you answer there are some things I have to tell you. BOSS, the all-powerful secret police, is fuming about your premature trial. They're at war with the department and the government over it. Bringing you to trial was a political maneuver to disarm public opinion, because your case is of international significance and interest. BOSS is absolutely determined to get your trial postponed so that they can get their hands on you for interrogation. You should know better than most what their methods of interrogation are. They've given you two days to make up your mind."

Andreas was shaking with rage and in his fury said thickly to the lawyer, "Mr. Bakos, do you remember what you said when I accepted your offer to defend me? What's made you change your mind? How dare you come to me with a proposal that I should betray the whole freedom movement and my dignity as a human being?"

"Andreas, don't jump to conclusions. I told you I was delivering that proposition as my duty but if you accept it, you'll have to get another lawyer to take your case!"

"Mr. Bakos, I know what my end will be and I'm thoroughly prepared for it. That is my final word on their offer!"

Bakos shook his hand, "Goodbye, Andreas. I'll see you soon."

Following Bakos's visit, Andreas felt trapped by two powerful voices within him competing for his attention. He sifted through his feelings trying to get his bearings. The first voice spoke to him seductively. It pleaded with him, "Life is short. Look after yourself. Be like your father," it said, "Enjoying all the pleasures of life. Drop all these crazy ideas of yours. Forget this nonsense. You're only a drop in the ocean. You'll just disappear."

As the first voice still echoed in his ears, the other went on scathingly, "Don't be a coward. You won't tolerate little kids with swollen bellies being thrown into jail for no reason. You can't allow injustice and oppression. Don't ignore your conscience and betray your fellow man by hardening your heart against his pain and suffering. Don't give up. Fight!"

"But I'm nothing. I'm just one individual. What can I do?" Andreas cried out in anguish.

"Don't waste your time with questions. Just believe. You're strong and you'll win. One individual is the starting point of everything. Drops become streams and streams become rivers, seas and oceans. You can help end this system of oppression."

Over the next few days, two serious events occurred in the center of the city and were reported in the media. A tremendously powerful bomb exploded among the numerous establishments of the newly built Carlton Center skyscraper, causing immense physical damage and an unknown number of casualties. Simultaneously, a group of three young blacks rushed into a department store with Scorpio-type automatic weapons. They scattered a pound of hot lead and let off half a dozen hand grenades, before the horrified eyes of the shop assistants and customers. The attack took five minutes, after which they walked out without haste, got into a taxi and disappeared. The commercial center was stunned. The police were mobilized to locate and arrest the perpetrators. At sunset, the Johannesburg Stock Exchange closed with the lowest prices since the great depression.

In the nearby John Vorster Square, Captain Kolradie was furious about the severe criticism and warning he had received from the prosecutor's office about the weakness of the evidence provided against the accused. He knew that the bastard was involved, up to his neck, in terrorist activities and that he was connected in one way or another with the bloody events that had shaken the country in the last few weeks. He and his team had spent endless hours searching the property, from one side of the farmhouse to the other, looking for incriminating evidence. They had been about ready to give up, when Shorty accidentally found the trapdoor to a secret compartment in the garage. There it was! A stockpile of evidence; guns, ammunition and furthermore a map of Johannesburg with circled targets of all the sabotage that had taken place. Captain Kolradie stormed into the Security General's office holding the map with circled target sites. Like a maddened bull, forgetting his office etiquette, he demanded the attention of the General.

"I was absolutely right General," he panted, "now I've got all the proof. Today's attacks were clearly planned and organized by our friend Magdalos before he was arrested."

Fury steamed from the Security General's ferocious face at the impertinence of his subordinate. "Who is involved? Have you arrested them?"

"Unfortunately, General, Magdalos is the only one who knows these people. The groups that operated with him were split up in such a way that none of them knew of the existence of the others and none of them had any contact with the Soweto doctor. These are the groups that carried out the executions in the ghetto as well as all the sabotage. Magdalos is the key to finding out who is involved."

"Are you sure about all that, Captain?" he frowned.

"As sure as we can see each other, everything starts and ends with Magdalos."

"What's the latest from the doctor?"

"Nothing yet General. He accepted responsibility for the troubles in Soweto but when it comes to Magdalos, he denies that he had anything at all to do with him. We're still working on him, but he's hard, very hard."

"I think you're right, Captain. Magdalos can solve a lot of our puzzles. In any case, the trial is a farce and the prosecutor wants our heads. I think I should go straight away and see the Minister of Police and ask him to postpone the trial. You wait in your office and I'll let you know as soon as I have any news."

That evening, the government made an announcement:

> *Given the emergence of new evidence against the terrorist Andreas Magdalos, who has been connected to the two terrorist actions that took place in Johannesburg today, the Ministry of Justice and Police has asked the Cabinet to postpone his trial, in order to allow for additional investigation. The Cabinet has acceded to the request and the trial has been adjourned until the relevant investigations have been concluded.*

Captain Kolradie was feeling very pleased with himself. He had got what he wanted. If Andreas talked, they would wipe out all rebellion in South Africa for many years. All attempts by Bakos to protest the legality of this decision fell on deaf ears.

Andreas was startled to see Norman and Shorty at his cell door, announcing to him ironically the postponement of his trial. His face remained expressionless but a thousand dark thoughts crossed his mind. They chained him and secretly transferred him to the thirteenth floor of John Vorster Square. Captain Kolradie was there waiting for him impatiently. He told the twins to leave him alone with Andreas, and then adopted the pose that Andreas knew so well. He went up to him amiably.

"Magdalos, you're a worthy opponent and I admire you! However, I have to confess, I underestimated you at our first meeting, but now we know one another better. I'll speak plainly and tell you straight out that if you talk and help me to arrest the whole of your gang, I shall have achieved a personal triumph which will automatically be followed by praise and promotion. Don't look so puzzled, I'm a very ambitious man, Andreas Magdalos. You've played and you've lost.

Life favors the victors, but if you co-operate with me, I promise you that I'll find some way of letting you escape so you can enjoy your father's millions in some other country."

The captain lit a cigarette and studied Andreas's reactions.

"Well?"

"Captain, I thought you were more intelligent? It looks as though I've made a mistake in overestimating you beyond your deserts. You're an implacable murderer without one trace of decency in you and you don't even deserve contempt. So let's drop your cheap flattery and let's get on with it, so we can get it over with."

"All right, Magdalos, let's leave the bullshit to someone else. Life is sweet and even Christ himself couldn't face the fear of death. But I'll tell you something. I'll make you beg for death! I promise you."

"Captain, I haven't the slightest doubt about what you intend to do. That's one of the reasons I'm not about to co-operate with you. I know how much you love your work and I wouldn't like in any way to deprive you of your pleasure."

Andreas felt an unprecedented calm, tranquility and courage. He knew that the only way for him to end his inevitable torture was by infuriating this man. He was not about to miss any opportunity. Norman and Shorty returned shortly and at a nod from the captain started their work while the strains of Wagner filled the room. They started with his lower extremities, and then moved to the upper, then to his torso and his genitals. Everything was coordinated and precisely timed, and Andreas's body jerked with pain. He bit his lip furiously to withstand the agony until the blood started to pour from his mouth. The captain and his assistants tirelessly and inventively applied their considerable experience and imagination to the task, working slowly and deliberately.

The torture continued at devilish pace to break him in, day and night, without leaving him alone for a single minute. Five sleepless days passed in a titanic battle of man and anti-man. Andreas was exhausted and he began to pray for death as a means of escape. His face had become utterly unrecognizable, beaten to a pulp and matted with dried blood, tears and the growth of his beard. His body had been reduced to a mash. His lips and tongue, because of the constant biting, had become swollen shreds full of pus. The doctor who stood by with his stethoscope in his ears was obliged to put plastic plaques in his mouth to prevent further injury. Present throughout like an orchestral conductor, he frequently examined the victim and told them when to start and when to stop.

The constant beatings and varied ill-treatments had produced a degree of immunity to pain and the captain, who was fully familiar with all the stages, ordered them to start the electrical torture. They wrapped Andreas in wet blankets, placed pieces of brass on selected places, attached the electrodes and turned on the invisible, insidious current, causing his body to twitch in spastic movements. Andreas's brain revolted with constant fainting fits. A little rest, and then it started again and again until he blacked out completely and his eyes rolled around stupidly and idiotically.

In one rare moment of lucidity, Andreas started to mutter quietly calling out names and places intermittently. The captain expectantly pressed his ear close to Andreas's mouth to hear what he was saying. Without warning, Andreas's teeth clamped fiercely on to his ear. The captain yelled with pain as blood spurted from the wound. Norman ran to his aid, trying to force Andreas's jaws apart. The captain, with tears in his eyes, punched Andreas's body, but the teeth held him fast. Shorty, in a panic, turned the control switch up higher than normal. Andreas's body arched horribly, the clenched jaws opened, and a wail of anguish escaped his mouth. His eyes bulged, his body collapsed again with a fearful death-rattle. Andreas lay still.

The papers came out with special editions bearing full-page headlines. The dangerous terrorist, Andreas Magdalos, while attempting to escape, fell to his death from the thirteenth floor of the John Vorster Square building. In an urgent application to the Supreme Court, the dead man's father, Frixos Magdalos, and the barrister George Bakos have demanded the release of the body for a post mortem. Security police have denied their requests citing that a public inquiry and burial may cause further unrest.

Epilogue

After a lifetime spent in prison on Robben Island, Mandela was free! It had all happened so quickly and unexpectedly. The structure of apartheid collapsed in a heap, like the tower of Babel. It had been built on the shallow foundations of racism and hatred.

"No vendettas. Forget the past," Mandela had requested, "the state of apartheid belongs to history. Whites and blacks will co-exist; we are going to build a new country of justice and opportunity for all."

All nations opened their doors to him. They welcomed him with heroic praises. He was a peacemaker and he engaged his hosts with his simplicity, gentleness and compassion. He asked for peace and cooperation and for people to live together. He immediately created the South African Truth and Reconciliation Commission under the leadership of Archbishop Desmond Tutu. Those who had committed crimes during apartheid, at least those who accepted responsibility for their wrongdoing, could ask for a pardon from the State and from the victims of their crimes. In the spirit of truth and reconciliation, amnesty would be given.

In the new South Africa, Matthew Matsimani shook his head in disbelief as he found himself converted from freedom fighter (or terrorist) to Director in the Department of the Ministry of Justice. Not even the most optimistic of people could have anticipated such unexpected and rapid changes. He could not accept or digest the new reality.

"From hunted to hunter, what an irony," said Matsimani to himself, "I worship Mandela. He is my leader, but I find it so difficult to follow his logic. I know well the Afrikaner mentality. I always believed that the road to freedom would be long, difficult and painful, washed with a river of blood and hundreds of deaths on both sides. The white minority put down their arms so unexpectedly, released Mandela from prison and just handed over the country. What was behind all this? What new games were the whites now playing? I longed for revenge. After all these difficult years, filled with humiliation, beatings and jail sentences, all the many close friends and relatives that I have lost from the blood stained hands of the security police; I planned how I was going to punish all the people that had made me suffer. Now I have to forget all this and forgive them? I am Christian but my Christianity does not reach that high. My father once told me that begging pardon was like taking half a shit. But I have no other choice but to follow the crazy laws, the new reality in South Africa."

With the privileges of his new job as Director of Justice, Matthew Matsimani had united a small flexible team. They traveled from one police station to another, from one side of the country to the other, collecting information from the security files of the secret police. He wanted to show the world how many inhuman crimes had been committed against his people.

Today was a great day, a significant day at the Truth and Reconciliation Commission. The security police officer, Colonel Snyman, had put forward his appeal for reconciliation relating to the death of Steve Biko. Matthew had made a special effort to be there. He sat in the front row of the prosecutor's bench in the provincial courtroom of the Centenary Hall of New Brighton in Port Elizabeth. The spectators numbered more than a thousand. Public interest remained high even though twenty years had passed. The old people had not forgotten and the young wanted to learn more. His gaze went all around studying each face until it stopped at that of the lawyer representing the family of the victim. George Bakos was one of few whites he respected and admired. The lawyer was also one of few men who through all the years had stood tall, ignoring establishment consequences. Time had put its marks on him. His hair had turned white and his chubby cheeks had become baggy. Only his eyes remained as Matthew remembered them, penetrating and glittery with a bright cleverness. He was of medium build, bulky, with a provincial appearance that created doubts as to whether he should be taken seriously. Matthew had never met with him close up until today. He felt happy and excited about the possibility.

Harold Snyman, the retired colonel of the previously powerful security police or BOSS, stood in the witness box protesting his innocence and maintaining that the death of Steve Biko was an accident.

"It was a simply a bad moment, Mr. Commissioner. I am innocent of this man's death." He was a man of around sixty, tall, slender and upright. He smelt like a policeman, even without his uniform. His hair was cut short and his grey moustache, just a touch of brush, scissored to perfection. A despotic, arrogant heretic, his strident voice challenged the spectators as he was talked in the forceful language of Afrikaans. His blue eyes were like cold steel under his thick lenses. He systematically avoided the eyes of the interrogator or the spectators in the room.

"My God, how much do these people all look alike," said Matthew to himself.

"Mr. Commissioner," Colonel Snyman was saying, "we did not have any reason to kill Steve Biko. We did not want to create even one more national hero, among those people. We knew very well how popular was this thirty year old man. He was the founder of the movement for black consciousness. We knew very well that he was a Messiah in the hearts of many of the young black students. Although we had many reasons to arrest Steve Biko, we had no intention to kill him. Our main concern was that he was distributing pamphlets and influencing students to stay away from schools. He intended to create mayhem and destruction by having them burn schools and public buildings. He was corrupting the youth and leading them to self-destruction. Our next concern was that the unrest had brought fear to the white population and was keeping potential foreign investors at bay.

"I ordered Steve Biko's arrest and we brought him for security reasons to a secret interrogation room on the sixth floor of a building in the industrial area of Port Elizabeth. Our purpose was to intimidate him and we believed that by taking him away from the scene, his disappearance might lead to a peaceful solution in the schools. As I told you Mr. Commissioner, we had no illusions. We well knew his power and in our opinion, he was among the leading agitators. We wanted to put him out of action and give time to the police to regroup and destroy the machine that he had created. We also knew that Biko was not your average man. He was a leader with a very strong personality and spiritual powers. As soon as we had captured him, I ordered my men to keep him awake and without food for a few days. We hoped that we could shake his power and determination. But my God, when we began the interrogation, he put up a tremendous resistance. He was like a wild bull irritated by our presence. He became exceedingly aggressive and non-cooperative. He ignored the order of interrogator, Captain David Slabert to remain standing while being questioned. Instead, he sat in the first available chair right in front of us, laughing sarcastically and swearing hideously in Bantu language. He told us that we had no power or right to arrest him or to interrogate him in this manner."

Snyman continued, "Captain Slabert disgusted by his arrogant behavior, grabbed him by the lapels of his jacket and lifted him up out of the chair. Then totally unexpectedly, the captive began punching Captain Slabert with uncontrolled and aggressive rage. His behavior left us motionless. Blood was pouring down Slabert's face, like a river, as Biko continued to punch him. The first person to come to his senses was Warrant Officer Beneke who leapt across the room and attacked him in a flying rugby tackle, using his elbow to bring him to the floor. Right away the remaining police ran to assist their blood-covered colleague and to bring the accused to order. Biko continued to fight with all his might using his hands, feet, head and teeth. He was a very strong man. At this moment, it is impossible to remember all the details, given that twenty years have passed, but from what I remember, one of the policemen managed to give him a blow to the side of the head that knocked Biko's head against the wall of the room. Biko appeared dizzy. His feet became unsteady and he collapsed on the floor. He looked like a boxer who had been knocked out."

The family lawyer, George Bakos, could not control himself any longer and he stood up enraged letting his glasses fall to the floor.

"Mr. Commissioner, what Mr. Snyman tells us is anything but the truth. I think he simply plays with our credibility. He is manufacturing a new story against all the evidence that has been produced. Worst of all, he does not seem to have the slightest remorse concerning his horrible and inhuman actions. We suggest that this application for reconciliation be terminated and that Mr. Snyman and all his henchmen be sent to the criminal justice court to be judged for the crimes that they have committed"

The Colonel, for the first time, lifted his eyes off the floor and looked directly at the Commissioners. "Mr. Commissioner, I have not harmed justice in any way," he exclaimed with passion. "I have readily and truthfully presented the facts as I remember, the way they took place concerning Steve Biko's death. Once again, I say that his death was just an accident, a bad moment when the police were trying to bring the captive to peace and order".

Bakos interrupted again, "Mr. Snyman, we have witnesses, some from your team, that have testified that three of your men grabbed the unfortunate young man in a horizontal position and they battered his head on the wall like a battering ram."

"Lies, lies," screamed Snyman at the top of his voice, spitting at the mouth, "nothing like that ever happened in my presence."

"Mr. Snyman," Bakos continued, " I want you to tell us if it is true or not, that when the martyr Steve Biko fell on the floor, instead of calling a doctor to give him medical aid, your men hung him like a slaughtered lamb, handcuffed by his wrists to the frame of the window."

Snyman trembling replied, "when he fell on the floor, we thought that he was putting on an act. He used to play like that, well, to make us appear stupid, so the officer thought it was appropriate to hang him up by his handcuffs for the rest of the day because the man was very dangerous."

Bakos said sarcastically, "Mr. Snyman, perhaps you did that to shake his morale, to make him workable and cooperative for a few days. I would like to ask you, just for the record, on what day did you eventually call the doctor to examine Steve Biko?"

"If I can remember, it was next day on the eleventh of September when the condition of Steve Biko continued to be the same. I called the doctor who told us, after examining him, that the prisoner was in good health. On the same day I received an order to transport him to Pretoria."

"Mr. Snyman, how far is Pretoria from Port Elizabeth? Can you tell us?"

"Certainly, Mr. Bakos, it is not a government secret. The distance is about seven hundred miles."

"Mr. Snyman, can you enlighten this Commission as to why you chose to transport a badly injured man in the back seat of a Land Rover for such a long distance?"

"Truly this...I don't know. I was just following orders from Pieter Goosen."

"Can you explain to us whether there was a specified reason as to why you transported the prisoner totally nude for all that distance, or why for that matter, why you held a man nude in your interrogation room?"

"As I told you Mr. Bakos, I was simply following orders."

"Mr. Snyman, can you tell us on what day Steve Biko died?"

"Twelfth of September," Snyman replied.

"Mr. Snyman, even here you are lying because the postmortem on the body of Steve Biko showed that your prisoner was in continuous torture for four days, so that his body was bruised from top to bottom with many lacerations to the head. So I ask you, during the four days did you not have any semblance of humanity to take the prisoner to a hospital?"

"As I told you Mr. Bakos, I was just a link in a very strong chain and I was just following the orders of my leader Colonel Pieter Goosen. It was he who told me to transport Steve Biko to Pretoria as soon as possible."

"Finally, Mr. Snyman, even if we accept, which we don't, that you are telling the truth and furthermore let's say that Steve Biko's death was an accident, why did you not notify his parents or put a notice in the newspapers?"

Snyman appeared very thoughtful and he said, "you are right Mr. Bakos, it would have been more human to do so, but Colonel Goosen had personally ordered me to camouflage the truth because it did not benefit the government to draw international attention to what had happened. Secondly, the announcement of his death would have exacerbated an already tense domestic situation. Thirdly, his death would have chased away potential investors so badly needed in South Africa."

"Mr. Snyman, can you tell me when your leader Colonel Pieter Goosen died?"

"Surely Mr. Bakos, somewhere in 1988."

"Very convenient for you because it is now so easy to hide behind a dead man! Mr. Snyman, you and your men should be standing in a court room for crimes against humanity."

"Mr. Bakos, I am seeking a pardon from the Reconciliation Commission because I am truly and deeply sorry about what happened. I really feel very badly that we acted in such an inhuman and barbaric manner toward Steve Biko. I beg forgiveness at this hearing, from his family and from his memory. I have nothing further to say."

"Mr. Snyman, I think that at this moment you have said the only truth that we have heard at this hearing, that you are inhuman and barbaric!" Finished, Bakos sat down.

"Mr. Snyman, you can be seated," said the Commissioner, "this committee will be in recession for thirty minutes."

Bakos, still furious, picked up his glasses and sighed.

Matthew felt as angry as he did, perhaps more so. "By God, I would not have hesitated to grab Snyman by the neck and snap it like a chicken."

Containing his rage, he approached the famous lawyer.

"Good morning Mr. Bakos. I am Matthew Matsimani," he said putting out his hand.

Bakos looked at Matthew inquisitively for a few minutes. Matthew was now in his early forties. He was well dressed and had managed to maintain his large athletic frame. Even through all the pain he had seen, he retained the warm, intelligent eyes and shy smile he'd had since he was a child. Matthew felt the keen eyes of Bakos bearing into his soul. The lawyer gave him a warm friendly smile and shook his hand.

"I am pleased to meet you Mr. Matsimani. By the way thank you very much for Biko's security file. It was very useful."

"Mr. Bakos, I believe you are just as angry with this truth and reconciliation option as I am," Matthew said.

Bakos looked at him skeptically for a while. "You are not wrong, Mr. Matsimani, perhaps I hate it more than anyone because I represented so many victims in the previous era. As a man of law, I am revolted when I see people like him get off scott free. This is my view, the view of a lawyer, the simple view. Mandela's view however, is the hard one, the more productive. What a man! He has overcome his wrath despite all those wasted years on Robben Island. He forgave his enemies for the good of this country and its people. He knows that what this country needs now more than ever is peace and cooperation, to stand on her feet and not to fall into the vortex of nationalism and hatred. The whites admire Nelson because he did what I could never do, bring back at last the compassion, humanity and peace so needed in this country."

Matthew followed what he was saying without speaking as Bakos continued, "nevertheless, it is not a small thing to see such a powerful and wicked man beg for forgiveness. It is at least some moral retribution for the victims and their families."

"Mr. Bakos, one of the reasons I wanted to meet with you was to tell you that Captain Kolradie, or as you called him the butcher of Soweto, has made an application for forgiveness. The hearing will take place before the Commission in a few days. I would like to request that you represent a person that we know in common, the doctor of Soweto."

Bakos screwed up his eyes and he asked with interest, "who must I represent, Mr. Matsimani?"

"I want you to represent the doctor of Soweto, Doctor Erickson; and also in the same application, Andreas Magdalos."

"Mr. Matsimani, you surprise me and without second thought, I tell you that I will represent them with joy, both your friend and Andreas Magdalos. I am amazed however. How do you know Andreas Magdalos?"

"Mr. Bakos, I have known him since we were children. We were friends and compatriots in the struggle."

Bakos showed some shadows of emotion in his eyes, "Matthew, I think you will allow me to talk to you quite plainly for even without knowing you, I feel as though I have known you for a long time just as I have also known of the famous doctor of Soweto. I actually represented Andreas at his first trial some twenty years back. As I recall he was reluctant at the time but his father prevailed upon me to persuade him. Don't you think however, that the request for me to represent him before the Truth and Reconciliation Commission should have come from Andreas's father?"

"Mr. Bakos you are right. I intend this week to visit Mr. Magdalos. I have to give him something that belongs to him. Searching through the security files in John Vorster Square, I found the personal diary of Andreas. I wanted to give it to him some time ago but I did not feel all that ready to meet with him. Perhaps I am afraid that he believes that I am to blame for what happened to his son. I have made a copy for you. I think that you might find it to be helpful"

George Bakos took the pile of papers and Matthew could see from his expression that the impact of the diary was going to be the same on the lawyer, as it had been on him.

* * *

A few days after the hearing, Matthew was overtaken by an overwhelming anger as he drove the government Mercedes on the dusty, gravel roads of Soweto. This place reminded him of the past, showed him all the work that still awaited the new South Africa in the present. The revolution, the victory, the abolition of the hated era of apartheid had led to overwhelming changes in his country. Their charismatic leader with wisdom and compassion had achieved so much in so little time. No one else could have achieved these gains and yet every time that Matthew drove into Soweto, he could see how little life had changed in the ghetto. At these times he felt an overwhelming despair. Poverty and misery were obvious in the childrens' pot-bellied tummies, a multitude of flies, mounds of garbage and a flagrant unemployment that inflamed crime. Matthew had dreamt so many times in the past of how the future would be different. He had shared hopes with the doctor of Soweto that they would demolish the depressing hovels of human degradation and that they would build small and cheerful homes, parks, schools, spiritual centers, libraries and sports facilities. All of these amenities had been missing from their lives and they had dreamed that these opportunities would be made available to the new generations. The sky was a fiery red and an enormous flaming sun was sinking slowly to its sunset. It was beautiful beyond imagination and yet it gave him no pleasure. The magnificent sunsets of the Transvaal highveld that had always helped him to forget his worries for a while, now had no effect upon him.

The corner of his eye fell on the half demolished castle of Tokoloshe. The vision enlightened his soul because this was a holy place. He stepped on the brakes and pulled to the side of the road. As though hypnotized, he emerged from the car and walked toward the ruin. It remained the only stone building in between the hovels and depressing municipal apartments. He felt at peace every time he came to this place and his emotions and memories streamed powerfully shaking the depths of his mind. He felt yet again his eyes to fill with tears. It was a sad monument to apartheid and he remembered clearly that the doctor and he had decided that the first spiritual center of Soweto would be located there. It had remained an unmet dream. Through his moist eyes, he thought he saw the image of his friend Samuel, the lawyer, standing in the gutted outside doorway, his bright clever eyes looking at him and smiling. He said that he had been forgotten. Samuel was one of the initial heroes in the struggle. The security police put a stop to his life at an early age. Matthew knew that his death and so many others had not been in vain. So much had happened but the hoped for changes were going forward so slowly. Democracy was still so new in South Africa. The country had inherited so many problems from the racist regime and crime had continued to rise to epidemic proportions.

Matthew had overwhelming anxieties about what would happen when Mandela was to resign. Would chaos erupt, like in so many other African countries? All was so fragile and it tortured him that except for the end of apartheid, nothing much had changed. The few had so much and the many still had nothing, except dreams and hopes. Naturally, in the change, many of the freedom fighters, like him, had become more comfortable. They were now working in civil service occupations with good salaries and luxurious cars. He was afraid that perhaps they would get used to the luxury and forget the many. So much worried him and he needed a friend, his spiritual father as much as ever. He felt the need to talk to him and to unburden himself and take advice. Six years in government and he was still not yet able to digest that all the barons of apartheid, those that had raped and plundered a whole nation were still free. He had not even digested the notion of reconciliation. The stone ghostlike building stood there golden in the sunset and the ghost of Samuel stood in the shadow looking at him.

Lively conversations from youthful voices interrupted his visions and returned him to reality. He heard the door of his car opening and he ran toward it. As he emerged from the ruined house, he saw five or six young tsotsis trying to steal his car.

"Ngizokushaya tsotsis! I will beat you!" he shouted in wrath. The youngsters stopped startled and looked at him. Puzzled and frightened, they ran away because not one had the courage to enter the house of the Tokoloshe.

"Bloody tsotsis," he said to himself as he drove away, "they have no respect for government property or for past freedom fighters."

Five minutes later, he stopped at the house Doctor Erickson. The same little garden was tended to perfection. The door still had the same faded blue color. It reminded him of the first time that Samuel had brought him here, and how his life had then changed forever. It was as though he was expected for as he approached the outer door opened and filled with the gigantic frame of a man. He was nude from the waist up and was still built with Herculean dimensions. His freshly shaved, proud head shining like black ebony.

"Matthew," he shouted and ran toward him with the flexibility of a gazelle. He grabbed Matthew in his enormous arms and lifted him out of the car with so much love and tenderness that did not match the appearance of such a rugged man.

"Matthew, how are you? You cannot imagine my joy."

Matthew tried to escape his deadly grip, to take a breath. They were about the same age, only that he was a head taller than Matthew and his physical breadth was twice his size. Matthew was by no means a small man and he eventually managed to escape from his grip. In turn he shouted,

"Zulu, my big brother and compatriot. It feels so good to see you again!"

Zulu grabbed his suitcase and said, "let's go in. Everyone is waiting for you and we have much to talk about."

"Is my car safe here?" Matthew asked.

"Don't worry about it at all. Even the worst tsotsi respects Doctor and Zulu."

Matthew looked again at his friend as though he could not get enough of him. Matthew heard Mama Rosa's joyful voice before she appeared. To him she looked as big and beautiful as ever.

"Matthew, my boy," she shouted and he found himself in her warm embrace. He laid his head on her enormous bosom and he felt as peaceful and calm as when he was a child.

"My sweet Mama Rosa. How much I've missed you!"

"Oh my God," she screamed. "What a beautiful car that is! Are you going to take us for a ride?"

They placed him between them with loud praises and laughter and he felt so good as though he was back in his own home. Doctor's house was as he remembered it. Nothing had changed. There were books and works of art everywhere, from woodcarvings to soap stone statues and paintings made by past patients and friends of the doctor. His friends were all there, Thomas in his wheel chair, Mafuta still wearing his ANC t-shirt, David, with his wife, Sithola, Winnie and Bill. They all rose and greeted him warmly with the exception of Doctor. It was a wonderful to feel so accepted and be greeted in such a warm manner from people so able, tried and tested in difficult moments. The large table was filled the scent of aromatic dishes, which had the stamp of Mama Rosa's labor; putu pap made out of mealie meal, which could be dipped in a bubbling beef stew, boerewors, babotie, curried fish, fried chips and vet cakes. There were pots filled with sour milk and homemade beer. The meal reflected the diverse and varied cuisine of the many cultures in South Africa. He embraced all his friends one by one, more especially his childhood friend, Thomas.

Afterward he turned toward Doctor Erickson who was sitting in a chair with a fixed empty gaze. He was looking into nothingness, totally disassociated from anybody. He kneeled before him and Doctor looked at him uneasily for a moment. He saw Matthew's familiar, although unknown, face before him and he continued his ceaseless rocking. Matthew took his hands in his and he squeezed them with love and tenderness.

"Doctor, my father. We need you as much now as ever. Return to us please, return to be with us."

His plea had no effect and a fierce anger gripped him once again. He wished once more to have his hands on the butcher of Soweto and his associates, who had tortured this once great man into this condition. He could have cut them into pieces to feed the dogs. Mama Rosa, his second mother who knew him so well, lifted him up tenderly.

"My boy, don't suffer needlessly. Whatever happened has happened. Don't poison your beautiful soul with ugly thoughts. Come, we need you all so much. We would like to hear your news and share your visions for our beautiful country."

Matthew knew that she was right. He gathered up his strength and turned toward his beloved friends.

Zulu approached him with two glasses of tswala and gave one to him.

"My brothers, let's drink to Nelson's health, to Matthew and to the future of our country," he said.

"To Nelson and to Matthew," they shouted in unison with joy.

"My friends," said Matthew "the main reason that I am with you the evening is to inform you about something unpleasant. The butcher of Soweto and his associates have finally placed their applications before the Truth and Reconciliation Commission. Their submission will take place in a few days and I believe that we should all attend."

Zulu reacted with a forceful and aggressive leap into the air and grimaced,

"I give you my word brothers that there they will find their end. They will never see the sun again!"

Mama Rosa inhaled a breath and she placed her two hands on her large hips.

"I'm not prepared to hear crazy talk from you Zulu or as a matter of fact from anybody else in here. As far as I am concerned, we buried the hatchet the day we as a nation went to the polls for the first time and elected as a free people the President, Nelson Mandela. On that glorious day, our country became free. What Mandela is doing is holy and has my signature. I was sick and tired of apartheid and I'm sick and tired of violence. I want peace. I want to forget all about the past and I want to build our country with compassion, self-respect and love, for us, for our children and for our grandchildren."

"You surprise me Mama, to hear you talking like this, of all people," replied Zulu with an angry voice. "How do you want me to forget? How can you forget the terrible doings, the rape of our country and our people? When I look at Doctor every day in his terrible plight, how can I forget? How can I forget what they did to Andreas and so many other young men and women? I am asking you? I am asking all of you, how can you forget? I think, Mama Rosa, that you are making so much money that you have turned your heart to be very tender. I never expected to hear that from you."

Knowing Mama Rosa and her hot temper, Matthew thought for a moment that she would grab the knife in front of her and slice Zulu. As he prepared to stop her, she surprised him with words that he would never have believed possible from her.

"Yes Zulu, if you want to know the truth my heart has become very tender. Would you like me to tell you when it happened? I will tell you and I am not at all ashamed. It was at the time that I stood in that long line on that hot day, waiting to vote for the first time. My God, what a feeling, I will never forget as long as I live that sweet moment, that magic moment. I cast my first vote and I turned into a free person. I felt that the world had become very small and I could ride on it, smiling with my happiness. I voted for Mandela, you voted for Mandela, all of us voted for Mandela, bringing democracy to our country. He is showing us the path that we have to follow."

Everybody stared at her in astonished reaction, and Matthew was even more amazed to hear Thomas continue, even though he was normally too shy to speak,

"Compatriots, you all know about the accident that befell me in my prime and marked my life forever. As you all know the people who did that to me were our people and they destroyed my body for just a few Rand. You know as well, that I am not the only one. A multitude like me became crippled for the easy profit of a few. When I had the accident, I was full of wrath at God, the tsotsis and the world. I've had a lot of time to think in this wheelchair, and I could write books with the ways I've imagined to revenge myself. For years my blood boiled with anger. As time passed however, my feelings became so overwhelming that I became obsessed with my anger, such that I nearly lost all my friends. I became a very miserable man. It took me some time to realize that I was imprisoned by my own hatred and that it had poisoned all of my being. One day, after I had hit bottom, I began to see things from another perspective. I had tamed my anger. I managed to forgive the people that injured me and suddenly I felt much lighter. I noticed the beauty of nature again, and of good people and I started living once more.

Nelson Mandela is a very wise leader and what he is trying to do is to take from us our anger and hate so that altogether, we will be able to build our country. He was a sufferer like me, and he wasted most of his life behind bars. He also hit his depths and he rose above with compassion and forgiveness because that is the only way to build. Hate brings hate, anger more anger and blood more blood."

Mafuta took a large gulp at his beer and he turned to Thomas, "All that sounds very well and good, but I still see the whites holding the best jobs, they own the factories and the land, with their beautiful homes and cars and we still have only our hopes and dreams and our poverty."

Thomas looked at him in the eyes and replied, "I agree with you David, things are still the same but with one difference. Now we are free, we no longer are forced to carry passbooks. We have broken the chains. We can work wherever we like and do whatever we like. We can send our children to good schools and universities. Furthermore, we can choose our own leaders and we can use our talents and creativity as we wish. For example, take myself and my sister Mama Rosa, we worked and believed in ourselves and already we own three restaurants.

Matthew suddenly became painfully aware of how the hate and anger that he carried was poisoning his life. He no longer smelt the sweetness of flowers, just as he had missed the majesty of sunset in evening's approach. Mama Rosa's and Thomas's compassion threatened to overtake him. He longed to throw the chains of hate that soured his new found freedom. He stood up and approached Zulu. They had shared so much over so many years.

"Zulu, my brother," Matthew said, "I share your justifiable rage. Those people have committed enormous atrocities and they would do it again in the right environment. Let me tell you that I have just returned from the Truth and Reconciliation Commission concerning Steve Biko's death. You would not believe their fear and how spineless they were when they begged for mercy and amnesty. I think the best punishment for these people is to take away their power. I agree with Mama Rosa and Thomas, we have to cleanse our souls of these terrible poisons and begin living and creating a new future for ourselves and our country."

Matthew felt Zulu's body ease. He filled their glasses with beer and he stared at Matthew in the eyes for a few seconds. He lifted his glass up high and shouted with his strong voice, "I drink to our new South Africa. N'kosi sikelel'i Afrika. (God save Africa)."

* * *

Early the next morning, Matthew rang the bell of a large cast iron gate at the driveway entrance to the house of Mr. Magdalos. He noticed the security camera following his doings and he heard a voice in the door's intercom,

"Who is it?" a voice said in English with an African accent.

"Mary, it's me," he said.

"Oh no," Mary said in disbelief, "is it you Matthew?"

"Yes, it is me," he said smiling.

"It's Matthew!" he heard her screaming, "our own Matthew. Oh God, I will go crazy."

"Mary, are you going to open the gate?" he asked.

"Oh Matthew, I'm sorry. I'm so excited!"

The heavy gates slid back silently on its well-oiled rails and Matthew drove the car into the property. The main door of the mansion was just opening and Mary appeared running as fast as she could despite her old age. Elizabeth and Jacob, the elderly gardener followed her. They all tried to embrace him at the same time, screaming loudly with excitement.

"Matthew, our boy. You have grown up so much. You are a famous person. We see you nearly every day on the television. How is your mother? She did not come to visit us this month. How is the rest of the family?"

They were all asking questions together at the same time and it was difficult for him to answer. Instead, he held them with affection and emotion. They were like his extended family. They had all worked together in this home for a long time. He looked with some nostalgia at the old mansion. It was still impressive and elegant. They took him on a tour starting with the garage. The golden Rolls Royce was still there, shining and beautiful. It was not until they reached Andreas's room however that Matthew was fully able to make contact with the past. It was exactly the same as he had last seen it and as he remembered it. He sat on the end of the bed and once again he was a small boy. Andreas was sitting sit next to him talking incessantly like always. It was hard to keep back his tears. This room was very significant for him as it was there that he had taken an oath that one day he was going to be free and equal.

"Where is Mr. Magdalos?" he managed to ask.

"Every day in cold or heat, he goes to the cemetery," Mary replied.

"You must wait for him. He will be very excited to see you. He always talks about you," Jacob added.

"I will go and meet him there," Matthew said.

The cemetery was a few blocks away from the house. He decided to walk because he needed time to be with himself and to think. He had not seen Mr. Magdalos for a long time.

The grave was simple and well cared for, mounted in white marble with small pedestal containing an icon, a photo of Andreas and a small burning candle. He looked so young, so full of life. Mr. Magdalos was sitting in a folding chair at the side of the grave, reading a book. He looked very frail for his age.

"Good morning Mr. Magdalos. I hope that I am not disturbing you?"

The old man turned toward him raising his hand to shield his eyes from the sun.

"Matthew," he said, "how nice to see you again. I thought you had forgotten us."

He sat next to him on the edge of the grave.

"Mr. Magdalos. How is your wife?"

"She is no longer with me. We have divorced. I believe she has remarried and now lives in Bloemfontein. It has been such a long time since I last saw you. What kept you away? You must be very busy with your new position?"

"I wanted to visit you a long time ago," Matthew replied in a rush, "but I was not ready. I was scared to face you. I thought you would hold me responsible for Andreas's death. Nevertheless, you must know that Andreas was never far from my mind. The reason that brings me here is that I have to tell you that Captain Kolradie and his accomplices have filed for amnesty before the Truth and Reconciliation Commission. Also I have come to bring something that I believe is rightfully yours. I discovered that Andreas was writing his story all along. I found his diary in the piles of security files at John Vorster Square. You have so much to feel proud about. I think that it would be good to get it published. The world must learn what it was like, for blacks and whites, to live under apartheid in South Africa."

"Matthew, I did not always feel proud of Andreas. I failed him many times because I just did not want to understand. Thank very much for coming and for all that you are doing. You must know that I always saw your mother as very close to my family. I hope you will continue to visit us. I'm feeling very tired now and overwhelmed with all this. I think I will head back home."

"Well I would like to stay a few moments alone with Andreas," said Matthew.

"Perhaps you could join me later and we will have some lunch," said Mr. Magdalos shuffling away with a halting step.

Alone, Matthew knelt on the white marble of the grave and closed his eyes. He began a silent conversation with his friend; the person with whom he had discovered that color, religion and nationality are not what makes us human. In the battle for freedom, by breaking these chains, we find a united purpose in seeking compassion for ourselves and each other no matter what price

Postscript

During the period portrayed in this book, a large number of prisoners met a similar death in South Africa while being detained for interrogation:

1. **Michael Shirute** His death was announced in Parliament by the Police Minister, Mr. L. Muller. According to this statement, the prisoner committed suicide on the evening of 16 June 19 (date unknown) after being arrested under the Anti-Terrorism Act.

2. **Jacob Monnakgotla** His death was announced in the course of the trial of ten blacks being tried under the Anti-Terrorism Act following the tribal unrest in the Transvaal. He died on (date unknown), the night before his trial began. During the trial, the police said he died of natural causes. The district doctor diagnosed death from thrombosis.

3. **Caleb Matesiko** Death from natural causes on 13 May 19 (date unknown) after eighteen days of detention under the Anti-Terrorism Act, according to the Police Minister's statement.

4. **James Lenkoe** Found hanged by his belt from his cell window on 10 March 19 (date unknown), five days after his arrest. Traces of brass found in his toes. Four doctors, one from abroad, said the wound in his toes could have been caused by electric shock. Secret police witnesses denied accusations that prisoners received electric shocks. Coroner brought in a verdict of death by hanging.

5. **Solomon Madipane** Died about three days after arrest on 25 February 19 (date unknown). No inquest. Coroner accepted certificate of death from natural causes. Police announcement claimed the dead man had slipped on a piece of soap.

6. **Nicodemus Kgoathe** died on 2 February 19 (date unknown)

after arrest on 7 November 1968. Spent two weeks in hospital before death. Autopsy showed death from pneumonia. The doctor who sent him to hospital during his interrogation testified that he found a number of injuries which in his opinion were caused by torture. Police sergeant said Kgoathe had stated that he had suffered torture at hands of members of secret police. Witnesses from the security police stated that the prisoner had slipped and injured himself in the shower. Magistrate ruled that there was insufficient evidence to ascribe responsibility for death of Kgoathe to anyone.

7. **J.B.Tubakwe** Died 11 September 1968, one day after arrest. Verdict: death from hanging.

8. **Ah Yan** Found hanged by his socks from shower water-pipe in his cell, 5 January 1967. Had been arrested November or December 1966. Official verdict: death by hanging.

9. **James Hamakwato** Suicide by hanging. Exact date of death not announced.

10. **Ahmet Timol** Died trying to escape from 10th floor of John Vorster Square building 27 (date unknown) 1971.

11. **Suliman Saltoojee** Died jumping from 7th floor of John Vorster Square building on 3 September 1964, two months after arrest under Anti-Terrorism Act. Security police who refused to answer certain questions put by defense lawyer categorically denied this man had been tortured. Coroner found that the man had died from multiple injuries after falling during interrogation. He could not state however whether Saltoojee committed suicide or was trying to escape. In general, there were no indications of torture.

12. **Looksmart Solwandle Ngudie** Died 5 September 1973 after three weeks imprisonment. Found hanged by his pyjama cord.

13. **Joseph Mduli** Died 19 March 1976 in Durban.

14. **Mapatla Mohapi** Died 5 August 1976 in King William.

15. **Luke Mazwambe** Died 2 September 1976 in Cape Town.

16. **George Botha** Died 19 December 1976 in Port Elizabeth.

17. **Nanoath Ntshuntsha** Died 9 January 1977 in Cape Leslie.

18. **Matthew Mabalane** Died 15 February 1977 in Johannesburg.

Steve Biko's was the 44th such death, in September 1977, while he was held by the security police. His death caused a storm of protest throughout the world.

These are among the known deaths. How many unknown others also lost their lives?